THE BRITISH
FANTASY SOCIETY:

A CELEBRATION

THE BRITISH FANTASY SOCIETY:

A CELEBRATION

Edited by Paul Kane & Marie O'Regan

Introduction by Stephen Jones.

This is a work of fiction. All characters and events portrayed in these stories are fictitious or used fictitiously.

The British Fantasy Society: A Celebration

Edited by Paul Kane & Marie O'Regan

Published by The British Fantasy Society
201 Reddish Road,
Stockport, SK5 7HR

www.britishfantasysociety.org.uk

Introduction © Stephen Jones.

Afterword © Paul Kane & Marie O'Regan.

All Other Material © Individual Authors

All rights reserved, including the right to reproduce this book, or portions thereof, in any form.

First Edition The British Fantasy Society © 2006

ISBN: 0953 868 16 8

Previous Publication History:

'Lost Souls' by Clive Barker. First appeared in *Cutting Edge* (ed. Dennis Etchinson, Futura, 1986)
'The Man Who Drew Cats' by Michael Marshall Smith. First appeared in *Dark Voices II* (eds Stephen Jones and David Sutton, Pan, 1990)
'The Cycle' by John Connolly. First appeared in *Moments* (ed. Ciara Considine, 2005)
'Days of the Wheel' by Peter Crowther. First appeared in *Strange Attraction* (ed. Edward E. Kramer 2000)
'Progeny' by Mark Morris. First appeared in *Close to the Bone* (Piatkus,1995)
'The Sustenance of Hoak' by Ramsey Campbell. First appeared in *Swords Against Darkness* (ed. Andrew J. Offutt, Zebra, 1977)
'This is Illyria, Lady' by Kim Newman. First appeared in *Shakespearean Whodunnits* (ed. Mike Ashley, Robinson, 1997)
'Ashputtle' by Peter Straub. First appeared in *Black Thorn, White Rose* (ed. Ellen Datlow & Terri Windling, Morrow AvoNova, 1994)
'Webs' by Neil Gaiman. First Appeared in *More Tales from the 'Forbidden Planet'* (ed. Roz Kaveney, Titan, 1990)
'Scarrowfell' by Robert Holdstock. First appeared in *Other Edens* (1987)
'Dust' by Richard Christian Matheson. First Appeared in *Scars and Other Distinguishing Marks* (Tor, 1987)
'Sundance' by Robert Silverberg. First appeared in *Fantasy & Science Fiction* (1969)
'My Repeater' by Stephen Gallagher. First appeared in *Fantasy & Science Fiction Magazine* (Jan, 2001)
'Partial Eclipse' by Graham Joyce. First appeared on SCIFI.COM (2000)
All other stories and material original to this publication.

All profits from the sale of this book go to the BFS and The 'Black Dust' Nqabakazulu Charity Project.

For the members of the British Fantasy Society,
the reason we do what we do.

Contents

Introduction - Stephen Jones xv

The Luxury of Harm - Christopher Fowler 21

Lost Souls - Clive Barker 28

Whisper Lane - Mark Chadbourn 41

The Man Who Drew Cats - Michael Marshall Smith 65

The Cycle - John Connolly 86

Days Of The Wheel - Peter Crowther 96

Now You See Him, Now You Don't - Juliet E. McKenna 106

Progeny - Mark Morris 115

The Sustenance of Hoak - Ramsey Campbell 128

Every Day A Little Death - Chaz Brenchley 157

This is Illyria, Lady - Kim Newman   174

Ashputtle - Peter Straub   180

Webs - Neil Gaiman   199

The Raffle - Simon Clark   207

Scarrowfell - Robert Holdstock   215

Building Sixteen - Brian Aldiss   236

Dust - Richard Christian Matheson   244

Sundance - Robert Silverberg   248

My Repeater - Stephen Gallagher   265

Partial Eclipse - Graham Joyce   282

Afterword - The Editors   299

By Way Of An Introduction
Stephen Jones

Stephen Jones lives in London, England. He is the winner of three World Fantasy Awards, three Horror Writers Association Bram Stoker Awards and three International Horror Guild Awards as well as being a sixteen-time recipient of the British Fantasy Award and a Hugo Award nominee. A former television producer/director and genre movie publicist and consultant (the first three *Hellraiser* movies, *Night Life*, *Nightbreed*, *Split Second*, *Mind Ripper*, *Last Gasp* etc.), he is the co-editor of *Horror: 100 Best Books* and its sequel *Horror: Another 100 Best Books*, *The Best Horror from Fantasy Tales*, *Gaslight & Ghosts*, *Now We Are Sick*, *H.P. Lovecraft's Book of Horror*, *The Anthology of Fantasy & the Supernatural*, *Secret City: Strange Tales of London* and the *Dark Terrors*, *Dark Voices* and *Fantasy Tales* series.

He has written *Creepshows: The Illustrated Stephen King Movie Guide*, *The Essential Monster Movie Guide*, *The Illustrated Vampire Movie Guide*, *The Illustrated Dinosaur Movie Guide*, *The Illustrated Frankenstein Movie Guide* and *The Illustrated Werewolf Movie Guide*, and compiled *The Mammoth Book of Best New Horror* series, *The Mammoth Book of Terror*, *The Mammoth Book of Vampires*, *The Mammoth Book of Zombies*, *The Mammoth Book of Werewolves*, *The Mammoth Book of Frankenstein*, *The Mammoth Book of Dracula*, *The Mammoth Book of Vampire Stories by Women*, *The Mammoth Book of New Terror*, *Shadows Over Innsmouth*, *Weird*

Shadows Over Innsmouth, Dark Detectives, Dancing With the Dark, Dark of the Night, White of the Moon, Keep Out the Night, By Moonlight Only, Don't Turn Out the Light, Exorcisms and Ecstasies by Karl Edward Wagner, *The Vampire Stories of R. Chetwynd-Hayes, Phantoms and Fiends* and *Frights and Fancies* by R. Chetwynd-Hayes, *James Herbert: By Horror Haunted, The Conan Chronicles* by Robert E. Howard (two volumes), *The Emperor of Dreams: The Lost Worlds of Clark Ashton Smith, Sea-Kings of Mars and Otherworldly Stories* by Leigh Brackett, *Clive Barker's A-Z of Horror, Clive Barker's Shadows in Eden, Clive Barker's The Nightbreed Chronicles* and the *Hellraiser Chronicles*. He was a Guest of Honour at the 2002 World Fantasy Convention in Minneapolis, Minnesota, and the 2004 World Horror Convention in Phoenix, Arizona. You can find his website at http://herebedragons.co.uk/jones/

Whenever a fledgling horror or fantasy writer comes up to me, at a convention or somewhere else, and asks me how they can get their work published, I invariably advise them that their first step should be to join The British Fantasy Society.

Unless you happen to be very, very lucky, or have one of the top literary agents in the business, then the best way to meet editors, publishers or even fellow writers is to *network*. A lot.

And that's where the BFS comes in. For more than thirty-five years, the Society has functioned as a gathering place and forum for people all over the world working in, or simply enjoying, every aspect of fantastic literature. It has not only achieved this through its multiple publications, but also from facilitating face-to-face meetings at the annual British FantasyCon or other social gatherings organised under its auspices.

Trust me, I know what I'm talking about here. After all, it worked for me.

I've written elsewhere, and at length, about how I first discovered The British Fantasy Society in the early 1970s. I responded to an advertisement – probably in Stan Nicholls' *Gothique* or some similar fanzine – and soon became a vocal critic of what the Society was doing. I didn't understand why, at a time when many small press magazines were going over to lithographic reproduction to give them a more professional appearance, the BFS was still putting out spirit-duplicated publications.

However, unlike many other members, I was willing to do something to try and change things. I soon began contributing news, articles and artwork to various BFS publications. Although my first attempt to get on the committee (after only being a member of the Society for less than a year!) failed ignominiously, I eventually found myself editing the Society's journal, *Dark Horizons*, quickly turning it into a classy-looking publication that rivalled such acclaimed American periodicals as *Whispers*, both in design and content. The fact that I was able to attract professionally published authors such as Ramsey Campbell and Brian Lumley to contribute to the title meant that we could quickly expand the scope of the magazine.

It also meant, although I didn't realise it at the time, that I was already on the road to eventually becoming a professional editor. (That happened in the late 1980s in a bar at FantasyCon, when a publisher approached me looking for new anthology projects.)

Over the next decade or so, I was involved in every aspect of The British Fantasy Society. I co-edited the regular *Newsletter* (reaching its pinnacle with an eighty-page special), designed and edited many of the individual booklets put out by the Society, chaired several FantasyCons (including combining two with the prestigious World Fantasy Convention) and instigated the popular Open Night meetings, which continue to this day. I even ended up running the Society on two separate occasions, the second time as something of a benevolent dictator.

I have also been very privileged to win quite a number of British Fantasy Awards along the way for both my fan and professional accomplishments. Voted for by the membership each year, these awards have for the most part thankfully remained free of the blatant

xvii

lobbying and obvious nepotism that affects some other prizes in our field.

And all the while, I was meeting new people, making new friends and working with numerous authors and artists – from rising stars to many of the Big Names in the genre.

I've previously recalled in print how I first encountered fellow Society members David Sutton, Ramsey Campbell and Brian Mooney (all professionally published at the time) at my very first science fiction convention, back in 1974. But being a member of the BFS also helped me meet a whole host of other names, many of whom I continue to work with all these years later.

Clive Barker, Kenneth Bulmer, Ramsey Campbell, Peter Crowther, Les Edwards, Jim FitzPatrick, Christopher Fowler, Neil Gaiman, Stephen King, Tim Lebbon, Tanith Lee, Brian Lumley, Michael Moorcock, Mark Samuels, Robert Silverberg, Michael Marshall Smith, Karl Edward Wagner, Manly Wade Wellman and Gene Wolfe are just a few of those who I initially met through my connection with the organisation.

And thanks to The British Fantasy Society, I am continuing to meet many exciting and upcoming talents today.

You only have to look at the names that have been assembled for this tribute volume to realise the influence the Society has had on the genre, and the many professionals who have benefited over the years from their own involvement with the BFS.

I would go so far as to claim that it has touched the lives and careers of almost every major figure in our genres, and the British Fantasy Award remains one of the most respected in our field.

From literature, to art, movies, television, comics, theatre, small press . . . the Society has always catered to every aspect of the genres. And let me be absolutely clear here: by "genres", I mean fantasy, horror and science fiction. You'll find all three ably represented in the various BFS publications, including this present volume.

The names of those involved in running the organisation may have changed over the years, and it has certainly suffered from its fair share of ups and downs, but The British Fantasy Society continues to grow and prosper, thanks to the many volunteers who give their time and effort for free. It is to those many committee members, often toiling unheralded behind-the-scenes, that we owe our gratitude – without them, there would not be a BFS as we know it today.

Although I may not always agree with the decisions made, the Society is still a democracy run for and by the membership. If anyone wants to influence the direction the organisation takes, they only have to stand for election to make their voices heard.

But now it is time to hear from some other voices – much more erudite and eloquent than mine. The celebrated contributors to this commemorative anthology have their own tales to tell, along with their individual memories of the BFS to recall.

So I'll end by saying a sincere "thank you" to The British Fantasy Society for helping to make me what I am today. When I joined, I was barely out of my teens and had no idea of how to discover more about my favourite genres, let alone how to become actively involved in the publishing industry. The BFS provided the signposts, and a great deal more besides.

Now, more than thirty years later, I find myself in the enviable position of having nearly ninety books to my name, along with a full-time career in my chosen field that is everything I always dreamed it would be.

I doubt I could have achieved it without being a part of The British Fantasy Society, which is why I continue to work alongside successive committees in an attempt to help influence the direction the organisation takes and promote it where and when I can.

So, if you're reading this and are not already a member, you should join up immediately. Especially if you are serious about working in this field in any kind of creative capacity.

You'll not regret it. That I guarantee. As I'm sure do the many respected names who appear over the following pages . . .

—Stephen Jones
London, England
June, 2006

THE LUXURY OF HARM
Christopher Fowler

Christopher Fowler was born in Greenwich, and now lives in King's Cross, on the Battlebridge Basin. He began his fiction career by penning humorous books including *How To Impersonate Famous People* and *The Ultimate Party Book*, before moving into the 'Dark Urban' sub-genre where he made his name. His first short story anthology, *City Jitters*, featured interlinked tales of urban malevolence, and further volumes of shorts have been published since: *City Jitters Two*, *The Bureau Of Lost Souls*, *Sharper Knives*, *Flesh Wounds*, *Personal Demons*, *Uncut*, *The Devil In Me* and *Demonized*. His novels include *Roofworld*, *Rune*, *Red Bride*, *Spanky*, *Psychoville*, *Disturbia* and the phenomenal *Calabash*.

His short story 'The Master Builder' was turned into a CBS movie starring Tippi Hedren and Marg Helgenberger entitled *Through The Eyes Of A Killer*. Another, *Left Hand Drive*, won Best British Short Film of 1993, while 'On Edge' became a short movie starring Doug Bradley. More recently, Christopher has been working on a series of novels featuring his recurring characters, the ageing detectives Bryant and May: *Full Dark House*, *The Water Room*, *Seventy-Seven Clocks* and *Ten Second Staircase*. In 1998 he won the BFS Best Short Story Of The Year Award, for 'Wageslaves'. In 2004, *The Water Room* was nominated for the CWA People's Choice Award, *Full Dark House* won the BFS August Derleth Novel Of The Year Award and 'American Waitress' won the BFS Best Short

British Fantasy Society: A Celebration

Story Of The Year. Finally, his novella *Breathe* won BFS Best Novella 2005. You can find out more about him and his fiction at www.christopherfowler.co.uk

Says Christopher: "One of the best things about FantasyCon is hardly ever mentioned.

"Like the ravens in the Tower of London, it's always there. Even if you can't make the event, you know in your heart it will be back in the calendar the following year, and there will be other nights when you can turn up in a pub and find friends who'll warmly greet you and start talking about something really peculiar, picking up an old conversation as if it had never stopped. The dutch have a word for this; *gezellig,* the pleasure of sociability. It's what separates FCON from other festivals and makes it such a pleasure; the knowledge that you can always find like-minded individuals who are literate, witty and as mad as an old man's trousers. I'd like to see FCON get bigger, with films being shown, a graphic novels sidebar, a web section, a membership drive, special events to encourage first time writers, and themed nights out in the nation's capital.

"Because FCON deserves to be enjoyed by all, and there's something very levelling here that allows first-timers to hang out with experienced writers and artists. Some years back I started to wonder if dark fiction was a spent force in the UK; now I'm sure it's on the rise, and FCON can rise with it. Writers know that anything is possible. It's time to spread the word."

When I was eleven, I was warned to stay away from a new classmate with freckles and an insolent tie, so naturally we became partners in disruption, reducing our educators to tears.

For eight years our friendship proved mystifying to all. Simon horrified our teachers by illegally racing his Easy Rider motorbike across the football field. We took the headmaster's car to pieces, laying it out as neatly as a stemmed Airfix kit in the school car park, and produced libellous magazines with jokes filched from TV

The Luxury Of Harm

programmes. Simon perverted me from learning, and I made his soul appear salvageable whenever he superglued the school cat or made prank phonecalls. I fretted that we would get into trouble, and he worked out how we could burn down the school without being caught.

Boys never tire of bad behaviour. Through the principals of economics and the theory of gravity, the Wars of the Roses and Shakespeare's symbolism, we cut open golfballs and tied pupils up in the elastic, carved rocketships into desks and forged each others' parental signatures on sick notes.

During puberty, Simon bought a mean leather jacket. I opted for an orange nylon polo-neck shirt with velcro fastenings. In order to meet girls, we signed for an operatic production staged in conjunction with our sister school. Simon met a blue-eyed blonde backstage while I appeared as a dancing villager in a shrill, offkey production of 'The Bartered Bride'. We double dated. I got the blonde's best friend, who had legs like a bentwood chair and a complexion like woodchip wallpaper. I rang Simon's girlfriends for him because he was inarticulate, and hung around his house so much that his mother thought I'd been orphaned. Our friendship survived because he gave me visibility, confidence and a filtered charisma that reached me like secondary smoking. He stopped me from believing there was no-one else in the world who understood me. And there he remained in my mind and heart, comfortable and constant, throughout the years, like Peter Pan's shadow, ready to be reattached if ever I needed it, long after his wasteful, tragic death.

But before that end came, we shared a special moment. I persuaded Simon to come to a horror convention with me, in a Somerset town called Silburton, where the narrow streets were steeped in damp mist that settled across the river estuary, and fishing boats lay on their sides in the mud like discarded toys. The place reeked of seaweed and dead fish, tar and rotting shells, and the locals were so taciturn it seemed that conversation had been bred out of them.

Of course, the hotel, a modern brick block that looked like a caravan site outhouse, had no record of our booking, and was full because of the convention. In search of a guest-house, we found a Bed & Breakfast place down beside the river ramps and lugged bags up three flights through narrow corridors, watched by the landlady in case we scratched her Indian-restaurant wallpaper.

By the time we returned to the hotel, the opening night party was in full swing. A yellow-furred rubber-suit alien was hovering uncertainly in the reception area, struggling to hold a pint mug in his claws, and a pair of local Goth girls clung to the counter, continually looking around as though they were afraid that their homies might wander in and spot them, raising their arms to point and scream like characters from *Invasion Of The Body Snatchers*.

Every year the convention had a theme, and this year it was 'Murderers on Page and Screen', so there were a few Hannibal Lectors hanging around, including a grinning lad with the top of his head sawn off. The bar staff took turns to stare at him through the serving hatch.

"Is this what you do for fun?" Simon asked me, amazed that I could take pleasure from hanging out with guys dressed as Jason and Freddie. "Who comes to these things?"

"Book people," I said simply, gesturing at the filling room. "Give it a chance," I told him. "There's no attitude here, and it gets to be great fun around midnight. Come on, you said you wanted to try something new."

Simon looked unsure; he hardly ever read, so the dealer rooms, the panels and the literary conversation held no interest for him. He could relate to drinking, though, and relaxed after a couple of powerful local beers that swirled like dark sandstorms in their glasses. Simon could drink for England. "So," he asked, "are they all writers looking for tips?"

"In a way. Take this year's theme. We're intrigued by motivation, method, character development. How do you create a realistic murderer? Who would make a good victim?" I tried to think of a way of involving Simon in my world. "Take the pair of us, for example. I'm on my home ground here. People know me. If I went missing, there would be questions asked. For once, you're the outsider. You're the tough guy, the bike riding loner nobody knows. That would make you the perfect victim."

"Why?" Simon wasn't the sort to let something beat him. His interest was piqued, and he wanted to understand.

"Because taking you out would take an act of bravery, and would be a show of strength. Killers seek notoriety to cover their inadequacies. But they also enjoy the remorse of loss."

Simon snorted. "How the hell does that work?"

"There's a strange pleasure to be taken in melancholy matters, don't you think? A kind of tainted sweetness. Look at the Goths and their fascination with death and decay."

"Okay, that's the victim sorted, so who's the killer?"

"Look around. Who would you choose?"

Simon scoped out the bar area. "Not the Jason or Freddy look-alikes. They're geeks who would pass out at the sight of a paper cut. They're happy to watch, but they wouldn't act."

"Good, keep going."

"And the Goths couldn't kill, even though they're professional mourners. They look tough but play gentle."

"Excellent."

"But him, over there." He tapped his forefinger against the palm of his hand, indicating behind him. "He looks like he's here to buy books about guys who murder their mothers. It wouldn't be such a big step to committing a murder."

"Yeah, we get a few of those at conventions. They sit in the front row at the Q&As, and are always the first to raise their hands with a question. There's one guy, a retired doctor, who even gives me the creeps. Over there." I pointed out the cadaverous Mr Henry, with his greasy combover and skin like the pages of a book left in the sun. He never missed a convention, even though he wasn't a writer or publisher, or even a reader. "He once told me he owns one of the country's largest collections of car crash photographs, and collects pictures of skin diseases."

"That's gross. I knew there would be freaks."

"Relax, he's too obvious. If there's one trick to serial killer books, it's making sure that the murderer is never someone you suspect. Have you noticed there are some very cute girls here?"

"You're right about that," Simon grudgingly admitted, watching two of them over the top of his glass.

"You should go and make their acquaintance," I suggested. "I'll just be here talking weird books with old friends, or the other way around."

I got into a long discussion/argument about the merits of *Psycho 2* and *3*, about Thomas M Disch and William Hope Hodgson and what makes a good story, and lost all track of the time. I only checked my watch when the waiter pulled shutters over the bar. Bidding farewell to my fellow conventioneers, I staggered off through the damp river mist toward the guest house. Somehow I managed to overshoot the path, and ended up on the seaweed-slick ramp to the harbour. The only sounds were the lapping of the water and the tinging of masts. The tide was coming in, and the boats were being raised from their graves like rising ghosts. Drunk and happy and suddenly tired, I sat down on the wet brown sand and allowed the mist to slowly reveal its secrets. It formed a visible circle around me, like the kind of fog in a video game that always stays the same distance no matter how hard you run. A discarded shovel someone had used to dig for lugworms stood propped against the harbour wall. Fishing nets, covered with stinking algae, were strung out like sirens' shawls.

And through the mist I gradually discerned a slender figure, his head lolling slightly to one side, one arm lower than the other, like the skeleton in Aurora's 'Forgotten Prisoner' model kit, the one that features on the cover of the Seventh Book of Pan Horror Stories. It was standing so still that it seemed to be more like the unearthed figurehead of a boat than a man.

There was a strong smell of ozone and rotting fish. The figure raised a ragged, dripping sleeve to its skull, rubbing skin to bone. It seemed as though it had ascended from the black bed of the sea.

"I fell off the fucking dock and tore my jacket. I am so incredibly slaughtered," said Simon, before tipping over and landing on his back in the sand with a thump.

The next morning, screaming seagulls hovered so close to my bedroom window that I could see inside their mouths. Shafts of sunlight bounced through the window, punching holes in my brain. My tongue tasted of duvet. I needed air.

I knocked on Simon's door, but there was no answer. Breakfast had finished, and the landlady had gone. The Easy Rider motorbike still stood in the car park behind the guest house.

The tide was out and the mist had blown away, leaving the foreshore covered in silvery razor-clams and arabesques of green weed. On the stone walkway above the harbour, an elderly lady in a teacosy hat marched past with a shopping bag. There was no-one else about. The gulls shrieked and wheeled.

Carefully, I walked across the beach to the spot where Simon had fallen, and knelt down. It took a moment to locate the exact place. Rubbing gently at a patch of soft sand, I revealed his sand-filled mouth, his blocked nostrils, one open shell-scratched eye that stared bloodily up into the sky. I rose and stood hard on his face, rocking back and forth until I had forced his head deeper into the beach. I carefully covered him over with more sand, smoothing it flat and adding some curlicues of seaweed and a couple of cockle shells for effect. Finally I threw the shovel I had used on his neck as far as I could into the stagnant water of the harbour.

As I headed back to the convention hotel, ready to deliver my lecture on 'Random Deaths: The Luxury Of Harm', a heartbreaking happiness descended upon me. I knew that there would be plenty of time to savour the full delicious loss of my friend in the days, the months, the years to come.

LOST SOULS
Clive Barker

Clive Barker is the best-selling author of twenty books, including *The Damnation Game*, *The Great and Secret Show*, *Imajica*, *The Thief of Always*, *Everville*, *Galilee*, *Coldheart Canyon* and the international betseller *Abarat*. He is also an acclaimed artist, film producer and director – notably of the British Fantasy Award-winning *Hellraiser* (based on his own *Hellbound Heart* novella), *Nightbreed* (based on his novel *Cabal*) and *Lord of Illusions*. In 1992 his short story 'The Forbidden', which also won a British Fantasy Award, was filmed as *Candyman* and went on to spawn two sequels. He burst onto the literary scene in the mid-80s with the publication of his groundbreaking *Books of Blood* series - and is working on a follow-up horror collection now called *The Scarlet Gospels*, featuring his two most popular characters: Pinhead and the detective Harry D'Amour (who also stars in the following story). Clive also introduced the BFS's 2005 Green Knight Calendar and contributed an extract to the BFS Horror Calendar 2006. He lives in sunny California with his partner, the photographer David Armstrong, and their daughter Nicole. His website can be found at www.clivebarker.info

Clive recalls: "My association with the BFS goes back a long way; it goes back with me to '84. I've never *not* had friends who were actively members. It's a way of keeping track and knowing where everybody is. It's nice to know people are growing old – I won't say gracefully – but at least getting on with the business of writing and living, and it's amazing how life passes so quickly.

"I tended to take a slightly low profile at the FantasyCons, at least that's my memory of how I performed; other people might think differently. But I've always been a lot more shy than my reputation suggests; I put on a bit of a public face, a sort of 'hail fellow, well met' kind of thing. But I'm actually wretchedly shy, which I've only recently comes to terms with and have sort of owned up to; I was really introspective. I think in many ways the art forms that I've chosen to practice, most strongly painting and writing, are attractive to me in no small part because they are solitary."

Everything the blind woman had told Harry she'd seen was undeniably real. Whatever inner eye Norma Paine possessed - that extraordinary skill that allowed her to scan the island of Manhattan from the Broadway Bridge to Battery Park and yet not move an inch from her tiny room on Seventy-fifth – that eye was as sharp as any knife juggler's. Here was the derelict house on Ridge Street, with the smoke stains besmirching the brick. Here was the dead dog that she'd described, lying on the sidewalk as though asleep, but that it lacked half its head. Here too, if Norma was to be believed, was the demon that Harry had come in search of: the shy and sublimely malignant Cha'Chat.

The house was not, Harry thought, a likely place for a desperado of Cha'Chat's elevation to be in residence. Though the infernal brethren could be a loutish lot, to be certain, it was Christian propaganda which sold them as dwellers in excrement and ice. The escaped demon was more likely to be downing fly eggs and vodka at the Waldorf-Astoria than concealing itself amongst such wretchedness.

But Harry had gone to the blind clairvoyant in desperation, having failed to locate Cha'Chat by any means conventionally available to a private eye such as himself. He was, he had admitted to her, responsible for the fact that the demon was loose at all. It seemed he'd never learned, in his all too frequent encounters with the Gulf and its progeny, that Hell possessed a genius for deceit. Why else had he believed in the child that had tottered into view just as he'd levelled his gun at Cha'Chat? – a child, of course, which had evaporated into a cloud of tainted air as soon as the diversion was redundant and the demon had made its escape.

Now, after almost three weeks of vain pursuit, it was almost Christmas in New York; season of goodwill and suicide. Streets thronged; the air like salt in wounds; Mammon in glory. A more perfect playground for Cha'Chat's despite could scarcely be imagined. Harry had to find the demon quickly, before it did serious damage; find it and return it to the pit from which it had come. In extremis he would even use the binding syllables which the late Father Hesse had vouchsafed to him once, accompanying them with such dire warnings that Harry had never even written them down. Whatever it took. Just as long as Cha'Chat didn't see Christmas Day this side of the Schism.

It seemed to be colder inside the house on Ridge Street than out. Harry could feel the chill creep through both pairs of socks and start to numb his feet. He was making his way along the second landing when he heard the sigh. He turned, fully expecting to see Cha'Chat standing there, its eye cluster looking a dozen ways at once, its cropped fur rippling. But no. Instead a young woman stood at the end of the corridor. Her undernourished features suggested Puerto Rican extraction, but that – and the fact that she was heavily pregnant – was all Harry had lime to grasp before she hurried away down the stairs.

Listening to the girl descend, Harry knew that Norma had been wrong. If Cha'Chat had been here, such a perfect victim would not have been allowed to escape with her eyes in her head. The demon wasn't here.

Which left the rest of Manhattan to search.

The night before, something very peculiar had happened to Eddie Axel. It had begun with his staggering out of his favourite bar, which was six blocks from the grocery store he owned on Third Avenue. He was drunk, and happy; and with reason. Today he had reached the age of fifty-five. He had married three times in those years; he had sired four legitimate children and a handful of bastards; and – perhaps most significantly – he'd made Axel's Superette a highly lucrative business. All was well with the world.

But Jesus, it was chilly! No chance, on a night threatening a second Ice Age, of finding a cab. He would have to walk home.

He'd got maybe half a block, however, when – miracle of miracles – a cab did indeed cruise by. He'd flagged it down, eased himself in, and the weird times had begun.

For one, the driver knew his name.

"Home, Mr. Axel?" he'd said. Eddie hadn't questioned the godsend. Merely mumbled, "Yes," and assumed this was a birthday treat, courtesy of someone back at the bar.

Perhaps his eyes had flickered closed; perhaps he'd even slept. Whatever, the next thing he knew the cab was driving at some speed through streets he didn't recognize, He stirred himself from his doze. This was the Village, surely; an area Eddie kept clear of. His neighbourhood was the high Nineties, close to the store. Not for him the decadence of the Village, where a shop sign offered 'Ear piercing. With or without pain' and young men with suspicious hips lingered in doorways.

"This isn't the right direction," he said, rapping on the Perspex between him and the driver. There was no word of apology or explanation forthcoming, however, until the cab made a turn toward the river, drawing up in a street of warehouses, and the ride was over,

"This is your stop," said the chauffeur. Eddie didn't need a more explicit invitation to disembark.

As he hauled himself out the cabbie pointed to the murk of an empty lot between two benighted warehouses. "She's been waiting for you," he said, and drove away. Eddie was left alone on the sidewalk.

Common sense counselled a swift retreat, but what now caught his eye glued him to the spot. There she stood – the

31

woman of whom the cabbie had spoken – and she was the most obese creature Eddie had ever set his sight upon. She had more chins than fingers, and her fat, which threatened at every place to spill from the light summer dress she wore, gleamed with either oil or sweat.

"*Eddie*," she said. Everybody seemed to know his name tonight. As she moved toward him, tides moved in the fat of her torso and along her limbs.

"Who are you?" Eddie was about to inquire, but the words died when he realised the obesity's feet weren't touching the ground. *She was floating.*

Had Eddie been sober he might well have taken his cue then and fled, but the drink in his system mellowed his trepidation. He stayed put.

"Eddie," she said. "Dear Eddie. I have some good news and some bad news. Which would you like first?"

Eddie pondered this one for a moment. "The good," he concluded.

"You're going to die tomorrow," came the reply, accompanied by the tiniest of smiles.

"*That's good?*" he said.

"Paradise awaits your immortal soul ... " she murmured. "Isn't that a joy?"

"So what's the bad news?"

She plunged her stubby-fingered hand into the crevasse between her gleaming tits. There came a little squeal of complaint, and she drew something out of hiding. It was a cross between a runty gecko and a sick rat, possessing the least fetching qualities of both. Its pitiful limbs pedalled at the air as she held it up for Eddie's perusal.

"This," she said, "is your immortal soul."

She was right, thought Eddie, the news was not good.

"Yes," she said. "It's a pathetic sight, isn't it?" The soul drooled and squirmed as she went on. "It's undernourished. It's weak to the point of expiring altogether. And *why?*" She didn't give Eddie a chance to reply. "A paucity of good works ... "

Eddie's teeth had begun to chatter. "What am I supposed to do about it?" he asked.

"You've got a little breath left. You must compensate for a lifetime of rampant profiteering-"
"I don't follow."
"Tomorrow, turn Axel's Superette into a Temple of Charity, and you may yet put some meat on your soul's bones."
She had begun to ascend, Eddie noticed. In the darkness above her there was sad, sad music, which now wrapped her up in minor chords until she was entirely eclipsed.

The girl had gone by the time Harry reached the street. So had the dead dog. At a loss for options, he trudged back to Norma Paine's apartment, more for the company than the satisfaction of telling her she had been wrong.

"I'm never wrong," she told him over the din of the five televisions and as many radios that she played perpetually. The cacophony was, she claimed, the only sure way to keep those of the spirit world from incessantly intruding upon her privacy: the babble distressed them. "I saw power in that house on Ridge Street," she told Harry, "sure as shit."

Harry was about to argue when an image on one of the screens caught his eye. An outside news broadcast pictured a reporter standing on a sidewalk across the street from a store ('Axel's Superette,' the sign read) from which bodies were being removed.

"What is it?" Norma demanded.

"Looks like a bomb went off," Harry replied, trying to trace the reporter's voice through the din of the various stations.

"Turn up the sound," said Norma. "I like a disaster."

It was not a bomb that had wrought such destruction, it emerged, but a riot. In the middle of the morning a fight had begun in the packed grocery store; nobody quite knew why. It had rapidly escalated into a bloodbath. A conservative estimate put the death toll at thirty, with twice as many injured. The report, with its talk of a spontaneous eruption of violence, gave fuel to a terrible suspicion in Harry.

"Cha'Chat ... " he murmured.

Despite the noise in the little room, Norma heard him speak.

"What makes you so sure?" she said.

Harry didn't reply. He was listening to the reporter's recapitulation of the events, hoping to catch the location of Axel's Superette. And there it was. Third Avenue, between Ninety-fourth and Ninety-fifth.

"Keep smiling," he said to Norma, and left her to her brandy and the dead gossiping in the bathroom.

Linda had gone back to the house on Ridge Street as a last resort, hoping against hope that she'd find Bolo there. He was, she vaguely calculated, the likeliest candidate for father of the child she carried, but there'd been some strange men in her life at that time; men with eyes that seemed golden in certain lights; men with sudden, joyless smiles. Anyway, Bolo hadn't been at the house, and here she was – as she'd known she'd be all along – alone. All she could hope to do was lie down and die.

But there was death and death. There was that extinction she prayed for nightly, to fall asleep and have the cold claim her by degrees; and there was that other death, the one she saw whenever fatigue drew her lids down. A death that had neither dignity in the going nor hope of a Hereafter; a death brought by a man in a grey suit whose face sometimes resembled a half-familiar saint, and sometimes a wall of rotting plaster.

Begging as she went, she made her way uptown toward Times Square. Here, amongst the traffic of consumers, she felt safe for a while. Finding a little deli, she ordered eggs and coffee, calculating the meal so that it just fell within the begged sum. The food stirred the baby. She felt it turn in its slumber, close now to waking. Maybe she should fight on a while longer, she thought. If not for her sake, for that of the child.

She lingered at the table, turning the problem over, until the mutterings of the proprietor shamed her out onto the street again.

It was late afternoon, and the weather was worsening. A woman was singing nearby, in Italian; some tragic aria. Tears close, Linda turned from the pain the song carried, and set off again in no particular direction.

As the crowd consumed her, a man in a grey suit slipped away from the audience that had gathered around the street-corner diva, sending the youth he was with ahead through the throng to be certain they didn't lose their quarry.

Marchetti regretted having to forsake the show. The singing much amused him. Her voice, long ago drowned in alcohol, was repeatedly that vital semitone shy of its intended target – a perfect testament to imperfectability – rendering Verdi's high art laughable even as it came within sight of transcendence. He would have to come back here when the beast had been dispatched. Listening to that spoiled ecstasy brought him closer to tears than he'd been for months; and he liked to weep.

Harry stood across Third Avenue from Axel's Superette and watched the watchers. They had gathered in their hundreds in the chill of the deepening night, to see what could be seen; nor were they disappointed. The bodies kept coming out: in bags, in bundles; there was even something in a bucket.

"Does anybody know exactly what happened?"' Harry asked his fellow spectators.

A man turned, his face ruddy with the cold.

"The guy who ran the place decided to *give* the stuff away," he said, grinning at this absurdity. "And the store was fuckin' swamped. Someone got killed in the crush – "

"I heard the trouble started over a can of meat," another offered. "Somebody got beaten to death with a can of meat."

This rumour was contested by a number of others; all had versions of events.

Harry was about to try and sort fact from fiction when an exchange to his right diverted him.

A boy of nine or ten had buttonholed a companion. "Did you smell her?"' he wanted to know. The other nodded vigorously. "Gross, huh?" the first ventured. "Smelled better shit;" came the reply, and the two dissolved into conspiratorial laughter.

Harry looked across at the object of their mirth. A hugely over-weight woman, underdressed for the season, stood on the periphery of the crowd and watched the disaster scene with tiny, glittering eyes. Harry had forgotten the questions he was going to ask the watchers. What he remembered, clear as yesterday, was the way his dreams conjured the infernal brethren. It wasn't their curses he recalled, nor even the deformities they paraded: it was the smell off them. Of burning hair and halitosis; of veal left to rot in the sun. Ignoring the debate around him, he started in the direction of the woman.

She saw him coming, the rolls of fat at her neck furrowing as she glanced across at him.

It was Cha'Chat, of that Harry had no doubt. And to prove the point, the demon took off at a run, the limbs and prodigious buttocks stirred to a fandango with every step. By the time Harry had cleared his way through the crowd the demon was already turning the corner into Ninety-fifth Street; but its stolen body was not designed for speed, and Harry rapidly made up the distance between them. The lamps were out in several places along the street, and when he finally snatched at the demon, and heard the sound of tearing, the gloom disguised the vile truth for fully five seconds until he realized that Cha'Chat had somehow sloughed off its usurped flesh, leaving Harry holding a great coat of ectoplasm, which was already melting like overripe cheese. The demon, its burden shed, was away; slim as hope and twice as slippery. Harry dropped the coat of filth and gave chase, shouting Hesse's syllables as he did so.

Surprisingly, Cha'Chat stopped in its tracks, and turned to Harry. The eyes looked all ways but Heavenward; the mouth was wide and attempting laughter. It sounded like someone vomiting down an elevator shaft.

"*Words,* D'Amour?" it said, mocking Hesse's syllables. "You think I can be stopped with words?"

"No," said Harry, and blew a hole in Cha'Chat's abdomen before the demon's many eyes had even found the gun.

"*Bastard!*" it wailed, "*Cocksucker!*" and fell to the ground, blood the colour of piss throbbing from the hole. Harry sauntered down

Lost Souls

the street to where it lay. It was almost impossible to slay a demon of Cha' Chat's elevation with bullets; but a scar was shame enough amongst their clan, Two, almost unbearable.

"Don't," it begged when he pointed the gun at its head. "Not the face,"

"Give me one good reason why not."

"You'll need the bullets," came the reply,

Harry had expected bargains and threats. This answer silenced him.

"There's something going to get loose tonight, D'Amour," Cha'Chat said. The blood that was pooling around it had begun to thicken and grow milky, like melted wax. "Something wilder than me."

"Name it," said Harry.

The demon grinned. "Who knows?" it said. "It's a strange season, isn't it? Long nights. Clear skies. Things get born on nights like this, don't you find?"

"*Where?*" said Harry, pressing the gun to Cha'Chat's nose.

"You're a bully, D'Amour," it said reprovingly. "You know that?"

"*Tell me...*"

The thing's eyes grew darker; its face seemed to blur.

"South of here, I'd say..." it replied. "A hotel .. ,"The tone of its voice was changing subtly; the features losing their solidity, Harry's trigger finger itched to give the damned thing a wound that would keep it from a mirror for life, but it was still talking, and he couldn't afford to interrupt its flow. "...on Forty-fourth," it said. "Between Sixth...Sixth and Broadway." The voice was indisputably feminine now. "Blue blinds," it murmured. "I can see blue blinds..."

As it spoke the last vestiges of its true features fled, and suddenly it was Norma who was bleeding on the sidewalk at Harry's feet.

"You wouldn't shoot an old lady, would you?" she piped up. The trick lasted seconds only, but Harry's hesitation was all that Cha'Chat needed to fold itself between one plane and the next, and flit. He'd lost the creature, for the second time in a month.

37

And to add discomfort to distress, it had begun to snow.

The small hotel that Cha'Chat had described had seen better years; even the light that burned in the lobby seemed to tremble on the brink of expiring. There was nobody at the desk. Harry was about to start up the stairs when a young man whose pate was shaved as bald as an egg, but for a single kiss curl that was oiled to his scalp, stepped out of the gloom and took hold of his arm.

"There's nobody here," he informed Harry.

In better days Harry might have cracked the egg open with his bare fists, and enjoyed doing so. Tonight he guessed he would come off the worse. So he simply said, "Well, I'll find another hotel then, eh?"

Kiss Curl seemed placated; the grip relaxed. In the next instant Harry's hand found his gun, and the gun found Kiss Curl's chin. An expression of bewilderment crossed the boy's face as he fell back against the wall, spitting blood.

As Harry started up the stairs, he heard the youth yell, "Darrieux!" from below.

Neither the shout nor the sound of the struggle had roused any response from the rooms. The place was empty. It had been elected, Harry began to comprehend, for some purpose other than hostelry.

As he started along the landing a woman's cry, begun but never finished, came to meet him. He stopped dead. Kiss Curl was coming up the stairs behind him two or three at a time; ahead, someone was dying. This couldn't end well, Harry suspected.

Then the door at the end of the corridor opened, and suspicion became plain fact. A man in a grey suit was standing on the threshold, skinning off a pair of bloodied surgical gloves. Harry knew him vaguely; indeed had begun to sense a terrible pattern in all of this from the moment he'd heard Kiss Curl call his employer's name. This was Darrieux Marchetti; also called the Cankerist; one of that whispered order of theological assassins whose directives came from Rome, or Hell, or both.

"D'Amour," he said.

Harry had to fight the urge to be flattered that he had been remembered.

"What happened here?" he demanded to know, taking a step toward the open door.

"Private business," the Cankerist insisted. "Please, no closer," Candles burned in the little room, and by their generous light, Harry could see the bodies laid out on the bare bed. The woman from the house on Ridge Street, and her child. Both had been dispatched with Roman efficiency.

"She protested," said Marchetti, not overly concerned that Harry was viewing the results of his handiwork. "All I needed was the child."

"What was it?" Harry demanded. "A demon?"

Marchetti shrugged. "We'll never know," he said. "But at this time of year there's usually something that tries to get in under the wire. We like to be safe rather than sorry. Besides, there are those – I number myself amongst them – that believe there is such a thing as a surfeit of Messiahs – "

"Messiahs?" said Harry. He looked again at the tiny body. "There was power there, I suspect," said Marchetti. "But it could have gone. either way. Be thankful, D'Amour. Your world isn't ready for revelation." He looked past Harry to the youth, who was at the top of the stairs. "Patrice. Be an angel, will you, bring the car over? I'm late for Mass."

He threw the gloves back onto the bed.

"You're not above the law," said Harry.

"Oh *please*," the Cankerist protested, "let's have no nonsense. It's too late at night."

Harry felt a sharp pain at the base of his skull, and a trace of heat where blood was running.

"Patrice thinks you should go home, D'Amour. And so do I."

The knife point was pressed a little deeper.

"Yes?" said Marchetti.

"Yes," said Harry.

"He was here," said Norma, when Harry called back at the house.

"Who?"

"Eddie Axel; of Axel's Superette. He came through, clear as daylight."

"Dead?"

"Of course dead. He killed himself in his cell. Asked me if I'd seen his soul."

"And what did you say?"

"I'm a telephonist, Harry; I just make the connections. I don't pretend to understand the metaphysics." She picked up the bottle of brandy Harry had set on the table beside her chair. "How sweet of you," she said. "Sit down. Drink."

Another time, Norma. When I'm not so tired." He went to the door. "By the way," he said. "You were right. There *was* something on Ridge Street ... "

"Where is it now?"

"Gone home."

"And Cha'Chat?"

"Still out there somewhere. In a foul temper..."

"Manhattan's seen worse, Harry."

It was little consolation, but Harry muttered his agreement as he closed the door.

The snow was coming on more heavily all the time.

He stood on the step and watched the way the flakes spiralled in the lamplight. No two, he had read somewhere, were ever alike. When such variety was available to the humble snowflake, could he be surprised that events had such unpredictable faces?

Each moment was its own master, he mused, as he put his head between the blizzard's teeth, and he would have to take whatever comfort he could find in the knowledge that between this chilly hour and dawn there were innumerable such moments – blind maybe, and wild and hungry – but all at least eager to be born.

Whisper Lane
Mark Chadbourn

Hailing from the Midlands and from a mining family, Mark Chadbourn interviewed scores of celebrities in his job as a journalist – from Paul McCartney, Bob Geldof and Elton John to Tim Burton, Catherine Zeta Jones and George Michael. His fiction-writing career took off when he won *Fear* magazine's Best New Author award for his first published short story, 'Six Dead Boys in a Very Dark World'. Critics have praised Mark Chadbourn for the astonishing detail and realism he brings to his novels. For his first novel *Underground*, set in an isolated mining community, he worked hundreds of feet beneath the earth. For *Nocturne* he spent time in the seedy underbelly of the Crescent City, New Orleans, meeting criminals, black magicians and voodoo practitioners. He viewed an autopsy and spent time among the Boiler Room sharp operators of London's financial district in preparation for *Scissorman*. And for his non-fiction book *Testimony*, Mark experienced the terrors of a real haunted house…

His bestselling fantasy trilogy, *The Age of Misrule* (*World's End*, *Darkest Hour* and *Always Forever*) has received acclaim not only for its detail, but also for its exhaustive historical research. *World's End* was nominated for the prestigious August Derleth Award for Best Novel, as was *Nocturne*, and Mark won the British Fantasy Award in 2003 for *The Fairy Feller's Master Stroke*.

He divides his time between writing for TV and penning bestselling novels, the latest of which – *Jack of Ravens* – begins another epic series. Mark Chadbourn currently lives in the heart of a forest where he indulges his passions for environmental campaigning and magic. His website can be found at www.markchadbourn.net

Mark tells us: "There is nothing like FantasyCon for stripping the patina of sophistication from even the most highly-regarded writer, editor or agent. FantasyCon is the great leveller, where all airs and graces are left at the door – along with dignity, usually. Case in point...

"In the late nineties when FantasyCon was still held regularly at a Birmingham city centre hotel, I witnessed award-winning author, raconteur and bon viveur Graham Joyce and award-winning publisher/editor/author ditto Pete Crowther running breathlessly down 14 flights of stairs, stopping off at each level to press the lift call button while laughing like hyenas. The point of this remarkable display of stamina – and, frankly, childish exuberance – was simply to torment a lift-full of leading editors and high-powered agents who had barrelled into the elevator ahead of a group of writers, artists and fans in a bid to get to the restaurant first.

"They emerged confused and cursing after their torturous journey down to be confronted by a lobby full of everyone they'd left behind. And naturally they got the seat in the restaurant next to the toilets...

"And if anyone says I was involved in that jape, they're lying."

Nine miles out, he pulled the car to the side and searched in the mirror for some sign of life. Blood moved beneath the skin and breath fogged the glass, but when he looked in his eyes he could see the truth.

The body was already in the ground by the time he made his way along increasingly run-down back streets, past a deserted industrial estate where a chemical smell hung in the air, and a boarded-up pub blackened by fire. He almost missed his destination. Someone had crudely attempted to whitewash over the sign indicating the turning, but 'Whisper Lane Estate' was just visible beneath the daubing. At the entrance road, a fire blazed in an oil drum. Behind it, graffiti was scrawled to warn the wary passer-by.

Beyond it, thick fog hung still and silent across the entire estate, trapped in place by some freakish microclimate. It only added to the dismal atmosphere. The social housing had once been proud and clean, but that time was more than forty years gone. Now gutters sagged and paint peeled, windows were patched with plywood or were filthy with dust that residents no longer had the energy to wipe off. More mindless graffiti scarred front walls and doors, tags feebly attempting to define fragile egos or abusive comments aimed at the residents. A pack of stray dogs ran by, barking wildly at something Jake couldn't see.

He was surprised to find his brother had been living in such a place. It had been many years since he had seen Peter, and perhaps hard times had crept up in the intervening years, but it still seemed too desperate a place for someone who had always been filled with life.

The day was fading out in a thin, grey light as Jake crept along at a funereal pace, peering at the names of the streets almost lost to the gloom. From out of the fog, a boy ran wildly into the middle of the road. Jake slammed on the brakes, his heart pounding at the near miss. The boy whirled to stare directly at Jake, but instead of the apologetic expression Jake was expecting, the boy's face was a snarl of hatred. He plucked a stone from the road and hurled it furiously. Jake threw up an arm to protect his face as the stone ricocheted off the windscreen. A large area was frosted. Jake swore loudly, but before he could get out for a confrontation, the boy had been swallowed up by the fog once more.

Rattled, Jake drove on.

Peter's house was as worn out as all the others. As Jake walked up the front path, muffled noises rose up away in the fog, and though there was something inherently disturbing about them, he couldn't quite put his finger on what it was. He hurried to the side door. His knock brought no reply, but he could see through the glass that a light was filtering under an inside door. Feeling oddly out of sorts, he tried the handle. It was open, and he slipped inside.

The lounge was glaringly lit from a single bare bulb. It was sparsely furnished and down-at-heel: an old TV playing with the sound down, a worn sofa, a threadbare carpet. On a dining chair in the centre of the room, a woman sat unnaturally still with her back to him. She was dressed in black.

"Hello?" Jake ventured.

The woman turned with stilted slowness and Jake could see it was Peter's wife Helen. Jake hadn't seen her in the ten years since the wedding, but she looked to have aged thirty years in that time. Though still in her thirties, her hair was filled with grey, and her face had the deep lines that could only be carved by hardship. She peered into Jake's face, and after a moment appeared to recognise him.

"Oh, it's you," she said flatly.

"I'm so sorry," Jake said. "I left in plenty of time to get to the funeral – "

"You shouldn't have come," she interjected.

"– but I kept getting lost. I'm sure the road signs aren't right. I asked for directions – "

"Nobody knows where this place is. They don't care," she said. "Good luck to them."

She turned away from him again, and Jake had to manoeuvre to get into her line of vision.

"Nobody came, you know. To the funeral. It was just me."

"I am sorry," he said. "You should have had some support. What about friends – ?"

"Round here?" she sneered.

Jake steeled himself. "Why did he do it, Helen?" She didn't reply. "Was there a note?"

"Just leave it."

"I was hoping to stay for a few days – "

"Spare room."

Jake couldn't tell if it was the grief or if she was on tranquilisers, but it was pointless talking to her. He got his bag from the car, then set off to find a pub he'd passed a couple of streets away. It was more difficult to locate in the fog than Jake imagined and he got turned around several times.

As he paused to get his bearings, an inexplicable atmosphere of unease crept up on him and the hairs on the back of his neck stood erect. He shrugged it off, but came to a halt after a few steps when he realised he was not alone. As the fog shifted in a slight breeze, he saw a woman in a black dress cross the road ahead of him. Her back was to him, but with the mourning outfit he at first thought it was Helen. Some instinct prevented him calling her name at the last, so he just watched as she was briefly illuminated in the diffuse glow of a streetlight.

Halfway across the road she came to a halt. She didn't move, or look around, and Jake had the odd sensation that she was waiting for him to call out to her, although she couldn't have known he was there. She continued to wait, and Jake watched, sure she would move soon, but she did not. He felt a strange urge to see her face, yet an equally odd repulsion. As he took a step closer, a feeling of great dread came over him. Unable to understand his reaction, he hurried away, glancing back only once, but the fog had already swallowed her up.

The Navigation was one of those pubs found on estates across the country that looked like they had been designed by someone who had never been in a pub in their life. It was too brightly lit, too cold, with too many open spaces that made it appear empty and unfriendly however many drinkers were there. That night only a handful of locals sat in ones or twos around the main bar area so that the place appeared even more desolate. Jake ordered a pint and stood at the bar, not quite sure why he had decided to stay on: was it to give Helen some support in the first few days after the funeral, or was it for himself?

Before he could find an answer, an argument broke out at the pool table. A short, stocky man with greasy hair was squaring up to another who towered over him like a bear. "You're letting me win," the short man shouted. "Don't you go doing me no favours."

The larger man protested angrily, but the row escalated with shocking rapidity until the shorter man punched the other in the genitals as if he was trying to fell a bull. As the larger man went down, the shorter one grabbed a pool ball from the table and hit the other in the face. Seconds later, the larger man was on the floor, feebly trying to protect himself as the ball was smashed repeatedly into his face. Blood and bits of tooth showered around.

Jake was stunned by the explosion of violence, and even more shocked by the way the other drinkers barely stirred from their pints. Sickened, Jake stepped forward to break up the fight.

A hand fell on his shoulder. "Don't."

A man in his fifties with an intelligent, compassionate face was standing behind him. "He's going to kill him," Jake protested.

"You can't get involved." The man's grip was firm on Jake's shoulder.

The bear-like man passed out. His stocky partner stormed off, hurling the dripping pool ball into a corner. The barman wandered out and dragged the prostrate figure to the toilets.

"Somebody should call the police," Jake said. "Why didn't anybody help?"

"Nobody will, round here." There was a strange tone to the man's voice that caught Jake's attention. He introduced himself as Frank Donaghy, a former teacher at the estate's school, since closed.

They retreated to a table in the corner away from the other drinkers and where Jake didn't have to look at the blood near the pool table, which the barman hadn't even bothered to mop up.

Frank appeared weary, but friendly. "What are you doing here?" he said. "Sorry, that sounded a bit brusque. It's just, we don't get many tourists at Whisper Lane." He smiled sardonically.

"Here for a funeral. Except I missed it," Jake said. "Got lost."

"That happens more than you might think round here." Frank sipped his lager without any relish. "Who – ?"

"My brother, Peter McKenzie. Do you know him?"

"Vaguely."

"Me too. I haven't seen him in ten years. Had a falling out just after his wedding. I didn't even know he'd moved here until I got the funeral notice from his wife."

"I'm sorry."

"You're sure you didn't hear about his death?"

"Should I have?"

"He poured petrol over himself and then set himself on fire in the middle of the street. I would think that would have got round."

"Ah." Frank stared into his lager. "Yes. I heard about that."

Jake felt relieved to talk to someone after the days of grief and the bottled-up emotions of the drive down. "I don't understand what happened. They say you never know, but Peter was always so positive...not the type who would take his own life."

"It's a mystery what goes on in people's heads."

The sickening circumstances surrounding the death were still too raw for Jake to consider easily. "He did it in broad daylight, outside his house. Before Peter struck the match, a postman went to stop him. His neighbours held the postman back. Why would they do that?"

"It was probably too late. Perhaps the postman would only have hurt himself."

Frank's eyes revealed that he knew all about Peter's death. It was understandable; in such an enclosed community, everyone would have heard all the gruesome details. He'd only pretended to spare Jake's feelings.

"Surely somebody could have done something to help him," Jake continued. Frank shifted uneasily. "What is it?" Jake pressed.

Frank weighed whether to respond. "Whisper Lane isn't a pleasant place to live. You need to understand that. It's not a pleasant place, and the people who live here aren't very pleasant either, me included. They deserve each other, you might say."

Jake didn't understand; Whisper Lane looked no worse than any other estate that needed a little cash spent on it. Frank saw his doubt and added, "Don't get in trouble here because no one will help you out. Ever. In Whisper Lane, you're on your own." He drained his beer in a hurry and stood up. "It's not the kind of place you want to stay around too long. Put some miles between you and here as soon as you can."

Back at the house, Helen was already slumbering in a tranquilised sleep so Jake found his way to the spare room. It was crammed with Peter's things that Helen had moved out en route to the dump or the charity shop, a relatively meagre collection of cheap clothes and shoes, mementoes, photos. The ones that had some weight were those Jake recalled from Peter's life before the wedding, and they looked oddly incongruous amid the worn and faded tatters of recent days, like gold shimmering in the gutter. Books, well-read but well-kept, classical CDs, a model plane that he had laboured over for days when he was sick in bed with chicken pox. That one affected Jake more than all the others: he recalled Peter painting it with the kind of love that had not been prevalent in their family. In an atmosphere of slaps and cold shoulders and long hours without adult supervision, every brush stroke felt like a revelation. Jake fought back the tears as he slipped into sleep.

He was woken by loud clanking from the kitchen. Grey light filled the room. The fog still wrapped Whisper Lane into a bleak, silent bundle. He wiped the moisture from the window; nothing moved outside.

Helen was preparing breakfast as if she was trying to punish someone, the crockery and cutlery clattering on the formica. She didn't look up when Jake entered.

"Any chance of some breakfast?" he asked.

"Get it yourself."

He blamed her attitude on the grief and set about making some toast. "Still foggy," he said to end the uncomfortable silence.

"It's always foggy."

"I suppose…this time of year…"

"No. It's always foggy. It never goes. It never will." She took her mug of strong tea to the table and stared into the middle distance as she drank.

After a moment, he said, "I need to understand why Peter committed suicide."

"Why does anybody commit suicide?"

"He must have been depressed, obviously. But he was always so upbeat, you know that. Of the two of us, he was the one who had hope things would turn out okay. Something must have changed him."

Helen sipped her tea, continued to stare into space.

"I can't rest until I find out what made him take his own life," he stressed.

Helen's eyes flickered towards him, and then she began to laugh coldly, growing more intense and hateful until she was barking and gasping for breath.

Jake couldn't stand to hear that sound. He left, and even when he was out on the street he could still hear her desperate laughter until the fog finally swallowed it up.

In the middle of the road outside the house, Jake found the unpleasant black smear that he had told himself he wouldn't seek out. Boiled human fat mixed with tarmac. No amount of hosing down by the emergency services would ever get rid of it. Jake could picture Peter rifling through the ramshackle wooden garage at the side of the house until he found the petrol can, then running into the road to pour the contents over his head. Jake could see the neighbours emerge from their homes into the fog, curious and slow, like ghosts. He watched as they restrained the postman trying to save Peter's life, and he wondered what depths of cruelty existed in that local gene pool that the spectacle of watching a man die was more valuable than saving his life.

Jake wanted to go to each door one after the other asking that very question, but he was afraid of the answer he would receive; afraid of what it would say about humanity; afraid that he would not be able to rest peacefully.

With his grief swelling once more, he moved away from that queasy smear. The streets of the place were so desolate the estate could have been abandoned, yet occasionally he glimpsed furtive movement behind the windows, impressions of lives being lived away from the light.

Eventually he found himself outside the bulk of the crumbling school, sealed off by a poorly-erected chain-link fence. Many of the windows had been boarded up and the walls were covered with graffiti, most of it highly offensive, some of it references to a girl, perhaps a former pupil. One wing had burned to the ground, and part of the remaining structure was blackened. Charred desks and chairs were scattered outside. The fire must have happened a while ago for scrubby weeds were pushing up through the soot-stained, broken concrete. Jake couldn't understand why it had not been repaired and brought back into use, but as it was, it was just another symbol of the terminal hopelessness that gripped the estate.

His attention was caught by movement in the shadows beyond the main doors that had been jammed open. Children, he thought, or a homeless person. But something piqued his curiosity and he felt the urge to investigate. As he started to push aside a ragged hole in the fence, he was startled by a voice behind him. "Don't go in there!"

A woman in her twenties watched him with a troubled uncertainty. Her dark hair was pulled back from a pale face that bore a scar above her right eye that looked like it had come from a knife. She could have been considered attractive if she made the most of herself, but she had the same beaten-down, couldn't be bothered air that afflicted everyone he had seen on Whisper Lane.

"I mean," she added with an uneasy hesitancy, "go in if you want. I'm not saying you shouldn't. If you want to risk it, it's up to you."

"Risk it?"

She grew more unsettled. "Forget I said anything."

She prepared to hurry off into the fog until Jake caught up with her. "I didn't mean anything by it," he said.

She grudgingly relented. "You're new here."

Jake introduced himself, and she told him her name was Megan. He explained about his brother's death, but her only response was, "When are you leaving?"

"Why does everyone want to know when I'm going?" he said.

"You can't stay." She shrugged, gestured at the bleak houses. "I mean, who'd want to stay? I'd pack my bag and go as soon as I can if I were you."

Jake noted a faked nonchalance in her words. Frank had exhibited the same attitude in the pub the previous night. "What's going on here?" he asked.

Fear lit her face briefly. They were interrupted by a loud cry.

The fog muffled it enough to make it hard to identify its origin, but it was followed by a couple of desperate shouts that gave him a bearing. "Somebody's in trouble," he said. Megan followed him reluctantly.

After a few minutes he came to a filthy canal that bounded the estate's eastern edge. The banks were so overgrown with bramble and fern the towpath was barely visible. Stinking and still, the black water beyond had the rainbow shimmer of oil pollutants. Plastic bottles floated and a shopping trolley, a sofa and various industrial barrels protruded like a tropical reef. Three children stood on the edge of the canal staring into the depths at something barely visible that resembled a large white fish. Its cries had been stilled, its struggling ended.

"Get him out!" Jake yelled. "Why aren't you helping him?" The boys looked at him with implacable eyes.

As Jake moved, Megan imposed herself between him and the steps down to the towpath, her eyes wide and desperate. "We've got to help," Jake said. "He's dying."

"It's too late. He's probably dead already."

Jake was disgusted by her response. He raced to the steps and a moment later he was in the freezing, greasy water, pulling the immobile form up from where it had been caught on the rusty springs of an old mattress. The boy was a little overweight and it was an effort for Jake to manoeuvre him up on to the towpath; even then no one came to help. His heart pounding, Jake gave mouth-to-mouth, not really knowing if he was doing it correctly, wishing someone else had taken the responsibility.

After what seemed too long, the boy convulsed, vomited water, then coughed and spat. His eyelids flickered open.

"It's all right," Jake said. He looked around in the expectation of sharing his relief, but Megan and the other boys had gone.

Shaking from his experience, the boy knocked Jake over as he scrambled to his feet.

"We need to get you to a hospital," Jake said.

The boy turned to Jake, his chubby face filled with contempt. "You've done it now," he said. "You stupid man!" Then he half-ran, half-staggered to the steps and was gone, leaving Jake overcome with confusion.

Jake changed out of his sodden clothes back at the house. Helen was not there, but all the doors were unlocked as if in recognition that there was nothing remotely worth stealing.

As he warmed himself against the single bar of an electric fire, Jake leafed through an old photo album he had found among Peter's things. There they were as children, together on Christmas morning; at some family birthday party when they were in their late teens, drunk on cheap wine; photos of them separately, still bright and accepting that everything always went right with the world, growing into the men they would become.

The memories were too painful, and Jake closed the album. Yet he had opened a long-sealed room and he could no longer prevent the escape of what lay within. He found himself turning to the events after Peter's wedding for the first time in many years, when he had killed the girl and everything had turned sour.

He was distracted from his thoughts by a sudden sharp pain in the middle of his back as if he had been poked hard by a bony finger. It was enough to make him leap to his feet, but when he examined the chair carefully there was nothing that could have accounted for it.

He put it down to a muscle spasm and decided to make his way to the pub for an early lunch. But as he left the house he was disturbed to see a large X had been daubed on the door in fresh red paint. It reminded him of one of the marks left on doors in the Middle Ages to denote the home of a plague-victim.

Along the street, two young girls playing in a front garden threw stones at him. An old woman dragging a shopping basket crossed the road to avoid him. The pub quietened several decibels at his entry, but no one looked his way. He jokingly asked the barman if he'd caught the pox or something. The barman took his money and poured his drink, but didn't acknowledge his presence in any other way.

Whisper Lane

For the rest of the day, Jake trawled the estate in search of anyone who might give him some insight into Peter's frame of mind before his death. But the story was the same wherever he went – the corner shop, the vandalised community centre, the fish and chip shop – frostiness that quickly turned to rage and threatened violence if he attempted to press himself upon anyone.

Night had fallen by the time he made it back to the house, and as Helen had predicted the fog had still not lifted. When he stepped through the door he found the house filled with a high-pitched, reedy crying. Helen had her head down on the kitchen table, sobbing uncontrollably. When she noticed him, she flew at him in a terrible rage.

"They painted the sign on the door!" she screeched, tearing at his chest with her nails. "It's you, isn't it?"

He grabbed her thin wrists. "What's wrong with this place?" he snapped.

She pulled herself away from his grip, turning her back on him. When she glanced over her shoulder, she reminded him of a cornered animal. "No good deed shall go unpunished," she hissed.

Wailing once again, she flew out of the room, sending a coffee mug smashing on the floor. He could hear that irritating thin sobbing coming from her room well into the night. He knocked once to see if she was all right, but the crying only got worse and he quickly retreated.

He slept fitfully. The senseless behaviour of the residents of Whisper Lane lay heavily on him; their motivations were mysterious, drifting in and out of the blanketing fog. Cold and uncaring, the faces of the boys watching as their friend slowly died. Megan trying to prevent him saving the boy. And then he was trapped in a circle of those uncaring faces while he burned alive; he was Peter and Peter was him.

He woke shortly after 3am, rigid as a board and slick with sweat. At first he didn't know where he was and a dull, unfocussed panic gripped him until the light from the streetlamp filtering through the curtains illuminated Peter's possessions. It was then he realised he was not alone.

In one corner hung a black, amorphous cloud that did not exist in any real sense, but felt like a patch on his vision, dead retinal cells obscuring what was really there. But he was paralysed, unable to move his head to look at it directly, or lift himself up, or swing his legs out of bed.

A suffocating dread fell across him as the springs protested at the foot of the bed. Something heavy crawled on to his legs, moving slowly up his body. A smell of damp and mould and wet bonfires enveloped him. Unable to cry out, he strained to look, but could only see a dense shadow. The weight pressed down on him, crushing his groin, his chest until he could barely breathe. Sharp, bony fingers pinched his flesh, working their way up to his face, tearing at his lips, prising open his mouth.

As the cloud loomed over him, he glimpsed a woman's face, soot-blackened, white eyes wide and staring and filled with a sickening hatred. They bore down on him, burning into his head, and then he blacked out from the unbearable dread.

When he woke, his face and jaw were in agony. He staggered to the bathroom to look in the bathroom mirror and saw dried blood caking his mouth. His upper left-hand incisor had been torn out by the root. He ran back to the bedroom and searched frantically for the missing tooth, but it was nowhere to be found.

A dull fear swelled inside him as he tried to make sense of what had happened. Helen had already gone out. Running out into the fogbound streets, he made his way to the corner shop where he scared the owner into directing him to Megan's house.

It was as run-down as all the others, but he could see through the windows that she'd made some attempt to brighten it inside. At first she wouldn't let him in, but when his anger gave way to dismay she finally relented. When she eventually met his eyes, Jake saw guilt there.

"I tried to warn you," she said hastily as if he was about to accuse her, but then she caught herself. "No, I didn't, not really. I couldn't."

He showed her the bloody hole where his tooth had been. "This happened last night. I don't understand what's going on, but you know something. You all do."

She led him through to the lounge, which smelled pleasantly flowery after the damp of Peter's house. "When you saved that boy you gave up your own life," she said flatly.

"You're not making any sense."

"None of it makes any sense!" Megan slumped on to the sofa, burying her head in her hands. "This isn't my home. I shouldn't even be here!" She struggled to modulate the hysteria that lay behind her voice. "I came here to stay with my boyfriend a year ago. Now I'm never going to be able to leave!"

Jake looked around, but could see no evidence of a male present in the house. "What did I see in my room last night?" Cold sweat ran down his spine. "What tore out my tooth?"

"That's just the first part," Megan said bitterly. "She'll keep taking things from you until there's nothing left. Some say she doesn't even stop then. You just move from one form of torment to the next."

"She?" That soot-blackened face, those hateful eyes.

"Annie, they call her. Black Annie."

He understood the implications of what she was saying, but he couldn't accept them. "Why was I attacked?"

"You saved that boy's life."

"That doesn't make any sense."

"No good deed shall go unpunished." Megan laughed humourlessly. "Annie has it in for everyone here…the whole of Whisper Lane. If anybody helps anybody else, Annie gives them her full attention. She gets her bony little claws in them, and she doesn't leave them alone until they're dead."

Jake's head was spinning and the ache in his jaw made him feel sick. "Why?"

"I don't know. It started before my time."

"What is it?" Jake asked desperately, but he already knew the answer and Megan merely gave him a contemptuous look.

Jake thought of the bleak mood that lay across the estate, of the mean-spirited residents looking after their own business as their community decayed. No good deeds. Nobody helping anyone else out. How long before that attitude took a grip and set off the relentless downwards spiral?

"I'll get away," he said.

"She won't let you leave, not now. You stay here for more than three days you're trapped for life. Or if you're marked by her."

"What could possibly stop me?"

"Someone tried to drive off a few months ago...not the first. Someone who'd moved here, like me, and didn't believe what they'd been told. They found the car on the edge of the estate. There was blood all over the inside of the windows. No sign of the driver."

Jake let this sink in. He didn't want to believe, but there was no escaping the lingering dread from the previous night. "So that's it for me?"

"There was a long pause and then Megan said quietly, "People say there's a way out. If you can get someone to do something good for you, Annie moves on to them and leaves you alone."

"But that means you've damned someone else. Who would do that?"

"You live here long enough you'll soon get an answer."

"And you don't know who she is and why she's doing this?"

Megan shook her head. Jake couldn't tell if she was lying. "Let me get you something for that tooth," she said, changing the subject. She caught herself. "There are painkillers in the bathroom cabinet if you want to help yourself."

"I get the message. I'm on my own."

He made to go, but Megan caught his arm. "Don't –"

Jake could see then how lonely she was, how lonely and miserable everyone on the entire estate must be. Whoever or whatever Annie was, she must hate them a great deal.

Megan made him a mug of tea and they talked for a long time, about mundane things to bring some normalcy back into their lives. Later she made him dinner and they drank a bottle of wine, and afterwards they had sex. There was no love, or any real attraction, just desperation for human comfort. The act was perfunctory and when it was over Megan cried.

It seemed she had something to tell him, but it took her an hour to get the words out. It was like a dam had broken. Between sobs she told him of her boyfriend, James, who had the misfortune to help their elderly neighbour when she slipped on an icy street.

"It started with a fingernail," she said. "By the time we'd accepted the truth of what everyone was telling us, he'd lost three toes, both thumbs and an eye. I had to watch him sobbing every day, scared, so scared, knowing he was just going to be…whittled down." She stared at him with red-rimmed eyes and he could see right into the horror of her experience. "And I sat by and didn't do a thing. I watched as he died, and I didn't give him any support or comfort in those awful final days, because I didn't want to bring it on myself. He was the man I loved, and all I thought about was myself. That's how worthless I am." She sobbed for another full minute and then added, "She likes it when she gets two. The one who dies…and the one who's left behind with their life ruined by guilt and self-loathing."

Jake wanted to comfort her, but there was nothing he could say. As she drifted into a troubled sleep, his thoughts turned to his own situation and he finally knew what had happened to Peter. His brother had always been the do-gooder who couldn't resist helping those in need, not like Jake. Peter must have resisted that impetus for much of his time on Whisper Lane, until finally it got the better of him. One good deed, one eternal punishment. He wondered how Peter would have felt with Black Annie coming night after night, taking things, cutting him down. Would it have driven such a decent man to the point of madness?

And so, when he could take no more, Peter poured petrol over himself and knelt in the middle of the street, desperately hoping someone would stop him striking a match. Not a neighbour, for they would know better. A postman, someone lost, a council worker, anyone. Good Peter was prepared to damn an innocent stranger to end his own suffering.

Was that Annie's mission, Jake wondered? To show everyone

the truth – that at the final reckoning everyone is as worthless as Megan said? All damned.

It took him a long time to go to sleep. And in the night he lost a finger.

In the morning, Megan cautiously cleaned and bound the bloody stump. Jake thought she was expecting him to cry with fear too, like James, but he was still a way from that.

At the door she asked him not to come back; she couldn't bear to watch another person being taken apart. Jake barely heard her. He was filled with a queasy desperation as the minutes of his life ticked away.

On the streets, he saw Whisper Lane with new eyes. At the entrance to the estate where the oil drum still blazed, the graffiti to which he had paid scant attention on his arrival now loomed up. *Stay away! Black Annie will get you.* It was there all over the school, which he had taken to be cruel children targeting one of their own. *Black Annie will get you.*

As he moved through the folding, silent fog, he had the unmistakeable impression that he was not alone. Behind him, lost in the dense grey cloud, someone followed, walking in his footsteps, matching him beat for beat, never deviating. He would stop, and the one pursuing him would stop. There was no sound to give it away, but Jake could feel the weight of it bearing upon his back. Once he turned and ran back, and he almost glimpsed it, a shiver of black retreating into the fog. He shuddered uncontrollably and did not attempt it again.

The rest of the estate continued to shun him, and Jake realised they knew exactly what walked with him. He drank alone in the pub, trying to still the waves of desperation. It was after his third pint that he began to make connections among the unbelievable information that had been given to him. The school was the source of Black Annie's power, he was sure of it; or at least that was what the residents believed. The vast amount of Black Annie graffiti that scarred the building suggested supplicants trying to fend off the attentions of an angry god. And Megan had been terrified that he might even consider entering the building. If the vengeful spirit existed anywhere, it was there.

In the dark, the burned-out hulk of the school was a brooding presence glowering from the depths of the fog. Jake tore aside the chain-link fence and slipped through, moving silently among the thistles to the gaping main doors. Despite the years that had passed, the damp air still held the charcoal smell of burning.

The creeping presence at Jake's back grew stronger as he moved slowly along the main corridor, stepping over rubble and broken glass, water-damaged text books and heat-twisted chairs and tables. It looked like no one had been inside since the fire.

Jake thought he saw movement in a classroom. An old lesson was still scrawled on the whiteboard. Outside the broken windows, the fog moved as if it had a life of its own, turned into mother-of-pearl by the diffuse illumination of the streetlamps.

The atmosphere in the school was unmistakeably altered; though he couldn't see Black Annie, he could feel her presence in every fibre of the building, sense her eyes on him. The dread was almost unbearable. He began to think that if he disturbed her in her lair, she would tear him apart in the same way that she had destroyed the person Megan told him about who had tried to leave the estate. He felt almost delirious from the intense fear, and though he wanted to run from there, he knew his only hope of survival was to lay her to rest, if that was at all possible.

He didn't know how he managed to search the school from top to bottom, and much of it passed in a queasy blur. Eventually there was only one place left to go, the boiler room, the black pit where all his greatest fears lay. Unconsciously he had left it till last for a part of him knew that was where he would find her. The door opened with a loud judder that resonated off the metres of pipework in the cavernous dark. Cautiously, he moved forward, trailing one hand along a cold, damp pipe for guidance, trying to focus on his feeble plan of confronting her with prayers in which he didn't believe.

There were too many distracting sensations and he didn't know exactly when his hand had moved from the chill ironwork on to something dry and rustling. But then the dark rose up filled with the foul smell he had first experienced two nights before, and in it he glimpsed something so terrible that his mind refused to cooperate. Blood flowed freely from his ragged cheek, but by then he was running, no longer capable of conscious thought.

By the time rationality returned to him, he was far from the school, struggling with fragments of memory: staring eyes, a hideous face, a *presence* that haunted deep in his unconscious. He made his way slowly back to the house through the fogbound streets, determined that he would stay awake and run when she next came for him.

But in the middle of the night as he sat on the bed, hugging his knees fearfully, he heard movement on the stairs, and a few seconds later sensed something lowering just outside the door.

That was all he could recall until he woke in the thin, grey light. This time Annie had taken two things to punish him for his audacity: the big toe of his left foot and his right eye.

Jake waited in the pub car park, swathed in the fog, not alone, never alone. The day had passed rapidly; he was almost delirious with the pain and the fear. A bloodstained bandage was tied at an angle to cover his missing eye, the socket aching as if someone had smashed it with a hammer. He supported himself on the rusty boot of a car and watched the pub's rear door.

After a couple of hours, Frank lurched out drunkenly, pausing briefly in the hazy golden light from the lamp above the door. He attempted to light a cigarette and then gave up. As he staggered into the car park, Jake walked up.

Frank was shocked to see Jake's condition, but then he shifted uneasily and stared at the ground.

"Don't worry, I'm not going to ask you to help me," Jake said.

"It's not that I don't want to," Frank began pathetically. Jake waved him quiet.

"I don't want to die, Frank, which is ironic because over the last few years I've thought about taking my life more than once."

"You're scared," Frank said. "That's understandable. You should be."

"Thanks. Three days ago you told me the people who live here aren't very pleasant, you included. Do you still hold with that?"
Frank smiled tightly. "Well, you're one of us now. Perhaps you've found your own." There was a snide tone underpinning his words that answered Jake's question.
Frank made to push by. Jake caught him and they struggled briefly, falling to the damp tarmac where Jake's frenzied desperation overcame Frank's drunkenness. After his head had been cracked against the hard ground three times, Frank lost consciousness.

Jake watched him come round in the gloom of the school boiler room. His confusion at the washing line that held his hands tight to one of the pipes gave way to mounting panic when he realised his location.
"Let me go," Frank squealed at Jake. His neck muscles grew taut as he strained to see into the dark with wide, terrified eyes. "You don't know what you're doing."
"I've got nothing to lose." Jake hid his shaking hands behind his back. "You were right. I fit in this place really well. My brother was the good one in the family, and even he gave into the vile mood of this place eventually. I'm already there. I'm home."
Frank launched into a frantic yanking, but the plastic line only bit deeper into his wrists.
"What's her connection to this place?" Jake's voice echoed eerily through the emptiness.
Frank swallowed twice before he could speak. "Will you let me go if I tell you?" Jake nodded. "I can tell you what the locals say, but I can't vouch for it being true."
"Go on."
"They say Annie came to work here as a teacher with underprivileged kids," he began desperately. "This would be back in the eighties. There were no jobs, no money to go around. Lots of kids were underprivileged. At the time they talked about a whole generation being wasted. She did a good job, by all accounts, tireless service to a good cause, the kind of dedication you rarely see these days." Frank's eyes were fixed on the dark depths of the boiler

room. "Then one of the children died," he continued tremulously. "Killed, I suppose. Everyone blamed Annie. She denied it, but there was supposed to have been some kind of evidence…an investigation was set in motion. I don't know. Annie ended up taking her own life. They found her hanging here. Everyone said that was proof enough – it was her guilt speaking."

"You're talking like she didn't do it," Jake said.

After a moment's silence, Frank replied, "The way people tell it, a while later some other evidence came up. It wasn't her at all. Somebody local was supposed to have killed the child, accidentally, I suppose. The community got together to protect their own and decided to blame the outsider."

"And now she's getting her revenge, is that what you're saying?"

"I don't know. It's just how people talk. Maybe it's just an urban legend…" His voice trailed off and he fought to compose himself. "…people trying to make sense of something that's completely senseless. All I know is it's been hell here for nearly as long as I can remember." He started to cry with silent, desperate sobs as if the well of his tears had dried up long ago.

"Centuries ago there used to be a folk tale about someone called Black Annis, some witchy figure who used to hunt and eat children. Maybe that's where it comes from," Jake said, recalling the inhuman face he had glimpsed the previous night. "Or maybe Whisper Lane has always been a stinking, horrible place and it just attracted something that felt at home here. Maybe bad places attract bad things. And bad people. Maybe that's just how it works."

Frank continued to whimper and strain at his bonds.

"When I was younger, I killed a girl." Jake's flat monotone echoed. "I was driving home late at night. I'd had a bit too much to drink. Not drunk, you understand, but too much, certainly. I didn't see her until the very last second. She was right against the hedgerow, dressed in dark clothes. There was no time to pull out. I hit her with the wing and she went up and over the car. I stopped…I did. I got out and checked and she was definitely killed instantly…well, there's no need to go into details. It wasn't a pretty sight.

"I was devastated. I drove straight home and phoned my brother.

Peter told me I should call the police straight away. That poor girl's family needed to know what had happened. They had to be able to try to put the whole thing to rest, and they couldn't do that without me owning up."

Jake picked up an old bottle and hurled it into the dark where it shattered loudly. Frank flinched as if he'd been shot.

"Peter was right," Jake continued. "I knew he was, even then, with me sobbing on the phone. But I couldn't bring myself to do it. I didn't want to be breathalysed, I didn't want to go to jail. It just came down to survival, and that took precedence over that girl's family.

"Peter never forgave me. He was so…moral. But I was his brother and he loved me. He wouldn't tell the police. So he had to carry around my burden, dealing with his own guilt that he couldn't wipe away. We didn't talk after that, but recently I wondered if that started his downward spiral. He was always on the way up before. And then he ended up here. Do you get what I'm saying, Frank? Peter earned his place in Whisper Lane with his guilt. Maybe everyone who lives here deserves to be here. I know I do. A bad place attracting bad people and broken people and haunted people, and giving them the punishment they think they deserve. What do you think about that? What's your particular guilty secret, Frank?"

Frank wouldn't meet Jake's gaze.

Jake sensed the presence at the far end of the boiler room before he noticed a shift in the quality of the dark. Frank saw Jake's sudden attention and began to scream in a manner that reminded Jake of pigs he had once heard at a slaughterhouse.

"Stop struggling. I'll free you," Jake snapped. The dark moved towards them.

His terror had taken away any signs of rationality from Frank's eyes; he was driven only by primal urges. Jake freed Frank and the two of them scrambled towards the exit, tearing at one another, crashing against the dead pipes.

At the door, Jake fell hard, tangling himself in Frank's legs and bringing Frank down too. Frank squealed and thrashed. Movement in the gloom behind them hinted at a shape, drawing closer, but it was impossible for Jake to tell if it was human or not; it seemed, from his strained perspective, to be a cloud of tattered rags blown by a wind that he could not feel.

Frank clawed his way to his feet. "Help me!" Jake yelled. "I've hurt my leg!" He extended a hand.

Instinctively, Frank hauled Jake to his feet and threw himself towards the door. He only realised what he had done when his hand closed on the handle. "No," he moaned. "Take it back. Take it back!"

Jake knocked him to one side and wrenched open the door. He ran up the stairs and along the corridor, without sense or reason and came to a halt when he was finally beyond the chainlink fence. There was one gut-wrenching scream deep in the bowels of the building, and then silence.

Jake felt no sense of elation, just a sickening recognition of what he had always feared to be the case about himself. He trudged back to Megan's house, thinking of the dismal years stretching ahead of him in that depressing place.

Megan answered the door, her expression fearful and mean-spirited.

"It's over." He felt bone-weary. "I've passed it on."

He half-expected some judgmental comments, but he should have known better. She opened the door wider to let him in. "You can stay here," she said coldly. "But don't you go being nice to me."

"Don't worry," he replied. "I won't."

THE MAN WHO DREW CATS
Michael Marshall Smith

Michael Marshall Smith was born in Knutsford, Cheshire, and grew up in the United States, South Africa, and Australia before moving to North London, where he currently lives with his wife Paula, their son, and two cats. After gaining a degree in philosophy from Cambridge University, he tried his hand at comedy writing and performing for BBC Radio. After winning the BFS Award for short story (see following) he went on to write three Science Fiction novels: *Only Forward* (which won the August Derleth and Philip K. Dick Awards), *Spares* (which was optioned by Steven Spielberg's Dreamworks SKG company) and *One of Us* (which was optioned by Warner Brothers). Under the name Michael Marshall he then penned the Sunday Times Bestselling *The Straw Men* (which Stephen King described as 'brilliantly written and scary as hell'), *The Lonely Dead* and *Blood of Angels*. He is one of the finest exponents of the short story working today and his collections include *What You Make It*, *Cat Stories* and *More Tomorrow and Other Stories*, listed in *Horror: Another 100 Best Books* (2005). His website can be found at www.michaelmarshallsmith.com

Says Michael: "'The Man Who Drew Cats' is a very significant story for me in at least two ways – the most obvious being that it was the first short story I ever wrote.

"I was on a three-month theatrical tour over the Summer of 1987, had just discovered Stephen King and was obsessively reading everything he'd written up to that point. The tour concluded in a two-week late-night run at the Edinburgh Fringe, and it was while wandering moodily around Prince's Street that I happened to hear a child crying – at the same time I was casting a desultory eye over the work of a pavement chalk artist. These two things collided to produce an idea for a story, which I started as soon as I got back home. I finished the first draft in a day and a half, edited it for a while, and finally realised that I'd actually written something.

"I had no idea what to actually *do* with a story, now I had one, and so just left it in longhand in my notebook. Over the next nine months I wrote a few more, which languished in the same way. Then I was lucky enough to meet Nicholas Royle (he happened to be leaving a company which I somewhat randomly arrived at to do temp work, and we got on immediately). He read the stuff I'd done, claimed it wasn't complete rubbish, and gave me encouragement and support without which I probably wouldn't now be a writer. He also gave me some pointers on where to send stories, and so I mailed 'The Man Who Drew Cats' to Kathy Gale, then working at Pan, in the hope of getting it to the guy editing the *Books Of Horror* series. The series had closed down, but she passed it on to the person who was putting together a replacement.

"That someone was Stephen Jones. He and David Sutton took the story, and it was published in *Dark Voices II*, in 1990. I can still very clearly remember getting the news it had been accepted: along with hearing I'd sold my first novel, and (much later) receiving a cover quote for *The Straw Men* from Stephen King, it counts as one of the four most jaw-dropping moments of my so-called career.

"The following year, Nick Royle encouraged me to come along with him to FantasyCon. I'd never had anything to do with the BFS before, never been to an open evening or convention of any kind, and I turned up to the hotel in London with absolutely no idea what to expect. Within half an hour I was standing at the bar, where I quickly met a number of people who've become lifelong friends – including, for the first time in person, Mr. Stephen Jones. I believe it was Steve who told me something *else* I'd had no previous conception of – that 'The Man Who Drew Cats' had been nominated for Best Short Story, and I'd also somehow been put up for the Best Newcomer Award.

"And the fourth high point? (You *were* counting earlier, right?) I had a pre-existing family commitment and so missed the Saturday at the convention, but came back for the banquet on the Sunday afternoon – where I was stunned to find myself winning both awards. I can vividly remember standing there, in front of all those people, and having absolutely no idea what to say. I'm not sure I've ever been so surprised, before or since.

"Winning a BFS Award emboldened me to approach Jane Johnson at HarperCollins (another tip from Nick) to see if she had any interest in publishing a collection of my short fiction. She politely refrained from saying 'A collection from a complete unknown? Are you out of your fucking mind?' – and instead encouraged me to send a novel, when I finished one. Turned out she'd actually been there at the banquet, when I won the awards.

"Three months later I finished *Only Forward*, sent it to her, and she accepted it. Lucky bastard, or what?"

"Yeah, I know. Though I've paid for it since."

"My wife and I sometimes have heated conversations about 'fate'. She believes in it, I don't (probably because I'm a Taurus, apparently. I don't believe in astrology either). One of the main reasons I tend to dismiss the idea of fate, however, is that it scares me. What if the past, that immutable other country, had worked out slightly differently? If I hadn't been standing at a particular point on an Edinburgh street almost twenty years ago, I wouldn't have written the story that follows. I'd've had nothing to talk to Nick Royle about, and we wouldn't have ended up being best man at each other's weddings. I wouldn't have wound up with Stephen Jones as friend and business partner. I wouldn't have attended my very first FantasyCon, and there met probably half the people I now count as mates – and gone back to the convention year after year to talk

about writing and reading and whose round it was next.
"You want to talk about horror stories? That works for me."

Tom was a very tall man, so tall he didn't even have a nickname for it. Ned Black, who was at least a head shorter, had been 'Tower Block' since the sixth grade, and Jack had a sign up over the door saying 'Mind Your Head, Ned'. But Tom was just Tom. It was like he was so tall it didn't bear mentioning even for a joke: be a bit like ragging someone for breathing.

Course there were other reasons too for not ragging Tom about his height or anything else. The guys you'll find perched on stools round Jack's bar watching the game and buying beers, they've known each other forever. Gone to Miss Stadler's school together, gotten under each other's Mom's feet, double-dated right up to giving each other's best man's speech. Kingstown is a small place, you understand, and the old boys who come regular to Jack's mostly spent their childhoods in the same tree-house. Course they'd since gone their separate ways, up to a point: Pete was an accountant now, had a small office down Union Street just off the Square and did pretty good, whereas Ned was still pumping gas and changing oil and after forty years he did that pretty good too. Comes a time when men have known each other so long they forget what they do for a living most the time, because it just don't matter. When you talk there's a little bit of skimming stones down the quarry in second grade, a whisper of dolling up to go to that first dance, a tad of going to the housewarming when they moved ten years back. There's all that, so much more than you can say, and none of it's important except for having happened.

So we'll stop by and have a couple of beers and talk about the town and rag each other, and the pleasure's just in shooting the breeze and it don't really matter what's said, just the fact that we're all still there to say it.

But Tom, he was different. We all remember the first time we saw him. It was a long hot summer like we haven't seen in the ten

The Man Who Drew Cats

years since, and we were lolling under the fans at Jack's and complaining about the tourists. Kingstown does get its share in the summer, even though it's not near the sea and we don't have a MacDonalds and I'll be damned if I can figure out why folk'll go out of their way to see what's just a quiet little town near some mountains. It was as hot as Hell that afternoon and as much as a man could do to sit in his shirt sleeves and drink the coolest beer he could find, and Jack's is the coolest for us, and always will be, I guess.

Then Tom walked in. His hair was already pretty white back then, and long, and his face was brown and tough with grey eyes like diamonds set in leather. He was dressed mainly in black with a long coat that made you hot just to look at it, but he looked comfortable like he carried his very own weather around with him and he was just fine.

He got a beer, and sat down at a table and read the town *Bugle*, and that was that.

It was special because there wasn't anything special about it. Jack's Bar isn't exactly exclusive and we don't all turn round and stare at anyone new if they come in, but that place is like a monument to shared times. If a tourist couple comes in out of the heat and sits down, nobody says anything – and maybe nobody even notices at the front of their mind – but it's like there's a little island of the alien in the water and the currents just don't ebb and flow the way they usually do, if you get what I mean. Tom just walked in and sat down and it was all right because it was like he was there just like we were, and could've been for thirty years. He sat and read his paper like part of the same river, and everyone just carried on downstream the way they were.

Pretty soon he goes up for another beer and a few of us got talking to him. We got his name and what he did – painting, he said – and after that it was just shooting the breeze. That quick. He came in that summer afternoon and just fell into the conversation like he'd been there all his life, and sometimes it was hard to imagine he hadn't been. Nobody knew where he came from, or where he'd been, and there was something real quiet about him. A stillness, a man in a slightly different world. But he showed enough to get along real well with us, and a bunch of old friends don't often let someone in like that.

Anyway, he stayed that whole summer. Rented himself a place just round the corner from the square, or so he said: I never saw it. I guess no-one did. He was a private man, private like a steel door with four bars and a couple of six-inch padlocks, and when he left the square at the end of the day he could have vanished as soon as he turned the corner for all we knew. But he always came from that direction in the morning, with his easel on his back and paintbox under his arm, and he always wore that black coat like it was a part of him. But he always looked cool, and the funny thing was when you stood near him you could swear you felt cooler yourself. I remember Pete saying over a beer that it wouldn't surprise him none if, assuming it ever rained again, Tom would walk round in his own column of dryness. He was just joking, of course, but Tom made you think things like that.

Jack's bar looks right out onto the square, the kind of square towns don't have much anymore: big and dusty with old roads out each corner, tall shops and houses on all the sides and some stone paving in the middle round a fountain that ain't worked in living memory. Well in the summer that old square is just full of out-of-towners in pink toweling jumpsuits and nasty jackets standing round saying 'Wow' and taking pictures of our quaint old hall and our quaint old stores and even our quaint old selves if we stand still too long. Tom would sit out near the fountain and paint and those people would stand and watch for hours – but he didn't paint the houses or the square or the old Picture House. He painted animals, and painted them like you've never seen. Birds with huge blue speckled wings and cats with cutting green eyes; and whatever he painted it looked like it was just coiled up on the canvas ready to fly away. He didn't do them in their normal colours, they were all reds and purples and deep blues and greens – and yet they fair sparkled with life. It was a wonder to watch: he'd put up a fresh paper, sit looking at nothing in particular, then dip his brush into his paint and draw a line, maybe red, maybe blue. Then he'd add another, maybe the same colour, maybe not. Stroke by stroke you could see the animal build up in front of your eyes and yet when it was finished you couldn't believe it hadn't always been there. When he'd finished he'd spray it with some stuff to fix the paints and put a price on it and you can believe me those paintings were sold before they hit the ground. Spreading businessmen from New Jersey or somesuch and their bored wives would come alive for maybe the first time in years, and walk away with one of those paintings and their arms round each other, looking like they'd found a bit of something they'd forgotten they'd lost.

Come about six o'clock Tom would finish up and walk across to Jack's, looking like a sailing ship amongst rowing boats and saying yes he'd be back again tomorrow and yes, he'd be happy to do a painting for them. He'd get a beer and sit with us and watch the game and there'd be no paint on his fingers or his clothes, not a spot. I figured he'd got so much control over that paint it went where it was told and nowhere else.

I asked him once how he could bear to let those paintings go. I know if I'd been able to make anything that good in my whole life I couldn't let it out of my sight, I'd want to keep it to look at sometimes. He thought for a moment and then he said he believed it depends how much of yourself you've put into it. If you've gone deep down and pulled up what's inside and put it down, then you don't want to let it go: you want to keep it, so's you can check sometimes that it's still safely tied down. Comes a time when a painting's so right and so good that it's private, and no-one'll understand it except the man who put it down. Only he is going to know what he's talking about. But the everyday paintings, well they were mainly just because he liked to paint animals, and liked for people to have them. He could only put a piece of himself into something he was going to sell, but they paid for the beers and I guess it's like us fellows in Jack's Bar: if you like talking, you don't always have to be saying something important.

Why animals? Well if you'd seen him with them I guess you wouldn't have to ask. He loved them, is all, and they loved him right back. The cats were always his favorites. My old Pa used to say that cats weren't nothing but sleeping machines put on the earth to do some of the human's sleeping for them, and whenever Tom worked in the square there'd always be a couple curled up near his feet. And whenever he did a chalk drawing, he'd always do a cat.

Once in a while, you see, Tom seemed to get tired of painting on paper, and he'd get out some chalks and sit down on the baking flagstones and just do a drawing right there on the dusty rock. Now I've told you about his paintings, but these drawings were something else again. It was like because they couldn't be bought but would be washed away, he was putting more of himself into it, doing more than just shooting the breeze. They were just chalk on dusty stone and they were still in these weird colours, but I tell you children wouldn't walk near them because they looked so real, and they weren't the only ones, either. People would stand a few feet back and stare and you could see the wonder in their eyes. If they could've been bought there were people who would have sold their houses. I'm telling you. And it's a funny thing but a couple of times when I walked over to open the store up in the mornings I saw a dead bird or two on top of those drawings, almost like they had landed on it and been so terrified to find themselves right on top of a cat they'd dropped dead of fright. But they must have been dumped there by some real cat, of course, because some of those birds looked like they'd been mauled a bit. I used to throw them in the bushes to tidy up and some of them were pretty broken up.

Old Tom was a godsend to a lot of mothers that summer, who found they could leave their little ones by him, do their shopping in peace and have a soda with their friends and come back to find the kids still sitting quietly watching Tom paint. He didn't mind them at all and would talk to them and make them laugh, and kids of that age laughing is one of the best sounds there is. It's the kind of sound that makes the trees grow. They're young and curious and the world spins round them and when they laugh the world seems a brighter place because it takes you back to the time when you knew no evil and everything was good, or if it wasn't, it would be over by tomorrow.

And here I guess I've finally come down to it, because there was one little boy who didn't laugh much, but just sat quiet and watchful, and I guess he probably understands more of what happened that summer than any of us, though maybe not in words he could tell.

His name was Billy McNeill, and he was Jim Valentine's kid.

The Man Who Drew Cats

Jim used to be a mechanic, worked with Ned up at the gas station and raced beat-up cars after hours. Which is why his kid is called McNeill now: one Sunday Jim took a corner a mite too fast and the car rolled and the gas tank caught and they never did find all the wheels. A year later his Mary married again. God alone knows why, her folks warned her, her friends warned her, but I guess love must just have been blind. Sam McNeill's work schedule was at best pretty empty, and mostly he just drank and hung out with friends who maybe weren't always this side of the law. I guess Mary had her own sad little miracle and got her sight back pretty soon, because it wasn't long before Sam got free with his fists when the evenings got too long and he'd had a lot too many. You didn't see Mary around much anymore. In these parts people tend to stare at black eyes on a woman, and a deaf man could hear the whisperings of 'We Told Her So'.

One morning Tom was sitting painting as usual, and little Billy was sitting watching him. Usually he just wandered off after a while but this morning Mary was at the Doctor's and she came over to collect him, walking quickly with her face lowered. But not low enough. I was watching from the store, it was kind of a slow day. Tom's face never showed much. He was a man for a quiet smile and a raised eyebrow, but he looked shocked that morning. Mary's eyes were puffed and purple and there was a cut on her cheek an inch long. I guess we'd sort of gotten used to seeing her like that and if the truth be known some of the wives thought she'd got remarried a bit on the soon side and I suppose we may all have been a bit cold towards her, Jim Valentine having been so well-liked and all.

Tom looked from the little boy who never laughed much, to his mom with her tired unhappy eyes and her beat-up face, and his own face went from shocked to stony and I can't describe it any other way but that I felt a cold chill cross my heart from right across the square.

But then he smiled and ruffled Billy's hair and Mary took Billy's hand and they went off. They turned back once and Tom was still looking after them and he gave Billy a little wave and he waved back and mother and child smiled together.

That night in Jack's Tom put a quiet question about Mary and we told him the story. As he listened his face seemed to harden from within, his eyes growing flat and dead. We told him that old Lou Lachance, who lived next door to the McNeill's, said that sometimes you could hear him shouting and her pleading till three in the morning and on still nights the sound of Billy crying for even longer than that. Told him it was a shame, but what could you do? Folks keep themselves out of other people's faces round here, and I guess Sam and his drinking buddies didn't have much to fear from nearly-retireders like us anyhow. Told him it was a terrible thing, and none of us liked it, but these things happened and what could you do.

Tom listened and didn't say a word. Just sat there in his black coat and listened to us pass the buck. After a while the talk sort of petered out and we all sat and watched the bubbles in our beers. I guess the bottom line was that none of us had really thought about it much except as another chapter of small-town gossip, and Jesus Christ did I feel ashamed about that by the time we'd finished telling it. Sitting there with Tom was no laughs at all. He had a real edge to him, and seemed more unknown than known that night. He stared at his laced fingers for a long time, and then he began, real slow, to talk.

He'd been married once, he said, a long time ago, and he'd lived in a place called Stevensburg with his wife Rachel. When he talked about her the air seemed to go softer and we all sat quiet and supped our beers and remembered how it had been way back when we first loved our own wives. He talked of her smile and the look in her eyes and when we went home that night I guess there were a few wives who were surprised at how tight they got hugged, and who went to sleep in their husband's arms feeling more loved and contented than they had in a long while.

He'd loved her and she him and for a few years they were the happiest people on earth. Then a third party had got involved. Tom didn't say his name, and he spoke real neutrally about him, but it was a gentleness like silk wrapped round a knife. Anyway his wife fell in love with him, or thought she had, or leastways she slept with him. In their bed, the bed they'd come to on their wedding night. As Tom spoke these words some of us looked up at him, startled, like we'd been slapped across the face.

Rachel did what so many do and live to regret till their dying day. She was so mixed up and getting so much pressure from the other guy that she decided to plough on with the one mistake and make it the biggest in the world.

She left Tom. He talked with her, pleaded even. It was almost impossible to imagine Tom ever doing that, but I guess the man we knew was a different guy from the one he was remembering. The pleading made no difference.

And so Tom had to carry on living in Stevensburg, walking the same tracks, seeing them around, wondering if she was as free and easy with him, if the light in her eyes was shining on him now. And each time the man saw Tom he'd look straight at him and crease a little smile, a grin that said he knew about the pleading and he and his cronies had had a good laugh over the wedding bed – and yes, I'm going home with your wife tonight and I know just how she likes it, you want to compare notes?

And then he'd turn and kiss Rachel on the mouth, his eyes on Tom, smiling. And she let him do it.

It had kept stupid old women in stories for weeks, the way Tom kept losing weight and his temper and the will to live. He took three months of it and then left without bothering to sell the house. Stevensburg was where he'd grown up and courted and loved and now wherever he turned the good times had rotted and hung like fly-blown corpses in all the cherished places. He'd never been back.

It took an hour to tell, and then he stopped talking a while and lit a hundredth cigarette and Pete got us all some more beers. We were sitting sad and thoughtful, tired like we'd lived it ourselves. And I guess most of us had, some little bit of it. But had we ever loved anyone the way he'd loved her? I doubt it, not all of us put together. Pete set the beers down and Ned asked Tom why he hadn't just beaten the living shit out of the guy. Now, no-one else would have actually asked that, but Ned's a good guy, and I guess we were all with him in feeling a piece of that oldest and most crushing hatred in the world, the hate of a man who's lost the woman he loves to another, and we knew what Ned was saying. I'm not saying it's a good thing and I know you're not supposed to feel like that these days but show me a man who says he doesn't and I'll show you a liar. Love is the only feeling worth a tin shit but you've got to know that it comes from both sides of a man's character and the deeper it runs the darker the pools it draws from.

My guess is he just hated the man too much to hit him. Comes a time when that isn't enough, when nothing is ever going to be enough, and so you can't do anything at all. And as he talked the pain just flowed out like a river that wasn't ever going to be stopped, a river that had cut a channel through every corner of his soul. I learnt something that night that you can go your whole life without realising: that there are things that can be done that can mess someone up so badly, for so long, that they just cannot be allowed; that there are some kinds of pain that you cannot suffer to be brought into the world.

And then Tom was done telling and he raised a smile and said that in the end he hadn't done anything to the man except paint him a picture, which I didn't understand, but Tom looked like he'd talked all he was going to.

So we got some more beers and shot some quiet pool before going home. But I guess we all knew what he'd been talking about.

Billy McNeill was just a child. He should have been dancing through a world like a big funfair full of sunlight and sounds, and instead he went home at night and saw his mom being beaten up by a man with shit for brains who struck out at a good woman because he was too stupid to deal with the world. Most kids go to sleep thinking about bikes and climbing apple trees and skimming stones, and he was lying there hearing his mom get smashed in the stomach and then hit again as she threw up in the sink. Tom didn't say any of that, but he did. And we knew he was right.

The summer kept up bright and hot, and we all had our businesses to attend to. Jack sold a lot of beer and I sold a lot of ice cream (Sorry ma'am, just the three flavours, and no, Bubblegum Pistachio ain't one of them) and Ned fixed a whole bunch of cracked radiators. Tom sat right out there in the square with a couple of cats by his feet and a crowd around him, magicking up animals in the sun.

The Man Who Drew Cats

And I think that after that night Mary maybe got a few more smiles as she did her shopping, and maybe a few more wives stopped to talk to her. She looked a lot better too: Sam had a job by the sound of it and her face healed up pretty soon. You could often see her standing holding Billy's hand as they watched Tom paint for a while before they went home. I think she realised they had a friend in him. Sometimes Billy was there all afternoon, and he was happy there in the sun by Tom's feet and oftentimes he'd pick up a piece of chalk and sit scrawling on the pavement. Sometimes I'd see Tom lean over and say something to him and he'd look up and smile a simple child's smile that beamed in the sunlight. The tourists kept coming and the sun kept shining and it was one of those summers that go on for ever and stick in a child's mind, and tell you what summer should be like for the rest of your life. And I'm damn sure it sticks in Billy's mind, just like it does in all of ours.

Because one morning Mary didn't come into the store, which had gotten to being a regular sort of thing, and Billy wasn't out there in the square. After the way things had been the last few weeks that could only be bad news, and so I left the boy John in charge of the store and hurried over to have a word with Tom. I was kind of worried.

I was no more than halfway across to him when I saw Billy come running from the opposite corner of the square, going straight to Tom. He was crying fit to burst and just leapt up at Tom and clung to him, his arms wrapped tight round his neck. Then his mother came across from the same direction, running as best she could. She got to Tom and they just looked at each other. Mary's a real pretty girl but you wouldn't have believed it then. It looked like he'd actually broken her nose this time, and blood was streaming out of her lip. She started sobbing, saying Sam had lost his job because he was back on the drink and what could she do and then suddenly there was a roar and I was shoved aside and Sam was standing there, still wearing his slippers, weaving back and forth and radiating that aura of violence that keeps men like him safe. He started shouting at Mary to take the kid the fuck back home and she just flinched and cowered closer to Tom like she was huddling round a fire to keep out the cold. This just got Sam even wilder and he staggered forward and told Tom to get the fuck out of it if he knew what was good for him, and grabbed Mary's arm and tried to yank her towards him, his face terrible with rage.

Then Tom stood up. Now Tom was a tall man, but he wasn't a young man, and he was thin. Sam was thirty and built like the town hall. When he did work it usually involved moving heavy things from one place to another, and his strength was supercharged by a whole pile of drunken nastiness.

But at that moment the crowd stepped back as one and I suddenly felt very afraid for Sam McNeill. Tom looked like you could take anything you cared to him and it would just break, like he was a huge spike of granite wrapped in skin with two holes in the face where the rock showed through. And he was mad, not hot and blowing like Sam, but mad and *cold*.

There was a long pause. Then Sam weaved back a step and shouted:

"You just come on home, you hear? Gonna be real trouble if you don't, Mary. Real trouble..." and then stormed off across the square the way he came, knocking his way through the tourist vultures soaking up the spicy local colour.

Mary turned to Tom, so afraid it hurt to see, and said she guessed she'd better be going. Tom looked at her for a moment and then spoke for the first time.

"Do you love him?"

Even if you wanted to, you ain't going to lie to eyes like that, for fear something inside you will break.

Real quiet she said: "No," and began crying softly as she took Billy's hand and walked slowly back across the square.

Tom packed up his stuff and walked over to Jack's. I went with him and had a beer but I had to get back to the shop and Tom just sat there like a trigger, silent and strung up tight as a drum. Somewhere down near the bottom of those still waters something was stirring. Something I thought I didn't want to see.

About an hour later it was lunchtime and I'd just left the shop to have a break when suddenly something whacked into the back of my legs and nearly knocked me down. It was Billy. It was Billy and he had a bruise round his eye that was already closing it up.

The Man Who Drew Cats

I knew what the only thing to do was and I did it. I took his hand and led him across to the Bar, feeling a hard anger pushing against my throat. When he saw Tom, Billy ran to him again and Tom took him in his arms and looked over Billy's shoulder at me, and I felt my own anger collapse utterly in the face of a fury I could never have generated. I tried to find a word to describe it but they all just seemed like they were in the wrong language. All I can say is I wanted to be somewhere else and it felt real cold standing there facing that stranger in a black coat.

Then the moment passed and Tom was holding the kid close, ruffling his hair and talking to him in a low voice, murmuring the words I thought only mothers knew. He dried Billy's tears and checked his eye and then he got off his stool, smiled down at him and said:

"I think it's time we did some drawing, what d'you say?" and, taking the kid's hand, he picked up his chalkbox and walked out into the square.

I don't know how many times I looked up and watched them that afternoon. They were sitting side by side on the stone, Billy's little hand wrapped round one of Tom's fingers, and Tom doing one of his chalk drawings. Every now and then Billy would reach across and add a little bit and Tom would smile and say something and Billy's gurgling laugh would float across the square. The store was real busy that afternoon and I was chained to that counter, but I could tell by the size of the crowd that a lot of Tom was going into that picture, and maybe a bit of Billy too.

It was about four o'clock before I could take a break. I walked across the crowded square in the mid afternoon heat and shouldered my way through to where they sat with a couple of cold Cokes. And when I saw it my mouth just dropped open and took a five minute vacation while I tried to take it in.

It was a cat alright, but not a normal cat. It was a life-size tiger. I'd never seen Tom do anything near that big before, and as I stood there in the beating sun trying to get my mind round it, it almost seemed to stand in three dimensions, a nearly living thing. Its stomach was very lean and thin, its tail seemed to twitch with colour, and as Tom worked on the eyes and jaws, his face set with a rigid

79

concentration quite unlike his usual calm painting face, the snarling mask of the tiger came to life before my eyes. And I could see that he wasn't just putting a bit of himself in at all. This was a man at full stretch, giving all of himself and reaching down for more, pulling up bloody fistfuls and throwing them down. The tiger was all the rage I'd seen in his eyes, and more, and like his love for Rachel that rage just seemed bigger than any other man could comprehend. He was pouring it out and sculpting it into the lean and ravenous creature coming to pulsating life in front of us on the pavement, and the weird purples and blues and reds just made it seem more vibrant and alive.

I watched him working furiously on it, the boy sometimes helping, adding a tiny bit here and there that strangely seemed to add to it, and thought I understood what he'd meant that evening a few weeks back. He said he'd done a painting for the man who'd given him so much pain. Then, as now, he must have found what I guess you'd call something fancy like 'catharsis' through his skill with chalks, had wrenched the pain up from within him and nailed it down onto something solid that he could walk away from. Now he was helping that little boy do the same, and the boy did look better, his bruised eye hardly showing with the wide smile on his face as he watched the big cat conjured up from nowhere in front of him.

We all just stood and watched, like something out of an old story, the simple folk and the magical stranger. It always feels like you're giving a bit of yourself away when you praise someone else's creation, and its often done grudgingly, but you could feel the awe that day like a warm wind. Comes a time when you realise something special is happening, something you're never going to see again, and there isn't anything you can do but watch.

Well I had to go back to the store after a while. I hated to go but, well, John is a good boy, married now of course, but in those days his head was full of girls and it didn't do to leave him alone in a busy shop for too long.

And so the long hot day drew slowly to a close. I kept the store open till eight, when the light began to turn and the square emptied out with all the tourists going away to write postcards and see if we

The Man Who Drew Cats

didn't have even just a *little* MacDonalds hidden away someplace. I suppose Mary had troubles enough at home, realised where the boy would be and figured he was safer there than anywhere else, and I guess she was right.

Tom and Billy finished up drawing and then Tom sat and talked to him for some time. Then they got up and the kid walked slowly off to the corner of the square, looking back to wave at Tom a couple times. Tom stood and watched him go and when Billy had gone he stayed there a while, head down, like a huge black statue in the gathering dark. He looked kind of creepy out there and I don't mind telling you I was glad when he finally moved and started walking over towards Jack's. I ran out to catch up with him and drew level just as we passed the drawing. And then I had to stop. I just couldn't look at that and move at the same time.

Finished, the drawing was like nothing on earth, and I suppose that's exactly what it was. I can't hope to describe it to you, although I've seen it in my dreams many times in the last ten years. You had to be there, on that heavy summer night, had to know what was going on. Otherwise it's going to sound like it was just a drawing.

That tiger was out and out terrifying. It looked so mean and hungry, Christ I don't know what: it just looked like the darkest parts of mankind, the pain and the fury and the vengeful hate nailed down in front of you for you to see, and I just stood there and shivered in the humid evening air.

"We did him a picture," Tom said quietly.

"Yeah," I said, and nodded. Like I said, I know what 'catharsis' means and I thought I understood what he was saying. But I really didn't want to look at it much longer. "Let's go have a beer, hey?"

The storm in Tom hadn't passed, I could tell, and he still seemed to thrum with crackling emotions looking for an earth, but I thought the clouds might be breaking and I was glad.

And so we walked slowly over to Jack's and had a few beers and watched some pool being played. Tom seemed pretty tired, but still alert, and I relaxed a little. Come eleven most of the guys started going on their way and I was surprised to see Tom get another beer. Pete, Ned and I stayed on, and Jack of course, though we knew our loving wives would have something to say about that. It just didn't seem time to go. Outside it had gotten pretty dark, though the moon was keeping the square in a kind of twilight and the lights in the bar threw a pool of warmth out of the front window.

Then, about twelve o'clock, it happened, and I don't suppose any of us will ever see the same world we grew up in again. I've told this whole thing like it was just me who was there, but we all were, and we remember it together.

Because suddenly there was a wailing sound outside, a thin cutting cry, getting closer. Tom immediately snapped to his feet and stared out the window like he'd been waiting for it. As we looked out across the square we saw little Billy come running and we could see the blood on his face from there. Some of us got to get up but Tom snarled at us to stay there and so I guess we just stayed put, sitting back down like we'd been pushed. He strode out the door and into the square and the boy saw him and ran to him and Tom folded him in his cloak and held him close and warm. But he didn't come back in. He just stood there, and he was waiting for something.

Now there's a lot of crap talked about silences. I read novels when I've the time and you see things like 'Time stood still' and so on and you think bullshit it did. So I'll just say I don't think anyone in the world breathed in that next minute. There was no wind, no movement. The stillness and silence were there like you could touch them, but more than that: they were like that's all there was and all there ever had been.

We felt the slow red throb of violence from right across the square before we could even see the man. Then Sam came staggering into view waving a bottle like a flag and cursing his head off. At first he couldn't see Tom and the boy because they were the opposite side of the fountain, and he ground to a wavering halt, but then he started shouting, rough jags of sound that seemed to strike against the silence and die instead of breaking it, and he began charging across the square – and if ever there was a man with murder in his thoughts then it was Sam McNeill. He was like a man who'd given his soul the evening off. I wanted to shout to Tom to get the hell out of the way, to come inside, but the words wouldn't come out of my throat and we all just stood there, knuckles whitening as we clutched

The Man Who Drew Cats

the bar and stared, our mouths open like we'd made a pact never to use them again. Tom just stood there, watching Sam come towards him, getting closer, almost as far as the spot where Tom usually painted. It felt like we were looking out of the window at a picture of something that happened long ago in another place and time, and the closer Sam got the more I began to feel very afraid for him.

It was at that moment that Sam stopped dead in his tracks, skidding forward like in some kid's cartoon, his shout dying off in his ragged throat. He was staring at the ground in front of him, his eyes wide and his mouth a stupid circle. Then he began to scream.

It was a high shrill noise like a woman, and coming out of that bull of a man it sent fear racking down my spine. He started making thrashing movements like he was trying to move backwards, but he just stayed where he was.

His movements became unmistakable at about the same time his screams turned from terror to agony. He was trying to get his leg away from something.

Suddenly he seemed to fall forward on one knee, his other leg stuck out behind him, and he raised his head and shrieked at the dark skies and we saw his face then and I'm not going to forget that face so long as I live. It was a face from before there were any words, the face behind our oldest fears and earliest nightmares, the face we're terrified of seeing on ourselves one night when we're alone in the dark and It finally comes out from under the bed to get us, like we always knew it would.

Then Sam fell on his face, his leg buckled up – and still he thrashed and screamed and clawed at the ground with his hands, blood running from his broken fingernails as he twitched and struggled. Maybe the light was playing tricks, and my eyes were sparkling anyway on account of being too paralyzed with fear to even blink, but as he thrashed less and less it became harder and harder to see him at all, and as the breeze whipped up stronger his screams began to sound a lot like the wind. But still he writhed and moaned and then suddenly there was the most godawful crunching sound and then there was no movement or sound anymore.

Like they were on a string our heads all turned together and we saw Tom still standing there, his coat flapping in the wind. He had

83

a hand on Billy's shoulder and as we looked we could see that Mary was there too now and he had one arm round her as she sobbed into his coat.

I don't know how long we just sat there staring but then we were ejected off our seats and out of the bar. Pete and Ned ran to Tom but Jack and I went to where Sam had fallen, and we stared down, and I tell you the rest of my life now seems like a build up to and a climb down from that moment.

We were standing in front of a chalk drawing of a tiger. Even now my scalp seems to tighten when I think of it, and my chest feels like someone punched a hole in it and tipped a gallon of ice water inside. I'll just tell you the facts: Jack was there and he knows what we saw and what we didn't see.

What we didn't see was Sam McNeill. He just wasn't there. We saw a drawing of a tiger in purples and greens, a little bit scuffed, and there was a lot more red round the mouth of that tiger than there had been that afternoon and I'm sure that if either of us could have dreamed of reaching out and touching it, it would have been warm too.

And the hardest part to tell is this. I'd seen that drawing in the afternoon, and Jack had too, and we knew that when it was done it was lean and thin.

I swear to God that tiger wasn't thin any more. What Jack and I were looking at was one fat tiger.

After a while I looked up and across at Tom. He was still standing with Mary and Billy, but they weren't crying anymore. Mary was hugging Billy so tight he squawked and Tom's face looked calm and alive and creased with a smile. And as we stood there the skies opened for the first time in months and a cool rain hammered down. At my feet colours began to run and lines became less distinct. Jack and I stood and watched till there was just pools of meaningless colours and then we walked slowly over to the others, not even looking at the bottle lying on the ground, and we all stayed there a long time in the rain, facing each other, not saying a word.

Well that was ten years ago, near enough. After a while Mary took Billy home and they turned to give us a little wave before they turned the corner. The cuts on Billy's face healed real quick, and he's a good looking boy now: he looks a lot like his dad and he's already fooling about in cars. Helps me in the store sometimes. His mom ain't aged a day and looks wonderful. She never married again, but she looks real happy the way she is.

The rest of us just said a simple goodnight. Goodnight was all we could muster and maybe that's all there was to say. Then we walked off home in the directions of our wives. Tom gave me a small smile before he turned and walked off alone. I almost followed him, I wanted to say something, but the end I just stayed where I was and watched him go. And that's how I'll always remember him best, because for a moment there was a spark in his eyes and I knew that some pain had been lifted deep down inside somewhere.

Then he walked and no-one has seen him since, and like I said it's been about ten years now. He wasn't there in the square the next morning and he didn't come in for a beer. Like he'd never been, he just wasn't there. Except for the hole in our hearts: it's funny how much you can miss a quiet man.

We're all still here, of course, Jack, Ned, Pete and the boys, and all much the same, though even older and greyer. Pete lost his wife and Ned retired but things go on the same. The tourists come in the summer and we sit on the stools and drink our cold beers and shoot the breeze about ballgames and families and how the world's going to shit, and sometimes we'll draw close and talk about a night a long time ago, and about paintings and cats, and about the quietest man we ever knew, wondering where he is, and what he's doing. And we've had a sixpack in the back of the fridge for ten years now, and the minute he walks through that door and pulls up a stool, that's his.

THE CYCLE
John Connolly

John Connolly was born in Dublin, Ireland in 1968 and has, at various points in his life, worked as a journalist, a barman, a local government official, a waiter and a dogsbody at Harrods department store in London. He studied English in Trinity College, Dublin and journalism at Dublin City University, subsequently spending five years working as a freelance journalist for *The Irish Times* newspaper, to which he continues to contribute. His first novel, *Every Dead Thing*, was published in 1999, and introduced the character of Charlie Parker, a former policeman hunting the killer of his wife and daughter. *Dark Hollow* followed in 2000. The third Parker novel, *The Killing Kind*, was published in 2001, with *The White Road* following in 2002. In 2003, John published his fifth novel – and first standalone book – *Bad Men*. In 2004, *Nocturnes*, a collection of novellas and short stories, was added to the list, and 2005 marked the publication of the fifth Charlie Parker novel, *The Black Angel*. John's seventh novel, *The Book of Lost Things*, was published in September 2006, with the next Parker novel, *The Unquiet*, following early in 2007. John Connolly is based in Dublin but divides his time between his native city and the United States, where each of his novels has been set. You can find his website at www.johnconnollybooks.com

John comments: "The Cycle came about as a dare. I think there might have been drink taken. There usually is when such things arise.

"An editor friend was putting together an anthology of short stories by Irish women writers, to be entitled *Moments*, in aid of tsunami relief. Over dinner, she suggested that it might be fun to slip in a story by a male author under a pseudonym, just to see if anyone would spot the interloper. It seemed like an interesting idea, at least until I sobered up, but by that point I'd already agreed to do it so I couldn't back out. I had recently published a collection of supernatural stories, *Nocturnes*, so 'The Cycle' represented a continuation of my fascination with the genre, and possibly the culmination of it too as it's the last such story that I've written.

"Curiously, when *Moments* appeared, the editor neglected to mention that a male author had been slipped in to the bunch, mainly because the anthology sold so well that it didn't need the extra publicity that the ruse might have brought. 'The Cycle' was complimented by a number of female reviewers, which was reassuring in one way and slightly disconcerting in another. Somehow, I had become an honorary woman, albeit without the potential trauma of dressing up in women's clothing or, indeed, the pleasure of hanging around locker rooms.

"*Moments* never made it beyond Irish shores as it sold out its print run in a matter of weeks, so this is the first chance that I've had to present it to a larger readership, flaws and all. It's particularly heartening that it should appear in this BFS collection, as the society was the first non-mystery organisation to extend a hand of welcome to me. I suppose I was best known, if I was known at all, as a mystery author, but I've always been curious about the possibilities of cross-pollinating genres and creating potentially interesting hybrids. In its support for my efforts, the BFS has been considerably more enlightened than some of its peers in the mystery field.

"So, having abandoned my female pseudonym (Laura Froom, the name of a vampire in one of the *Nocturnes* stories) I can no longer claim plausible deniability where 'The Cycle' is concerned. I can, though, blame it on my feminine side, assuming I have one. If

I do, I fear that it's not very gentle..."

The pain began almost as soon as she boarded the train. Usually, she planned these things so well. How could she not, after all these years? Today, though, had just been one of those bloody awful days, when nothing went according to plan. She had planned to get the five o'clock train, which would have seen her safely tucked up at home with the doors closed and a whole weekend of privacy and quiet to get over the curse. Instead, a crisis in the office meant that Dominic, her boss, had been forced to call an emergency meeting. Two days before a deadline, one of the agency's most important clients had decided that elements of the new ad campaign were 'inappropriate' and needed to be re-examined. That meant a brainstorming session which lasted until after seven, the beautiful autumn day outside slowly descending into shadows by the time she left.

She could feel it approaching, even as she left the building and headed for the station: a sense of unease, of dislocation, and a tenderness to her belly and her breasts. Her already short temper contracted even further, so that she almost bit off the head of the lazy clerk behind the ticket counter, the idiot apparently more concerned with picking his lottery numbers than ensuring that she made her train, the closing of unseen doors already signalling its imminent departure. She was forced to sprint to make it, and that had not helped matters at all. Running, fretting and snapping at morons seemed only to accelerate the pain.

She took a seat in the next-to-last carriage. The toilet was in the final carriage, right at the end, but the lights in the carriage were malfunctioning, flickering off and on with an angry buzzing sound, as though masses of bees were trapped within the fluorescent bulbs, so she had been forced to sit a little further forward than she would have liked. Still, perhaps it would be all right. It hadn't started yet, although it was close.

The train crawled slowly from the station. Her fellow passengers read books and newspapers, or talked nonsense loudly on their mobile phones, their lack of consideration annoying her still further

The Cycle

but providing a momentary distraction, an outlet for her frustration. She had a phone herself, of course, but she kept it switched off on trains and buses unless it was absolutely essential to leave it active, and even then she left it on vibrate and would step out of the carriage to answer it. She was very conscious of her privacy, and it constantly amazed her that people were prepared to discuss, at high volume, the most intimate details of their lives among strangers. Her father and mother would sooner have died than engage in a conversation upon which others might eavesdrop. In fact, her parents had rarely discussed anything of consequence on the telephone. They were resolutely old-fashioned in that sense. If something was important, then it was worth discussing face-to-face. Their telephone conversations, except in exceptional cases like bereavement or illness, rarely lasted for longer than a minute or two. Their daughter had learned from them the importance of discretion in certain matters.

The raised voices were nagging at her hearing. Her senses always seemed to be more acute at this time of the month, so that even moderately loud noises became difficult to tolerate, and she was more aware than usual of distinctive smells and tastes. She wondered if others experienced it the same way she did. She could only assume that she was not unique in these sensations, although she was not the kind of person who would discuss such matters with another, even if she were not so solitary by nature.

Towns flashed by. They were making good time. She allowed herself a little sigh of relief, and breathed in deeply. As she did so, something rippled inside her. She grimaced, and shifted on her seat. Hell. The train slowed, disgorging passengers at another station. Others rarely got on to replace them at these provincial towns, and she was used to spending most of her journeys in empty carriages, especially as her destination was the last stop on the line, her house a mere stone's throw from the station. It allowed her to sleep a little later than most in the mornings, and made the trip home a little easier to bear.

She closed her eyes. Sometimes she felt lonely, living in the little village where every face was familiar to her, where every name was echoed dozens of times in the form of cousins, brothers, uncles, grandparents. Her parents had always kept themselves slightly aloof from the life of the community on the principle that good fences made good neighbours, and she was grateful to them for that. The round of meetings, charity drives, garden parties and festivals was not for her, but her desire to remain at one remove had given her a reputation around the village, particularly since she also chose to politely deflect the attentions of its menfolk. She had no intention of ever dating a man from the village, of permitting him access to the secrets of her life. She knew these men too well, and was not anxious to become one of their conquests. She had enjoyed some relationships in the city, but none that lasted. She liked men who were prepared to let her keep her distance when she chose, who wanted their own space as much as she wanted hers, but such men were harder to find than one might think. The demands that she made led her to attract those who were merely seeking casual one-night flings, or those who claimed that they appreciated her desire for independence even though, as time went on, these types inevitably grew more and more uncomfortable with it, and tried to impose their own rules. She had quickly learned that when a man said he valued a woman's independence, what it really meant was that he valued his own, and would only indulge her taste for it when it suited him to do so.

Another station passed, bringing her another mile nearer to home. The gnawing pain was stronger now, and she had a coppery taste in her mouth. She hated the cycle, the inescapable incovenience of it. It really was a curse, but, as her mother had said to her in those first awkward months of adolescence, "what cannot be cured must be endured." Looking back now, she remembered the shock and amazement that she felt at the realization that her own body could do this to her, could wound her from deep within and bring her discomfort, pain and embarrassment, even as her mother had instructed her on what to do and how to prepare for it so that she was not taken by surprise. It was always easier to put up with in your own home, her mother had said, surrounded by familiar things, but you could not let it dictate how you lived your life. Yet, for the first few months, that was precisely what had happened: she was grateful

The Cycle

and relieved once it had passed, but the relief only lasted for a week or two until it commenced, once again, its inevitable approach. It was different for the other girls: they seemed to take the changes to their bodies in their stride, and she envied them that. It was simply beyond her own capacities to do the same.

The train arrived at Shillingford, the last stop before home. Soon she would be able to lock the door and remain within the walls for the entire weekend. By Monday, it would all be over, and normal life would resume.

The door at the head of the carriage opened as the train moved off, and two young men entered. They were probably still in their late teens, although one wore a ragged line of scruffy facial hair on his upper lip, a nasty little excuse for a moustache that made him look shifty and untrustworthy. His companion, taller and bulkier, had acne pimples on his chin, bloodied where he had picked at them. They wore cheap leather jackets, and jeans that were baggy and flared.

"Alright, love?" one of the boys said. She did not look at him, but she could see him reflected in the glass. It was the one with the moustache. Neither of them had taken their seats. They stood, craning their necks to catch sight of her face and body. She drew her coat a little more tightly around her.

"Aw, don't do that," said the spotty one. "Give us a look."

She bit her lip. Something contracted inside her, and she jerked slightly in her seat. Her skin began to itch.

"Go on, smile," said the one with the moustache. "It can't be that that bad. I've got something that will make you smile."

He sniggered.

"Dyke," said the other. He smirked at his wit.

"Nah," said his mate. "She's not a dyke. They're ugly. She's not that bad."

He pointed his chin at her.

"You're not a dyke, are you?"

"Get lost," she said, despite herself. She didn't want to be drawn into an argument with them, but they had just picked the wrong evening to confront her. It was only after she had spoken that she realised how dangerous it might be to antagonise them, to draw them upon her.

"Touchy," said Moustache to his friend. "Must be her time of the month. They all get a bit like that."

He returned his attention to her.

"Is that it, darlin'? Time of the month? The old curse?"

His smile slowly faded, to be replaced by something infinitely more unpleasant.

"Don't bother me," he said, so softly that she thought she might have misheard, until he repeated himself. "Don't bother me one little bit ..."

Suddenly, the train ground to a halt. For a moment, there was only silence, and then a voice came over the public address system.

"We would like to apologise to all passengers for this slight delay. This is due to a temporary signal failure on the line ahead of us, which means that we have to wait for the southbound train to pass before we can continue. Again, we would like to apologise for any inconvenience caused, and assure you that we will be on our way very shortly."

She couldn't believe it. She pressed her face to the window and thought that she could almost see the lights of the station in the distance. She could walk to her house from here, but the old manually operated doors were long gone and she, like all the others, was a prisoner of new technology. She felt nauseous, and the coppery taste in her mouth was growing more pronounced. It was now dark outside. She looked at the night sky. There were no stars visible, although a telltale edge of brightness had begun to show in the north as the clouds began to thin. This was bad, very bad. She could hear the boys whispering, and she risked a glance at them. The one with the pimples was looking over at her, and she could see the lust in his eyes.

"Unnnhhh."

The groan of pain caused the boys to stop their conversation. She winced. The delay was just unbearable. What a bloody nuisance. She almost howled in frustration. There was no other choice: she rose, grabbed her briefcase, and headed for the last carriage. If she could get to the toilet, then she could do whatever was necessary and wait things out until the train got into the station, then slip onto the platform through the back door, avoiding the young men and the stink of their desire. She stepped into the space between the carriages, opened the door, and entered the empty compartment, the buzzing unbearably loud, the flickering of the lights paining her eyes.

Behind her, the two teenagers exchanged a look, then stood and followed her into the carriage.

Their names were Davey and Billy. Davey was the older one, the smarter one, and he was proud of his carefully cultivated facial hair. The moustache was sometimes the difference between being served in a bar or being refused, and he was very proud of it. Billy was bigger than his friend, but dumber and more brutal. They often saw women on the trains late at night, some of them a bit the worse for wear and unlikely to put up much of a fight, but somehow the opportunity they sought had never presented itself, until now. The woman was alone, the train was stopped: even if she cried out, no one would hear her. It was perfect.

They entered the carriage. The fluorescent lights flickered and buzzed then, finally, gave up the ghost, artificial light yielding to the moon's luminescence as a great disc of white cleared the cover of the clouds and shone down upon the woods, the fields, and the silver body of the unmoving train. The toilet was ahead of them, at the far end. It wouldn't have much of a lock on it. On trains, they never did.

They were halfway down the carriage when the noise came from behind them. Something moved in the space between two seats, previously hidden from the young men by the shadows, the moonlight not yet penetrating its reaches. They turned as it unfolded itself, slowly rising up before them, taller than they were, and infinitely more powerful. There was a sharp animal smell in the carriage, and they heard a sound like a dog might make if someone threatened to remove the bone from between its paws. As Davey's eyes grew accustomed to the gloom, he saw clawed feet, longer than a human's and covered with fine dark hair that shone in the moonlight, and muscular legs that bent sharply at the knee, rising up to a flat crotch, a taut stomach, and small, pale breasts. Even as he watched, more fine hairs erupted from the pores of the skin, colonising the white spaces and turning them all to black. The tattered remains of a dress hung from the figure's arms and back, and as its fingernails curled in on themselves Davey thought he saw traces of purple varnish upon them. The hair on its upper body was thicker than that upon its legs and belly as the breasts slowly disappeared beneath it: it was denser, and tinged with white and grey, as though a great cape had been placed across its shoulders.

Then it emerged from the darkness, slowly advancing upon them, and the moonlight shone upon the woman's face. It was still changing, the features transforming before them, so that she remained clearly recognisable to Davey, like a figure glimpsed in a funhouse mirror, distorted yet familiar. Her face was lengthening, the tips of her ears extending and tufting with hair, her nose and chin elongating to form a lupine jaw, the teeth within growing sharper and shining whitely, thick strands of saliva and blood dripping from the tips. Her hands, the fingers gnarled and taloned, gripped the edges of the seat before her as her body shuddered, the change now almost complete as Davey heard four words emerge from deep in her throat, their meaning almost lost to him as she the animal overcame the woman.

Almost.

"Time of the month," she said, and Davey thought that the words were followed by something that might have been laughter before that too was transformed, becoming a growl filled with hunger and the promise of death. Her eyes turned to yellow, and the full moon was reflected in their depths. She raised her head and howled just as, too late, the boys tried to run. Davey pushed Billy out of the way, using his size to squeeze past him before Billy even realised what he was doing. A splash of warmth struck Davey's hair and back as Billy's life ended with the rending of claws, but he kept moving, never looking behind him, his gaze focused on the rectangle of glass ahead of him, and the silver handle of the door. He was almost close enough to touch it when a great weight landed on his back, forcing him to the ground. The train jerked into motion as

The Cycle

Davey felt hot breath upon his skin, and sharp teeth upon his neck. In his final moments, he was struck, oddly, by the realisation that he had always been afraid of women. Now, at last, he thought that he understood why.

And then Davey screamed as he took his place in the great cycle of living and dying, and the world was filled with redness.

DAYS OF THE WHEEL
Peter Crowther

Author, editor, critic/essayist, poet and now – with the multiple BFS award-winning PS imprint – publisher, Peter Crowther has edited more than 20 anthologies and produced almost 100 short stories and novellas (two of which have been adapted for British TV while two more are scheduled to begin filming for the big screen in 2006), plus *Escardy Gap* (in collaboration with James Lovegrove) and *Darkness, Darkness*. He's currently busy writing story notes for *Dark Times*, his fifth collection, while working on the second instalment of his *Forever Twilight* SF/horror series, a mainstream novel, a couple of new anthologies and another TV project. Pete lives about 500 yards from the sea on the east coast of England with his wife, Nicky and an unfeasibly large collection of books, comics, DVDs, record albums and CDs.

Peter informs us: "I suppose I came a little late to the BFS and, most importantly, to this wonderful constant commune that is FantasyCon.

"It was 1988. I'd had a few things published – mainly non-fiction in the shape of interviews and reviews…mostly in the old *Fear* magazine – and, years before that, I'd had a few stories published in the small press efforts of the day. But I didn't really *know* anyone, except for Ramsey, whom I'd interviewed for *Midnight Graffiti*.

Days Of The Wheel

"Nicky and I had attended a few EasterCons in the very early 1970s and WorldCon in 1979 in Brighton, so we knew the ropes...but there was something immediately obviously different about FantasyCon – and you know, it's still there. You can smell it, almost cut it with a knife it's so thick. And even though they've maybe been a little smaller and writers and publishers have been a little thinner on the ground, successive FantasyCons have maintained that same spirit...an air of camaraderie and companionship, of like-minded souls...all intermingling. If you could bottle that up, capture the feeling, the excitement, the elation...you could sell it.

"I made friends on that first weekend...friends I still see now, along with other friends I've made at subsequent FantasyCons along the years, when we meet up conventions or at bookstores on one of our occasional reading (and curry-eating) appearances. It sounds clichéd and perhaps a little shmaltzy but FantasyCon is a home you left when you were younger that you come back to once a year, like at Christmas or Thanksgiving. And the people there – and the memories of the good and lovely and much-missed people we've lost along the way – well...they're family. It's as simple as that."

The days of a Ferris wheel are long, long in twenty-four hour terms and long in the life of the world... to which a wheel is not dissimilar, neither in purpose – of which it has none – nor in the way it moves, turning slowly on its fixed axis, day in and day out, ever the same, never changing, never tiring, never feeling.

Most of all, never feeling.

The woods that come together in its construction are traditionally as varied and various as those that may be found anywhere on the world, soft and hard, dark and light, their sap spent and only the bile of old-age left, the aftertaste of life, like the wrinkled old folks now watching as a parade struts down the Main Street of Forest Plains, folks like Miriam Greenhoff and Miranda Matthews,

Joseph Montgomery and Duane Patterson, watching through bifocals from the windows of the Forest Plains Home For The Elderly, across lawns with grass cut so short you'd think someone had crouched there all night with scissors, whispering to the moon and the stars as the world moved on oblivious.

The eyes of these septuagenarian, octogenarian and even nonagenarian bundles of stick-bones and parchment-skin travel without moving, across picket fences white-painted by a hundred Tom Sawyer lookalikes, watching all that life and energy pass them by on the horizon of their vision, clasping mottled hands – shaped and mis-shaped like birds' feet covered in mottled flesh – placed on scrawny laps, their fingers wrestling silently with each other, embittered siblings never able to agree as their owners listen to the now dulled thud of their hearts, each thud sounding more faltered and more unsure, a syncopated and discordant tune that is not a tune at all, at least not any more than all the sounds that are the world are tunes, wondering whether this beat... or this one or one coming along any time now, already stacked up and waiting, will be the last.

At times like this, Miriam and Miranda, Joseph and Duane... and all the old folks in all the small towns, towns scattered across the country like duck-down from a pillow burst in a midnight fight, huddle together in the collective sentience of their souls wondering how death will feel when it comes to sit with them, how kind it will be, how understanding and gentle, and how cold or painful its touch, and they think back, while they wait, to their youth, those dim and distant days of seemingly endless sunshine, when skies were an unbroken blue and the summer stretched like taffy between the tall-tree days of spring and fall.

And they try to remember what it used to feel like riding the carnie rides.

They half-imagine, these old timers, these 'senior' citizens referred to by many as Pop or Ma, old man, old woman – and by sycophantic talkshow hosts and phone-in radio deejays as being 83 or 77 or 91 years *young* – they half-imagine that they can once more smell the fun of the fair over and above the cloying scent of sickness that surrounds them, the drifting aroma of peppermint

and clocks winding down, remembering, in that faraway cobwebby place at the back of their minds, the amalgam of motor fumes, axel-grease, hot dogs and cotton candy mixed in with their own cheap drugstore cologne or perfume, cigarette smoke and well-chewed *Juicy Fruit* gum... half-imagining they can hear the barkers' calls
> *step right up!*
> *just one thin dime!*
> *one tenth of a dollah!*

to brave the Ghost Train and the Ferris Wheel and all the other clanking rides, to see the tattooed lady and the two-headed boy, to throw wooden balls at coconuts glued onto tall pedestals, to stand in line for a fortune read by an old crone wearing too much face powder and lipstick and who talks in an incessant rehearsed whine that speaks of Des Moines or Brooklyn or Austin or Duluth and never of exotic places with exotic names, places that Miriam and Miranda and Joseph and Duane and all their kind in the myriad small towns that make up the time-embroidered quilt of America, places they only ever saw or read about in old many-owned textbooks or well-thumbed dog-eared copies of *National Geographic* back when they were all at school here in Forest Plains and able to move quickly through life and able to see so much of it waiting ahead of them, curled up like an old dog lazing in the summer sun just waiting to be called upon.

And at night, when the lights are turned down in their rooms and the time comes that, occasionally, when the conditions are just right, they're visited by friends and relations long since forgotten who sit on the edges of their beds without leaving an imprint and who cast no shadows on the wall in the light patch thrown by the moon through their windows... at night they sense the carnival again and feel the wind in their hair, hair long since grown gray and wiry, sparse and thin, like the grasses in the park outside the Library, only it's not the library any more because the Library has gone, they suddenly remember... now it's a fast food restaurant and a savings and loan outlet and something else they forget, even though they maybe only saw it yesterday or maybe the day before when they were out in town, walking along the sidewalk feeling out of breath, cringing at the sounds of the motorcar horns and the strange rhythms blaring out of the music store onto the street.

They sit back, Miriam and Miranda, the two Emms who have buried three husbands and four children between them, and old Joe and deaf Duane, who thinks that every woman – even the steely-eyed and square-jawed Mizz Russell, the aptly-named, straight-backed matron, whose rustling, sibilant underclothes are the only quiet thing they ever seem to be able to hear... because, in some strange way

here we come... here we come for you!

it speaks to them of fear – is the wife he lost to cervical cancer long before it became fashionable and that every man is one of the two sons he lost in Korea and who visit him, from time to time, to tell him about what it feels like when a bullet enters the stomach or when a grinning madman slices off the eyelids so that the many interesting experiments he plans need not be missed by an involuntary muscle spasm brought on by exquisite and unimaginable pain... they sit back from the window, and Miriam gives a crooked half-smile to nobody in particular, seeing her reflection mimic the smile in the glass before her and wondering where the girl went that used to live behind those lips, wondering if she still lives here somewhere, wondering if maybe images never truly die the way she's heard that no sound ever truly dies but only keeps on getting fainter and fainter until only a half-crazed dog can hear it on the night winds.

And for a minute or a second or some other infinitesimal measurement of time gone by, time stored by old folks which, in the wealth of their experience, carries no true value because it represents such a tiny, tiny portion of all they have known, Joseph Montgomery – who, despite being called 'Old Joe' is no older than any of the others and is even younger than many who refer to him thus – feels a once-familiar but now almost completely forgotten stirring, a thin and crusty unfurling of old skin stretching and old muscles hardening... an old friend come to visit, come to ask difficult questions

what happened to us?
to me?

Days Of The Wheel

where did I go?
where have I been?

and Miriam feels a sudden quickening and a moist warmth amidst the wizened parchment of her most private area, a crawling anxiety... a secret anticipation, a race-memory hoarded by the body to tantalize and depress.

And in that fragile moment, the four of them... the untold *millions* of them, all pulled back from windows as though hearing the sound of approaching footsteps behind them, footsteps that do not always seem to have owners when they creak arthritically around to look, they see a group of strangely attired men and women, some big, some small, a flurry of long tail-coats and stovepipe hats, ruffled neckties and flowing dresses, carrying amongst their unsmiling number a model Ferris wheel, which, large though it may be in terms of its portability to a man or woman bent by age and aches, is but a fraction of the size of the real thing, a sample-sized version of the monolithic structure pictured on the side of their horse-drawn wagon

a horse-drawn wagon in this day and age: I ask you!

depicting a structure of wooden beams and spokes seemingly carved to look like bones... old bones brittle with age and feisty with longing for life, and crazy-headed nuts and bolts that look for all the world like yellowed teeth and eyes laced with veins and the milky blue of cataracts, and tear-repaired mock-leather upholstery that resembles bruised skin mottled with brown whorls; it is a structure – the poster proclaims – that will soon grace the field behind the park on the edge of town, over beyond the turnpike and the old pond, a field that was once stronger and younger than it is now

than any of us are now!

a tired expanse of corn stubble... like an old man's beard, hard and abrasive and unforgiving.

Behind them – and behind the unending number of like-minded like-bodied aged folks in all the nursing homes, and in all the tenement rooms whose windows are open to the uncaring streets below, and huddled in all the nighttime department store doorways nursing a brown-bagged dose of memory-erasing liquid oblivion, and even in all the small one-room homes given over in plush houses owned by progeny who wear their familial allegiance on their pocketbook covers – life goes on, creaking and swishing in a familiar potpourri of disinfectant and urine and cooking food, a familiar static of radio phone-ins and TV reruns and the muted chatter of voices scarred and dimmed by age... it goes on oblivious to the spectacle outside the window or up the street or around the block, ignorant of the parade.

But not so the old people.

They see all too clearly the incarcerating struts and beams, the cold metal supports and tensile girders, the restrictive ground pinions and trammeled swing mechanisms, the formaldehyde upholstery of the seats glistening in the sunlight... they see the huge balls of Regret, finely spooled into boulder-sized twine-weaves; they see the steaming paste-pots of Dissatisfaction, and smell its pungent odor of sun-baked carcass and dried semen wafting invisibly and unstoppably through window-jams and door-sealings; they see the filigreed masking tapes of Hope and Envy, their cumulative binding power a heady brew of sunlight and shadow, of possibilities light and dark.

The parade pauses across the street, halts in its progress as all eyes turn to the window and meet the eyes of Miriam Greenhoff and Miranda Matthews, Joseph Montgomery and Duane Patterson – and, in a million other towns and cities at different times and in different settings, the eyes of countless scores of other people all nearing the end of one ride and reaching for the next... reaching with unsteady hands and nervous hearts – and for a second, all of them catch the breath in their throats as the entourage waves to them, waves its hands like a many-armed single entity, like corn blowing in the fields, moving in meticulous unison... the skeleton man and the angel, the harlequin and the harpy, the vampire and the ticket collector, the lamia and the ringmaster, the tattooed lady and the two-headed boy, a clutch of Siamese triplets joined at the head in a huge bulbous dome, their bodies bent outwards, warped by time into a gnarled normalcy, the sideshow barker waving his cane and tapping it against his straw hat, the exotic dancer switching her hips in a flurry of crinoline, eyes flashing menacingly

Days Of The Wheel

(*and enticingly*, Duane Patterson thinks to himself, feeling that movement again beneath his old work pants)
    and all the others, and the ringmaster throws something into the air, a brief flutter of paper caught on the breeze and carried, wafting like a winged seed, across the pavement and the sidewalk and the closely-cut grass of the nursing home lawns – flying as it has flown over and around all the doorway litter and strewn washing-lines tethered across alleyways, and across the silent memory-festooned night-time rooms borrowed from sons and daughters, and over narrow hospital walkways between drips and blinking machines, and over church pews whose straight-backed seat-shelves contain leathery volumes of hymn and prayer whose covers are worn and stained by a million million hopeful and expectant fingers, and across highways littered with cars and buses, and over oceans topped by salt-spray foam, and along train tracks humming with the possibility of places to come and the memory of places gone behind – and in the Forest Plains Home For The Elderly it finds a way in, an entrance, finding a heel in this nursing-home-Achilles as it has done so many times before in all the myriad 'safe' places... finding the slightest gap betwixt wood and frame, glass and holding cement, brick and mortar.
    It spirals down and up and across, catching currents and riding the air-draughts, unseen to all but those for whom the carnival waits, those for whom the Ferris wheel turns, its smooth and cold metal arm-handle wound and pulled by hands old when even the world was young, young in both world terms and the terms of the cosmos that contains it... until, at last, it falls, this breeze- and breath-carried epistle, falls onto the scrawny arms and into the clawlike hands of
    Miranda Matthews!
    one of the ancient spectators.
    And then the cries ring out
    a parade!
    a carnival!
    my, will you just look *at those folks!*
    and Miriam and Miranda, who now holds the airborne object to her eyes but who has not yet read the swirling writing and curlicued script it bears, and Old Joe and Deaf Duane look around in surprise,

wondering how it is that the others can see and thinking that maybe this is not their time, that this is nothing more than a simple parade, a circus perhaps, a fair come to their town to spread cheer and merriment and laughter, but then, as Miriam frowns and curls up her nose, they hear another cry, a muted call unsure of what it says:
gas!, the call echoes, *can you smell gas?* - a question voiced to any who might respond

and in that same flickering instant, that same pause between now and soon, when anything and everything is possible, Miriam Greenhoff glances up the room towards Wilbur Portain, scrunched down in his wing-backed armchair, deaf to the world and uncaring of it, oblivious to the parade in the street outside, busy tamping down the tobacco in his curved Meerschaum with a blackened thumb, a worn silver lighter in his other hand, placing the pipe into his wizened mouth between teeth worn down and yellowed by time and nicotine, lifting the lighter to the bowl, flicking it... once, when it doesn't catch – and Miriam wants to cry out

no! leave the pipe, don't strike the light!

and then she glances to her side, sees Miranda reading the simple card in her hand, sees Old Joe leaning across blinking through his reading glasses, sees Deaf Duane staring out of the window, a slight smile on his face as he lifts his hand to return the waves from the street... and she turns back – and he tries a second time... Wilbur Portain, whose son and daughter-in-law put him into this place so long ago and never so much as a birthday card let alone a visit, and this time Miriam does not want to cry out but instead is suddenly concerned that the increasingly louder cries of something smelling around the silent room of old people might halt Wilbur Portain in his efforts, and then, still unsuccessful, he tamps the tobacco some more and shakes the lighter as Miriam looks around and Miranda looks up from the swirling letters, a frown and a smile fighting for control of her face, and Old Joe reaches over to take the card as Deaf Duane calls out his wife's name, watching the word spiral across the manicured glass at the other side of the window... spiral across the street to the waiting fair folk, one of whose number he has suddenly recognized, her face peering over the shoulders of the sideshow barker, and...

Days Of The Wheel

The click of the lighter is drowned beneath a tidal wave of fire, buried beneath an avalanche of flying masonry and wood-splinters, swept up in a tornado of spinning reading glasses, photo frames, favorite books, letters from dutiful sons and daughters and brothers and sisters, each filled with awkward words and phrases... the air outside the Forest Plains Home For The Elderly is black with debris and smoke, the carefully-manicured lawn covered with smoldering remnants of furniture, building materials and people, and the wind carries the smell of toasted meat out over the rooftops of the houses across the street, out over the turnpike and the old pond, out across the fields to the stubbled corn.

Listen:

Far away beneath the sound of the first sirens speeding along Sycamore, and a dog barking and someone crying, you can hear a calliope droning its sombre-sweet melody into the October wind, hear the step-right-up banter of the sideshow barker, hear the click and groan of the gears of the Ferris wheel...

ride!

Now You See Him, Now You Don't
Juliet E. McKenna

Juliet E. McKenna was born in Lincolnshire in 1965, later moved to Dorset, and now lives in West Oxfordshire with her husband Steve and their sons, Keith and Ian. She attended Parkstone Girls' Grammar School, Poole, where her favourite subjects were History, English and Latin – having started reading folk tales and Greek myths at about age five. Away from school she read as much fantasy and SF, crime and thrillers as she could get her hands on. She studied Greek and Roman history and literature at St Hilda's College, Oxford, taking up table top and live role playing and joining the Oxford University Speculative Fiction Group. There she also took up Aikido, a Japanese martial art based on principles of defence, developed from ju-jitsu. After finishing her degree, Juliet moved into recruitment and personnel work and married Steve, who she met through aikido and role playing. Increasingly, she wrote the table top scenarios they played and the couple ran an invitation-only LRP club where they developed a fantasy world to be the on-going background for all the adventures and events. It was during this time she wrote her first complete novel, a classic 'youth leaves home, rites of passage' tale and sent it to various agents and publishers, who told her that though well written there was nothing to distinguish it from the other fantasies that landed on their desks every week.

Now You See Him, Now You Don't

After starting a family and working in her local Ottakar's as a part time bookseller, she began working on ideas for something different in a traditional fantasy setting – it would turn into *The Thief's Gamble* which she again tried with agents and publishers, gaining a more positive response. Through contacts she had made at Ottakar's, the book ended up at Orbit who not only published it, but offered her a two book deal. She sat down and immediately drew out an outline for *The Swordsman's Oath*. The success of those two books lead to a contract for another three Tales of Einarinn: *The Gambler's Fortune*, *The Warrior's Bond* and *The Assassin's Edge*. She is currently working on a new series, *The Aldabreshin Compass*. Juliet was a Guest of Honour at 2006's FantasyCon and is an integral member of 'The Write Fantastic' (along with Chaz Brenchley and Mark Chadbourn) set up to promote the fantasy genre. You can visit their website at www.thewritefantastic.com and Juliet's site at www.julietemckenna.com

Juliet maintains: "I don't do horror. Not the modern schools of visceral and psychological horror anyway. Doug Bradley's fascinating talk on movie monster make-up and masks at FantasyCon 2000 is as close as I'm ever going to get to seeing Pinhead. But I can occasionally be tempted by a good old-fashioned creature-feature, or one of the Universal classics...Hence this story."

"I'm really no' sure about this, gentlemen." Standing in the doorway, the speaker jangled a ring of keys.

"Come on man, it has to be tonight. Now!" The man loomed menacingly over the rotund policeman, even though he was standing on the step below him.

"Now then, sir." Unnerved, the policeman groped for his whistle chain among the silver buttons on his dark blue serge tunic.

The second man awaiting admittance put a restraining hand on the tall man's black sleeve. "Officer, this villain is responsible for killing four young women of good family and irreproachable character."

Where the constable's accent was that of a gruff lowlander of humble origins, both the other men spoke with the precision of education at Fettes and Oxford.

"Oh aye." The policeman huffed through his ferociously bristling moustache and his breath clouded the cold night air. "But gentlemen..." He shook his head uncertainly.

"Come and see for yourself. We'll do no damage." The black-clad man plucked the ring of keys from the constable's unwary fingers and unlocked the door himself. "Hurry!"

Ignoring the policeman's protests, he hurried away through the ground floor of the tall narrow building tucked into the grandeur of Edinburgh's Royal Mile.

"I'm sorry." The second man smiled apologetically. "But we really don't have time to waste." He ran after the tall man, both of them heading for the stairs.

The constable muttered something under his breath and followed, after turning to close the door securely behind him.

"Hurry, James." The tall man was taking the steps two or three at a time, the tails of his black evening dress lashing as he took the turns. Despite the autumn chill he wore no hat, gloves or overcoat.

"She's my sister, Arthur," the second man snapped back. He wore a tweed covert-coat, leather gloves and trousers more suited to a grouse moor than polite society. As he ran up the seemingly endless flights of stairs, he snatched off his brown bowler hat.

Reaching the building's pinnacle, Arthur searched the ring of keys for the one that would open the camera obscura itself. The starched white linen of his shirt front shone, diamond studs brilliant, as the full moon above sailed blithely through a cloudless sky.

"Hurry!" Now it was James who was impatient, lighting a shuttered oil lamp with an angry scrape of a match against his boot sole.

"You, in here." As the puffing policeman climbed laboriously onto the roof, Arthur grabbed his shoulder to pull him into the closeted darkness of the camera obscura.

"Now, sir – " the constable protested.

Now You See Him, Now You Don't

"Have you ever been up here before?" Arthur found the levers to control the mechanism high above their heads.

"No," the constable began. "What – " He fell silent, open-mouthed, as a vision of the Castle Esplanade appeared on the wide white circular table in the centre of the room. "Now will ye look at that," he breathed in wonder.

"Stand by the door." Hawk-like with his prominent nose and intense dark eyes, Arthur was studying the minute figures crossing the cobbled expanse in the image. "No, don't open it, not more than a crack. We need darkness in here."

"How does it work, sir?" The constable meekly complied. "Is it mirrors?"

"The image is brought to the table by means of a prism in the apex of the roof." Out on the roof, James obliged with an explanation, determinedly courteous. "It's what the scientists call refraction, rather than reflection. The man we're following has no reflection. Possibly because of the silvering used to make mirrors – "

Arthur interrupted without apology. "James, is Robert down there?"

James was standing by the rail guarding the edge of the roof. He lifted his lantern and snapped the shutter once, twice and a third time. Down in the darkness in front of the castle gate a light blinked twice in answer. "Yes." His voice cracked with relief. "Can you see Isobel? Is there enough moonlight?"

"I told you. The moon's brighter tonight than it's been for eighteen years, and than it will be for another eighteen." Arthur bent to study the tiny images more closely. "Yes, I see her."

His eyes followed a figure wearing a billowing evening cloak. The hood wasn't raised to avoid disturbing the young woman's high-piled hair so frivolously dressed with feathers. Clasped low on her breast, the cloak had slipped to one side to reveal a glimpse of white shoulder.

"Can you see him?" James's voice thickened with loathing.

"Not yet." Arthur's reply was clipped.

"But ye say this man's a murderer," the policeman protested breathlessly. "Why has there been no hue and cry? I've heard nothing – "

109

"Because the medical profession calls it *chlorosis*." Arthur's contempt resonated around the high ceiling. "Green sickness; an afflication peculiar to virgins. Because doctors have no more wit than to wring their hands, watch their patients die and then send in their bills as swiftly as possible thereafter."

"Can you see him?" demanded James from out on the roof.

"Wait." Arthur's eyes had not moved from the round table carrying the image of the esplanade. "Yes, there he is."

"How close?" James rasped.

"Who is he?" The policeman took a step towards the table. "Is it poison, then? How he kills them?"

"There." Arthur pointed. As his sleeve cast a black shadow across the image, a tiny figure walked across his white cuff, lifted up from the table beneath.

"How does this thing work?" The constable looked upwards once again, quite bemused.

"How close is he to Isobel?" James's words cracked with anger.

"She's safe at present, James," Arthur said tersely. "Wait until I give the word. We won't get a second chance."

"I won't lose a second sister," James hissed.

The constable watched the figure Arthur had identified as the murderer. "You're waiting for him to make some move? That'll give ye proof?" As his fingers strayed to the handcuffs at his belt, his gaze flickered to the solitary female walking steadily up the esplanade. "The lassie's his sister, ye say? Couldn't ye find some trollop and pay her to lure the brute? They risk death and worse every night – "

"Whores are old before their time, foul and diseased." Arthur was still watching intently. "This monster wants pure blood and unsullied flesh."

"Pure, ye say?" The constable stirred, his splendid moustache now bristling with disquiet. "You've a man down there, though? This Robert? Will he save the lassie if needs be?"

"He won't be able to." As Arthur shook his head slowly, his eyes never left the tiny figures on the table. "Any more than you could arrest him, my good fellow. As soon as he locks eyes with someone, man or woman, he can wipe their memory of him clean away."

Now You See Him, Now You Don't

"That's what they call hypnotism?" The constable groped for understanding. "Mesmerism?"

"Call it what you will, you'd be left standing there wondering what you'd been thinking of doing – " Arthur broke off as the image dulled and wavered before fading altogether. "Damnation! What's happening? James?"

The only answer from the roof was a paroxysm of coughing.

The constable pushed open the door to reveal choking skeins of sooty smoke swirling around the lofty structure. "Aye, the wind's changed. That's Auld Reekie for ye." His voice quavered between tight-throated apprehension and a certain satisfaction that these educated gentlemen had foolishly overlooked Edinburgh's notorious pall of chimney smoke. "Are ye all right, sir? And what about the lassie?"

James couldn't reply, doubled over with coughing, the back of one gloved hand pressed to his eyes.

"Shut the door, man!" Arthur bellowed, scowling ferociously.

Startled, the constable did as he was bid. As he did so, all was darkness, no hint of light or life on the camera obscura table.

"Oh God." Arthur's voice rose on a note of uncertainty for the first time. "Open the door! James!" he shouted, "it's no good! Signal to Robert – "

The table shivered and the vision of the esplanade reappeared.

"There!" The constable stabbed an urgent finger at the image. "Him in the tall hat, that's him, isn't it? And there's the lassie."

"Good man." Arthur fixed his burning gaze on their target. "Stand ready to open the door. Tell James – no, wait, not till I give the word…"

"What's the lassie going tae do?" the constable asked dubiously. "If it's some kind of assault – "

"Now!" yelled Arthur.

"Robert!" There was no hope of James's hoarse and desperate shout reaching their distant ally but the light flashing from the frantic shutter of his lantern spoke for him.

Down in the darkness by the castle gate, the second lamp reflected the frenzied signal.

The girl in the evening cloak whirled around, one forearm raised

111

to shield her eyes. Her other hand brought a heavy glass and silver bottle out from the concealing folds of heavy silk.

The man in the tall hat had been reaching for her slender shoulders. He recoiled, throwing up his own hands. It was to no avail. The moonlight caught a glittering spray of liquid soaking him from head to toe. The man lurched away, weaving from side to side. He staggered a few paces and then fell to his knees, hands pressed to his face.

"Vitriol!" The constable choked, aghast. He threw open the door.

"No, wait." Arthur abandoned the mechanism of the camera obscura and the image vanished.

"Please." James spread beseeching hands and moved to intercept the policeman, tears borne of his coughing fit still glistening on his cheeks.

"Out o' the way!" The constable shoved him aside with a firm hand to the chest and ran for the stairs, his heavy boots resounding on the treads. James rushed after him, slower and still audibly wheezing.

Arthur followed, taking the time to lock the doors, to the camera obscura and to the building itself as he emerged onto the Royal Mile.

Up on the Castle Esplanade, he heard a single breathless blast of a police whistle, suddenly cut short. That prompted him to pick up his pace, frowning darkly.

Up on the esplanade, a knot of men had gathered around Isobel, several in uniform, the silver spikes and chain straps on their helmets shining in the moonlight. Even that brief alarm had summoned rapid assistance.

Arthur joined them and tapped the closest policeman on one shoulder. "What's going on, officer?"

It was the hapless constable who'd accompanied them up to the camera obscura. "You, you..." He struggled for words, bristling moustache eloquent with outrage and confusion.

"Some villain was about to attack my sister," James explained to the newly assembled policemen, his face wholly open and innocent, apparently breathless in his urgency.

"I saw him." Robert stepped forward, all honest concern in his

Now You See Him, Now You Don't

frock coat and top hat. "The villain ran off." He shook his head regretfully.

"Ran off?" the constable expostulated wrathfully. "Miss, just what have you got there?"

Isobel looked at him, limpid blue eyes wide. "A *gazogène*."

"A soda siphon, officer," Arthur added helpfully.

"We were at dinner and it was such a curious thing." Within the loose neck of her cloak, it was plain she was wearing a pale pink evening gown, the wide neck trimmed with scarlet satin roses. "I was bringing it to show James – " Isobel shivered violently and not merely from the cold. There was nothing feigned about the shock racking her.

"I told you to wait for me," Arthur scolded her nevertheless.

"Let me see that." The constable growled as he pulled on his white gloves with suppressed violence. He took the silver and glass device from her unresisting hands and sniffed cautiously at it.

"I've only just arrived in town," James explained with a rueful gesture at his clothing. "The near-side horse went lame – "

"He ran off, ye say?" One of the other officers turned to scan the empty expanse of the esplanade. The others were already drifting away, glowering at the dark alleys leading away all around. "Would you know him again, miss?"

"I – I don't believe so." Isobel looked quite woebegone as she clutched at her silken cloak with demure lace-mittened hands, drawing the slippery cloth up under her chin.

"You, sir?" The policeman demanded of Robert.

He shook his head regretfully. "I was too concerned with assisting Miss Murray to get a good look at the scoundrel."

"Ay well, we'll see if we can find him all the same." The helpful officer gave her a grimly encouraging nod.

As the other police all departed, intent on the hunt, the constable thrust the soda siphon at Arthur with a scowl. "Water? He ran off because the lassie sprayed him with fizzy water."

"Holy water, officer." Arthur smiled with vicious satisfaction as he took the device. "And no, he didn't run off."

"Then where is he?" cried the constable, exasperated. "How's this to stop these killings you speak of?"

"He won't be killing any more innocent girls." Isobel stirred a slough of fine dust with one dainty satin-slippered toe. "All that's left of him lies here under our feet." A single tear slid down her porcelain cheek before she broke into violent sobs.

Robert folded her in a firm embrace.

"Now then." The constable's moustache bristled with indignation at such an unseemly display.

"They are engaged to be married," James said firmly.

"As I was, to the eldest Miss Murray," Arthur said with cold composure. "Before this monster sapped the life from her and we laid her in an early grave."

"We knew he couldn't resist following me." Isobel's voice was muffled against the lapels of Robert's coat. "We knew I was the only one who could get close enough to douse him."

"As long as she didn't look at him and risk meeting his gaze." James gestured vaguely in the direction of the lofty camera obscura. "He'd know any of the rest of us, and use his hypnosis to disable us. We had to watch him from a distance and use lamp signals to let Isobel know he was about to pounce."

"But who was he?" The constable was beside himself with frustration.

"A better question would be '*what* was he?'," Arthur began.

James took pity on the hapless policeman. "There's a novel you should read, my good fellow. It was published in London last May. That should answer all your questions."

"Excuse me, but we should get Isobel home," Robert said firmly.

"Oh aye," the constable said, now quite bemused. "This book, ye say?"

James turned to speak over his shoulder as the three men departed, Isobel safe between them. "The chap who runs the Lyceum wrote it. It's called *Dracula*."

With thanks to Gail Nina Anderson, for idly speculating over dinner about the difference between mirrors and a camera obscura when it comes to vampires. And to Chaz Brenchley for gracefully yielding the idea to me, and for helpful comments on the story in progress.

PROGENY
Mark Morris

Mark Morris was born in the mining town of Bolsover in 1963, and spent his childhood in Tewkesbury, Hong Kong, Newark and Huddersfield. He became a full-time writer in 1988 on the Enterprise Allowance Scheme, and a year later saw the release of his first novel *Toady*. Since then he has had ten further novels published to great acclaim, including *Stitch, The Immaculate, The Secret of Anatomy, Mr Bad Face, Longbarrow, Genesis, The Dogs, The Uglimen, Nowhere Near an Angel* and *Fiddleback* (writing as J.M. Morris) – as well as collections such as *Close to the Bone*. He is also editor of the *Cinema Macabre* book in which authors, editors, actors and film-makers write about their favourite horror films. The book includes contributions from such names as Simon – *Shaun of the Dead* – Pegg, Mark – *- League of Gentlemen* – Gatiss, Muriel Gray, Neil Gaiman, Stephen Jones, Peter Atkins and many others. He lives near York with his wife, the artist Nel Whatmore, and their two children.

Mark states: "To me the BFS is synonymous with laughter and friendship and camaraderie. It was Ramsey Campbell who first suggested I attend its annual shindig, the British Fantasy Convention, after I'd sent him a series of fan letters back in 1987. I arrived at the

British Fantasy Society: A Celebration

Midland hotel in Birmingham a callow youth (well, I was 24), nervous and uncertain, not sure where to go or what to do. After a somewhat inauspicious first meeting with Ramsey (which you can read about in my introduction to the PS edition of his wonderful novel, *The Overnight* (plug, plug)), I was taken under the kindly collective wing of George Budge, Mike Chinn and the legendary Whispering John Carter. Too terrified to snub John's incredible generosity, I was soon consuming pints of beer so rapidly that one of the bar staff burst into flames trying to keep up with our increasingly slurred demands. The next morning I was to experience what has become a long-held and much-revered tradition at these events: the FantasyCon Hangover. I recall lying on the bathroom floor of my hotel room and watching a beetle amble unhurriedly towards my face. Unable to move a muscle, I simply closed my eyes, and when I opened them again some time later the beetle had gone.

"It was at this FantasyCon that I met the first of many of the best friends a fellow could ever hope to have. I'd seen Nicholas Royle's photograph in *Fear* magazine, accompanying one of his typically erudite and unsettling stories. It was an arty profile of his sharp-boned face and long neck. His bio described him as a 24 year old writer and actor, who lived in London. He was the same age as me and yet he looked austere and sophisticated. From his photo I imagined someone tall and willowy, dressed in black. I was delighted when a grinning, bespectacled skinhead the same height as I was (5'7) came up to me on the Saturday night and said, "You're Mark Morris. You've sold a novel." Turned out we were both equally in awe of each other, but we soon got over that. By the end of the weekend we'd become great mates, and we still are. That's what happens at FantasyCon. Those two short days are often spent forging friendships that last a lifetime. For me, it is this enduring sense of community, of family, that epitomises the BFS. That is why I am incredibly proud to continue to be a part of it, and to share in these celebrations."

I miss you, Dora. I miss you so much. Why did it have to happen like this?

His first sensation was of an incredible lightness, as though, for him alone, gravity had lessened. He was vaguely aware of the floor below him, but had to concentrate hard before he had any perception of his own feet touching that floor. Even then he seemed ephemeral, as though he were suspended from the ceiling and could reach the ground only with his tip-toes. The room at first was like something in a dream: an impression. Something flimsy and insubstantial, like a hastily constructed set. Unpainted. Undetailed.

Gradually, however, a focus established itself. A bed. And, more importantly, the girl *in* the bed. He immediately felt guilt, shame, fear. At the sight of her solemnly sleeping face, her blonde hair spread over the pillow like a princess's, he felt anguish grip him. Seeing her like this, so serene, appeared to indicate that she had not been traumatised by what she had been through. Nevertheless he knew that she was changed. Irrevocably. Somewhere deep inside. He had seen the evidence, suffered it every day. They shared the scars, the hurt, the ever-booming echo of that dreadful mindless moment.

The dependence. The incapacitation. That was the second thing he noticed. It had gone. All gone. Yet it seemed as though he was nothing but...but an outline. A shell. Full of emptiness.

His brain, his mind, whatever it was up there, sent a message to his arm, told him to raise it. Methodically he imagined the procedure, the arm coming up, the fingers straightening. His eyes (he must have eyes; he could see, couldn't he?) looked at the place where the arm should be. There was no sense of strain in the eyes, no foggy patina of approaching cataracts as there had been previously.

And yes, he *could* see the arm. Dimly, hazily, but it was there, wasn't it?

Well, wasn't it?

His uncertainty troubled him. Why did he feel so strange? He let the arm drop – or at least he thought he did (the instant he stopped

117

thinking about it, the arm seemed to...to go away. To be discarded. To...to...to dissolve?).
I don't think, therefore I may not be.
Sudden anger. The girl in the bed. She was the important one, not his bloody arm. He wasn't here to establish the fact of his own existence.
So what *was* he here for? What was he supposed to do? Surely not that? No, please God, he wouldn't. He just wanted all this to end. He'd rather die before he put her through that again.

I know what you think of me, Rachel, and I only wish that I could use my voice, or even hold a pen, that I could communicate my regret to you in some way. The last ten years have been hell, partly because of my situation but largely because I can see how it's eating you up, growing and blackening inside you, mutilating your mind. I never meant to do what I did, Rachel. You must believe that, though I know you never will. If only you could read my thoughts. If only I could talk to you. Just ten minutes, that's all I would ask for. I would give my life for just ten minutes of articulation.
Don't you think I've asked myself over and over again why I did it? Well I have. And each time I come up with the same answer – I just don't know. It happened, that's all, it just seemed to progress naturally, which in a way is the most horrifying thing of all. I was perfectly sane, perfectly clear-headed, or at least I thought I was. Mind you, they say the mad always think they're sane, don't they? It's only the sane who worry that they might be going crazy.
All I would like to do, Rachel, is to give you my version of what happened that day, to take you through it step by step. I wouldn't ask you to condone what I did, or even to understand it. I would just ask you to listen to me, that's all, to listen to my side of things. Maybe it would help, I don't know. Or maybe nothing would change. If I could go back and make things different, I would. Believe me, I would.
This is how it happened. I took you out around twelve, twelve-

thirty that day. It was a sunny day and I was as happy as I could be under the circumstances. I know it seems that I planned it all from the start, but it's not true, Rachel, you must believe that. If you think I planned it, then it makes me a bigger monster than I already am, but nothing could have been further from my mind, *nothing*, and that's God's honest truth. So what *were* you thinking about? I hear you ask. Just how *did* you feel?

Well, like I say, happy enough. Just being with you made me feel that way, and there's nothing to be ashamed of in that. I loved your innocence, your exuberance. You didn't exactly make me feel young (in fact you quite exhausted me sometimes), but you made me feel as though the *world* was still young, as though there were still wonders in it, wonders that only children could see.

I suppose you reminded me of *my* childhood. Yes, that's it, I think. But not in a sad or wistful way like we sometimes remember our youth. In a happy way, a nostalgic way, as though you were living what I'd had to give up. Does that make sense to you? Because that's exactly how I felt, no more, no less.

The drive was uneventful, so I'll start from the funfair. I'm sure you think it was there where I started to get my ideas, but that's not true either. Oh, you can argue it was a warm day, there were lots of young girls in shorts and those t-shirts they wear without sleeves (halter-tops are they called? Anyway, it doesn't matter), and lots of couples having fun, their arms around each other, some even kissing, I suppose. But honestly, Rachel, I never really noticed any of those things, and even if I did none of them affected me. None of them "got me thinking" or anything like that.

You were being your normal lovely self. Laughing a lot. Asking lots of questions. Pointing at things, your eyes as big as dinner plates.

I bought you an ice-cream and some candy floss and a toffee apple, and I let you ride on whatever you wanted. I knew I was spoiling you but I thought: grandad's prerogative. I decided that the worst that could happen was that you would be sick on the big dipper or the ferris-wheel, and I thought that that was a small price to pay for all the fun.

The only ride we went on where there was any real physical contact was the Ghost Train, and that was because you got scared and grabbed my hand. There was nothing unusual in it, nothing funny. It was only a natural thing. When we came out of that tunnel, back into the daylight and the noise, all the other kids were holding their parents' hands too.

Should I stay here or move closer? What if she sees me and starts to scream? Oh God, won't someone please tell me what to do?

The room unveiled its details one by one, unwrapped them as though they were presents or secrets. It was a colourful room, gaudy even, filled with innocently smiling images that to him seemed somehow desperate. The Wombles cavorting on the curtains to his left seemed to be denying the existence of the black night. On the pink carpet objects were strewn – or perhaps arranged, carefully placed, like childish charms against evil spirits. There was a fluffy blue dog, a Raggedy Ann on its back, a storybook opened to a picture of the Sleeping Beauty, a pair of small white shoes laid toe to toe.

The shoes. He looked at them and a sensation overcame him. In other circumstances he might have started to shake. A lump might have obstructed his throat. Perhaps even tears might have fallen.

Yes, they were *the* shoes. There was no doubt about it. They were the shoes she'd been wearing on that day.

He moaned, or thought he did, and his gaze skittered, as always, back to the girl. Once again he stared at her face, tried to discern some residue, some mark left by what had occurred. The fact that he couldn't profoundly distressed him. If she had let her feelings show – her confusion, her trauma – then perhaps the badness might have flowed out of her, left her for ever. But her innocence had buried the trauma, secreted it in the deepest darkest part of her mind. Which meant that her scars ran deep, that somewhere in the bubbling brook that was her childhood a capsule lurked, a flimsy fragile thing, ready at the slightest whisper to crack and spread its poison.

Why? he whispered (thought he whispered). Why oh why oh why?

The girl made a small sound, frowned, twisted slightly, as though a breeze had passed over her face.

He froze. A thought came to him: What *was* he doing here? Why *had* he come back? Surely the strength of his curiosity, his need to see, to know, had not dragged him here? No, he couldn't believe that of himself. Even after what he'd done he found it impossible. He was no slavering ghoul, no voyeur, no gloater. God knew, there were enough of them around, people who revelled in the misery of others, but surely he could not be counted amongst their number? Those people were disturbed, mad, spiteful. But that day, *that day*, he must have been too. And if he had been then, why not now? Why was he here, after all? *Why was he here?*

He moved a little closer to the bed.

* * *

Can you recall what we did after the funfair? We walked along the promenade for a bit and then we went down on the beach. Starmouth beach is lovely. Smooth sand, hardly any pebbles, a pier you can walk right underneath, and lots of caves and rock pools.

You loved it. You picked up some shells and some bits of glass. The glass was all rough and rounded, do you remember? I explained this was because the sea had moved it around a lot and the salt and the tide had worn it down. I said the glass had probably come from a foreign country, that it had been washed miles and miles, right across the ocean. You looked at me, wide-eyed. "Which country, grandad?" you asked. I told you America or China or maybe even Russia. "Wow," you said and looked out to sea, shielding your eyes with your hand. I think you thought that you would be able to see the coastline of one of those countries just peeping over the horizon.

I remember that moment so clearly: the way you looked. You had your blonde hair tied back in...what do you call them? Ponytails? Bunches? Anyway, tied back with these little bits of elastic with plastic butterflies on them. Your dress was flapping around your knees because of the wind coming off the sea and your white shoes were covered in sand. I told you we'd have to clean those shoes before we came home or Mummy wouldn't be pleased, but you just shrugged and pouted. I remember teasing you, telling you what a little madam you were, making you laugh.

I think of that laugh now. So childish. So carefree. How could I have done what I did? What in God's name drove me to it?

Anyway, I'll carry on, tell you the rest.

We walked along to the caves and the rock pools. You wouldn't go further than any of the cave entrances, especially when I told you about the dinosaur skeleton they'd found in one of them. In a rock pool we came across a big crab with only one claw, half-hidden by an overhang of stone. You found a stick or a reed or something and lowered it down, right in front of the crab. I bet you remember that, don't you? The crab didn't pay any attention, so you swirled the stick around a bit, disturbing the sand. All at once the crab's claw shot out and grabbed the stick. You should have seen your face! You jumped and let go of the stick and let out a little scream. Then you looked up at me and started laughing and laughing.

We walked back along the beach. You took off your shoes and socks and started splashing along the sea's edge. You kept trying to kick water up at me but the wind caught it and scattered the droplets. We walked under the pier, which smelt all seaweedy, and then, believe it or not, you announced that you were hungry again so we made our way back to the promenade. I gave you the choice of doughnuts and lemonade or some proper fish and chips from a seafront cafe. You chose the fish and chips, so after we'd found a bench where you could brush the sand off your feet and put your shoes and socks back on, we made our way to a cafe.

I don't want all this to happen again. I don't. I truly don't. My only crime – my only true crime – was that I loved her far too much.

The girl's eyes opened. They looked straight at him. He froze, suddenly more terrified, more ashamed, than he'd ever thought it possible to be.

"Mummy," the girl shouted. "Mummy, where are you?" She sat up, blonde hair falling to her shoulders, snatching at the pillow and holding it to her chest like a shield.

Movement in the corridor outside. Mowgli and Balloo and King Louie and Bagheera lay flat on the wallpaper, framing a pink door. The door opened. Light fell into the room. A woman entered, sleepy-eyed, tousle-haired, a dressing-gown draped over her shoulders like folded diaphanous wings.

He felt, in that instant, a crushing desperate terrible shame. To be found here, to be discovered by this woman, the product of his own seed...No. No, it was too awful to bear. He wanted to shrink, to dissolve, to burst. Felt he would be struck down the moment he saw the lightning bolt of accusation in her glaring eyes.

But he was spared all that. The woman didn't even look at him. Instead she crossed straight to the bed, took the girl in her arms, whispered, "Sh now, sh. Mummy's here. What's the matter?"

The girl clutched the woman. Held tight to her sleeves. Half-buried her stricken face in the woman's breasts. Through a mouthful of thumb she murmured, "Someone was here, Mummy. Standing by my bed. I think he came out of the wardrobe."

The woman turned. Looked straight at him. *At him!* He felt like screaming.

He waited. For the anger. The hate. Perhaps even the violence. But:

"There's no one there," the woman said. "You've had a bad dream, darling, that's all."

He listened, amazed. No one there? What did she mean? Why was she lying? He heard her continue:

"Do you want to sleep in Mummy's bed where it's warm? Shall we go and wake Daddy up? Get him to read us a story?"

The girl gave a sulky half-nod.

"Come on then. My, you're getting to be a big girl, aren't you? Hold tight. Do you want Raggedy Ann to come too?"

Chatting quietly to her daughter, allaying her fears with a weave of words, the woman carried the girl across the room and out, closing the door behind her.

He stood for a moment, wondering. Listened to the murmurs finally dwindle to silence. Then he crossed to the bed, sent a message to his hand, saw – or thought he saw – - the hand lying flat on the place where the girl had lain.

And suddenly he understood. Thought he did. Wasn't sure. He felt the girl's warmth, felt it dissipate little by little. Felt the bed become cool. Cooler. Cold.

I'm sorry, he said, though he could hear no sound. *I'm sorry, I'm sorry, I'm sorry.*

You had fish and chips and mushy peas. A child's portion. And bread and butter and a strawberry milkshake. Despite what you said about being hungry, you couldn't eat it all, which didn't surprise me after all that stuff at the funfair. You pushed the food around your plate with your fork until I'd eaten mine, now and then stopping to have a sip of your milkshake. You had a funny look on your face, a sort of faraway look, as if you were leading up to something, thinking about something you wanted to ask. Sure enough a few seconds later you put down your fork and looked straight at me. Then you said, "Grandad, where's Nanna gone?"

Well, as you can imagine, the question threw me. I had to think about it a bit before answering. I wasn't sure what to tell you - how much you would really understand and how much I wanted you to know. It surprised me, coming three months after Dora's death. I would never have thought a six-year-old would keep such a question bottled up so long.

Eventually I said, "She's gone to Jesus, pet. Didn't Mummy explain?"

"Yes," you said with a frown on your face, "but I don't know where Jesus is."

I nearly laughed at that but I stopped myself just in time. You looked deadly serious and I didn't want you to think I was making fun of you. I was about to tell you that Jesus was a person, not a place, but then I realised it would sound as though Dora had run off with the milkman or something. Eventually I said, "Jesus is God's son, pet. They live in the sky. In Heaven. That's where your Nanna's gone."

You frowned. "You mean with the angels?" you said.

"Yes," I said, "with the angels. Your Nanna's one of them now."

"But doesn't she want to come and see us any more?" you asked.

"Of course she does," I said, "but once you get to Heaven you have to stay there. You can't leave."

"Then I think Heaven's horrible," you said. "And I think God's horrible too. She's my Nanna, not his."

I felt as though I hadn't explained things very well. Children do that to you sometimes. You try to be delicate, try to skirt round the real facts because you think you're protecting them, when all you're really doing is confusing them, avoiding taboos not for their sake but for your own, and succeeding only in tying yourself into knots.

Does that make sense? I hope so. The reason I'm telling you all this is because it was due to this conversation that I gave you a hug in the car. Again, I didn't mean anything by it. It was just a hug, that's all. I suppose I was frustrated because I couldn't explain things and because I just sort of loved you all of a sudden, loved your childishness, your innocence. Even now I wasn't thinking anything. You were just a little girl, my grand-daughter, and I loved you only because of that.

We started to drive home. It was about six, seven o' clock. You were pointing at things, asking questions, and then bit by bit the questions tailed off and you went very quiet. I thought you must be sleepy but when I looked over I noticed you were a bit green around the gills, so I asked if you felt all right. You said, "No, I feel sick." I drove another fifty, sixty yards, then pulled into a layby.

I unbuckled your seat-belt, then reached over and opened the car door. We were in the countryside by now. There were fields and hedges and trees, a couple of distant farmhouses and not many cars on the road. You leaned right out of the car and was sick on the ground outside. And that's when it happened. Right there while you were bringing up toffee apple and fish and chips and candy-floss and ice-cream.

Your dress got kind of bunched up and I could see brown legs and white pants and something just sort of clicked inside me. I've been through it time and again in my mind and I just can't explain it any other way. One minute I was thinking what a nice day we'd had and working out what time we'd get home, and the next I was doing those awful things.

Even now when I think about those things it makes me want to die in shame. I hope you won't feel the same way for ever, but I think that you might, I truly truly do. In a way I still can't believe I really did anything. It's as though it was someone else there that day, someone who looked like me but wasn't me. Someone who pushed aside my control and who used my body and my brain for their own degraded purpose.

But saying that is crazy, and much too easy. Of course it was me. I have no excuse for what I did and no explanation. It happened, that's all. It happened. I just want you to know it wasn't planned, it wasn't pre-meditated. It was terrible, I admit that. It was unforgivable. But I'm sorry. I've suffered enough. I know what it's like to be a victim and now I just want some peace.

I'm drifting. Can feel myself going back. No, I don't want to. I can't stand it any more.

* * *

He woke with a jolt when the door slammed. For a moment the sound made him forget who or where or when he was. The door was as wide and as blank as his mind. There was colour to the left of the door — pink flesh, blue denim, yellow and black bee-stripes.

Rachel.

He remembered then, and was struck, as he often was, by their separate perception of a shared world. Time for him was an endurance, a boulder he was forced to drag in his wake. For her it was nothing, or at worst a feather which she could blow from her cupped palm and watch float away. Was she really seventeen? It seemed inconceivable. And yet in her swift maturing he had crossed deserts of anguish, oceans of pain.

As best he could he regarded himself. He saw as always the blanket covering his wasted legs, his hands like roots entwined in his lap. If only he had some autonomy he wouldn't mind the wheelchair. But no; the stroke had been as merciless, as uncaring and as permanent as his actions over a decade earlier. Of course he'd rather have died, but that would not have been suitable retribution. He ached at the sight of her golden hair. If only. If only...

She walked across the room, staring at him as ever with dreadful accusation. She never spoke but then she had no need to. Her hate seemed to spill like poison from her cold eyes. Monster, freak, beast, betrayer, pervert: he saw all this in her gaze. He could close his own eyes but that was somehow worse, knowing she was there, watching.

She sat cross-legged on the floor before the wheelchair and stared at him. She was motionless, expressionless. He could have believed she was an automaton, bled of all emotion, if he had not heard her laughing with her friends. This was the moment each day when their worlds conjoined, when time for them both ran parallel. This was their shared hour, a time for remembering. For him it was the longest hour of all.

THE SUSTENANCE OF HOAK
Ramsey Campbell

The Oxford Companion to English Literature describes Ramsey Campbell as 'Britain's most respected living horror writer'. He has been given more awards than any other writer in the field, including the Grand Master Award of the World Horror Convention and the Lifetime Achievement Award of the Horror Writers Association, as well as being a multiple recipient of the British Fantasy Award.

In *Supernatural Literature of the World* S. T. Joshi writes 'With a prose style of unexcelled fluidity and quiet power, an ability to draw character in a few deft strokes, and a seemingly inexhaustible fluidity of imagination, Campbell begs comparison with Poe, Blackwood and Lovecraft as the preeminent author of supernatural horror in all literary history.'

Among his novels are *The Face That Must Die*, *Incarnate*, *Midnight Sun*, *The Count of Eleven*, *Silent Children*, *The Darkest Part of the Woods*, *The Overnight*, *Secret Stories* and *The Grin of the Dark*. His collections include *Waking Nightmares*, *Alone with the Horrors*, *Ghosts and Grisly Things* and *Told by the Dead*, and his non-fiction is collected as *Ramsey Campbell, Probably*. His novels *The Nameless* and *Pact of the Fathers* have been filmed in Spain.

Ramsey Campbell lives on Merseyside with his wife Jenny. He reviews films and DVDs weekly for BBC Radio Merseyside. His

The Sustenance Of Hoak

pleasures include classical music, good food and wine, and whatever's in that pipe. His web site is at www.ramseycampbell.com

As President of the BFS Ramsey says: "I took no part in the founding of the British Weird Fantasy Society, but perhaps I planted a seed in a nearby field that may have had some effect. In 1969 I wrote a single-page polemic that was printed in *Gothique* magazine that year and handed out in the form of a flyer at the London Eastercon in 1970. *Zombies Awake!* was my rude title, very possibly one reason why some members refused to accept a copy, John Brunner among them. The handout called on fantasy fans to form a society independent of the British Science Fiction Association. Next year several people did.

"The first British Fantasy Society – actually devoted to science fiction – was founded in 1942 by Mike Rosenblum and Ted Carnell. This may explain the addition of the Weird to the new organisation's name, which was founded by Keith Walker, Phil Spencer and Rosemary Pardoe, with Dave Sutton soon making up the gang of four. Before long the adjective was sloughed, and nobody seemed confused. The genial Ken Bulmer was elected President, and in time I took over from him, though few could have inherited his energy. I'm just a figurehead fronting the voyage of the Society into fantastic seas.

"It looks quite a trip to me now, one compounded of nostalgia and adventure. I still remember the first FantasyCon, a day's event for which all the attendees were locked into a smoky room... the increasingly decrepit Midland Hotel in Birmingham, a chunk of urban Gothic (though not architecturally) that could hardly have been more appropriate to the Society's horrific side... the legendary Mythcon, an attempted coup that lasted a weekend and sent off Dennis Etchison to receive an award in the Suttons' back garden... the woes of finding the motorway exit to the hotel in the wilds of Walsall... Tom Monteleone and his bottle... Mark Timlin and the Malaysians, who appeared to offend him as much as P. D. James famously did... the perennial panel on the future (or the death) of horror... I'll stop before all these ellipses turn me dotty, but believe me, they imply that much more could be recalled. May the Society enjoy another thirty years, and then another when I shall be a memory or less than one. I hereby undertake to haunt all the FantasyCons I can. It's been fun, and I hope it stays that way for everyone."

"If we ever reach the treasure," Ryre said with bitter humour, "we'll have earned it and twice again."

Glode's mouth opened, but nothing emerged except a thread of blood. He was trying to raise himself against the tree where Ryre had propped him; his fists crushed the earth, his arms trembled like trees, their thick veins swelled. "Keep down," Ryre said as a flight of arrows tore through the leaves overhead. "I'll get you in there if I have to stick the lot of them on their own arrows," he said, gazing narrow-eyed though the trees at the gate of the town of Hoak.

And it might come to that, he thought, crawling through the undergrowth. Heat throbbed through the forest like blood, slow and viscous. He remembered how they'd decided to come to Hoak.

Like most of the mercenaries who'd helped win the war against the pirates on the Sea of Shouting Islands, they had been drinking their pay and complaining of its meagreness when talk had turned to the treasure of Hoak. The treasure was buried beneath the town; a now long-lost map showing its location had been found attached to the leg of a migrating bird; the people of Hoak (someone had said, trying to out-shout jeers) were willing to give the treasure to whoever found it; nobody who had sought it had returned. Silence followed that, quickly broken by bantering. Ryre and Glode had jeered with the rest, but later they'd agreed that the rumours felt more like the truth than did most tales of treasure. And they knew that unless they moved on they would have to vow allegiance to the local lords, or fight those of their companions who had done so. As for the vanished seekers – they must have failed and been too ashamed to return empty-handed. Ryre and Glode had smashed their

The Sustenance Of Hoak

wine-mugs in the street below the inn, splashing the boots of a cursing sailor, and had made their way to the wharves. Next day they had left the continent of Drobond for Thabbe.

Ryre was at the edge of the forest now, two hundred yards from the gate of Hoak. The trees around him were scraggy; the forest must once have been cut further back from the town. Peering across the parched grass, he saw that the gate beneath the archers had been patched with planks, leaving gaps. The town wall was of growing trees, the gaps plugged with logs. His lips pulled back thinly. It would be enough.

Once on Thabbe they'd bought steeds at the port of Zizir. The trader had smiled sadly on hearing where they were bound, but had told them the route readily enough. They had been six days into the forest that covers half of Thabbe, and less than a day from Hoak, when in a long avenue bandits had dropped like ripe fruit from the trees. Ryre and Glode had swerved between them, slashing them as they fell. The bandits must have been used to slower and meeker prey. But some had had blowpipes as well as knives; one dart had spilled the last of the water while another, finding a chink in the leaves of Glode's armour, had lodged deep in his guts. Since then he had ridden doubled over, his silence like a cry in Ryre's ears.

He was still propped against the tree, sitting bent low over his stomach, his fist clenched white around a fistful of earth. "I can break the gate," Ryre said, collecting dry twigs and grass and tying them in a bun at the head of a lopped-off branch. He untied their steeds and brought Glode's to him. "Bid him farewell," Ryre said. "He will help save you."

At the edge of the forest he lit the tip of the firebrand with a flint from the pouch at his belt, then slapped Glode's steed out into the open. At once the arrows responded. The few he had time to watch looked too high for an attack, more like a warning. Certainly he thought it was an inexpert bowshot that spiked the animal's neck.

But he was riding, lying low behind his own steed's broad head. Air streamed smarting over his eyes; the brand dwindled into roaring fire at his shoulder. He was squeezing more speed from his mount with his thighs, urging the implacably distant gate closer as the archers swung toward him; he felt the grass beneath his steed's pads hindering him like water. He was there, and the song of the bowstrings had failed. He plunged his blazing club into the gate.

Here his plan was weakest. His steed was rearing now that the fire which had driven it had sprung before its face, dilating furiously. Above him he heard moving stone, grunts of exertion. During the war against the pirates he'd learned how to coax his steed through fire, but this was another steed, *Hakkthu*, he swore between defiant blasphemy and plea, and covered the beast's eyes with his hands, its ears with his forearms.

It quieted uneasily. Overhead he heard the unmistakable sound of heavy stone poised on wood. Then, as a wave of heat surged out from the collapsing gate, Ryre's steed flinched back stumbling, yards clear of the protection of the wall.

He heard the first stones fall. It took him a moment to realize they had fallen within the gate. The defenders didn't want to kill him, only to keep him out. Why? He grinned and shrugged, snarling.

The gate sagged on the dropped stones with a shout of flame. The defenders were scrambling down from scorching branches. One of them was shouting, directing the others to fetch water from a well, to throw earth on the fire, to bring axes; now he was monkey-climbing down a trunk.

He saw Ryre coming at him through the frame of fire: all six and a half feet of him, reflected fire streaming over the predator's mane that widened in a V from his shaved crown to his shoulders, fire pouring down his long grimly grinning face and over his flexed muscles, tensed for an easy spring. The man twisted; his feet found a branch from which to launch him upward again. Ryre chopped the branch from beneath him and catching him as he fell, stunned him with his sword-hilt.

"Move again, any of you," Ryre shouted, "and I'll knock you down with his head." They were a sorry-looking lot, even the hostage: grimy, dull-faced, ragged. Their shuffling approach had been disordered, tentative. Behind him another tree snatched the fire, cackling. Their faces flickered like embers as they watched him, their gazes plucked fretfully at the fire; shovelfuls of earth drooped from their hands, narrow-necked vessels of water drained.

"My friend is injured, " he shouted above the chorus of fire.

"Have your best healer ready for him. I shall bring him in now. This man stays with me until my friend is healed. If I've reason even to suspect any of you, we'll see if this man can walk while he's holding his guts from tripping him up."

The growing crowd, fifty or so of them, now, was milling as if turned up from beneath a stone. "We'll help," a voice said just audibly within the mass; then, as if drawing strength from its concealment, more loudly: "We promise. Don't take him out."

"He stays with me until my friend is well," Ryre shouted.

They were turning uneasily toward someone in the narrow dry earth street between the low square houses: their leader, Ryre thought - then saw that it wasn't a man at all. It was a stump of wood planted in the street, shaped near the top into a fat mouthless face; instead of ears, limp-looking branches hung. The black wood looked wet and was patched with white, as if stretched pale; specks of reflected fire burned in the wide whitish stare. Their god, no doubt.

"Please, not out," someone was muttering; others joined in. "Please."

Ryre had never seen such insularity, not even on the Sea of Shouting Islands. "I will protect him from anything out there," he shouted, riding toward the leap through the blazing gap, "keep your word and he is safe. If I think you haven't," (their paling faces showed he had found the words to command them) "I'll leave him out there."

Glode was lying beside the tree. His lips were so pale that Ryre couldn't distinguish the slit between them from their trailing threads of blood. He didn't move when Ryre supported his head. Ryre frowned; he had counted on Glode's being conscious and able to hold onto the hostage before him on Ryre's steed. He pondered, stroking the beast's neck. Heat sank thickly through the branches.

As he pondered, his hostage began to move. The man pushed at the beast's ribcage to raise himself. When he saw where he was, he started to flail his limbs and scream incoherently. He lay draped over the animal's spine, screaming and wriggling wildly, then he fell to the ground.

"Be quiet and listen." Ryre had to push the sword's point into the man's neck before he would stop thrashing about. "We are going back to Hoak now. You will ride this steed. You will carry my friend, who is injured. If you loosen your grip on him, or try to ride faster than I walk, I shall cut you down and leave you outside the wall."

Ryre had once seen one of the steeds set ablaze by the warriors of Gurj and sent screaming into enemy camps to cause injury and demoralization: he had seen its staring eyes, piteously rolling. He had hoped never to see such terror again, but it was here, in the eyes of the hostage. The man's arms gripped Glode and his entire body shook as if caked with ice; he gazed in supplication at the distant wall pacing closer, at the gap where men were chopping away the charred section of the wall. Glode's inert body trembled with him.

Ryre felt himself to be a stretched rein, holding the man back from utter reckless panic. His sword was out and ready; its point winked a warning beside his hostage. He curbed his mind from pondering the source of the man's terror. *Hakkthu*, he thought, *if I'm going to know I'll know without tempting it nearer*. Behind him he felt the hot bright forest and plain, silently poised.

The healer was waiting in the street. He'd brushed away dust from a space and laid planks there. He was an old nearly bald man, scrawny as if he'd melted himself down in losing a long fight; grey hair made a tidemark around his skull. "Put him there," he told Ryre indifferently.

"Haven't you a house of healing?" Ryre demanded.

"Outside is better." Townspeople were clambering exhausted down the singed trunks. Ryre prodded his panting hostage into lowering Glode from the steed.

"Help him, some of you. Now you get down, slowly. And you, hold my steed." As the hostage dismounted the others were still holding Glode's unconscious body. "Give him to your healer," Ryre said with tight control *Hakkthu*, he thought, *one day they'll forget how to dung until someone tells them.*

"What's wrong with him?" the healer asked.

"A dart in the gut. Bandits attacked us, half a day from here." Dust eddied around the restless crowd and crept toward Glode. "Keep still," the healer shouted. Ryre felt the beginnings of trust.

The Sustenance Of Hoak

What he'd taken for indifference in the healer wasn't the apathy that weighed down the watching faces, but harassed weariness. In the man's eyes alertness still glinted faintly.

Someone was murmuring at Ryre, as if in sleep: a large-boned man with a face like a square slab of rock that might once have looked chiselled but now was less weathered than moss-smoothed by beard, and slackly bland. "That's who we thought you were," he was saying. "The bandits. They want our treasure. But you can't get at it from inside the town. We wish they'd take it. It's only trouble for us. We're happy without it. We try to keep the bandits out so they'll search outside and take it."

"What is this treasure?"

"Jewels," another voice said. "A cave full of jewels."

"And how is it reached?"

"There are tunnels," the slab-faced man said. "They're easy to find. We can tell you where."

"You're so anxious to keep people out you've convinced me there's something in here worth defending."

Ryre turned his back, dismissing them all. The healer had parted the hard yet flexible leaves of Glode's armour, had lifted the shirt beneath and was probing Glode's stomach.

The crowd was fraying, wandering away; people plodded into the low houses. Ryre disliked the way windows were blocked with old wood. The kneeling hostage shifted gingerly beneath his sword. Ryre prodded him toward a house. "Knock the wood out of that window, " he said.

The wood scattered clattering, and Ryre laughed grimly. The scene within seemed so typical of Hoak: a man lying on a plank bed in a bare room, drinking from a long-necked vessel, blinking timidly at the intrusion. Apart from the bed, and dust and tracked-in mud, there was nothing in the low-ceilinged room but a replica of the stumpy god from the street. About two feet high, it stood in a corner as if growing through the floorboards, its eyes closed in sleep. Ryre knew instinctively that nothing more sinister was happening behind the masked windows of the other houses.

A woman was carrying a vessel to the healer. Glode's head turned tottering toward the vessel. "Give me drink," he said, his tongue

135

protruding weakly, dry as a sand-burrower's tail. The healer shrugged sadly, and rose.

Glode took one gulp, Ryre's hand behind his head. Then he coughed the liquor into the dust, mixed with what might have been a stomachful of blood. He fell back, unconscious.

For a moment Ryre dreaded that the healer had never intended to drink. He sniffed at the mouth of the vessel: a sharp vinous smell. The healer and the remnants of the crowd were watching him. He put the mouth to his lips.

He was tipping the vessel against his tongue-stopped lips, watching for their reaction, when the hostage knocked the vessel from his hands. He scrabbled after it on all fours, seized it and began to gulp, his throat working like a climber's hand on a parting rope. By the time Ryre had bullied it from him he knew it couldn't be poisoned. His own throat was chafing and pleading, but he pointed his sword to Glode.

"The dart's lodged deep," the healer said. "It's in his stomach, too deep to get out. All he can do is rest. It may work itself out before he starves."

Ryre felt frustrated anger mass within him. He knew from battles that if the dart had lodged so, there was nothing they could do. He tipped the vessel, gulping. Thick liquor spread through his throat. A warmth rushed through him, tingling his fingertips.

The healer turned away; he looked disappointed, somehow betrayed. Let him thirst, Ryre thought savagely. His mouth was full of a meadish taste; light sparkled on slow drops of cloudy amber liquid spilling from the vessel's mouth. The squat houses and encircling trees, the dust and dancing ash, seemed to have snapped into closer clarity, as if the light had hardened. "We need a room," he shouted, to halt the retreating crowd.

"We have one," a girl said. Like the rest she was dressed in shapeless rags, almost colourlessly browned by use and the sun; she was thin and stooped as if by an insistent gale. Only a trace of youth in her face, which was shaped like a starved heart, convinced Ryre she was younger than twenty. She stood beside the slab-faced man, no doubt her father. As she gazed at Ryre, he caught sight of a dull glint of desire.

The Sustenance Of Hoak

The house was a dozen housefronts away up the street – more accurately, the trudged path. Each house was surrounded by twice its own area of earth, baked to a cracked crust, in which tufts of grass and weeds browned. Apart from the small procession behind which he was leading his steed, the hot flat blinded streets were deserted.

When they reached the house Ryre let the hostage go. If he needed to defend a room he could best do so without the hindrance of the man. He walked though the house, cursing loose boards, knocking the wood from the windows to admit light. Each room was the same: the plank bed, the sleeping god in the corner, the liquor-vessel, bareness. The first room, into which the sagging street door opened, was entirely bare.

Ryre chose the fourth room, which could be approached only through all the others. It could be a trap of sorts, but at least there was only one doorway to defend. He beckoned the bearers to lay Glode down, then gestured them out. He draped Glode's cloak and his own over his unconscious friend. He called for a bed to be brought for himself. He tethered his steed outside the window, and propped the wood he'd knocked down so that any attempt at entry though the window would send it clattering.

The girl, whose name was Yoce and whose father's was Vald, peered in while Ryre was eating some of the food his steed had carried. The second time, he held out a chunk of cheese to her. He'd seen no food or plates in the house. But she shook her head and went back into the next room. *She needn't think she'll come to me in the night*, Ryre thought, gazing anxiously at Glode. Later, in the twilight, he heard her sucking at her liquor-vessel.

Darkness muffled the houses. The dry ground breathed out thick heat. Ryre sat on the bed with his back against the door, gazing at the god in the corner.

Of everything he'd seen in Hoak he disliked that face most of all. It looked like the face a slow growth on a treetrunk might have: fat and somnolently sated. Beneath the eyes it swelled featurelessly, like a bladder. The branches hanging limply looked obscene, as if flaunting their impotence. It summed up Hoak. He couldn't truthfully believe he would be attacked during the night. He sipped at the liquor-vessel, pondering the contradictions of Hoak. Before him the mouthless face sank sleepily into the embrace of night.

It was late next day when he awoke, and Glode was dead. Glode's faded eyes stared into a glare of sunlight. His face was slack as melting fat. On his cheeks and beneath his head were the marks of a last bloody cough.

There was no mark of further violence, no culprit on whom Ryre could take revenge; he could only rage dully. Sweat had gathered within the leaves of his armour; they felt close and clammy, he felt closed in upon himself, his emotions muffled. He strained to mourn Glode. But as he gazed at the limp face his grief seemed dulled.

He grabbed the liquor-vessel. Glode would have a mercenary's mourning. Ryre laughed harshly, staring out at the desiccated street. Sometimes an unwary passer-by would scoff at a mercenary's tears, and die for it; such deaths were a tribute to the mourned. Ryre hoped someone of Hoak would dare to scoff. He sucked the vessel, which someone had refilled.

He was still trying to drink grief into himself when footsteps sounded in the outer room. Vald and three other men appeared, peering warily; beside them Yoce gazed. Vald thrust the girl into the room. Ryre's nearness quickened her breath; her eyes were wide with awe of him. "They've come to bury your friend," she said too loudly, nervously.

Burial ought to be swift, in this heat. Ryre gestured brusquely to the men. They hefted Glode as if he were a heavy plank, and hurried him out; his sword lay on his chest. Ryre followed, gulping liquor to hasten his mourning. Voce hung back, in the house.

He hurried after the bearers. Hakkthu, they were anxious to be done with the burying! Hot dust puffed up from their scurrying feet and settled over figures squatting beside the path. All the figures were blankly intent on their hands, which were whittling arrows. It was the only occupation Ryre had seen practiced here. Once, so the trader in Zizir had told him, Hoak had been renowned for the skill of its carvers.

The Sustenance Of Hoak

None of the whittlers glanced at the burial-party. Ryre felt numb rage at their indifference, all the more because it seemed to have infected him: he stared at Glode, at the sword jogging on his friend's chest, and could feel nothing.

The town was infecting him. Everywhere he saw slumped apathy: in the parched streets, the senile houses, the whittlers like hollow jerking dummies draped with sacking. Even the well from which water had been drawn to douse the fire was used as a communal cloaca. Yet once, the trader had told him, Hoak had been a station on a trade route between the coast and the interior, until its people had grown sullenly hostile.

It must be the liquor that had brought apathy. Ryre had seen no other food or drink. He supposed it was brewed from the trees in the town walls - there seemed to be no other healthy growth. No wonder the people were dull, if liquor were their only food. He would drink no more of it once Glode was buried. He'd need all his wits to find the treasure.

The bearers stumbled rapidly onward. They had carried Glode almost half a mile; they were nearly at the centre of Hoak. Ahead Ryre saw a group of small figures scattered among the whittlers, dressed in torn knotted rags of larger clothes. He had to peer closely to tell they were children.

They were the only children he'd seen here – hardly three dozen of them. On their faces, which looked already pinched and old, apathy was set like identical masks. They sat or lay in the dust; one child stared flatly from a window. When their muddy eyes moved, it was always to a liquor-vessel standing near them. They drank mechanically. Beside a dull-eyed mother, Ryre saw an infant sucking at a vessel as though it were a breast.

Fury swelled in him; he trembled. Behind the child in the window he saw a stump and its sleepy contented face, the flaccid branches dangling. Perhaps all the drinking was a religious tribute to their self-satisfied god. He would storm into the house and lop off the mouthless head-

He checked himself. However deplorable they were, gods were something whose revenge one couldn't fight. But he smashed his own vessel to the ground.

Some of the children watched the swiftly dwindling stain; a few of the adults gave him a glance like a faint sad shrug. The bearers were trudging ahead indifferently. He stamped angrily in pursuit.

Above the roofs he saw a shiny dome, swaying closer in imitation of his stride. Here at the centre the houses were even more dilapidated. Among them he saw bare patches where houses had stood. In each patch was a deep socket; had that housed a godstump? the bearers had halted in a wider space. Ryre hurried there.

It was the old market-place. Remnants of stalls and tethering-rails poked from the ground, like bones from a boneyard. At the centre of the space a patch of dark moist earth, no more than twenty yards square, stood out from the dry surround. From this earth protruded a pillar whose crown was the shiny dome. The pillar wriggled with heat-haze. Ryre gaped at it, breathing harshly.

It stood twice his height, half again as broad as his chest. Its domed crown was a pale bubble swelling up through the black cracking mud of its bark. On the side nearest him, formed of the same lividly patched substance, was the flabby contented face, several times enlarged. Its left cheek was bloated out of shape by a large fibroid growth, giving it a fattened cheek-pouched appearance. Ryre felt grubs of disgust crawling over him.

There were no branches sprouting beside the face, nor any room for them. Four faces bulged at various heights on the pillar, identical except for blemishes and variations in size. That on the north side – the one he'd first seen – looked to be encroached upon by the larger fibroid eastern face, which seemed to be eating into its cheek.

Ryre felt passionately that the entire festering thing ought not to be here in the sunlight, but buried beneath tons of earth. He had a sudden crawling notion that the substance of the thing had not ceased growing. He clutched his sword-hilt to feel cold metal amid the soft sticky embrace of the heat.

Vald and the others were digging. Glode lay in the dust. His loose face upturned. They meant to bury him beneath the bunch of swollen faces. Ryre felt harsh rage – but wherever Glode lay in Hoak he would be overlooked by the omnipresent stump. Better he should lie here in this rich tended earth than in the parched ground.

The Sustenance Of Hoak

He stood over his friend's body, sword bared in tribute, as they dug.

They were digging hastily, exhaustingly, near the foot of the pillar. Ryre had time to wonder at the size of the burial ground, which seemed bewilderingly small, before the diggers turned up a flat rock. The top of it looked like a fleshless hand. Peering, Ryre saw that it was indeed a hand, rotted at the wrist and stuck to the rock. One man scraped it off with his spade and threw it back into the hole. Then they grounded their spades and picking up Glode's body, carried him across to roll him, sword and all, into the hole.

"Not like that!" Ryre roared. His sword trembled between them, darting at their throats. "Make him a coffin!"

They gazed blankly. "A box for him to lie in!" he shouted, prodding them with their burden to the edge of the ground. "Make him a box," he said with cold fury, "and bring it here."

He waited, glaring at the introverted faces on the pillar. Heat rose from the moist ground, fluttering about them; the edge of the fibroid face seemed to bulge, creeping like a grub across its neighbour's cheek. As they had made to drop Glode into the hole Ryre had imagined he glimpsed the eyes of the northward face opening, a blink, closing before he'd glared at them. It must have been the antics of the heat.

He gazed across the market-place. On the side which he had yet to explore stood a house full of piled timber. Some of the wood looked delicate. Crushed between stacked planks he saw elaborate ladles, stringed instruments, minute figures. One figure lay in a niche between planks, almost unharmed: the figure of a swordsman, poised in easy but assured defense. Its tiny perfect face, hardly the size of Ryre's smallest fingernail, was stern yet peaceful. Ryre slid the figure from its niche. Rough handling had crippled it; one leg was snapped off at the knee.

The burial party returned, carrying a crude box from which protruded bent and rusty nails. They lifted Glode into the box and nailed down a plank for a lid. Then they dropped the box into the hole.

Ryre's fury drained quickly. He saw how they must feel about death. He gestured them back and nicking his forearm with his

141

sword-blade, held his fist above the coffin as his blood dripped. He lifted earth from the grave and sprinkling it over the wound, let the mud of blood fall on the coffin. When they had filled in the grave, he stood the carved swordsman on the mound and watched over it while they wandered away.

Still he had not mourned Glode. His mind seemed to have lost its grasp on his friend. When he managed to recapture a few of their exploits – Glode saving him from a knife-thrust in a dark temple; Ryre trying to swing himself onto Glode's shoulders to snag the ropes that were lowering them into a pit of snakes – they seemed flat, unconvincing. Now the liquor was making him feel light, unconcerned, unburdened. He would mourn Glode when he was free of Hoak – when he had made sure their journey had not been in vain. He must find the treasure.

The sun was low. The shadow of the pillar lay across the glistening patch, like the shadow of a cankered tree. It pointed toward the far side of Hoak. The treasure must be there, where he hadn't explored.

He searched, trying to outdistance night. The earth was grey and cracked as the skin of a senile corpse. Few of the windows were blocked; these he knocked open. He stared into room after room, at fallen planks, at the hole like a burrow in the corner of each floor. The rooms were dimming; twilight rose in them like a mist with which the dark burrows merged. The twilight was heavy with silence, the silence of midnight in a dead and windless forest.

The heads of the surrounding still trees peered at Ryre over the nearby wall. Desolation waited silently behind him wherever he turned. His mind was chattering: it isn't here, not in these houses, there's nothing here, go back.

And this was all that was left of Hoak: scarcely a hundred people, isolated on this barren island amid the enormous forest. Then he realized something else. The vanished population must be buried in the square, all of them, piled up and rotting beneath the contented pillar. He shrugged off a shudder at the thought of the earth in which Glode lay, and hurried back toward the centre. He had words to scare the truth of the treasure out of slab-faced Vald.

The faces on the pillar were set in the twilight as in plush. Ryre

The Sustenance Of Hoak

spat in the dust. Corpse-candle of a god, he blasphemed the pillar. He glanced toward Glode's grave. At once he was striding across the yielding ground, clutching his sword. The mound had vanished. The carved swordsman still lay on the earth. As he snatched it up he heard a faint muffled creaking. It came from the grave. Was Glode pushing his way out of the box, rising up through the soil to punish Ryre's negligence? Blotting out his terror with anger, he began to gouge out the grave with his hands.

The grave was shallow, but his progress seemed slow as the creeping twilight. As the soil squeezed through his fingers he remembered the hand that had been thrown into the hole. At last he reached the box. The lid had split open; soil had widened the split and fallen through. Cursing the makeshift coffin, Ryre lifted the pieces of the lid.

At first, in the twilight, he couldn't distinguish what was in the box. A mixture of earth and pale objects: the pale things were entangled – there were large glistening pale surfaces and paler forms coiled about them. The pale thick tendrils were dragging the larger object, or objects, through the bottom of the coffin. One extremity of the large object slipped an inch lower in the hole, amid a strained creaking and a rattling of earth. Although the large object was losing its form, as if melting, it had Glode's face.

Ryre screamed in fury and brought his sword crashing down on the tangle within the coffin. Tendrils parted and whipped into the earth like pale worms. When Ryre had finished chopping, there was nothing recognizable in the hole. Weeping, ablaze with shame, he kicked earth into the grave.

The cancerous faces loomed above him, at his back. He rushed at the pillar, brandishing his sword. The faces waited, untroubled. Suddenly full of panic and nausea, Ryre fled toward the gate.

His steed waited outside Vald's house, chewing in its foodsling. Ryre reined back his panic; he must retrieve his satchel of food, which was lying beneath the plank bed. In the dim deserted street that throbbed wakefully with the sound of his heart, Ryre felt the need for stealth. Somewhere he could hear a slow muffled trickling. He shook his head impatiently and paced around to the outer door.

Vald was prostrate on his bed, fingers hanging limply to the floor. Ryre thought he was dead until his nails scraped the boards feebly. Padding softly, Ryre had almost crossed the room before he saw Yoce. She was standing with her back to him, in the corner where the face stood. As Ryre strode loudly toward her, she turned.

The branches dangling from the head were swollen, pale, almost transparent. They glimmered in the dimness. Yoce had been thrusting the neck of a liquor-vessel over one branch; now she pulled the vessel away. Snatching it, Ryre saw that it was brimming with liquor. A drop hung at the tip of the branch.

Yoce grabbed the vessel before he could smash it, and carried it to Vald. Ryre was less horrified by his discovery than by the yearning of his own parched throat for the liquor. "You do that!" he shouted through his nausea, hand at his sword.

"What else can I do for him?" Yoce said furiously. "Where's another food?"

When her words reached him, his hand slumped on the hilt. "What is this town?" he demanded thickly.

Liquor was spilling from Vald's mouth. She stood the vessel beside him, then she took Ryre's hand simply and led him into the inner room. Her fingers read the moist earth on his hand. "You've seen what it does," she said. "To your friend."

The face hung like a clot of the dimness, inscrutable eyelids swollen. "It can't hear us," she said reassuringly. "Anyway, it's dead. It died when my mother did. That's what happens when you die. This was her room. She died a few days ago, I think. I can't remember time very well."

Ryre sat on the bed, away from the face. He shook himself; this wasn't what he wanted to know. "That thing in the burial ground," he snarled.

"Nobody knows what it is. You know it's the same as the ones in the houses. They grow from it."

He felt the dimness closing about him as though it were the heavy exhalation of the faces. "Why do you need to drink that filth?" he shouted, then answered himself dully, "Because you need more and more of it."

"I don't," Yoce said indignantly.

The Sustenance Of Hoak

That explained her comparative vitality. "Yes. But there must have been a time once when someone could have killed that thing," he said impatiently. "When it first began growing."

"We could never kill it. It wouldn't let us."

He felt her words giving power to the face. Ripping a splinter from the wood beneath the window, he lit it with his flint. He thrust the flame into the corner, peering. But the face hung on the stump, slack and puffy.

He was about to shake out the flame when the eyes opened. The lids rose heavily, with the faintest of moist creaks. The widening crescents of dull white looked to Ryre exactly the colour of the marsh-fungus he'd once seen growing on a corpse in a swamp. The eyes were open now, swollen globes of thick white in which he could see no life at all. They seemed to watch the flame. All at once he caught up a stick, lit it from the splinter and thrust it into the face.

The wood, if such it were, of the stump began to sputter. Threads of fire squirmed across it, and vanished. The eyes were still, but the lids shivered. Then the stump caught fire; a spot of flame grew and flared up across the face. The eyes burst. In a minute the stump was a dwarf of fire, twisting and writhing as it crumpled into ash.

Ryre kicked the ash down the hole in the floor, laughing harshly. Hot ash crawled on the sides of the hole, and he glimpsed a charred stump retreating, dousing itself with earth. "What can the rest of it do now?" he demanded.

Yoce was sitting unmoved on Glode's bed. "It won't do anything. It only does if you attack it in the burial ground. That one was dying, anyway. If it had anyone to feed it would have grown again."

He grinned into the darkness. He was the thing's master now. He could destroy it whenever he wanted to, and he would. But first — "It must have made your people forget where they'd hidden the treasure," he said. Do you know where it is?"

"There isn't any. There never was."

"There is. You've just forgotten, if you ever knew."

"I haven't! I remember that! They made up the treasure so people would come from outside. To kill the eater."

145

"Then why did your men try to keep us *out*?"

"Because you can't kill it from inside the wall. You have to go underneath. And when people came here they'd drink the milk, even if our people tried to stop them. Then they'd stay and not be able to go out. That's why the men keep people out. Only they've forgotten why. They think there really is a treasure."

Everything he'd seen confirmed her words. He felt too defeated by Hoak even to be angry. "If you managed to keep some people out," he said desultorily, "why didn't they kill it?"

"Maybe they didn't get far enough. Or maybe they were frightened. You have to go all the way under the burial ground. There was a map that said the treasure was there."

"Why can't you kill it from up here?"

"Someone tried, a long time ago." She had lowered her voice; the darkness leaned closer. "It ate his woman. He set fire to the one in her room. He was sleeping there, so it grew again for him. Then he tried to set fire to it at the burial ground, but it reached out of the ground and ate him while he was still alive. "

"How do you know all this?" Ryre demanded.

"Trome the healer told me. He tries not to drink much, like me. He helps babies to come and gives them names, and he tries to teach people how to do things. The man you took out, he was one Trome taught. He helped me to remember all the things he'd told me, so I could tell you. He said you wouldn't kill me."

Ryre was silent. Heat and darkness and Hoak gathered on him like mud. Yoce came and sat beside him. "I'm sorry there isn't a treasure for you," she said. "I never liked stories that weren't true. Vald used to tell me when I was little that I'd be able to go outside the wall, to stop me crying." She took his hand and pressed herself against his side.

"Does your healer expect me to kill that thing for you?" Ryre asked, letting the disbelief of his words soak into him.

"You could do it for us," she said, gripping his hand. "For your friend."

Suddenly he grabbed her shoulders and threw her against the wall. "You called the men to bury my friend!" he shouted.

"I didn't," she said. "It calls in your head when it wants its food."

The Sustenance Of Hoak

She began sobbing like an exhausted child – exhausted perhaps by the effort of talking to him. Irritably he grabbed her and pulled her roughly to him until she ceased shaking. All of a sudden she was straddling him, her hips gulping. "Have me," she said plaintively. "Nobody else can."

His body was shouting yes, yet he hesitated. Had they reached the true reason why Trome had sent her? Ryre didn't object to even so meagre a bribe, nor did his feeling that she was still a child trouble him. But he felt insulted by her eagerness, in a sense; he could be any man except a eunuch.

"Please," she said. "I always used to wonder. I knew it made some girls happy, until they stopped feeling it. Trome said the milk did that. So I didn't drink much, only as much as I had to. But all the boys did, so they couldn't have me, they didn't work. Trome tried when I asked him, but he was too old."

Even with Voce's clothing laid over them the floor-boards were harsh against Ryre's knees. But once she'd closed around him he felt nothing but their union. She was eager as a parched throat; his heart seemed to be pounding all his blood into his genitals. It was quickly over. Both of them cried out.

They lay together until dawn. "You weren't a virgin," he said drowsily; then, sensing her blankness: "Not sealed. "

"I did that myself," she said proudly.

As they neared the gate Trome formally wished Ryre, "Your day of triumph." At the gate Yoce said, "Good fortune. What's your name?"

He was unwilling to leave his name where it might be at the mercy of Hoak. "You don't need my name. You want the deed," he said and, reaching into his pouch, handed her the carved swordsman. "Say that was me," he said.

Waiting for Trome to wrench open the repaired wall, he felt a cancer of panic growing within him swiftly as fire. It was the effect of the liquor; it infuriated him. Yet it was only a taste of the panic that ruled Hoak. He averted his face from Yoce as he rode out. He wouldn't betray his fear to her. She had enough of it already.

147

The baked plain drank his sweat avidly. The forest took him with a slow suffocating hiss of leaves. Foliage swayed like drowned tentacles, luring him in. When he closed his eyes he felt the cooler moist air settle over him like a clammy shroud. His breath racked his throat. He breathed harder to distract himself. By the time his steed led him to a stream he was a flayed tube of thirst.

The soothing drink felt distant, merely a concept separate from the dull unchanging panic. But the very dullness of the panic helped him by enraging him. He must act. He had dreaded tunnelling beneath the eater; now this seemed less daunting. He had come out of Hoak: he could do anything.

Even the sight of the tunnel entrance failed to daunt him. He passed it once, covered as it was by a tangle of green shoots. But a large mound of earth and a pile of timber showed its position. Beneath the shoots the tunnel descended for a few feet at a steep angle, eased by steps of wood driven into the earth, then levelled into darkness.

Ryre filled his satchel with faggots and dry grass. He lifted the two rusty spades from his steed. Strapping the satchel to his back, he gazed through the trees at Hoak. Trome had left the gap open. Ryre gazed at it, then he climbed down into the earth.

He had made tapers in Hoak. He lit one with his flint and peered ahead. The taper burned feebly, sputtering. At least the flame was slow. The light plucked at the tunnel: a quivering hole of darkness that drew the walls and roof into itself. The roof was roughly but adequately shored with a thick length of timber, supported by two others forced beneath it, against the walls. It was too low for him to stand upright.

He clambered out and began to collect shoring from the pile. Birdsong was scattered over the forest like light on water. His panic at leaving Hoak was ebbing somewhat, baffled.

He climbed down with an armful of props, grinning sourly. Whoever had opened the tunnel must have believed they were outwitting the guardians of the treasure. He would make sure, he vowed grimly, that they were among those who had outwitted the eater of Hoak.

He stuck a burning taper in the earth near the entrance, then

The Sustenance Of Hoak

hefted his shoring. The burden hardly taxed him, but this was only the first journey. He debated taking off his armour. But it was light, though few blades could cut its flexible leaves, which grew harder under pressure. It might save him – from what, he refused to think. He pulled the taper from the earth and holding it before the pile of shoring on his arms, stooped quickly into the tunnel.

The taper was burning more steadily now, though feebly. He had to walk slowly for fear of extinguishing it. His view ahead was cramped by the pile of wood, which was almost as broad as the tunnel; he could see a dim box surrounding him and keeping pace, shaking as if crumpled by the weight of earth above. At least it was excellent wood, he reassured himself; neither the shoring around him nor the pile outside had rotted.

The dim box swung slightly about him. Its featurelessness lulled him, stealing his sense of time and of how far he'd come. He strained to look back. His shadow flickered forward from the blinding darkness. Within it he thought he could see a tiny point of light, the tunnel entrance. Then it was gone.

He drove himself onward, trying to measure his distance from Hoak by the count of his steps. He had to trust the judgement of those who had dug the tunnel. Assuming that they had followed the original map, the course of the tunnel should lead to a point directly beneath the eater – unless the thing had grown downwards since.

His back was beginning to resent its cramping. In the dim browned light his eyes felt as if mud were gathering on them. His hearing felt muffled, suffocated. Even his legs felt hobbled, for he had to tread carefully on the uneven floor.

He dreaded that the thing knew he was approaching. He felt its vast bulk somewhere above him, and it seemed impossible that it could not sense him. He was struggling so fiercely with his unease that he had almost touched the tendril with the taper before he saw it.

It was a limply coiled pale thread, drooping through a crack between the shoring of the roof. As the flame approached, the tendril drew itself up jerkily and flattened against the wood, groping about convulsively. Ryre flinched back, almost dropping taper and props. Surrounding him beyond his cage of faint light, he heard a muffled

149

creaking whose rhythms imitated the convulsions of the tendril. He lowered his pile of wood to the floor and kneeling, rested on it, willing the spasms of the tendril to subside.

At last they did so, and the cracking faded: but not until half the taper had burned. Ryre walked more deliberately now, his strained gaze urging forward the dim sluggish wave of light. Darkness swelled up solidly beyond it, but yielded only darkness. When something more solid loomed into the glow, he was prepared and hardly started. It was a white root, blocking the centre of the tunnel.

It had forced its way between the shoring, bulging itself a hole. Earth was sprinkled on the floor beneath, but the root had plugged the gap it bad made. It spanned the tunnel, fat and glistening white.

He planted the taper. Then he slid the props past the root on their edges, letting them down gently beyond. He pulled up the taper and holding it beyond the root, inched himself past. The root might have felt him if he'd touched it. In any case, he couldn't bear the thought of doing so.

The darkness ahead bobbed closer, thickening, bulging between the props, refusing to give way to the advancing light. He had reached the end of the tunnel, a couple of hundred yards past the root. Ahead sloped a ragged wall of earth, somewhat smoothed by time.

He dropped the timber from his aching arms. After a while he took a taper from his pouch and lighting it from the first, stuck the latter in the floor. He glanced back at the light as he made his way toward the entrance.

There he rested. Light lapped the swaying foliage above him. Should he have left the taper? Wouldn't a flame left underground starve the air? He was arguing himself out of going down again, he knew.

He saw himself spading out the tunnel, carrying back the earth, spading out, trying to prop the tunnel – but was he exaggerating the task? It might have been his fear confusing his feelings, yet he felt the tunnel had almost reached its goal. He'd lost count of his steps at the tendril.

He remembered the carving he'd given Yoce. But his words didn't require him to be like the carving. He thought of Yoce and Trome,

The Sustenance Of Hoak

trapped within the open wall. He thought of the children, and of Glode. If Ryre succeeded, he would have a tale in which to hold Glode fast and give him power. Already Glode must feel nothingness closing about him as Ryre's words of him slipped away, dwindling to nothing. Ryre refilled his satchel and picked up the spades, then walked into the tunnel.

He'd hoped the taper he had left would look encouraging. But its glimmer swam forward like marsh-gas, emphasizing the enormous darkness. He set the two tapers at opposite sides of the tunnel. The darkness massed behind him, seeping into his brain, reminding him of the deceptive stillness of the white tendril, of the way the plump root seemed to have moved and swollen since the first time he'd passed it. He began to dig.

A taper burned down to the floor, and another. He filled his satchel with earth, which he scattered in the dark beyond the flames: again, again. His breath felt rougher than the earth; muddy sweat poured over him; pain clamped his muscles, tightening. He had been digging until the dark felt thickened by midnight when the creaking began.

It was all about him, muffled. It grew, a dull immense writhing mass of sound. Ryre felt as if the darkness were pressing down on him, as if the flimsy tunnel were sinking into depths where the pressure would burst the walls, flooding him with tons of earth, letting in the insidious source of the creaking.

This must be what had scared the dung out of his predecessors. As a youth he'd suffered the lightless hold of a ship for days; if this were the eater's defence it was already defeated. He dug.

The creaking trailed away, leaving the silence thick and close. There was no sound except a sprinkling of earth, ahead of him. The hard earth roof, which had held up uncomplainingly while he dug the softer earth below, was cracking.

He grabbed a length of shoring and swung it up against the roof. He ground his shoulders against it and reaching back, forced lengths of timber into place alongside him, propping the roof. Beyond it a shadow reached out for him, glistening with earth. He hurried back and brought the tapers forward.

He dug and shored another length of tunnel. Then panic flooded him. He was suddenly sure that the next thrust of the spade would touch the eater. It was waiting for that moment, to close on him. Or it might play with him, filling the tunnel with hungry tendrils, until it chose to block his way entirely.

Perhaps the thing was stealing these fears into his mind, or perhaps the darkness was thinking for him. He thrust the spade in furiously, but couldn't help closing his eyes. Glode and Yoce and the rest had fled his mind, leaving him alone.

The spade gouged the earth. Another spilling spadeful of earth for his satchel; another. Then the spade plunged into softness. Ryre fell forward, then threw himself back, wrenching out the spade. But a sliding of earth had already begun. The end of the tunnel was collapsing. He had turned to flee in case the props gave way, or before something emerged, when he realized that the wall was collapsing away from him. He had dug his way into a hollow.

When the sound of scattering earth had ceased he lit a new taper and held it low through the gap. Within was a hollow of moist earth, about seven feet in diameter. Its walls sloped up to a pale ceiling, a soil-smudged whitish object swollen with dozens of almost translucent veins. He was beneath the eater.

Appalled fascination paralyzed him. The surface was bloated like a great veined belly. Amber liquid coursed through some of the veins, others were empty and flabby. He forced himself away, back to his satchel. Emptying it of earth, he stuffed it with faggots and dry grass, and strapped it on.

He bullied himself into leaving the taper in the entrance to the hollow. If he took it in, the thing might act to defend itself. He scrambled down into the hollow, disliking the moistness of the earth. It was only ordinary good earth, he told himself, unlike the dry earth above, which the thing's hunger had drained. But he couldn't forget that the burial ground was above him. Liquor pumped through the whitish ceiling.

He piled the kindling at the centre, wondering uneasily why the hollow was there at all. It didn't matter. One last trudge to collect kindling, then he would lay a fuse to the hollow. At last all the effort which had led here would be justified; Glode would live in the tale. Ryre was making for the taper, thinking of words that would preserve

The Sustenance Of Hoak

the power of the deed, when the tunnel collapsed.

There was a violent splintering, and a heavy fall of earth. When he seized the taper he saw that the walls of the tunnel twenty yards away had been crushed. Among the debris writhed thick whitish tubes. He kicked at the collapsed wall, and the tubes closed about it, squeezing the earth. He knew that they would crush him even if he managed to broach the barrier.

Now that it was open battle the darkness lost some of its power. He felt it, solid on every side, but he could plan. The thing blocked the tunnel, but could he distract it? He grinned hungrily. He knew what the thing feared.

He slid down into the hollow, carrying a taper. He was about to throw the taper into the kindling – but no, the flame might not catch. Better to venture all the way in. He had almost reached the pile when he heard air moving in the tunnel, a hollow muttering. Suddenly the dim tunnel mouth was a black hole. Air swept across his face, and the taper he was holding went out.

The darkness rushed into his lungs, choking him. Above him he heard a vast creaking, no longer muffled. He scrabbled in his pouch and found the flint. He struck it, struck it again; the creaking lowered toward him. The taper flamed.

When he looked up he saw why there had been a hollow. At some time the eater, perhaps not content to feed through its tendrils, had raised itself bodily toward the burial ground. Now it was descending on him, having trapped him at last. A few tendrils crept down from the edge of the dwindling hollow. The cold moist belly sank and touched his forehead.

Ryre roared wordlessly. He ran, cramped and stooping, to the fuel and thrust in the taper.

A flame groped over the pile. In a minute it was a mound of fire. The fire rushed at the white belly, which sputtered and crackled, blackening. What happened then, hideous as it was, filled Ryre with grim triumph. The thing was raising itself on its roots, which its haste exposed all round the hollow, as if it were a vast bloated spider raising itself on its web. But its retreat worked the fire like a bellows, and the flames followed it up, flaring higher, roaring.

Fire sprang out from the midst of the belly, snatching whitish fuel that writhed. Veins popped, hissing. A whole piece of the thing fell on the edge of the hollow, torn away by an arc of fire that had charred through its roots. Clods tumbled through the torn gap, smoking, blocking the gap as Ryre considered dashing toward it.

The thing had raised itself above the level of the tunnel. Falling earth had closed the tunnel mouth, but there was still a small gap, and the wall of earth looked weak. Ryre scrambled over the shifting floor. Above him the centre of the belly was drawing up and in, trying to flee its agony; fire rushed into the drawn-in pit, splitting it open. Fire was dividing the eater along its veins, consuming each patch.

Ryre launched himself at the tunnel mouth, but slithered back. As he gathered himself to spring again the fire above him shouted, crackling and popping. It rushed above him, embracing a patch. He heard it give way, and the blazing chunk fell toward him. He tried to throw himself out of its way, but it fell full on him, smashing him into darkness.

He was buried alive. His face was full of earth. A crushing weight lay on him. He clawed at the earth, which squeezed beneath his nails, and the weight moved. His shoulders felt like an open sore, but when he raised them the weight toppled away. It was the fallen wood, quenched by soil. Propping himself on all fours, he looked about.

He was at the bottom of a hollow perhaps fifteen feet deep, open to the sky. Its sides had collapsed, and within it lay mounds of fallen earth and chunks of smouldering wood. Ash flocked over all; he beat away a settling cloud. Opposite him, where most of the earth had slid, leaned the central pillar. It was little more now than smouldering ash that retained its shape. Empty sockets smoked; a face of ash was crumbling in the wind.

Ryre dragged himself upward. His body throbbed with bruises, his mane was charred, but the fallen wood and his armour had protected him from the fire. He reached the lip of the hollow. The people of Hoak were milling about nearby, wandering blankly,

The Sustenance Of Hoak

halting, starting constantly as if from traps of sleep. He groped for a hold to pull himself up. Suddenly Yoce and Trome were lifting him.

The girl's left foot was bound – in a shirt patterned with swords, that Glode had worn. His fury faded quickly: Glode would have given it to her, and they must need cloth. "What's wrong with your foot?" he asked.

"Someone smashed it," Trome said.

"I broke all the milk vessels," Yoce interrupted, so swiftly Ryre could tell she didn't want revenge. "So we couldn't save any milk. Now we'll have to go outside." She saw Ryre's hunger for vengeance, gleaming in his eyes. "You mustn't kill anyone," she said. "There are too few of us. "

Trome hurried to fetch ointment. Ryre hobbled to a window and, knocking out the wood, began to chop brands. "Come here," he shouted at the wandering crowd. "All of you! Here!" He handed out the brands and lit them. The crowd stood gazing; nothing about them but the flames. "Wherever you find that thing's head," he shouted, "burn it. Let one live and by Hakkthu, I'll feed you to it in pieces. When I'm gone, Trome has a sword to rule you. Quickly!" he shouted as they stumbled away.

Trome was staring uneasily at him. "Haven't you my friend's sword?" Ryre demanded. "Then use it as wisely as he did."

Trome fussed about him, salving and binding.

"Enough, enough. I'll live, unless you smother me to death. Bring the children to the gate," he said to Yoce.

Ryre felt no qualms as he passed the wall. The power of the eater was dead. At the tunnel mouth he untethered his steed, then he filled his scorched satchel with fruit. Some hard-shelled fruit were as big as his head; the halves of the shell could be used to carry water.

Yoce was standing with the children just inside the gate. Adults stood nearby, restless and threatening; Trome was holding them back with the sword. Ryre piled the fruit a few feet outside the gate. He bit into the largest and juiciest fruit. Then he held it out to Yoce.

She stepped forward hesitantly. As she reached the wall fear

155

clamped over her face like a mask. Behind it he could see her struggling. The mask's forehead puckered. Sweat streamed from it. Then she stumbled forward, eyes closed, across the boundary. She gripped Ryre's arm, bruising it, and opened her eyes.

Fear still pinched her face like a claw, but she managed to smile. She bit into the fruit. Juice trickled from her mouth, tears from her eyes. She held out the fruit to the children.

They shuffled, glancing away. Suddenly the youngest ran out and grabbed the fruit. Her sister ran to drag her back. The older girl halted abruptly, gaping, as she realized where she was. But Voce stuffed a fruit into her open mouth.

Ryre showed Yoce the use of the half-shells, and pointed toward the stream. In time they would venture there. Trome forced himself to emerge, breathing heavily, and exchanged swords for a moment with Ryre in farewell. All the children were out now; their parents were scurrying timidly to rescue them, glancing suspiciously at the pile of fruit, sniffing at it, snatching a fruit and nibbling like rodents afraid of a trap. Ryre looked at Yoce, but she was rounding up the children, who were laughing hysterically, discovering their voices. He rode away.

Just within the forest he halted on a rise. By a caprice of the heat he could see Hoak vividly, minute and detailed. A group of people were lustily smashing the pillar of ash, while near the gate the guardian stump was ablaze. Some old men sat obstinately by the burial ground, arms huddled over their heads, refusing to move. Yoce was leading the children into the town, pointing in the direction in which he'd ridden, showing them a small object. It was the carved swordsman. He turned and rode into the forest, toward the sea.

Every Day a Little Death
(Or The Clockmaker's Apprentice)
Chaz Brenchley

Chaz Brenchley has been making a living as a writer since he was eighteen. He is the author of nine thrillers, most recently *Shelter*, and two major fantasy series: *The Books of Outremer* (which include the novels *Tower of the King's Daughter*, *Feast of the King's Shadow* and *Hand of the King's Evil*) based on the world of the Crusades, and *Selling Water by the River*, set in an alternate Ottoman Istanbul. A winner of the British Fantasy Award, he has also published three books for children and more than 500 short stories in various genres. His time as Crimewriter-in-Residence at the St Peter's Riverside Sculpture Project in Sunderland resulted in the collection *Blood Waters*. He is a prizewinning ex-poet, and has been writer in residence at the University of Northumbria, as well as tutoring their MA in Creative Writing. His novel *Dead of Light* is currently in development with an independent film company; *Shelter* has been optioned by Granada TV. He was Northern Writer of the Year 2000, and lives in Newcastle upon Tyne with a quantum cat and a famous teddy bear. His website can be found at www.chazbrenchley.co.uk

Comments Chaz: "Like most of the good things in my life (pauses to extract hand from jaws of hellcat, to whom this also applies), the

BFS happened to me by accident.

"Thing was, I was quite happy being a crime writer at the time, late eighties/early nineties. But I was writing serial-killer thrillers, back before 'The Silence of the Lambs' had really established the genre in the UK, and my publishers weren't quite sure what to do with me. They ended up putting horror-style covers on the books, so as often as not I was finding my titles in the horror section of bookshops. At that point it just seemed to make sense to write some proper horror, though initially I did it under another name; and from there it followed naturally, that I should join the BFS. I've always liked that slightly old-fashioned idea of a society, with regular mailings and a sense of community, even if it was a community that lay a little out of my reach. Two things, about joining an established group: first off, the active ones all know each other already, so alienation is built in for the new guy; and second, events do tend to congregate down the bottom end of the country. I live in Newcastle. All the interesting stuff happens at the margins, by definition, in the borderlands, which is one reason why I'm here, but distance is also insulation from the core of things.

"I had to be bullied into going to my first FantasyCon (see above, under 'alienation'; add chronic shyness and a tendency to run away when scared, and you will understand). I am vulnerable to bullying, so I did go; but I went with chips carefully balanced on both shoulders, muttering 'I don't want to be here and I want to go home.' And walked into the hotel, and – oh, I don't know, just started meeting people. And learned quickly that some of my favourite writers were as erudite, as articulate, as argumentative off the page as on, which is scary but satisfying; that most of them like a drink almost as much as I do, which fuels all the above, unless it only seems to; that a book room is a fine place to hang out, on all sorts of levels; that BFS politics is as scabrous, as virulent, as entertaining as the straight stuff, and the gossip is better; that the generosity of certain key members – you know who you are – is only rivalled by the generosity of their partners; that...

"Oh, you get the picture. Some of my favourite writers transmuted into some of my favourite people, as did some of those who don't write at all. The BFS is a community of readers, after all; the writers are just a subset. And it's a broad church; I joined as a horror writer, but I haven't been flung out now that I'm largely writing fantasy. Indeed, it was through the BFS that I met a bunch of other fantasy writers, and so we formed The Write Fantastic, to promote our own work and the genre in general to readers outside the community. Socially and professionally both, the Society has been a boon and a blessing to me; more importantly, it flies a flag for genre fiction at a time when fiction of all kinds is being squeezed. It's a meeting-place for small presses and mid-list writers, for the not yet published and the grand old names together; it's a kind of Babylon 5 for the fantasy & horror community, a core that carries a seed. It might even be our last best hope."

When we count the clocks that tell the time, there are always more than we think. We find them everywhere we can; we watch the sun, we watch a shadow lengthen on the ground to say how late it is. We keep calendars to say how many days there are to come, and journals to say how we have used what days we've had. We calculate moveable feasts, and give names to the days when the seasons turn. We're more nervous than we know. We try to pin time down with numbers, with measurements, with standing stones and mechanical devices, candle-clocks and water-clocks and pendulums and bells.

There is a reason for it, for this obsession, and it makes good sense if you happen to be human. Monkey see, monkey do; we learn by imitation, we've always been best at mimicry, and we look for comfort in homoeopathic doses, hollow copies of the real thing. We bottle history in plays and songs, we tell each other stories that make-believe the world – and we surround ourselves with toys that cut time into smaller and smaller slices, separate and survivable moments that are short enough to do no harm, only to help ourselves forget that in the end there is just the one clock for each of us, one clock that counts.

Abu bin Hassid was a clockmaker in Baghdad. Did I say a clockmaker? No, I malign him. He was *the* clockmaker, the fat one, the king of his craft. He had served kings; he could have lived in the palace and served the Sultan himself and drunk pearls in vinegar all his days, as the saying is. But he was a proud one, the fat one, and he preferred to have the Sultan come to him. He had started his life in the suk, he said, and he would end it there. He did, he said that, often. Of course he had started as a thief before the old clockmaker caught him and kept him, beat the worst out of him and beat his own trade in. Abu didn't often tell that part of the story. And of course in the end he was hardly in the suk at all, building his own little palace of a craft-house within sight of the Sultan's, with high walls and barred windows and great mutes for guards at the gate and no one knew what secrets kept within, along with the gold and the jewels and the precious tools of his work. He might speak expansively of his people – "the poor are my tribe," he said, especially when he was speaking to the rich – but he took care to keep them outside his house. His was a private showroom, and the less money you had the more private it became.

His guards were carefully trained to keep it so. They might have no voices to plot against him, but it was remarkable how expressive a silent giant with a massive scimitar could be, when he was seeking to suggest that your purse was too light to work the latch on the gate.

Accordingly, our Abu felt a twinge of annoyance one hot afternoon, when he came in from the courtyard to find a man looking around in the workshop. It was a tall man, a stranger, dressed in a dusty and unpromising robe. At first sight, he should never have talked his way past the guards. If second sight had shown him to be wealthier than he appeared – a traveller, perhaps, who carried his money in diamonds and preferred not to show it in his clothes, no foolish precaution in these troubled times – then Abu should have been summoned immediately. In any event, the man should never have been allowed to wander freely this way, into the workshop or the warerooms or who knew where. Abu was at a loss to understand how that had happened, when he himself had been in the courtyard and had seen not a shadow move; his men would be at pains, indeed at extreme pains to explain it to him later, with whistles and gestures in lieu of words, grunts and shapeless cries in lieu of – well, in lieu of nothing, really. Grunts and cries could be whipped up from anyone, whether or not they had the gift of tongues.

Still, the man was here, whether or not he ought to be; and he had a precious thing in his hands, a confection of frothy gold and diamond.

"Sir, sir, please, put that down..."

The man showed no signs of doing so, but turned it over in his fingers as though he had never seen such a thing before. Well, and so he had not; it was unique.

"What is it?"

The voice must of course have come from below the hood, where his face was hidden in shadow. It didn't feel that way. It felt as though it spoke from everywhere at once, as though the world itself had spoken very, very softly, and the echo of it resounded in Abu's bones.

"It's a clock, sir, a very special clock..."

"It looks like a castle. A castle made of sand."

"Yes, sir, yes, a clock in the shape of a sandcastle. See, the turrets turn to show how the minutes pass, flags rise to show the hours; and all the case is gold with diamond slices for the windows, and please, sir, it is very precious and fragile," by which Abu meant 'valuable', "so if you wouldn't mind just setting it down quite carefully on the workbench there..."

"I am accustomed to handling fragile things," the man said mildly, "and someone always thinks them precious."

"Even so, sir. It is not for sale. It is a gift for His Magnificence the Sultan," by which Abu meant that his own skin depended on its safe delivery, and that therefore it was very precious indeed.

"I do not want it. It pretends to be one thing pretending to be another, sand shaped into a castle, when it is neither; and it pretends to do something more, which is to count the passage of time, which it cannot."

"Pretends? Sir, I make the finest timepieces in all Baghdad! And this one is a true clock, it strikes the hours as the flags rise..."

Indeed it did so now, ticking and whirring and chiming suddenly in the man's hands, raising its little flags of jewel-chippings on a gold ground in designs that flattered the Sultan and God in equal measure, because Abu was a careful man. The man's sleeves fell back as he held the clock up into a fall of sunlight; Abu blinked, and tried to tell himself that it was just the dazzle deceiving him. The man was gaunt, no more than that, no doubt a desert traveller; if he seemed bone-bare, well, that was just a metaphor. Wasn't it...?

Abu had been a thief and a liar all his life, but he still found it hard to deceive himself, and in honesty the sunlight wouldn't do it for him. If beauty was only skin deep, this man should perhaps not keep a mirror in his house.

"Remarkable," the man said gravely. "Such noise, such fuss – and all such nonsense, to pretend that time can run mechanically, always the same distance between one sunset and the next, to be counted off by cogs and spindles. I prefer sand, myself." There was sand in his voice, like the tides of ages, dry and merciless.

"Sir, if you have no interest in my work..." He meant to sound angry and dismissive; he was afraid that the words came out more pleadingly.

"That was what I came to discover. I have heard speak of Abu bin Hassid, and I came to see what it was that you did. Well, now I have seen, and it is not worth the doing. No matter. I do not judge. The world may miss your clocks, but no doubt there will be others."

"Sir, who are you, to come into my house and speak so?" Like any dishonest man, Abu liked to be sure of his ground. He had a fear in him now, and he needed to be certain that he should.

"I have been called the clockmaker's apprentice," the man said, as though he had puzzled over the title himself, "because I sweep up what God discards. You may play at being God, with your machines that hammer time into a chain of links; but time moves on unregulated, sand slides through glass and I do my work as I must. Abu bin Hassid, we shall meet again."

"How, how soon...?"

"What, can your clocks not tell you? At the time appointed, then. It will not be long delayed."

Then the man turned and was gone, and it was hard to say whether he had walked away or not, whether he had passed through the door into the court or gone some other way not open to Abu. This much was certain, that there would be no point in challenging the guards. If they had seen the stranger coming, they could not have stopped him; Abu thought that they would not have seen him leave. He knew many stories of those who tried to keep a watch on Death, to bar him from their houses, from their lives. They never could.

No, Death must come. The trick was not to be there, when he did...

Abu sat for hours while his clocks chimed all through the house, while the sky grew as dark and secret as his thoughts, while the moon rose like the lamp that his servant brought to lighten the little space around him, though that only served to make the great house darker yet to his eyes. He had always seen the span of a man's life like a thread, wound around a spool by the steady ticking of a clock. Now he could see his own life like a thread cut free, and the loose end winding closer. It was hard to think, against that brutal ticking. But still, he was a clockmaker, and so was God; had Death not said so? He understood the workings of the world, none better. And there was no one better able to adjust them, given the proper tools...

So he sat all night and drew intricacies in his head, because a clockmaker is a man of hidden ways and subtle understanding. And in the morning, he washed his head and hands and went out into the city without his breakfast. He really didn't think that he would need to eat.

First he went down to the river quarter, where the real poor could be found, and the powers that live among the poor if you know where to find them. Abu had a mind like one of his own clocks, it ticked over and over and never allowed that a moment passed was a moment lost; he remembered everything.

He remembered to leave his bodyguards behind him, which was good for a man who did not wish to die. He remembered to turn left here and right here, and not to look behind him as he went. He remembered the smells of these alleys, all the separate smells, the damp and the food and the dirt and the fear. He remembered his own fear, those times he had ventured further than he had excuse or courage for.

Above all he remembered this particular door, and who waited behind it. Old witch, old crone, old meddler: she had always been old, he thought. She was old when he was young, she would be old now but still perhaps no older, he thought she had reached a perfectibility of age and had no need to add to it in this world. For sure, he thought, she would never trouble herself with dying.

He hoped that she might help him now, though not with her own solution. He had no interest in growing witheringly old. He thought that he would rather do the other thing, and step away from Death by stepping back.

Abu bin Hassid, clockmaker to the court, to His Magnificence himself and emperors of other lands: his steady, ticking mind was curious to see how scared he was, as he passed through that door.

An hour later he came out again, unchanged, unless perhaps she had given him something more to be frightened of, after Death and her. Something at least she had given him; he carried it in a pouch inside his robe. What he had given her, we need not enquire. Some things never were meant to be told in stories.

He went from there to the cattle market, outside the city walls. He bought a fine she-camel, he who was too fat and satisfied to travel, and ordered her sent to his house with saddle and reins and riding-stick, all that might be needful and all of the best quality. The dealer was doubtful, managing to imply without ever quite saying that she would never stand beneath his weight. Abu was a hard man to deny, though, and his gold was a soft persuader.

Then he walked on, he who never walked anywhere, past the horse-lines and the ox-pens to the slavers' compound, where he visited his old adversary Muazzar bin Muazzar in his tent. Muazzar was a lean man, a quiet man, and if he had vices they were not of the flesh. He and Abu despised each other, but each was pre-eminent in his trade, and each liked to buy the best. When Muazzar had need of a clock – usually for a gift, to flatter a reliable client; he was not a man for trinkets – he would come to Abu; when Abu needed more guards or other servants for his house, he brought his trade to Muazzar and no one else.

On this day they drank coffee together, ate sweetmeats, exchanged news and pretty compliments; and when time came for business, Abu said, "Muazzar, I want a boy today."

"Do you, indeed? To what end?"

Abu chuckled. "I shall make an apprentice of him, and pass on all my skills. It is time I made provision for my age."

"That may be true, but as I remember, the last boy I sold you for that purpose, you strangled him."

"He was stealing from me."

"The sweepings from your floor, I believe, Abu."

"Even so." Abu's face clouded; the phrase had an uncomfortable echo. "The sweepings from my workshop floor are dusted with gold and precious things. I sweep my own shop now. This boy shall not touch a broom, I promise you; nor shall I harm him. I will be as careful of his health as I am of my own."

"Well, I do have a boy that might suit, a bright lad, well set up, only unfortunate in his choice of father. The man is a drinker of arak; it is a sin expensive of health, of position and of money, and he is made bankrupt by it. His creditors have seized his goods, his house and household by way of restitution. I had the boy cheap, and I will not sting you for him."

"None the less, you must be recompensed for time and trouble.

You know that I am generous with my purse, Muazzar." This was how the two men expressed their contempt for each other, in a duel of underpricing and overpaying. To come off worst in a deal was a victory; their struggles tended to counteract each other, so that victories were few and far between and most of their exchanges were grudgingly allowed to be fair.

"Well. Let us see the boy."

A clap of the hands, a word to the servitor, and the boy was fetched. He had perhaps been too hungry for too long and he had some growing still to do, but his body was straight and his eye was sharp. He was a little sullen and a little scared, but that mattered nothing. Abu was pleased, and offered a price in gold; Muazzar was appalled, outraged that an old and favoured client should so cheat himself. He refused to take anything more than the same number of coins in silver, and that was too high...

And so they bargained, and came at last to a figure that satisfied neither of them, by virtue of its being more or less the market price for a boy not trained to any work.

The boy was called Hussein. Abu took him first to the offices of the city scribes, to adopt him legally into his household and name him heir to all that he possessed. While Hussein was still gaping, they went on to Abu's tailor, where new clothes were ordered to replace the shabby rags that he was wearing; everything from riding boots to a traditional clockmaker's welchet, and all to be delivered that same day.

And so home, where Abu introduced Hussein to all his staff with the strict injunction that they were to obey the boy in all things, as scrupulously as they did himself. Then, just the two of them, they went to the strongest of his store-rooms, where there were no windows and the door was iron-barred. "I will show you my treasures, lad," he said; but first he locked the door behind them, and then he opened the pouch that he had bought that morning, at what cost we do not know.

Storytellers need not be spies, under an obligation to report all that they have seen. No matter what Abu did in that dark room, or with what craft he did it. For us it is enough to say that the door opened again in the twilight of the day, and it was the boy Hussein who came out smiling. He locked the door behind him with great care, and summoned all the household.

"A dreadful thing has happened to our master," he announced. "An 'ifrit came and took possession of him, and he raves. He is sleeping now, but mark me, when he wakes you must not listen to his madness. Nor should you fetch him imams or a doctor or a lawyer, whatever he may demand. Only feed him through the bars here and see to his comforts as best you can; I have the only keys, for fear that his blandishments should move you to a dangerous kindness. Do not under any circumstances seek to force the door, or the 'ifrit will destroy you all. I ride to find a magician who can drive the creature out. In my absence, be watchful, beware! Let no one in to see him, and above all, do not let him out!"

And then he dressed himself in his fine new clothes and saddled the camel in the yard and rode away, and all the house stared after him in mute astonishment.

For days he rode and nights he slept in caravanserais, buying his food and entertainment with Abu's coin. When he came to Samara, it seemed he felt that this was far enough. He sought out the finest clockmaker in the town and showed him a paper written in Abu's hand, commending his son Hussein as a skilled apprentice, highly trained, needing only experience in another man's workshop now.

The clockmaker – a good man, you will be pleased to hear, whose name was Sharif al Tarkas – grunted, and said, "Abu bin Hassid's name is known throughout the sultanate. I have seen his clocks. But I had not heard that he ever had a son."

"I am adopted, sir. The city scribes will confirm it, if you ask."

"What, shall I send all the way to Baghdad to have some pox-scarred clerk's warranty? Those are easier forged than this," and he waved Abu's paper dismissively. "I will believe it when I have seen you at work. Come, here is an old clock, foul with dust and sand; let me watch you clean it."

That done, there was a bezel to cut, an ornate clockwork to be assembled, all the testing tasks that Sharif could conceive. By the day's end he was exhausted, but the boy was still smiling. Sharif did not quite like that smile, but he was an honest man, as well as a good one; he said, "Well, lad, I have tested what I can, and I would keep you without the name you bring, without the certification. You have the eye, the gift, the skill; your father must have trained you all your life, to bring you on so far so young. I suppose you must go back to him one day, but till then, your home is with me. Come back now, and my wife will find us food and a place in my house for you to spread your blanket."

A few days later, the boy was watching his new master's stall in the general market, where they sold mostly simple timepieces to simple people. He was pining a little, perhaps, because Samara is not Baghdad. Then he saw a familiar hand trail among the clocks on the stall, touching, assessing, dismissing: a hand that might never have known any sins of the flesh, or the fleshy.

He was nervous, but he had always been bold; he lifted his head and met the stranger, eye to eye.

For a moment too short to measure, he thought perhaps that he had startled Death.

Then, "You have changed your face, Abu bin Hassid."

"I have, and my body too. I left the old one for you in Baghdad."

"Did you so? I have not been to see; our appointment was here in Samara. And I have found you here. You are still yourself, Abu bin Hassid. You cannot hide from me."

"I don't need to hide," our Abu said, with a kind of anxious smugness. "You have found me, of course – but you cannot take me now, out of this borrowed body. I am not Abu bin Hassid, I am the boy Hussein, his adopted son. Hussein is not fated to die today; God himself would not allow it. You need old Abu's body, the fat one. Go back to Baghdad, you will find it there, penned up and waiting for you."

"With the boy's spirit trapped inside it – and as you said, he is not meant for me today."

"It is a puzzle for you," Abu said, smiling and satisfied. "But you cannot save him, I have come too far; take my spirit and this body dies, before you can fetch him to it. You need one body between the two of us today. Take his, take Abu's. It is written so, and men at least will understand it. Otherwise he is a madman, an old man pleading to be a boy; and the boy might live another sixty years in that body, which would make him the oldest man in the world before you would let him die. It is a wicked trick of mine, I am sure, and God will punish me; I will face that when my time comes."

"Your time has come."

"But not yet gone," said Abu, picking up one of his master's clocks from the stall and turning the hands backwards, to show Death where they stood. The clock was more intricate than any other here, and was surmounted by a clockwork figure that struck a bell to mark the hours; and yet the whole device was only pocket-sized, if you had deep pockets. Your pockets would need to be deep, to pay its price. It was a showpiece, not really meant for sale, only to catch the eye; but Death said,

"What cost would that command?"

"Oh, I thought you were not interested in our work?"

"Suddenly," Death said, "I find it very interesting indeed." And he drew, from what must have been a very deep pocket indeed, a purse holding nothing but pennies. "How many of these do you want?"

In Baghdad, in the strongest storeroom in the city, a fat old man sat huddled in a corner, surrounded by the most precious wreckage imaginable. He had begged and wept, he had raged and cursed, he had broken open boxes and poured jewels out through the bars on the door, but he could not buy his freedom. The more he raved, the more the guards backed away from him. Of course they could not speak, to urge him to be patient, to be at peace, to pray and trust in

169

God and the boy Hussein, who had gone to seek help for his affliction. Before long their silence had driven him to smash boxes for the simple sake of smashing, for the chance to break anything that was Abu's.

His great body was too heavy to bear such passion for so long. His hands trembled now, his heart laboured in his chest, and his spirit was almost broken. The tears had dried in his unaccustomed beard, and he had no more weeping in him; bewildered and exhausted and afraid, he barely raised his head when he realised that he was suddenly no longer alone in the storeroom, although the door most certainly had not been opened.

He had no light in there, beyond what was grudgingly let in through the door's bars, but the figure before him seemed to blaze in the shadows, as though it stood in another kind of darkness altogether.

"I know who you are," he said, shying almost at the sound of the voice that said it, Hussein's words from Abu's mouth. "But I am not, I am not the man you want, the monster Abu..."

"This I know," Death said. "And yet, that body has to die today, it cannot live; and your own is far from here, where you could never reach it."

A lost spirit is a desperate thing, restless beyond recovery, fading and howling in the desert. The thin boy choked in the fat man's body, but he made no further protest. Let it be as it was written; his was a cursed life, and he could not change it now.

Death reached into his pocket, and drew out a clock that gleamed darkly golden in the eerie light. Hussein would rather have expected a timer of glass and sand, his life equally frail and equally short.

While his eyes were still on the clock, he was aware of Death's other hand in motion suddenly. So swift the movement was, he couldn't say whether there had been an implement used, something long and bright that existed only at that margin where speed was a measurement of sharpness, or whether it was the hand itself that he saw, blurring as it stretched towards him. Nor could he say quite what was done, what was cut or pinched off or plucked out. But it seemed to him that the hand, unless it was a tool, had slipped somehow inside this vast body that he inhabited now, and yet he had not felt it; and while in there, in here, that tool – unless it was a hand – had done something drastic and irrecoverable. He felt like a ship cut loose, adrift; there was abruptly nothing solid under his hands, no certainty in him anywhere. He was detached even from his misery, from his despair.

He stood up, if you could call it standing; he looked down, and saw Abu's body slumped on the floor at his feet, and thought lightly that this would probably be a powerful moment in a man's life, if that were his own body that he looked down on. And then he saw that he had no feet, no body at all that he could register, and suddenly it was a powerful moment in his own life, except that he thought that he couldn't really call it life. More like the other thing, though he didn't want to use the word, with Death standing right beside him. It would have seemed like lèse majesté, and might possibly have led to confusion.

Instead, gazing at the figure of Death which was somehow brighter now, or else the world was more shadowy, he said, "Isn't the clock supposed to chime or something, to show that my time is up?"

"That might have been a good idea," Death said, "if it were true. But I have stopped the clock. You would need to chime it yourself."

And Death's hand moved again, and this time it was clearly empty. Hussein felt it close around him like a cage, like bitter iron, constricting, squeezing; and then it was gone but the grip was not, he was held and confined in a cold world, a world of wheels and teeth. For a timeless moment, nothing moved. Then, one by one, those terrible wheels began to turn...

The day was not over, though the sun was very low. Abu in his stolen body had packed up his timepieces and carried them back to his master's house, with a small sack full of pennies. Now he was cutting cogs in the last of the light, smelling what vagrant aromas slipped into the yard from the kitchen to promise good eating to come, wondering how vagrant his master's younger daughter might prove to be if he could slip her from the kitchen and out into the dark. He was hardly at all thinking of Death and his great defeat, the long-awaited triumph of man over the oldest enemy. Or the triumph of one man, rather. He didn't intend to share it.

Nor did he at all expect a cold shadow to fall across his work, especially as the sun was behind his shoulder. He glanced up and felt his young heart race for a moment, before he could control it.

"I have said, you cannot have me today."

"And yet I will. Your body I have already, back in Baghdad; now I want your spirit."

"If you slay this body, you slay the boy; and that you cannot do. Have you forgotten?"

"I forget nothing. And I did not speak of slaying. You left your proper body, to borrow his; I have brought him with me, to reclaim it."

A silence, brief and wary; then, "I have not finished with it yet."

"Neither have I finished with you."

Death took the clock from his pocket, and Abu almost, almost understood. "In there? But how — ? It is a mechanical contrivance, a toy..."

"And what more is your body, or the boy's? God is called the great clockmaker, remember, and I am his apprentice." The little bell struck, light and silvery: once and again and then again, erratically, although it had been better made than that and the hands of the clock were moving not at all and stood nowhere near the hour.

And it seemed Death was tired of talking then, or else he was irritated by the chimes. His other hand reached out and might perhaps have seemed to slide within the body of the boy, unless it passed behind, if it could be behind from every imaginable perspective. It came out clenched around something that could not be seen, although it was transparently there; and it passed into the clock and came out empty. And then it reached for the clockwork figure that struck the bell, that was striking and striking. It drew something forth from there, and slipped that into the boy's body.

The boy caught himself suddenly, on the very edge of falling, like a man who is dozing and startles awake. He shuddered, and rubbed his hands across his face, and then drew back and looked at the hands minutely. Then, because he had nice manners and was perhaps still a little bewildered, he lifted his head and said, "Thank you, sir. But, please – what am I to do now?"

"I think you are to be a clockmaker's apprentice," Death said.

"But, but I do not, I have not the skill..."

"You will find that the hands remember, they have had a master craftsman guide them; and the head can learn. It is probably a better life than a slave's. There is property that belongs to you in Baghdad, but you should not claim it yet. You might prefer not to claim it at all, as there will be some uncomfortable questions that come with it. If you stay to make your life here, your new master is called Sharif al Tarkas, and I understand that he has a daughter. The rest you must discover for yourself."

And then he turned and was gone, as though he had stepped from sunlight into shadow, but all the shadow had been his own. Hussein blinked, and gazed down at his hands for a while. Then he picked up a small brass cog and a delicate tool, and sat cutting teeth until a dark girl with teasing eyes came to call him in to supper.

If Death had a house, there would be a room in that house where he would keep a table, which would be Death's table, and he would sit at it; and at his back there might be the ever-swelling hiss of sands, innumerable sands, but on his table there would be a clock. Just the one, and with a muffled bell. And Death would be aware, he would count its every tick, as he is aware, he counts every grain of sand that slips by for each of us; and Death's clock would never need winding, and every tick would be a little, just a little as though the pendulum were a razor, and with every swing it scythed the finest imaginable shaving from an endless, breathless, unstoppable scream.

THiS iS ILLYRiA, LAdY
Kim Newman

Kim Newman was born in 1959 in London, raised in Aller, Somerset, and educated at Dr. Morgan's Grammar School in Bridgewater, before studying English at the University of Sussex. As well as making a name for himself as one of the most informed and noteworthy genre critics of the past twenty five years, writing for countless magazines and journals, as well as appearing in documentaries on television, he has carved out a successful career as a novelist and short story writer. He attributes his interest in the horror genre to seeing Tod Browning's Dracula at age eleven, which probably explains why he chose that particular character to focus on for his alternate history work – epitomised by *Anno-Dracula*, in which Dracula has succeeded in becoming ruler of England, *The Bloody Red Baron* and *Dracula, Cha Cha Cha*. His other books include *The Night Mayor* – his first published novel from 1989 – *Bad Dreams*, *Jago*, *Famous Monsters*, *The Quorum* and the semi-autobiographical *Life's Lottery* in which the protagonist's life story is determined by the reader's choices. He has won the Bram Stoker Award and the International Horror Guild Award, and has been nominated for the World Fantasy Award. In 2006 he was a Guest of Honour at World HorrorCon in the US. The following tale is a spin on *Twelfth Night*, told as only Kim could. His website can be reached at www.johnnyalucard.com

This Is Illyria, Lady

Her deception was over, but they'd never trust her entirely. Not even – no, especially not – those who loved her. She was not a part of this place. Really, they didn't know her.
    She was thinking of herself as a woman again.
    Provisionally, as usual. Since coming to these shores, she'd been in a flux. The Duke assumed the dissembling part of her life was finished, that this was the real woman. For the moment, it was and she was.
    But only, she knew, for the moment.
    It would be pleasing to settle.
    But the deceiver never did. The other deceiver. It was her lot to follow wherever he led. Arrive with a shipwreck, depart with an exeunt of attendants. At first, she'd thought she could thwart him, save innocents, avert tragedies. But as cycles repeated, she knew that would never happen. Her purpose was to explore the human wreckage the deceiver left behind in his wake, to understand.
    In her, deception was defence. In the other, attack.
    He liked to taunt her with their similarities. The argument didn't wash and wouldn't hold.
    She hurt no one but herself.
    (She thought.)
    All was for the best.

He had got away with it, of course. The deception had been seen as a joke that ran away with itself, and all the blame seemed shouldered by the fathead uncle, the drunken reprobate 'punished' by marriage to a servant. The uncle was one of the comicals, as much deceived as deceiver, flattered and flattering, blustering through with his coterie of hangers-on, siezing on some scheme or other without thinking where the suggestion came from. There was real malice in jests, unappreciated by the beery conspirators.
    Everybody in Illyria prized wit above all else.
    But the flame of wit comes invariably from the spark of cruelty.
    She knew she was looking for a wit.

Not a fool, a clown.
A whisperer.

This Illyria was a desert town of glass and stone and light, inland from a jagged coast. Its hostels and gambling dens rose in tiers above paved streets, thin white sand on thick black tar, fountains of water bursting around red or green lights. The hours of the clock meant little. The people slept in shifts. There was harsh music everywhere, and the wave-like crash of coins, fortunes turning over.

Her throat was always dry, the food always salted. Bottled water was precious.

There were hot outbursts at every intersection. Drawn swords, red slashes in tight shirts. Instant quarrels instantly settled, blooming and ending in death like accelerated desert flowers.

These were the squabbles and tantrums of children, nothing like the elegant schemes of the deceiver, which might end with sword-strokes but always began with whispered words, with ideas planted in minds and cultivated with care.

... are you sure your wife is faithful? ... might you not be elevated to your true worth? ... she says she loves you. ... would you not kill in a good cause?

She had walked here, from a muddy sea, salt-heavy skirts chafing her legs.

Now, she had her cooled penthouse and her Duke.

For the moment.

She had known at once that the deceiver was here. It was the sort of city he loved, the sort of people who appealed to him, whose chaotic interrelationships were like scattered puzzle-pieces he could break and fix together in a grotesque, cruel pattern.

They were always wary of each other.

She was not allowed to interfere, just rebuke.

As she found herself ensared by her own deceptions, caught

between the Duke and the Lady, separated from her male shadow self, she was lulled.

Story was always a trap.

Here, story grew and wound around them all. The deceiver slipped through the gaps, to work his own story, a sub-plot, to strike swiftly like an adder and pull back, uncaring, unpunished, at the end.

Madhouses were always the places to find his leavings.

No one could like the steward. She had mixed with him briefly, a tussle of words at a reception desk. He was in her way, refusing to help, citing the limitations of his job, using the rules to excuse a simple lack of fellow-feeling. He was the type common to everywhere, a petty obstruction. She saw self-importance, not self-deception.

Even now, she could not pity the broken man.

The Lady wished to take him back into her household, but there was no one to take back. A personality, puffed by feeble attempts at self-creation, had been expertly shredded away and trampled.

He was no one now.

She glimpsed the skeleton figure at four in the morning, at a crossroads at the edge of town, torn between all four streets. Talking with him was useless. He would most likely have no idea who did this to him, probably not quite realise that anything had been done. He might think on revenge, might even escalate the quarrel, murdering his persecutors real and imagined until he was himself brought down. It was not likely, though. The steward was not one of the great ones, nor ever could be even in his own self-deceptions.

In other countries, other cities, she had seen the deceiver's masterpieces, worlds skillfully woven around great men, worlds that superimposed upon their realities and drove them to self-destruction. The lesson he wished to teach was that all human personality was malleable, was what he could make of it. Kingdoms could be brought to ruins, but it was the men who were the victims.

The story was done, here.

She found the deceiver in the deserted lobby of a large hostel, in drab motley. Here, he was a clown. Without an audience, he was restless.

"My lady," he greeted her.

"Fool," she acknowledged.

He smiled, mocking the steward's rictus grin.

"You have to handle these people carefully," he said. "They break so easily. The game is often over too quickly for my taste."

"You still think of it as a game?"

He cocked his head.

"Don't you, my lord-or-lady? They can love as easily as hate."

"Can you?"

"I feel nothing. Just a mild interest. The essence of play is that it should be idle.'

That was the difference between them.

(She thought.)

She was a part of her stories. She felt for people, she loved and hated. She bled and died.

The other puppeteered and passed on.

"This was just a diversion," he said, plucking banjo strings. "A what-you-will."

"You just pretend indifference. You are culpably cruel."

He shrugged.

She put a sword-point to his adam's apple.

"Tell me why I do not end this now?"

He remained indifferent, even to the threat to his own life.

"You unpick your own question in the forming of it. You admit you will not end it, by your own choice. As to the why, that's for you to know."

"You could make me kill you."

He laughed, genuinely, shockingly.

"That would be novel. Perhaps, eventually, it will have to come to that. Often, I have included myself among my victims. I could as well be principle as player."

He was gone, and she was left behind.

She felt the pull. Soon she would doff her current mask and move on. This place would close down, street by street, waiting again.

Heigh-ho, the wind and the rain…

There was an attendant, as always. She had grown used to seeing them in the corner of her eye, standing respectfully, rushing in or out with messages, listening.

"Why?" she asked. "This arbitrariness? This indulgence of cruelty? This acceptance of the casual smashing of one man by others? Why?"

The attendant shrugged.

"This is Illyria, Lady."

It was as good an answer as any.

ASHPUTTLE
Peter Straub

Born March 2, 1943 in Milwaukee, Wisconsin, bestselling author Peter Straub's first fiction was in the literary mainstream in the mid-1970s with the novels *Marriages* and *Under Venus* – the latter not published until after he had gained fame for his horror writing. Peter Straub initially dabbled in the supernatural with *Julia* (1976) and *If You Could See Me Now* (1977), then came to widespread public attention with his fifth novel, *Ghost Story* (1979), which was a critical success and loosely adapted into the 1981 film starring Fred Astaire. Novels such as *Shadowland*, *Floating Dragon* – for which he won a British Fantasy Award – *Koko*, *Mystery*, *The Throat*, *The Hellfire Club*, *Mr X*, *Lost Boy, Lost Girl* and *In the Night Room* – as well as collections like *Houses Without Doors* and *Magic Terror* followed. He also co-wrote the international bestsellers *The Talisman* and *Black House* with Stephen King. Peter now lives in New York with his wife, Susan, director of Project Read to Me. His website can be found at www.peterstraub.net

---

People think that teaching little children has something to do with

Ashputtle

helping other people, something to do with service. People think that if you teach little children, you must love them. People get what they need from thoughts like this.

People think that if you happen to be very fat and are a person who acts happy and cheerful all the time, you are probably pretending to be that way in order to make them forget how fat you are, or cause them to forgive you for being so fat. They make this assumption, thinking you are so stupid that you imagine that you're getting away with this charade. From this assumption, they get confidence in the superiority of their intelligence over yours, and they get to pity you, too.

Those figments, those stepsisters, came to me and said, *Don't you know that we want to help you?* They came to me and said, *Can you tell us what your life is like?*
These moronic questions they asked over and over: *Are you all right? Is anything happening to you? Can you talk to us now, darling? Can you tell us about your life?*
I stared straight ahead, not looking at their pretty hair or pretty eyes or pretty mouths. I looked over their shoulders at the pattern on the wallpaper and tried not to blink until they stood up and went away.
What my *life* was like? What was *happening* to me?
Nothing was happening to me. I was *all right.*
They smiled briefly, like a twitch in their eyes and mouths, before they stood up and left me alone. I sat still on my chair and looked at the wallpaper while they talked to Zena.
The wallpaper was yellow, with white lines going up and down through it. The lines never touched – just when they were about to run into each other, they broke, and the fat thick yellow kept them apart.
I liked seeing the white lines hanging in the fat yellow, each one separate.

When the figments called me *darling,* ice and snow stormed into my mouth and went pushing down my throat into my stomach, freezing everything. They didn't know I was nothing, that I would never be like them, they didn't know that the only part of me that was not nothing was a small hard stone right at the center of me.

That stone has a name. MOTHER.

If you are a female kindergarten teacher in her fifties who happens to be very fat, people imagine that you must be truly dedicated to their children, because you cannot possibly have any sort of private life. If they are the parents of the children in your kindergarten class, they are almost grateful that you are so grotesque, because it means that you must really care about their children. After all, even though you couldn't possibly get any other sort of job, you can't be in it for the money, can you? Because what do people know about your salary? They know that garbage men make more money than kindergarten teachers. So at least you didn't decide to take care of their delightful, wonderful, lovable little children just because you thought you'd get rich, no no.

Therefore, even though they disbelieve all your smiles, all your pretty ways, even though they really do think of you with a mixture of pity and contempt, a little gratitude gets in there.

Sometimes when I meet with one of these parents, say a fluffy-haired young lawyer, say named Arnold Zoeller, Arnold and his wife, Kathi, Kathi with an *i,* mind you, sometimes when I sit behind my desk and watch these two slim handsome people struggle to keep the pity and contempt out of their well-cared-for faces, I catch that gratitude heating up behind their eyes.

Arnold and Kathi believe that a pathetic old lumpo like me must love their lovely little girl, a girl say named Tori, Tori with an *i* (for Victoria). And I think I do rather love little Tori Zoeller, yes I do think I love that little girl. My mother would have loved her, too. And that's the God's truth.

Ashputtle

I can see myself in the world, in the middle of the world.
I see that I am the same as all nature.

In our minds exists an awareness of perfection, but nothing on earth, nothing in all of nature, is perfectly conceived. Every response comes straight out of the person who is responding.

I have no responsibility to stimulate or satisfy your needs. All that was taken care of a long time ago. Even if you happen to be some kind of supposedly exalted person, like a lawyer. Even if your name is Arnold Zoeller, for example.

Once, briefly, there existed a golden time. In my mind existed an awareness of perfection, and all of nature echoed and repeated the awareness of perfection in my mind. My parents lived, and with them, I too was alive in the golden time. Our name was Asch, and in fact I am known now as Mrs. Asch, the Mrs. being entirely honorific, no husband having ever been in evidence, nor ever likely to be. (To some sixth-graders, those whom I did not beguile and enchant as kindergarteners, those before whose parents I did not squeeze myself into my desk chair and pronounce their dull, their dreary treasures delightful, wonderful, lovable, above all *intelligent,* I am known as Mrs. Fat-Asch. Of this I pretend to be ignorant.) Mr. and Mrs. Asch did dwell together in the golden time, and both mightily did love their girl-child. And then, whoops, the girl-child's Mommy upped and died. The girl-child's Daddy buried her in the estate's church yard, with the minister and everything, in the coffin and everything, with hymns and talking and crying and the animals standing around, and Zena, I remember, Zena was already there, even then. So that was how things were, right from the start.

The figments came because of what I did later. They came from a long way away – the city, I think. We never saw city dresses like that, out where we lived. We never saw city hair like that, either. And one of those ladies had a veil!

One winter morning during my first year teaching kindergarten here, I got into my car – I *shoved myself* into my car, I should explain; this is different for me than for you, I *rammed myself* between the seat and the steering wheel, and I drove forty miles east, through three different suburbs, until I got to the city, and thereupon I drove through the city to the slummiest section, where dirty people sit in their cars and drink right in the middle of the day. I went to the department store nobody goes to unless they're on welfare and have five or six kids all with different last names. I just parked on the street and sailed in the door. People like that, they never hurt people like me.

Down in the basement was where they sold the wallpaper, so I huffed and puffed down the stairs, smiling cute as a button whenever anybody stopped to look at me, and shoved myself through the aisles until I got to the back wall, where the samples stood in big books like the fairy-tale book we used to have. I grabbed about four of those books off the wall and heaved them over onto a table there in that section and perched myself on a little tiny chair and started flipping the pages.

A scared-looking black kid in a cheap suit mumbled something about helping me, so I gave him my happiest, most pathetic smile and said, well, I was here to get wallpaper, wasn't I? What color did I want, did I know? Well, I was thinking about yellow, I said. Uh-huh, he says, what kinda yellow you got in mind? Yellow with white lines in it. Uh-huh, says he, and starts helping me look through those books with all those samples in them. They have about the ugliest wallpaper in the world in this place, wallpaper like sores on the wall, wallpaper that looks like it got rained on before you get it home. Even the black kid knows this crap is ugly, but he's trying his damnedest not to show it.

I bestow smiles everywhere. I'm smiling like a queen riding through her kingdom in a carriage, like a little girl who just got a gold and silver dress from a turtledove up in a magic tree. I'm smiling as if Arnold Zoeller himself and of course his lovely wife are looking across my desk at me while I drown, suffocate, stifle, bury their *lovely, intelligent* littleTori in golden words.

Ashputtle

I think we got some more yellow in this book here, he says, and fetches down another big fairy-tale book and plunks it between us on the table. His dirty-looking hands turn those big stiff pages. And just as I thought, just as I knew would happen, could happen, would probably happen, but only here in this filthy corner of a filthy department store, this ignorant but helpful lad opens the book to my mother's wallpaper pattern.

I see that fat yellow and those white lines that never touch anything, and I can't help myself, sweat breaks out all over my body, and I groan so horribly that the kid actually backs away from me, lucky for him, because in the next second I'm bending over and throwing up interesting-looking reddish goo all over the floor of the wallpaper department. Oh God, the kid says, oh lady. I groan, and all the rest of the goo comes jumping out of me and splatters down on the carpet. Some older black guy in a clip-on bow tie rushes up toward us but stops short with his mouth hanging open as soon as he sees the mess on the floor. I take my hankie out of my bag and wipe off my mouth. I try to smile at the kid, but my eyes are too blurry. No, I say, I'm fine, I want to buy this wallpaper for my kitchen, this one right here. I turn over the page to see the name of my mother's wallpaper - Zena's wallpaper, too - and discover that this kind of wallpaper is called 'The Thinking Reed.'

You don't have to be religious to have inspirations.

* * *

An adventurous state of mind is like a great dwelling-place.

To be lived *truly,* life must be apprehended with an adventurous state of mind.

But no one on earth can explain the lure of adventure.

Zena's example gave me two tricks that work in my classroom, and the reason they work is that they are not actually tricks!

The first of these comes into play when a particular child is disobedient or inattentive, which, as you can imagine, often occurs in a room full of kindergarten-age children. I deal with these infractions in this fashion. I command the child to come to my desk. (Sometimes, I command two children to come to my desk.) I stare at the child until it begins to squirm. Sometimes it blushes or trembles. I await the physical signs of shame or discomfort. Then I pronounce the child's name. "Tori," I say, if the child is Tori. Its little eyes invariably fasten upon mine at this instant. "Tori," I say, "you know that what you did is wrong, don't you?" Ninety-nine times out of a hundred, the child nods its head. "And you will never do that wrong thing again, will you?" Most often the child can speak to say *No.* "Well, you'd better not," I say, and then I lean forward until the little child can see nothing except my enormous, inflamed face. Then in a guttural, lethal, rumble-whisper, I utter, "OR ELSE." When I say "OR ELSE," I am very emphatic. I am so very emphatic that I feel my eyes change shape. I am thinking of Zena and the time she told me that weeping on my mother's grave wouldn't make a glorious wonderful tree grow there, it would just drown my mother in mud.

The attractiveness of teaching is that it is adventurous, as adventurous as life.

My mother did not drown in mud. She died some other way. She fell down in the middle of the downstairs parlor, the parlor where Zena sat on her visits. Zena was just another lady then, and on her visits, her "social calls," she sat on the best antique chair and held her hands in her lap like the most modest, innocent little lady ever born. She was half Chinese, Zena, and I knew she was just like bright sharp metal inside of her, metal that could slice you but good. Zena was very adventurous, bur not as adventurous as me. Zena never got out of that town. Of course, all that happened to Zena was that she got old, and everybody left her all alone because she wasn't pretty anymore, she was just an old yellow

Ashputtle

widow-lady, and then I heard that she died pulling up weeds in her garden. I heard this from two different people. You could say that Zena got drowned in mud, which proves that everything spoken on this earth contains a truth not always apparent at the time.

The other trick I learned from Zena that is not a trick is how to handle a whole class that has decided to act up. These children come from parents who, thinking they know everything, in fact know less than nothing. These children will never see a classical manner demonstrated at home. You must respond in a way that demonstrates your awareness of perfection. You must respond in a way that will bring this awareness to the unruly children, so that they too will possess it.

It can begin in a thousand different ways. Say I am in conference with a single student – say I am delivering the great OR ELSE. Say that my attention has wandered off for a moment, and that I am contemplating the myriad things I contemplate when my attention is wandering free. My mother's grave, watered by my tears. The women with city hair who desired to give me help, but could not, so left to be replaced by others, who in turn were replaced by yet others. How it felt to stand naked and besmeared with my own faeces in the front yard, moveless as a statue, the same as all nature, classical. The gradual disappearance of my father, like that of a figure in a cartoon who grows increasingly transparent until total transparency is reached. Zena facedown in her garden, snuffling dirt up into her nostrils. The resemblance of the city women to certain wicked stepsisters in old tales. Also their resemblance to handsome princes in the same tales.

She who hears the tale makes the tale.

Say therefore that I am no longer quite anchored within the classroom, but that I float upward into one, several, or all of these realms. People get what they need from their own minds. Certain places, you can get in there and rest. The classical was a

187

cool period. I am floating within my cool realms. At that moment, one child pulls another's hair. A third child hurls a spitball at the window. Another falls to the floor, emitting pathetic and mechanical cries. Instantly, what was order is misrule. Then I summon up the image of my ferocious female angels and am on my feet before the little beasts even notice that I have left my desk. In a flash, I am beside the light switch. The Toris and Tiffanys, the Joshuas and Jeremys, riot on. I slap down the switch, and the room goes dark.

Result? Silence. Inspired action is destiny.

The children freeze. Their pulses race – veins beat in not a few little blue temples. I say four words. I say, "Think what this means." They know what it means. I grow to twice my size with the meaning of these words. I loom over them, and darkness pours out of me. Then I switch the lights back on, and smile at them until they get what they need from my smiling face. These children will never call me Mrs. Fat-Asch; these children know that I am the same as all nature.

Once upon a time a dying queen sent for her daughter, and when her daughter came to her bedside the queen said, "I am leaving you, my darling. Say your prayers and be good to your father. Think of me always, and I will always be with you." Then she died. Every day the little girl watered her mother's grave with her tears. But her heart was dead. You cannot lie about a thing like this. Hatred is the inside part of love. And so her mother became a hard cold stone in her heart. And that was the meaning of the mother, for as long as the little girl lived.

Soon the king took another woman as his wife, and she was most beautiful, with skin the color of gold and eyes as black as jet. She was like a person pretending to be someone else inside another person pretending she couldn't pretend. She understood that reality was contextual. She understood about the condition of the observer.

One day when the king was going out to be among his people, he asked his wife, "What shall I bring you?"

"A diamond ring," said the queen. And the king could not tell who was speaking, the person inside pretending to be someone else, or the person outside who could not pretend.

"And you, my daughter," said the king, "what would you like?"

"A diamond ring," said the daughter.

The king smiled and shook his head.

"Then nothing," said the daughter. "Nothing at all."

When the king came home, he presented the queen with a diamond ring in a small blue box, and the queen opened the box and smiled at the ring and said, "It's a very small diamond, isn't it?" The king's daughter saw him stoop forward, his face whitening, as if he had just lost half his blood. "I like my small diamond," said the queen, and the king straightened up, although he still looked white and shaken. He patted his daughter on the head on his way out of the room, but the girl merely looked forward and said nothing, in return for the nothing he had given her.

And that night, when the rest of the palace was asleep, the king's daughter crept to the kitchen and ate half of a loaf of bread and most of a quart of homemade peach ice cream. This was the most delicious food she had ever eaten in her whole entire life. The bread tasted like the sun on the wheatfields, and inside the taste of the sun was the taste of the bursting kernels of the wheat, even of the rich dark crumbly soil that surrounded the roots of the wheat, even of the lives of the bugs and animals that had scurried through the wheat, even of the droppings of those foxes, beetles, and mice. And the homemade peach ice cream tasted overwhelmingly of sugar, cream, and peaches, but also of the bark and meat of the peach tree and the pink feet of the birds that had landed on it, and the sharp, brittle voices of those birds, also of the effort of the hand crank, of the stained, whorly wood of its sides, and of the sweat of the man who had worked it so long. Every taste should be as complicated as possible, and every taste goes up and down at the same time: up past the turtledoves to the far reaches of the sky, so that one final taste in everything is *whiteness*, and down all the way to the mud at the bottom of graves, then to the mud beneath that mud, so that another final taste in everything, in even peach ice cream, is the taste of *blackness*.

* * *

From about this time, the king's daughter began to attract undue attention. From the night of the whiteness of turtledoves and the blackness of grave-mud to the final departure of the stepsisters was a period of something like six months.

I thought of myself as a work of art. I caused responses without being responsible for them. This is the great freedom of art.

They asked questions that enforced the terms of their own answers. *Don't you know we want to help you?* Such a question implies only two possible answers, 1: no, 2: yes. The stepsisters never understood the queen's daughter, therefore the turtledoves pecked out their eyes, first on the one side, then on the other. The correct answer – 3: person to whom question is directed is not the one in need of help – cannot be given. Other correct answers, such as 4: help shall come from other sources, and 5: neither knowledge nor help mean what you imagine they mean, are also forbidden by the form of the question.

Assignment for tonight: make a list of proper but similarly forbidden answers to the question *What is happening to you?* Note: be sure to consider conditions imposed by the use of the word *happening*.

The stepsisters arrived from the city in grand state. They resembled peacocks. The stepsisters accepted Zena's tea, they admired the house, the paintings, the furniture, just as if

Ashputtle

admiring these things, which everybody admired, meant that they, too, should be admired. The stepsisters wished to remove the king's daughter from this setting, but their power was not so great. Zena would not permit it, nor would the ailing king. (At night, Zena placed her subtle mouth over his sleeping mouth and drew breath straight out of his body.) Zena said that the condition of the king's daughter would prove to be temporary. The child was eating well. She was loved. In time, she would return to herself.

When the figments asked, *What is happening to you?* I could have answered, *Zena is happening to me.* This answer would not have been understood. Neither would the answer, *My mother is happening to me.*

* * *

Undue attention came about in the following fashion. Zena knew all about my midnight feasts, but was indifferent to them. Zena knew that each person must acquire what she needs. This is as true for a king's daughter as for any ordinary commoner. But she was ignorant of what I did in the name of art. Misery and anger made me a great artist, though now I am a much greater artist. I think I was twelve. (The age of an artist is of no importance.) Both my mother and Zena were happening to me, and I was happening to them, too. Such is the world of women. My mother, deep in her mud-grave, hated Zena. Zena, second in the king's affections, hated my mother. Speaking from the center of the stone at the center of me, my mother frequently advised me on how to deal with Zena. Silently, speaking with her eyes, Zena advised me on how to deal with my mother. I, who had to deal with both of them, hated them both.

And I possessed an adventurous mind.

The main feature of adventure is that it goes forward into unknown country.

Adventure is filled with a nameless joy.

Alone in my room in the middle of Saturday, on later occasions after my return from school, I removed my clothes and placed them neatly on my bed. (My *canopied* bed.) I had no feelings, apart from a sense of urgency, concerning the actions I was about to perform. Perhaps I experienced a nameless joy at this point. Later on, at the culmination of my self-display, I experienced a nameless joy. And later yet, I experienced the same nameless joy at the conclusions of my various adventures in art. In each of these adventures as in the first, I created responses not traceable within the artwork, but which derived from the conditions, etc., of the audience. Alone and unclothed now in my room, ready to create responses, I squatted on my heels and squeezed out onto the carpet a long cylinder of fecal matter, the residue of, dinner not included, an entire loaf of seven-grain bread, half a box of raisins, a can of peanuts, and a quarter pound of cervelat sausage, all consumed when everyone else was in bed and Zena was presumably leaning over the face of my sleeping father, greedily inhaling his life. I picked up the warm cylinder and felt it melt into my hands. I hastened this process by squeezing my palms together. Then I rubbed my hands over my body. What remained of the stinking cylinder I smeared along the walls of the bedroom. Then I wiped my hands on the carpet. (The *white* carpet.) My preparations concluded, I moved regally through the corridors until I reached the front door and let myself out.

I have worked as a certified grade-school teacher in three states. My record is spotless. I never left a school except by my own choice. When tragedies came to my charges or their parents, I invariably sent sympathetic notes, joined volunteer groups to search for bodies, attended funerals, etc., etc. Every teacher eventually becomes familiar with these unfortunate duties.

Outside, there was all the world, at least all of the estate, from which

Ashputtle

to choose. Two lines from Edna St. Vincent Millay best express my state of mind at this moment: *The world stands out on either side / No wider than the heart is wide.* I well remember the much-admired figure of Dave Garroway quoting these lovely words on his Sunday-afternoon television program, and I pass along this beautiful sentiment to each fresh class of kindergarteners. They must start somewhere, and at other moments in their year with me they will have the opportunity to learn that nature never gives you a chance to rest. Every animal on earth is hungry.

Turning my back on the fields of grazing cows and sheep, ignoring the hills beyond, hills seething with coyotes, wildcats, and mountain lions, I moved with stately tread through the military rows of fruit trees and, with papery apple and peach blossoms adhering to my bare feet, passed into the expanse of the grass meadow where grew the great hazel tree. Had the meadow been recently mown, long green stalks the width of caterpillars leapt up from the ground to festoon my legs. (I often stretched out full length and rolled in the freshly mown grass meadow.) And then, at the crest of the hill that marked the end of the meadow, I arrived at my destination. Below me lay the road to the unknown towns and cities in which I hoped one day to find my complicated destiny. Above me stood the hazel tree.

* * *

I have always known that I could save myself by looking into my own mind.

I stood above the road on the crest of the hill and raised my arms. When I looked into my mind I saw two distinct and necessary states, one that of the white line, the other that of the female angels, akin to the turtledoves.

The white line existed in a calm rapture of separation, touching neither sky nor meadow but suspended in the space between. The white line was silence, isolation, classicism. This state is one half of what is necessary in order to achieve the freedom of art, and it is called the Thinking Reed.

The angels and turtledoves existed in a rapture of power, activity, and rage. They were absolute whiteness and absolute blackness, gratification and gratification's handmaiden, revenge. The angels and turtledoves came streaming up out of my body and soared from the tips of my fingers into the sky, and when they returned they brought golden and silver dresses, diamond rings, and emerald tiaras.

I saw the figments slicing off their own toes, sawing off their heels, and stepping into shoes already slippery with blood. The figments were trying to smile, they were trying to stand up straight. They were like children before an angry teacher, a teacher transported by a righteous anger. Girls like the figments never did understand that what they needed, they must get from their own minds. Lacking this understanding, they tottered along, pretending that they were not mutilated, pretending that blood did not pour from their shoes, back to their pretend houses and pretend princes. The nameless joy distinguished every part of this process.

Lately, within the past twenty-four hours, a child has been lost.

A lost child lies deep within the ashes, her hands and feet mutilated, her face destroyed by fire. She has partaken of the great adventure, and now she is the same as all nature.

At night, I see the handsome, distracted, still hopeful parents on our local news programs. Arnold and Kathi, he as handsome as a prince, she as lovely as one of the figments, still have no idea of what has actually happened to them – they lived their whole lives in utter abyssal ignorance – they think of hope as an essential component of the universe. They think that other people, the

Ashputtle

people paid to perform this function, will conspire to satisfy their needs.

A child has been lost. Now her photograph appears each day on the front page of our sturdy little tabloid-style newspaper, beaming out with luminous ignorance beside the columns of print describing a sudden disappearance after the weekly Sunday school class at St.-Mary-in-the-Forest's Episcopal church, the deepening fears of the concerned parents, the limitless charm of the girl herself, the searches of nearby video parlors and shopping malls, the draggings of two adjacent ponds, the slow, painstaking inspections of the neighboring woods, fields, farms, and outbuildings, the shock of the child's particularly well-off and socially prominent relatives, godparents included.

A particular child has been lost. A certain combination of variously shaded blond hair and eyes the blue of early summer sky seen through a haze of cirrus clouds, of an endearingly puffy upper lip and a recurring smudge, like that left on corrasable bond typing paper by an unclean eraser, on the left side of the mouth, of an unaffected shyness and an occasional brittle arrogance destined soon to overshadow more attractive traits will never again be seen, not by parents, friends, teachers, or the passing strangers once given to spontaneous tributes to the child's beauty.

A child of her time has been lost. Of no interest to our local newspaper, unknown to the Sunday school classes at St.-Mary-in-the-Forest, were this moppet's obsession with the dolls Exercise Barbie and Malibu Barbie, her fanatical attachment to My Little Ponies Glory and AppleJacks, her insistence on introducing during classtime observations upon the cartoon family named Simpson, and her precocious fascination with the music television channel, especially the 'videos' featuring the groups Kris Kross and Boyz II Men. She was once observed holding hands with James Halliwell, a first-grade boy. Once, just before naptime, she turned upon a pudgy, unpopular girl of protosadistic tendencies named Deborah Monk and hissed, "Debbie, I hate to tell you this, but you *suck*."

A child of certain limitations has been lost. She could never learn to tie her cute but oddly blunt-looking size 1 running shoes

195

and eventually had to become resigned to the sort fastened with Velcro straps. When combing her multishaded blond hair with her fingers, she would invariably miss a cobwebby patch located two inches aft of her left ear. Her reading skills were somewhat, though not seriously, below average. She could recognize her name, when spelled out in separate capitals, with narcissistic glee; yet all other words, save *and* and *the*, turned beneath her impatient gaze into random, Sanskrit-like squiggles and uprights. (This would soon have corrected itself.) She could recite the alphabet all in a rush, by rote, but when questioned was incapable of remembering if *O* came before or after *S*. I doubt that she would have been capable of mastering long division during the appropriate academic term.

Across the wide, filmy screen of her eyes would now and then cross a haze of indefinable confusion. In a child of more finely tuned sensibilities, this momentary slippage might have suggested a sudden sense of loss, even perhaps a premonition of the loss to come. In her case, I imagine the expression was due to the transition from the world of complete unconsciousness (Barbie and My Little Ponies) to a more fully socialized state (Kris Kross). Introspection would have come only late in life, after long exposure to experiences of the kind from which her parents most wished to shelter her.

An irreplaceable child has been lost. What was once in the land of the Thinking Reed has been forever removed, like others before it, like all others in time, to turtledove territory. This fact is borne home on a daily basis. Should some informed anonymous observer report that the child is all right, that nothing is happening to her, the comforting message would be misunderstood as the prelude to a demand for ransom. The reason for this is that no human life can ever be truly substituted for another. The increasingly despairing parents cannot create or otherwise acquire a living replica, though they are certainly capable of reproducing again, should they stay married long enough to do so. The children in the lost one's class are reported to suffer nightmares and recurrent enuresis. In class, they exhibit lassitude, wariness, a new unwillingness to respond, like the

Ashputtle

unwillingness of the very old. At a schoolwide assembly where the little ones sat right up in front, nearly everyone expressed the desire for the missing one to return. Letters and cards to the lost one now form two large, untidy stacks in the principal's office and, with parental appeals to the abductor or abductors broadcast every night, it is felt that the school will accumulate a third stack before these tributes are offered to the distraught parents.

Works of art generate responses not directly traceable to the work itself. Helplessness, grief, and sorrow may exist simultaneously alongside aggressiveness, hostility, anger, or even serenity and relief. The more profound and subtle the work, the more intense and long-lasting the responses it evokes.

Deep, deep in her muddy grave, the queen and mother felt the tears of her lost daughter. *All will pass.* In the form of a turtledove, she rose from grave-darkness and ascended into the great arms of a hazel tree. *All will change.* From the topmost branch, the turtledove sang out her everlasting message. *All is hers, who will seek what is true.* "What is true?" cried the daughter, looking dazzled up. *All will pass, all will change, all is yours,* sang the turtledove.

In a recent private conference with the principal, I announced my decision to move to another section of the country after the semester's end.

The principal is a kindhearted, limited man still loyal, one might say rigidly loyal, to the values he absorbed from popular music at the end of the nineteen sixties, and he has never quite been able to conceal the unease I arouse within him. Yet he is aware of the respect I command within every quarter of his school, and he has seen former kindergarteners of mine, now freshmen in our trisuburban high school, return to my classroom and inform the awed children seated before them that Mrs. Asch placed them on the right path, that Mrs. Asch's lessons would be responsible for seeing them successfully through high school and on to college.

Virtually unable to contain the conflict of feelings my announcement brought to birth within him, the principal assured me that he would that very night compose a letter of recommendation certain to gain me a post at any elementary school, public or private, of my choosing.

After thanking him, I replied, "I do not request this kindness of you, but neither will I refuse it."

The principal leaned back in his chair and gazed at me, not unkindly, through his granny glasses. His right hand rose like a turtledove to caress his graying beard, but ceased halfway in its flight, and returned to his lap. Then he lifted both hands to the surface of his desk and intertwined the fingers, still gazing quizzically at me.

"Are you all right?" he inquired.

"Define your terms," I said. "If you mean, am I in reasonable health, enjoying physical and mental stability, satisfied with my work, then the answer is yes, I am all right."

"You've done a wonderful job dealing with Tori's disappearance," he said. "But I can't help but wonder if all of that has played a part in your decision."

"My decisions make themselves," I said. "All will pass, all will change. I am a serene person."

He promised to get the letter of recommendation to me by lunchtime the next day, and as I knew he would, he kept his promise. Despite my serious reservations about his methods, attitude, and ideology – despite my virtual certainty that he will be unceremoniously forced from his job within the next year – I cannot refrain from wishing the poor fellow well.

WEBS
Neil Gaiman

Neil Gaiman is a critically acclaimed and multi-award-winning British author who first came to the attention of the masses as the writer of the Sandman comics, which featured an incarnation of Morpheus – the dream king – as well as a very Goth-looking Death (who looks set to star in her own film soon). His bestselling novels include *Neverwhere* (also a major BBC drama series starring Lenny Henry), *Stardust* (which has just been turned into a movie starring Claire Daines and Robert De Niro), the phenomenal New York Times best-selling *American Gods*, and most recently *Anansi Boys* which, like the following short story, dealt with the topic of arachnids. His collections are *Angels and Visitations*, *Smoke and Mirrors* and, most recently, *Fragile Things*, plus he has written the successful children's books *Coraline*, *The Day I Swapped My Dad for Two Goldfish* and *The Wolves in the Walls*. He also recently scripted *MirrorMask* directed by long-time collaborator and friend, artist Dave McKean. He writes a live journal for his website www.neilgaiman.com which is read by millions, and he now lives in Minnesota with his family and his cats.

Neil recounts: "I found FantasyCon almost accidentally. I was 22, and it was in Birmingham, in October '83, at a long gone hotel called the New Imperial, and I was mostly there to interview GoH Robert Silverberg for Penthouse.

"I did not know that these were My People when I arrived. I'd never been to a convention before, didn't know anyone, but I was fortunate enough to have been commissioned to write an article about FantasyCon VIII for a pop-culture magazine the name of which I forgot over 20 years ago. Because I was writing an article, I didn't have to be shy, and I got to find interesting people and talk to them – Peter Nicholls, Steve Jones, David Sutton, Ramsey Campbell, Jo Fletcher, and many others. Steve Jones raffled off Blue Thunder hats on the Saturday Night. It was like discovering there were other people out there who shared my cultural identity, who were part of the same odd race. They were family, and they were friends. It was almost like coming home, except going to Birmingham is never like coming home (as Kim Newman and I discovered, the following year, on the way to FantasyCon IX, as we stepped over the just-knifed body at the top of the escalators coming out of New Street Station).

"After that first one, the sequence of FantasyCons turns into a blur of bars and panels and late-night conversations, of strange and wonderful films I'd never seen before.

"The publisher- editor of the London-based pop culture magazine phoned to say she loved the article I did on FantasyCon, and would I come in to the office and talk about being a regular columnist? So I did, only to find her sadly putting the last of the office furniture into her Dad's van, and locking the offices behind her. She said she couldn't give a forwarding address in case any creditors got hold of it, but if the article was ever published, she'd let me know."

In the web-covered halls of the King of the Spiders, Lupita spent a most memorable year. She had servants in attendance upon her, and a jerkin covered in chryolanths, a present from the King. Lupita was a guest of one of the Dark Lords, although nobody seemed to know which one; it was the subject of much court speculation:

"Today, milor' Lupita abased herself perhaps a trifle too low before Lord Caryatid."

"Ah, but yesterday she was seen publicly to ignore Lord Tistatte, and on one of the dark days: surely there is a sign of favour?"

"Or of other protection. Perhaps she is in lien to one of the Lords of shifting position..."

And all would be silent, and watch Lupita as she walked across the hall, strands of webbing adhering to her cape and drifting behind her like fronds of plants from the Slow Zone: old man's folly, perhaps, or tiger-whiskers, a plant spoken of in the classics as possessing certain unusual properties, although no one today knew nor cared what they were.

It was the uncertainty about Lupita's status that had kept her safe from court intrigues; for, after all, no one would dare to risk their status on a cheap guess. Blood was the Dark Lords' tithe from those who worshipped them, and few were overly eager to hasten the communion by involvement in the complicated and shifting game the Lords played. Instead they mirrored it, or thought they did, aped what they presumed they saw, with their petty little cliques, and their treacherous little factions.

Although the webs did much to mute sound in the endless corridors of the Palace of Spiders, there was always a soft susurrus, a sly whispering as alliances were formed, the hiss of betrayals discovered and bought, the kiss of character assassination (and possibly of assassination of another kind, for sometimes bodies could be seen lolling high in the webs of the halls, wrapped around in pale silken strands like empty insects in some old larder, although no one ever climbed the webbing to find out who it was that had been left there. The bodies were always gone in a week, or two at most).

In her time in the palace Lupita formed a number of oblique

on the floor of the corridor, and waited.

The crowd stared at her, enraptured, waiting with amazement for her next trick. It was all so new, so daring. Someone at the back began to applaud, swallowing gulps of air and belching loudly, but the noise was quickly shushed.

By the time the stone was struck for evening meal, the last onlooker had given up, and wandered off. Lupita was still waiting, sitting in the shadows, pale eyes gazing up at the shrouded body.

When the last stone was struck for deep night a servant came by and replaced the food and water Lupita had consumed on her vigil.

On the third night it seemed to Lupita almost as if the servant were about to speak to her, but the servant did no such thing, So Lupita spoke to the servant.

"Do you know what I will find?"

The servant shrugged.

"Do you care?"

"It is," admitted the servant, "not something that will affect my lot one way or another."

Lupita nodded dismissal, and the servant backed away.

It is said that at that time Lupita slept, and dreamed a dream. But a dream is a private matter, and we shall not concern ourselves with it. Be that as it may, Lupita was either woken, or not woken but alerted, an hour after this, by a tugging on the thread about her thumb. Looking up she could just make out the cat-cadaver lurching up the web. She let out loops of thread from her thumb, like someone coaxing a nervous kite to fly, until she saw the shape vanish in the webbing, pulled inside by a dark and spindly limb.

It was then that Lupita hand-over-handed up the web (which would have caused apoplexy, and perhaps a chorus of eructation, had an audience been there to observe), trying, and not altogether failing, to move at random, as if she were merely a rip in the net, old bones and gnawed skulls slipping and shifting from the turbulence in the web caused by the recent passage of the cat.

She waited near the spot where the mammal's body had vanished, until the thread was tight around her thumb (which she could feel was losing feeling), then she let out the last couple of loops, and pushed into the web. Strands of the stuff stuck to her eyelashes, her face, her hair. She screwed her eyes together tightly, then pulled her cloak in front of her face, and moved forward into the space.

She had expected a tunnel.

Instead she found herself disoriented, moving through something that felt like a waterfall, but which was composed of light and something else, not matter. It seemed like something was brushing her lightly from the soles of her feet to her head. It tickled, but it was a tickling inside, not outside, not on her skin.

Her eyes were still tight shut, but colours formed inside them, seeping like river mists of blue, of green, of peach and viridian, then exploding like fire inside her head.

She said nothing, and was still. When her inner world had calmed down she lowered her cloak, and opened her eyes. The world had turned silver: lights shone silver from mirrored panels, illuminated silver switches and buttons, cast silver reflections on silver surfaces and spilled to the silver floor around dark grey shadows.

In a corner, next to a vast metal ship, its silver sails fluttering in a nonexistent breeze, sat two huge spiders, white spots on splotchy brown abdomens; angular knobby-jointed legs waving gently in the air; emerald eyes gleaming with hunger and greed.

They had divided the cat between them, and were eating it in a most unpleasant fashion.

Lupita pulled her knife from her belt, and threw it at the largest of the spiders, hitting it in the abdomen. White stuff began to ooze from the cut, dripping onto the metal floor. The creature ate on, not noticing the wound, not even when the pale substance (in appearance, Lupita observed, somewhere between pus and jelly) oozed as far as the cat, and the spider continued its meal with itself as sauce and condiment.

Since her knife attack had done no apparent good, Lupita slowly began to circle the spiders, walking as quietly as was possible. She circled them once, twice, three times, then she ran, hard, as fast as she could toward a far wall.

She turned around, and winced. The thread had performed its function, but while one of the spiders – the one with the wounded belly – had been neatly sliced in two, yellow organs swimming in mucus now slipping and spilling onto the floor, the other had been less fortunate. The thread had slid down, so that, instead of encircling the body, it had merely noosed the legs. The final tug had pulled seven of the eight legs off, and they lay stiff and ghastly on the ground, stacked up like dreadful brushwood against the spider's shivering body. The last leg twitched and spasmed, spinning the spider around on the silver floor.

Lupita went close enough to it to retrieve her knife, then, keeping well clear of the mouth, which was opening and closing in impotent and silent fury, she slit the creature's belly wide open, with a cry,

"Haih!" and jumped back, pulling up her cloak as she did so to avoid the tumbling organs splashing it.

She tried to untie the thread from her thumb, but it had been too tightly wound for too long, and her thumb was blue and cold. The thread had been pulled too tight to untie and was too tough to cut, although she produced a respectable amount of blood in trying.

In the end she had to cut the thumb off. She cauterised it in spider-spit, which took away the pain and stopped the bleeding, although it made her feel strangely distant, as if she was not participating in her life, but was merely an interested spectator, watching her own actions from over her shoulder. This feeling, which was new to her, was to recur several times in later life.

She wiped the knife on her leg, returned it to her belt, and climbed out the way she had come.

The next day it was observed that neither the King nor the Lord Chamberlain were to be found in the palace environs; however this realisation was rapidly overshadowed by the discovery that a certain antique Dark Lord had gone into fugue, and was apparently blown out.

It was widely assumed that Lupita had cut off her thumb in order to appear mysterious, and the court, unable to cope with further mysteries, agreed to find this in faintly bad taste.

Worse was to follow:

That evening Lupita left the palace. Before she went, as she passed through the hall of the Dark Lords, she was seen to stroke the casing of the Lord-in-fugue.

The court gathered in an observation tower to watch her leave; they stared after her until she had crossed the borderline and was lost in the mists; but the sky remained curiously free from lightning, there were no awful screams or terrible cries, and the earth did not part and swallow her up.

They went back to their halls feeling slightly let down. Later they polished the Dark Lords: Iliaster and Baraquely, Zibanitutula, Ettanin, Bodstieriyan, and the rest.

It was then that one of the lesser courtiers was foolish enough to be heard praying that Lupita be punished for her lack of respect. Prayers of any kind were anathema to the Dark Lords, and he was turned to twisted stone where he stood.

The people waited for their king and his chamberlain to return to them.

The webs collapsed and rotted in the halls near to where Lupita (now just an enigmatic memory) had had her chambers. But other webs were being spun; they were all over the palace, if you knew where to look for them.

THE RAFFLE
Simon Clark

Simon Clark was born in Wakefield in 1958, and now lives in Doncaster, South Yorkshire, with his family and a jet-black dog. As a child he was inspired by a radio broadcast which recited lines from Dylan Thomas's famous poem *And Death Shall Have No Dominion* – which might explain his later fascination for all things zombie-like. The young Clark was also intrigued by legends about a skull buried under the family's garage. He attended Whitwood Technical College and wrote stories in his spare time, breaking into the small press and publishing his first collection *Blood and Grit* in 1990. Four years later Hodder and Stoughton picked up his first two novels, *Nailed by the Heart* and *Blood Crazy* and he hasn't looked back since. His subsequent novels include *Darker, King Blood, Judas Tree, Vampyrrhic, Stranger, Vampyrrhic Rites, In This Skin, The Tower* and *London Under Midnight*. In 2003 he won the British Fantasy Award for his novel *Night of the Triffids*, which continues the story of the classic Wyndham adventure, and also for his novella 'Goblin City Lights' which was later reprinted in his *Hotel Midnight* collection for Robert Hale. Simon was also Guest of Honour at 2005's FantasyCon. His website can be found at www.bbr-online.com/nailed

"This happened fifteen years ago," remembers Simon, "when I had to leave FantasyCon mid-afternoon for my train. That year the convention was held in central Birmingham so it was only moments' walk to the station. The train never appeared, leaving me with forty minutes until the next one, so I decided to nip back to the hotel where the closing event was taking place. I crept unobserved into the function room. Everyone was still there listening to a closing speech but I no longer felt part of the convention. Was this how a spirit feels when it returns to earth to take a secret peek at family and friends? It was a strangely powerful experience and seemingly inexplicable. I'd only left the convention thirty minutes ago, yet here I was suddenly an outsider, observing those convention-goers as if seeing them for the first time.

"And that was the moment, as I lingered invisibly at the back of the room full of friends, that I realized how important the BFS and FantasyCon had been to me.

"Last year I was fortunate enough to be a guest of honor at FantasyCon in Walsall. As I hadn't been to the convention for a while I wondered if it'd still mean as much to me. I did, however, enjoy it enormously – and it was in the leaving after FantasyCon that once more it was driven home how important those conventions are to me. I'd been on the train for about an hour when I realized all those subtle bonds formed at the convention were breaking. I wouldn't see that band of like-minded souls for another twelve months. That's when I experienced painful pangs of separation.

"One of the FantasyCon events, which has become legendary, is our unique raffle. As well as a bonding experience it raises money for good causes. This year I could not resist being inspired by them to write a short story entitled *The Raffle*, which is presented for you in this volume now."

Dedicated with deep respect to the membership of the British Fantasy Society.

The Raffle

*'Without lie, certain and most true:
What is below is like what is above, and what is above is like what is below...'*
From the Hermetic Emerald Tablet

The convention's near legendary – no make that *totally legendary* raffle was held that night in the hotel's main function room. There were twenty tables that each seated ten people. As was my wont, I sat at the back of the room near the bar. Outside, lightning seared the night sky, while thunder stalked like a vengeful god hunting backsliders and idolaters and sinners of every shape and persuasion. While the raffle tickets were given a final mix round in an ice bucket before the master of ceremonies took the mic I chatted with my fellow raffle jockeys.

Sitting at my table were Mr. Lovecraft, Mr. Machen, Mr. Hodgson, Mr. Tolkien, Dylan ("Don't you call me mister, boyo.") Thomas, Mrs. Jackson, Mrs. Bronte and Mr. Poe. Mr. Bela Lugosi had just popped to the gents.

"Damn, that flaming draught. Close the window." Mr. Hodgson recovered colored strips of paper from the floor. "My bloody raffle tickets are going all over the place."

"I only bought a strip of five," Mr. Lovecraft intoned as he sipped from a glass of water. "Times are hard."

Mr. Poe was perspiring. "I don't think I can take this. I've heard these raffles go on until after midnight."

Dylan Thomas carelessly flicked his raffle tickets at Mr. Machen. "If you have the endurance for a convention raffle then you can endure anything. Absolutely bloody anything."

Mr. Machen ducked to avoid the balled-up raffle ticket striking him in the eye. "I can take the hint, sir. My round. What's everyone having?"

As Mr. Arthur Machen bought the drinks I should explain. Ordering the pints of lager, the vodka and cokes and the Baileys wasn't *really* the author of the *Great God Pan, The White People* and other tales of fabulous literature. This time at the UK Arcanum Convention for fans of the outré and the fantastic it had been decided to combine a masked ball with the raffle. Our masks had been assigned by chance; that is to say they were in the goodie bag with the free books and program. Happily, I found I'd drawn Boris Karloff's Frankenstein Monster, which was now fixed to my head with something that looked suspiciously like knicker elastic.

As Dylan Thomas waited for the drink he looked out of the window and declaimed, "Starless and Bible black it is. I can see bugger all."

Mrs. Jackson retorted with, "Shouldn't that be 'I can see Llareggub'?"

"Very witty, Mrs. Jackson," Mr. Tolkien said. "Uh, the raffle's starting. Good luck, team mates."

"I bet I win damn well nothing," Mr. Hodgson thundered. "I never do."

Mr. Poe wrung his hands in anguish. "They've got to stir the raffle tickets up. If they don't, the same people will keep winning. I tell you, I don't know if I can take it!"

Mr. Machen delivered the drinks. "Mr. Poe, you were the Baileys and ice, weren't you?"

"Cheers." Poe dropped the tortured poet angst but lifted his mask a little so he could sip the fawn liquor. "Thanks, Big Mac."

Mr. Machen sniffed. "Sir, I doubt whether Arthur Machen would have answered to Big Mac."

The amplified voice of the mc boomed out as thunder crashed. "Everyone ready? We've a table full of prizes generously donated by all and sundry." The mc shed his mask so he could speak into the microphone without bashing Quasimodo's cock-eye against it. "And we have special mystery prizes donated by an individual who wishes to remain anonymous. The mystery prizes are the crimson tickets...that's the *crimson* tickets. Okay, ladies and gentlemen, time to begin our legendary raffle..."

As lightning flashed and thunder fell like the hammer of God the mc began.

* * *

The Raffle

The storm was at its height. Even though lightning blazed against the windows accompanied by pounding thunder the convention raffle was going well. The mc called out winning numbers, winners shouted, "Here!" and runners delivered prizes of books, DVDs, posters and T-shirts from a table piled high with goodies.

Then Mr. Poe won a mystery prize. He held up his hand with the crimson ticket, "Here!"

"Ah, this is a different sort of prize, Mr. Poe," announced the mc. "You have to collect it in person."

"By Jove." Mr. Poe put down his Baileys and headed for the podium to applause from the audience in their masks.

The mc read the back of the blood-red ticket he'd pulled from the ice bucket. "Lucky winner, go to the glass elevator and claim your prize."

Mr. Poe was anguished. "But the glass elevator has been out of order since we got here."

"Those are the instructions. I'm sure you'll be fine." As Mr. Poe trotted toward the hotel lobby the mc delved into the ice bucket once more. "Green ticket. Number eighty-eight. Who's got eighty-eight? Come on, someone must have it."

"Here," shouted Mr. Lugosi.

Time marched towards midnight to the rhythm of the thunderstorm. More and more of the blood-red tickets were drawn. The winners sallied forth to collect their mystery prize from the glass elevator.

At five minutes to twelve Mr. Tolkien leaned toward me and whispered, "Have you noticed, those who go to collect their mystery prize never come back?"

I shrugged. "The mystery prize will be a room party."

"Free drinks," Dylan Thomas mumbled into his beer. "Free drinks and canapés for all."

The mystery prize winners now formed a slow but indefatigable exodus. From two hundred in the room we'd dwindled to less than a hundred. But the mc wasn't to be thwarted. He still had a heap of prizes to dispose of. Untiringly, he delved into the ice bucket. "Crimson ticket, number fifty-eight."

"Here!" I shouted in surprise. "That's me. And I never ever win

211

anything."

Mr. Machen chuckled. "Then it's your lucky day."

I collected my crimson ticket and headed for the glass elevator. With the time approaching midnight the hotel lobby was empty. Even the reception desk was a desolate expanse of black marble, the clerk obviously taking a break in a back office. Through the glazed doors I could see rain swirling down a deserted street. Thunder still grumbled; a restless giant woken from its sleep.

As instructed I went to the glass elevator. The doors were open as if it expected a new passenger. I glanced back down the corridor to the function room in case someone else won a mystery prize and we could ride the elevator together but there was nobody in sight. The doors had closed and I could hear the mc's voice no longer. Maybe Dylan Thomas was right about the room party. I pictured the canapés and realized I was more than ready to eat. Eagerly, I entered the elevator. The glass doors swished shut and it began to descend. Odd, I thought, shouldn't it be ascending? Through the transparent walls I saw the brick-lined shaft. Maybe I collected my mystery gift from the basement? Perhaps the elevator had been pre-programmed to deliver me there? Okay, I'd wait and find out what awaited me down below.

The elevator descended into a stark void with a concrete floor and wheeled cages containing dirty laundry. Nobody there – not a soul.

Then the strangest thing…

The elevator continued downward. I stared out through the glass walls as it passed into the earth beneath the hotel. It was like sinking through a brown ocean. Suspended there were shards of broken pottery from medieval times, then ancient foundations of what might have been a Roman villa with blocks of stone, red splinters of roof tile and fragments of mosaic floor that revealed the screaming face of a snake-haired gorgon. Down, down, down… layers of creamy clay slid by as my little transparent vessel descended into the earth. Now I saw boulders the size of cars that had been deposited by glaciers ten thousand years ago. Scattered here and there in the subterranean ground-scape were mammoth tusks and the formidable skulls of other primeval

The Raffle

beasts that died long before humans had speech.

It was only as the elevator began to slow to a stop that I punched the 'lobby' button. Of course, it was too late. Here I was: my final destination. The doors slid back to reveal a gloomy underworld. Fossilized plants and tree trunks made from coal soared toward a basalt 'sky.' As if impelled by some force I could not identify I stepped out into cold, moist air.

A moment later the elevator vanished into the gloom above my head. There was nothing else I could do but move forward in the hope I could find some other escape route to the surface. Then I paused, because looming through the forest made of coal was a shadowy figure. A second later it emerged from the gloom; a hideous creature that bristled silver hair and possessing a single gelatinous eye.

Before I could react it opened its drooling lips and hissed, "My name is ... was John Aitken. Once I was a man like you. Get away from here while you can." Then the figure slunk away into the shadows again.

That did it. I started running. The glossy black tree trunks were uncompromisingly hard. I cannoned against them more than once as I charged through that cold, dead forest of coal and fossil ferns.

A moment later I staggered into an opening in the brittle jungle. That was when I experienced a surge of relief because standing there were dozens of my fellow convention goers. These were the mystery prize winners that had preceded me into the glass elevator. Strangely, they paid no attention to me blundering into their midst. No, their eyes were fixed on dozens of creatures sitting at tables carved from solid blocks of coal. I saw satyrs sharing tables with beasts that were part man, part hog with little piggy eyes and curling tusks. Squatting amongst them were giants clad in rust-covered armor. And sitting around and under more glossy black tables were an assortment of demons, elves, goblins, spider-faced women, ghouls, fishoid squid-backed men, and chimera that chattered, grimaced, hissed and rolled their baleful eyes.

I was ready to run like hell only I saw the bars of a cage had formed around us luckless conventioneers.

On top of a jet-black boulder a wizard reached into his pointed

213

hat made from human skin. He stirred his clawed hand round and around as he announced: "The offerings have arrived. So let the ritual begin!" He pulled out a slip of parchment. "Number fifty-eight. Who has the raffle ticket number fifty-eight?"

SCARROWFELL
Robert Holdstock

Robert Holdstock was born in Kent in 1948 (from East of the Medway). His childhood was spent between the dense woods of the Kentish hearthlands and the bleak expanse of the Romney Marsh, near which he was born. After nine years of being a student, specialising in medical Zoology, Robert became a full-time writer in 1975. His early novels include *Eye Among the Blind*, *Where Times Winds Blow* and *Necromancer*. His short stories are collected in *In the Valley of the Statues* and *The Bone Forest*. He has written a variety of Celtic, Nordic, Gothic and Pictish fantasy, a series of occult thrillers: *Night Hunter*, and the novel of John Boorman's film *The Emerald Forest*. He has won many awards but his most famous work is *Mythago Wood*, for which he won the World Fantasy Award in 1985. This novel was described by Michael Moorcock as 'the outstanding fantasy book of the 80s', and the following novel in the cycle, *Lavondyss* won the British Science Fiction Association's award. He now lives in North London, collects masks, and escapes to the forests and the wilds whenever possible. Robert was a Guest of Honour at 2004's FantasyCon in Walsall. His website address is http://robertholdstock.com

Robert has this to say: "I was more of a BSFA man than a BFS man

– sf having been an adolescent passion – but I always enjoyed the BFS meetings and conventions I went to (the Docklands convention especially.) I never made a distinction between horror, myth and science fiction, and mixed and matched in my work according to whim. Heavily influenced, of course, by the TV series' *Quatermass* (a fact never denied). What appealed about the British Fantasy Society? I always felt I was among storytellers, interested in storytelling and the 'dark'. The sf animal in many writers of my generation hungered for 'future time'. But the dual appetite could only be sustained with a dish or two of 'primal urge'.

"I wrote 'Scarrowfell' for a Halloween reading evening at Chris Priest's. The words of the song are from Morris On, a spin-off group from The Albion Dance Band, and I had the tape of the eerie music to play in and out of the reading. A performance piece. It amused. But then, Morris Dancing usually does. The story got me into small trouble when first published in the US, because of its pagan version of the Lord's Prayer. A few years later, when reprinted, nobody seemed bothered. Two years ago it had its first French translation, and won a prize. Good old French. Tastes and moods change so fast. But never abandon a story because it seems to belong to another time. Somewhere in the world its time will be coming.

"And it's a pleasure indeed to contribute to this celebration book for the BFS."

1

In the darkness, in the world of nightmares, she sang a little song. In her small room, behind the drawn curtains, her voice was tiny, frightened, murmuring in her sleep:

> *Oh dear mother what a fool I've been...*
> *Three young fellows...came courting me...*
> *Two were blind...the other couldn't see...*
> *Oh dear mother what a fool I've been...*

Tuneless, timeless, endlessly repeated through the night, soon the nightmare grew worse and she tossed below the bedclothes, and called out for her mother, louder and louder, *Mother! Mother!* until she sat up, gasping for breath and screaming.

"Hush, child. I'm here. I'm beside you. Quiet now. Go back to sleep."

"I'm frightened, I'm frightened. I had a terrible dream…"

Her mother hugged her, sitting on the bed, rocking back and forward, wiping the sweat and the fear from her face. "Hush…hush, now. It was just a dream…"

"The blind man," she whispered, and shook as she thought of it so that her mother's grip grew firmer, more reassuring. "The blind man. He's coming again…"

"Just a dream, child. There's nothing to be frightened of. Close your eyes and go back to sleep, now. Sleep, child…sleep. There. That's better."

Still she sang, her voice very small, very faint as she drifted into sleep again. *"Three young fellows…came courting me…one was blind…one was grim…one had creatures following him…"*

"Hush, child…"

Waking with a scream: "Don't let him take me!"

2

None of the children in the village really knew one festival day from another. They were *told* what to wear, and *told* what to do, and *told* what to eat, and when the formalities were over they would rush away to their secret camp, in the shadow of the old church.

Lord's Eve was different, however. Lord's Eve was the best of the festivals. Even if you didn't know that a particular day would be Lord's Eve day, the signs of it were in the village.

Ginny knew the signs by heart. Mr. Box, at the Red Hart, would spend a day cursing as he tried to erect a tarpaulin in the beer garden of his public house. Here, the ox would be slaughtered and roasted, and the dancers would rest. At the other end of the village, Mr.

Ellis, who ran the Bush and Briar, would put empty firkins outside his premises for use as seats. The village always filled with strangers during the dancing festivals, and those strangers drank a lot of beer.

The church was made ready too. Mr. and Mrs. Morton, usually never to be seen out of their Sunday best, would dress in overalls and invade the cold church with brooms, brushes and buckets. Mr. Ashcroft, the priest, would garner late summer flowers, and mow and trim the graveyard. This was a dangerous time for the children, since he would come perilously close to their camp, which lay just beyond the iron gate that led from the churchyard. Here, between the church and the earth walls of the old Saxon fort – in whose ring the village had been built – was a tree-filled ditch, and the children's camp had been made there. The small clearing was close to the path which led from the church, through the earth wall and out onto the farmland beyond.

There were other signs of the coming festival day, however, signs from outside the small community. First, the village always seemed to be in shadow. Yet distantly, beyond the cloud cover, the land seemed to glow with eerie light. Ginny would stand on the high wall by the church, looking through the crowded trees that covered the ring of earthworks, staring to where the late summer sun was setting its fire on Whitley Nook and Middleburn. Movement on the high valley walls above these villages was just the movement of clouds, and the fields seemed to flow with brightness.

The wind always blew from Whitley Nook toward Ginny's own village, Scarrowfell. And on that wind, the day before the festival of Lord's Eve, you could always hear the music of the dancers as they wended their way along the riverside, through and around the underwood, stopping at each village to collect more dancers, more musicians (more hangovers) ready for the final triumph at Scarrowfell itself.

The music drifted in and out of hearing, a hint of a violin, the distant clatter of sticks, the faint jingle of the small bells with which the dancers decked out their clothes. When the wind gusted, whole phrases of the jaunty music could be heard, a rhythmic sound, with the voices of the dancers clearly audible as they sang the words of the folk songs.

Ginny, precariously balanced on the top of the wall, would jig with those brief rhythms, hair blowing in the wind, one hand holding on to the dry bark of an ash branch.

The dancers were coming; all the Oozers and the Pikers and the Thackers, coming to join the village's Scarrowmen; and it was therefore the day of Lord's Eve: the birds would flock and wheel in the skies, and flee along the valley too. And sure enough, as she looked up into the dark sky over Scarrowfell, the birds were there, thousands of them, making streaming, spiral patterns in the gloom. Their calling was inaudible. But after a while they streaked north, away from the bells, away from the sticks, away from the calling of the Oozers.

Kevin Symonds came racing around the gray-walled church, glanced up and saw Ginny and made frantic beckoning motions. "Gargoyle!" he hissed, and Ginny almost shouted as she lost her balance before jumping down from the wall. "Gargoyle" was their name for Mr. Ashcroft, the priest. A second after they had squeezed beyond the iron gate and into the cover of the scrub the old man appeared. But he was busy placing rillygills – knots of flowers and wheat stalks – on each gravestone and didn't notice the panting children just beyond the cleared ground, where the thorn and ash thicket was so dense.

Ginny led the way into the clear space among the trees in the ditch. She stepped up the shallow earth slope to peer away into the field beyond, and the circle of tall elms that grew at its center. A scruffy brown mare – probably one of Mr. Box's drays – was kicking and stamping across the field, a white foal stumbling behind it. She was so intent on watching the foal that she didn't notice Mr. Box himself, emerging from the ring of trees. He was dressed in his filthy blue apron but walked briskly across the field toward the church, his gaze fixed on the ground. Every few paces he stopped and fiddled with something on the grass. He never looked up, walked through the gap in the earth-works – the old gateway – and passed, by doing so, within arm's reach of where Ginny and Kevin breathlessly crouched. He walked straight ahead, stopped at the iron gate, inspected it, then moved off around the perimeter of the church, out of sight and out of mind.

"They've got the ox on the spit already," Kevin said, his eyes bright, his lips wet with anticipation. "It's the biggest ever. There's going to be at least two slices each."

"Yuck!" said Ginny, feeling sick at the thought of the gray, greasy meat.

"And they've started the bonfire. You've got to come and see it. It's going to be huge! My mother said it's going to be the biggest yet."

"I usually scrub potatoes for fire-baking," Ginny said. "But I haven't been asked this year."

"Sounds as if you've been lucky," Kevin said. "It's going to be a really big day. The biggest ever. It's *very* special."

Ginny whispered, "My mother's been behaving strangely. And I've had a nightmare…"

Kevin watched her, but when no further information or explanation seemed to be forthcoming he said, "*My* mother says this is the most special Lord's Eve of them all. An old man's coming back to the village."

"What old man?"

"His name's Cyric, or something. He left a long time ago, but he's coming back and everybody's very excited. They've been trying to get him to come back for ages, but he's only just agreed. That's what Mum says, anyway."

"What's so special about him?"

Kevin wasn't sure. "She said he's a war hero, or something."

"Ugh!" Ginny wrinkled her nose in distaste. "He's probably going to be all scarred."

"Or blind!" Kevin agreed, and Ginny's face turned white.

A third child wriggled through the iron gate and skidded into the depression between the earth walls, dabbing at his face where he had scratched himself on a thorn.

"The tower!" Mick Ferguson whispered excitedly, ignoring his graze. "While old Gargoyle is busy placing the rillygills."

They moved cautiously back to the churchyard, then crawled toward the porch on their bellies, screened from the priest by the high earth mounds over each grave. Ducking behind the memorial stones – but not touching them – they at last found sanctuary in the freshly polished, gloomy interior. Despite the cloud-cover, light was bright from the stained-glass windows. The altar, with its flowers, looked somehow different from normal. The Mortons were cleaning the font, over in the side chapel; a bucket of well-water stood by ready to fill the bowl. They were talking as they worked and didn't hear the furtive movement of the three children.

Kevin led the way up the spiralling, footworn steps and out onto the cone-shaped roof of the church's tower. They averted their eyes from the grotesque stone figure that guarded the doorway, although Kevin reached out and touched its muzzle as he always did.

"For luck," he said. "My mother says the stone likes affection as much as the rest of us. If it doesn't get attention it'll prowl the village at night and choose someone to kill."

"Shut *up*," Ginny said emphatically, watching the monster from the corner of her eye.

Michael laughed. "Don't be such a scaredy-hare," he said and reached out to jingle the small bell that hung around her neck. Her ghost bell.

"It's a small bell and that's a big stone demon," Ginny pointed out nervously. Why was she so apprehensive this time, she wondered? She had often been up here and had never doubted that the stone creature, like all demons, could not attack the faithful, and that bells, books and candles were protection enough from the devil's minions.

The nightmare had upset her. She remembered Mary Whitelock's nightmare a few years before – almost the same dream, confided in the gang as they had feasted on stolen pie in their camp. She had not really liked Mary. All the same, when she had suddenly disappeared, after the festival, Ginny had felt very confused...

No! Put the thought from your mind, she told herself sternly. And brazenly she turned and stared at the medieval monstrosity that sat watching the door to the church below. And she laughed, because it was only frightening when you *imagined* how awful it was. In fact, it looked faintly ludicrous, with its gaping V-shaped mouth and lolling tongue, and its pointed ears, and skull cheeks, and its one great staring eye…and one gouged socket…

Below them, the village was a bustle of activity. In the small square in front of the church the bonfire was rising to truly monumental heights. Other children were helping to heap the faggots and broken furniture onto the pile. A large stake in its center was being used to hold the bulk of the wood in place.

Away from where this fire would blaze, a large area was being roped off for the dancing. The gate from the church had already been decked with wild roses and lilies. The Gargoyle himself always led the congregation from the Lord's Eve service out to the festivities in the village. Ginny giggled at the remembered sight of him, dark cassock held up to his knees, white bony legs kicking and hopping along with the Oozers and the local Scarrowmen, a single bell on each ankle making him look as silly as she always thought he was.

At the far end of the village, the road from Whitley Nook cut through the south wall of the old earth fort and snaked between the cluster of tiled cottages where Ginny herself lived. Here, two small fires had been set alight, one on each side of the old track. The smoke was shattered by the wind from the valley. On the church tower the three children enjoyed the smell of the burning wood.

And as they listened they heard the music of the dancers, even now winding their way between Middleburn and Whitley Nook.

They would be here tomorrow. Sunlight picked out the white of their costumes, miles distant; and the flash of swords flung high in the air.

The Oozers were coming. The Thackers were coming. The wild dance was coming.

<u>3</u>

She awoke with a shock, screaming out, then becoming instantly silent as she stared at the empty room and the bright daylight creeping in above the heavy curtains of her room.

What time was it? Her head was full of music, the jangle of bells, the beating of the skin drums, the clash and thud of the wooden hobby poles. But now, outside, all was silent.

She swung her legs from the bed, then began to shiver as unpleasant echoes of that haunting song, the nightmare song, came back to her.

She found that she could not resist muttering the words that stalked her sleeping hours. It was as if she had to repeat the sinister refrain before her body would allow her to move again, to become a child again...

"Oh dear mother...three young men...two were blind...the third couldn't see...oh mother, oh mother...grim-eyed courtiers...blind men dancing...creatures followed him, creatures dancing..."

The church bell rang out, a low repeated toll, five strikes and then a sixth strike, a moment delayed from the rest.

Five strikes for the Lord, and one for the fire! It couldn't be that time. It couldn't! Why hadn't mother come in to wake her?

Ginny ran to the curtains and pulled them back, staring out into the deserted street, crawling up onto the window ledge so that she could lean through the top window and stare up toward the square.

It was full of motionless figures. And distantly she could hear the chanting of the congregation. The Lord's Eve service had already started. Started! The procession had already passed the house, and she had been aware of it only in her half sleep!

She screeched with indignation, fleeing from her bedroom into the small sitting room. By the clock on the mantelpiece she learned that it was after midday. She had slept...she had slept fifteen hours!

She grabbed her clothes, pulled them on, not bothering with her hair but making a token effort to polish her shoes. It was Lord's Eve. She *had* to be smart today. She couldn't find her bell necklace. She had on a flowered dress and red shoes. She pulled a pink woollen cardigan over her shoulders, grabbed at her frilly hat, stared at it, then tossed it behind the hat rack...and fled from the house.

She ran up the road to the church square, following the path that, earlier, the column of dancers must have taken. She felt tears in her eyes, tears of dismay, and anger, and irritation. Every year she watched the procession from her garden. *Every year!* Why hadn't mother *woken* her?

She loved the procession, the ranks of dancers in their white coats and black hats, the ribbons, the flowers, the bells tied to ankle, knee and elbow, the men on the hobby horses, the fools with their pigs' bladders on sticks, the women in their swirling skirts, the Thackers, the Pikermen, the Oozers, the black-faced Scarrowmen...all of them came through the smoldering fires at the south gate, each turning and making the sign of peace before jigging and hopping on along the road, keeping time to the beat of the drum, the melancholy whine of the violin, the sad chords of the accordion, the trill of the whistles.

And she had missed it! She had slept! She had remained in the world of nightmares, where the shadowy blind pursued her...

As she ran she *screamed* her frustration!

She stopped at the edge of the square, catching her breath, looking for Kevin, or Mick, or any others of the small gang that had their camp in the earthen walls of the old fort. She couldn't see them. She cast her gaze over the ranks of silent dancers. They were spread out across the square, lines of men and women facing the lych-gate and the open door of the church. They stood in absolute silence. They hardy seemed to breathe. Sometimes, as she brushed past one of them, working her way toward the church where Gargoyle's voice was an irritating drone in the distance, sometimes a tambourine would rattle, or an accordion would sigh a weary note. The man holding it would smile and glance at her, but she knew better than to disturb the Scarrowmen when the voice was speaking from the church.

She passed under the rose and lily gate, ducked her head and made the sign of peace, then scampered into the porch and edged toward the gloomy, crowded interior.

The priest was at the end of his sermon, the usual boring sermon for the feast day.

"We have made a pledge," Mr Ashcroft was intoning. "A pledge of belief in a life after death, a pledge of belief in a God which is greater than humankind itself..."

She could see Kevin, standing and fidgeting between his parents, four pews forward in the church. Of Michael there was no sign. And where was mother? At the front, almost certainly...

"We believe in the resurrection of the dead, and in a time of atonement. We have made a pledge with those who have died before us, a pledge that we will be reunited with them in the greater Glory of our Lord."

"*Kevin!*" Ginny hissed. Kevin fidgeted. The priest droned on.

"We have pledged all of this, and we believe all of this. Our time in the physical realm is a time of trial, a time of testing, a testing of our honor and our belief, a belief that those who have gone are not gone at all, but merely waiting to be rejoined with us..."

"*Kevin!*" she called again. "*Kevin!*"

Her voice carried too loudly. Kevin glanced around and went white. His mother glanced around too, then jerked his attention back to the service, using a lock of his curly hair as her means. His cry was audible to the Gargoyle himself, who hesitated before concluding.

"This is the brightness behind the feast of the Lord's Eve. Think not of the Death, but of the Life our Lord will bring us."

Where was her mother?

Before she could think further someone's hand tugged at her shoulder, pulling her back toward the porch of the church. She protested and glanced up, and the solemn face of Mr. Box stared down at her. "Go outside, Ginny," he said. "Go outside, now."

Inside, the congregation had begun to recite the Lord's Prayer.

He pushed her toward the rose gate, beyond which the Oozers and Scarrowmen waited for the service to end. She walked forlornly toward them, and as she passed the man who stood closest to her she struck at his tambourine. The tambours jangled loudly in the still, summer square.

The man didn't move. She stood and stared defiantly at him, then struck his tambourine again.

"Why don't you *dance*?" she shrieked at him. When he ignored her, she shouted again. "Why don't you make *music?* Make *music!* Dance in the square! Dance!" Her voice was a shrill cry.

4

There was no twilight. Late afternoon became dark night in a few minutes and a torch was put to the fire, which flared dramatically and silenced all activity. Glowing embers streamed into a starless sky and the village square became choking with the sweet smell of burning wood. The last smells of the roasted ox were banished and in the grounds of the Red Lion the skeleton of the beast was hacked apart. A few pence each for the bones with their meaty fragments. In front of the Bush and Briar Mr. Ellis swept up a hundredweight of broken glass. Mick Ferguson led a gang of children, chasing an empty barrel down the street, toward the south gate where the fires still smoldered.

For a while the dancing had ceased. People thronged about the fire. Voices were raised in the public houses as dancers and tourists alike struggled to get in fresh orders for ale. A sort of controlled chaos ruled the day, and in the center of it: the fire, its light picking out stark details on the gray church and the muddy green in the square. Beyond the sheer rise of the church tower, all was darkness, although men in white shirts and black hats walked through the lych-gate and rounded the church, talking quietly, dispersing as they reemerged into the square. Here, they again picked up sticks, or tambourines, or other instruments of music and mock war.

Ginny wandered among them.

She could not find her mother.

And she knew that something was wrong, very wrong indeed.

It came as scant reassurance when a bearded youth called to the Morrismen again, and twelve sturdy men, all of them strangers to Scarrowfell, jangled their way from the Bush and Briar to the dancing square. There was laughter, tomfoolery with the cudgels they carried, and the whining practice notes of the accordion. Then they filed into a formation, jiggled and rang their legs, laughed once more and began to hop to the rhythm of a dance called the *Cuckoo's Nest*. A man in a baggy, flowery dress and with a big frilly bonnet on his head sang the rude words. The singer was a source of great amusement since he sported a bushy, ginger beard.

He wore an apron over the frock and every so often lifted the pinny to expose a long red balloon strapped between his legs. It had eyes and eyelashes painted on its tip. The audience roared each time he did this.

As Ginny moved through the fair toward the new focus of activity, Mick Ferguson approached her, grinned, and went into his Hunchback of Notre Dame routine, stooping forward, limping in an exaggerated fashion and crying, "The bells. The bells. The jingling bells..."

"Mick..." Ginny began, but he had already flashed her a nervous grin and bolted off into the confusing movement of the crowds, running toward the fire and finally disappearing into the gloom beyond.

Ginny watched him go. Mick, she thought... Mick...why? What was going on?

She walked toward the dancers and the bearded singer and Kevin turned around nervously and nodded to her. The man sang:

"Some like a girl who is pretty in the face
And some like a girl who is slender in the waist..."

"I missed the procession, Ginny said. "I wasn't woken up."

Kevin stared at her, looking unhappy. He said, "My mother told me not to talk to you..."

She waited, but Kevin had decided that discretion was the better part of cowardice.

"Why not?" she asked, disturbed by the statement.

"You're being denied," the boy murmured.

Ginny was shocked. "Why am I being denied? Why me?"

Kevin shrugged. Then a strange look came into his eyes, a horrible look, a man's look, arrogant, sneering.

The man in the hideous dress sang:

"But give me a girl who will wriggle and will twist
Each time I slap my hand upon her cuckoo's nest..."

Kevin backed away from Ginny, making "cuckoo" sounds.

"It's a *rude* song," Ginny said.

Kevin taunted, "*You're* a cuckoo. *You're* a cuckoo..."

"I don't know what it means," Ginny said, bewildered.

"Cuckoo, cuckoo, cuckoo," Kevin mocked, then jabbed her in

the groin. He cackled horribly then raced away toward the blazing bonfire. Ginny had tears in her eyes, but her anger was so intense that the tears dried. She glared at the singer, still not completely aware of what was going on except that she knew the song was rude because of the guffaws of the adult men in the watching circle. After a moment she slipped away toward the church.

She stood within the lych-gate watching the flickering of the fire, the highlit faces of the crowds, the restless movement, the jigging and hopping...hearing the laughter, and the music, and the distant wind that was fanning the fire and making the flames bend violently and dangerously toward the south. And she wondered where, in all this chaos, her mother might have been.

Mother had been so supportive to her, so gentle, so kind. During the nights when the nightmare had been a terrible presence in the house by the old road, where Ginny had lived since her real parents had died in the fire, during those terrible nights the Mother had been so comforting. Ginny had come to think of her as her own mother, and all grief, all sadness had faded fast.

Where *was* the mother? Where *was* she?

She saw Mr. Box, walking slowly through the crowd, a baked potato in one hand and a glass of beer in the other. She ran to him and tugged at his jacket. He nearly choked on his potato and glanced around urgently, but soon her voice reached him and, although he frowned, he stooped down toward her. He threw the remnants of his potato away and placed his glass upon the ground.

"Hello Ginny..." He sounded anxious.

"Mr. Box. Have you seen mother?"

Again he looked uncomfortable. His kindly face was a mask of worry. His mustache twitched. "You see...she's getting the reception ready."

"What reception?" Ginny asked.

"Why, for Cyric, of course. The war hero. The man who's coming back to us. He's finally agreed to return to the village. He was supposed to have come three years ago, but he couldn't make it."

"I don't care about him," she said. "Where's mother?"

Mr. Box placed a comforting hand on her shoulder and shook

his head. "Can't you just play, child? It's what you're supposed to do. I'm just a pub landlord. I'm not part of the Organizers. You shouldn't even...you shouldn't even be *talking* to me."

"I'm being denied," she whispered.

"Yes," he said sadly.

"Where's mother?" Ginny demanded.

"An important man is coming back to the village," Mr. Box said. "A great hero. It's a great honor for us...and..." he hesitated before adding, in a quiet voice, "And what he's bringing with him is going to make this village more secure..."

"What *is* he bringing?" Ginny asked.

"A certain knowledge," Mr. Box said, then shrugged. "It's all I know. Like all the villages around here, we've had to fight to keep out the invader, and it's a hard fight. We've all been waiting a long time for this night, Ginny. A very long time. We made a pledge to this man. A long time ago, when he fought to save the village. Tonight we're honoring that pledge. All of us have a part to play..."

Ginny frowned. "Me too?" she asked, and was astonished to see large tears roll down each of Mr. Box's cheeks.

"Of course you too, Ginny," he whispered, and seemed to choke on the words. "I'm surprised that you don't know. I always thought the children knew. But the way these things work...the rules..." He shook his head again. "I'm not privileged to know."

"But why is everybody being so horrible to me?" Ginny asked.

"Who's everybody?"

"Mick," she said. "And Kevin. He called me a cuckoo..."

Mr. Box smiled. "They're just teasing you. They've been told something of what will happen this evening and they're jealous."

He straightened up and took a deep breath. Ginny watched him, his words sinking in slowly. She said, "Do you mean what will happen to *me* this evening?"

He nodded. "You've been *chosen*," he whispered to her. "When your parents were killed, the Mother was sent to you to prepare you. Your role tonight is a very special one. Ginny, that's all I know. Now go and play, child. Please..."

He looked suddenly away from her, toward the dancers. Ginny

followed his gaze. Five men, two of whom she recognised, were watching them. One of them shook his head slightly and Mr. Box's touch on Ginny's shoulder went away. A woman walked toward them, her dress covered with real flowers, her face like stone. Mr. Box pushed Ginny away roughly. As she scampered for safety she could hear the sound of the woman's blows to Mr. Box's cheek.

5

The fire burned. Long after it should have been a glowing pile of embers, it was still burning. Long after they should have been exhausted, the Scarrowmen danced. The night air was chill, heavy with smoke, bright with drifting sparks. It echoed to the jingle of bells and the clatter of cudgels. Voices drifted on the wind; there was laughter; and around and around the Morrismen danced.

Soon they had formed into a great circle, stretched around the fire and jigging fast and furious to the strident, endless rhythm of drums and violin. All the village danced, and the strangers too, men and women in anoraks and sweaters, and children in woolly hats, and teenagers in jeans and leather jackets, all of them mixed up with the white-and-black-clothed Oozers, Pikers, Thackers and the rest.

Around the burning fire, stumbling and tottering, shrieking with mirth as a whole segment of the ring tumbled in the mud. Around and around.

The bells, the hammering of sticks, the whine of the violin, the Jack Tar sound of the accordion.

And at ten o'clock the whole wild dance stopped.

Silence.

The men reached down and took the bells from their legs, cast them into the fire. The cudgels, too, were thrown onto the flames. The violins were shattered on the ground, the fragments tossed into the conflagration.

The accordions wept music as they were slung onto the pyre. Flowers out of hair. Bonnets from heads. Rose and lily were stripped off the lych-gate. The air filled suddenly with a sharp, aromatic scent...of herbs, woodland herbs.

In the silence Ginny walked toward the church, darted through the gate into the darkness of the graveyard...Around between the long mounds to the iron gate...

Kevin was there. He ran toward her, his eyes wide, wild. "He's coming!" he hissed, breathlessly.

"What's going on?" she whispered.

"Where are you going?" he said.

"To the camp. I'm frightened. They've stopped dancing. They're burning their instruments. This happened three years ago when Mary...when...you know..."

"Why are you so frightened?" Kevin asked. His eyes were bright from the distant glow of the bonfire. "What are you running from, Ginny? Tell me. Tell me. We're friends..."

"Something is wrong," she sobbed. She found herself clutching at the boy's arms. "Everybody is being so horrible to me. *You* were horrible to me. What have I done? What have I done?"

He shook his head. The flames made his dark eyes gleam. She had her back to the square. Suddenly he looked beyond her. Then he smiled. He looked at her.

"Goodbye, Ginny," he whispered.

She turned. Kevin darted past her and into the great mob of masked men who stood around her. They had come upon her so quietly that she had not heard a thing. Their faces were like black pigs. Eyes gleamed, mouths grinned. They wore white and black...the Scarrows.

Unexpectedly, Kevin began to whine. Ginny thought he was being punished for being out of bounds. She listened, and then for one second...just one second...all was stillness, all was silence, anticipation. Then she reacted as any sensible child would react in the situation.

She opened her mouth and screamed. The sound had barely echoed in the night air when a hand clamped firmly across her face, a great hand, strong, stifling her cry. She struggled and pulled away,

231

turned and kicked until she realized it was the Mother that she fought against. She was no longer wearing her rowan beads, or her iron charm. She seemed naked without them. Her dress was green and she held Ginny firmly still. "Hold quiet, child. Your time is soon."

The iron gate was open. Ginny peered through it, into the darkness, through the grassy walls of the old fort and toward the circle of great elms.

There was a light there, and the light was coming closer. And ahead of that light there was a wind, a breeze, ice cold, tinged with a smell that was part sweat, part rot, and unpleasant in the extreme. She grimaced and tried to back away, but the Mother's hands held her fast. She glanced over her shoulder, toward the square, and felt her body tremble as the Scarrows stared beyond her, into the void of night.

Two of the Scarrows held tall, hazel poles, each wrapped around with strands of ivy and mistletoe. They stepped forward and held the poles to form a gateway between them. Ginny watched all of this and shivered. And she felt sick when she saw Kevin held by others of the Scarrows. The boy was terrified. He seemed to be pleading with Ginny, but what could she do? His own mother stood close to him, weeping silently.

The wind gusted suddenly and the first of the shadows passed over so quickly that she was hardly aware of its transit. It appeared out of nowhere, part darkness, part chill, a tall shape that didn't so much walk as *flow* through the iron gate. Looking at that shadow was like looking into a depthless world of dark; it shimmered, it hazed, it flickered, it moved, an uncertain balance between that world and the real world. Only as it passed between the hazel poles held by the Scarrows, and then into the world beyond, did it take on a form that could be called…ghostly.

Distantly the priest's voice intoned a greeting. Ginny heard him say, "Welcome back to *Scarugfell.* Our pledge is fulfilled. Your life begins again."

A second shadow followed the first, this one smaller, and with its darkness and its chill came the sound of keening, like a child's crying. It was distant, though, and uncertain. As Ginny watched, it took its shadowy form beyond the Scarrows and into the village.

As each of them had passed over, so the Scarrowmen closed ranks again, but distantly, close to the fire in the square, an unearthly howling, a nightmare wind, seemed to greet each new arrival. What happened to the spirits then, Ginny couldn't tell, or care.

Her mother's hand touched her face, then her shoulder, forced her around again to watch the iron gate. The Mother whispered, "Those two were his kin. They too died for our village a long time ago. But Cyric is coming now..."

The shadow that moved beyond the gate was like nothing Ginny could ever have imagined. She couldn't tell whether it was animal or man. It was immense. It swayed as it moved, and it seemed to approach through the darkness in a ponderous, dragging way. Its outlines were blurred, shadow against darkness, void against the glimmering light among the trees. It seemed to have branches and tendrils reaching from its head. It made a sound that was like the rumble of water in a hidden well.

It seemed to fill her vision. It occupied all of space. Its breath stank. Its single eye gleamed with firelight.

One was blind...one was grim...

It seemed to be laughing at her as it peered down from beyond the trees and the earth walls that surrounded the church.

It pushed something forward, a shadow, a man, nudged it through the iron gate. Ginny wanted to scream as she caught glimpses, within that shadow, of the dislocated jaw, the empty sockets, the crawling flesh. The ragged thing limped toward her, hands raised, bony fingers stretched out, skull face open and inviting...inviting the kiss that Ginny knew, now, would end her life.

"No!" she shouted, and struggled frantically in the Mother's grip. The Mother seemed angry. "Even now it mocks us!" she said, then shouted, Give the Life for the Death. Give it now!"

Behind Ginny, Kevin suddenly screamed. Then he was running toward the iron gate, sobbing and shouting, drawn by invisible hands.

"Don't let him take me! Don't let him take me!" he cried.

He passed the hideous figure and entered the world beyond the gate. He was snatched into the air, blown into darkness like a leaf whipped by a storm wind. He had vanished in an instant.

The great shadow turned away into the night and began to seep back toward the circle of elms. The Mother's hands on Ginny's shoulders pushed her forward, toward the ghastly embrace.

The shadow corpse stopped moving. Its arms dropped. The gaping eyes watched nothing and nowhere. A sound issued from its bones. "Is she the one? Is she my kin?"

Mother's voice answered loudly that she was indeed the one. She was indeed Cyric's kin.

The shadow seemed to turn its head to watch Ginny. It looked down at her, then reached up and pulled the tatters of a hood about its head. The hood hid the features. The whole creature seemed to melt, to descend, to shrink. Ginny heard the Mother say, "Fifteen hundred years in the dark. Your life saved our village. Our pledge to bring you back is honored. Welcome, Cyric."

Something wriggled below the tatters of the hood. The Mother said, "Go forward, child. Take the hare. *Take him!*"

Ginny hesitated. She glanced around. The Scarrows seemed to be smiling behind their masks. Two other children, both girls, stood there. Each was holding a struggling hare. Her Mother made frantic motions to her. "Come on, Ginny. The fear is ended, now. The day of denial is over. Only you can touch the hare. You're the kin. Cyric has chosen you. Take it quickly. Bring him over. Bring him back."

Ginny stumbled forward, reached below the stinking rags and found the terrified animal. As she raised the brown hare to her breast she felt the flow of the past, the voice, the wisdom, the spirit of the man who had passed back over, the promise to him kept, fifteen hundred years after he had lain down his life for the safety of *Scarugfell*, also known as the *Place of the Mother*.

Cyric was home. The great hunter was home. Ginny had him now, and *he* had her, and she would become great and wise, and Cyric would speak the wisdom of the Dark through her lips. The hare would die in time, but Cyric and Ginny would share a human life until the human body itself passed away.

And Ginny felt a great glow of joy as the images of that ancient land, its forts, its hills, its tracks, its forest shrines, flooded into her mind. She heard the hounds, the horses, the larks, she felt the cold wind, smelled the great woods.

Scarrowfell

Yes. Yes. She had been born for this. Her parents had been sacrificed to free her and the Mother had kept her ready for the moment. The nightmare had been Cyric making contact as the Father had brought him to the edge of the dark world.

The Father! The Father had watched over her, as all in the village had often said he would. It had been the Father she had seen, a rare glimpse of the Lord who always brought the returning Dead to the place of the Lord's Eve.

Cyric had come a long, long way home. It had taken time to make the Lord release him and allow Cyric's knowledge of the dark world back to the village, to help Scarrowfell, and the villages like it keep the eyes and minds of the invader muddled and confused. And then Cyric, too, had waited...until Ginny was of age. His kin. His chosen vehicle.

Ginny, his new protector, cradled the animal. The hare twitched in her grasp. Its eyes were full of rejoicing.

She felt a moment's sadness then, for poor, betrayed Kevin, but it passed. And as she left the place of the gate she joined willingly in reciting the Lord's prayer, her voice high, enthusiastic among the rumble of the crowd.

Our Father, who art in the Forest,
Horned One is Thy name.
Thy Kingdom is the Wood, Thy Will is the Blood
In the Glade, as it is in the Village.
Give us this day our Kiss of Earth
And forgive us our Malefactions.
Destroy those who Malefact against us
And lead us to the Otherworld.
For Thine is the Kingdom of the Shadow, Thine is the
Power and the Glory. Thou art the Stag which ruts
with us, and we are the Earth beneath thy feet.
Drocha Nemeton.

BUILDING SIXTEEN
Brian Aldiss

The legendary science fiction writer Brian Aldiss has been in print since the mid-1950s, when a number of pieces he wrote for a booksellers trade journal came to the attention of British publishers Faber and Faber, and he won a competition run by *The Observer* to set a short story in the year 2500. His first SF book *Space, Time and Nathaniel* – a collection of stories – was published in 1957, with his first novel *Non-Stop* following in 1958. He was voted the 'Most Promising New Author' at the World Science Fiction Convention that same year, and elected President of the British Science Fiction Association in 1960. In the intervening years he has given us such books as *Hothouse*, *The Airs of Earth*, *Earthworks*, *The Eighty-Minute Hour*, *Brothers of the Head*, *Moreau's Other Island*, *Forgotten Life* and *Remembrance Day*. His 1973 novel *Frankenstein Unbound* was turned into a film by Roger Corman in 1990, and his short story *Supertoys Last All Summer Long* formed the basis of the 2001 Kubrick/Spielberg film *AI Artificial Intelligence*. Brian Aldiss has won most of the prizes and awards in the SF field and also gained an O.B.E. Now into his eighties he shows no sign whatsoever of slowing down.

Says Brian of the following original piece: "My own life is happy enough – happier maybe than I had any right to expect. 'Building

Building Sixteen

Sixteen' is about misery, the misery that springs from tyranny. "Tyranny is never banished from the world. Do we fend it off by thinking and talking about it? Well, we certainly don't fend it off by pretending it doesn't exist.

"Or maybe I am making excuses. Maybe I was drawn to fantasy because it allows you to write nakedly about forms of wretchedness, and the ingenuity that forms of wretchedness can take."

That whole building disappearing! I've never got over the horror of it. It changed my life.

We lived rather cramped, Pazin and I. One room and a landing. We let out the landing to a little aparatchik called Gaspod Hussein. Hussein lived on the landing quietly enough. He played music into his ears. He was only young, mid-twenties and thin as a post.

I felt sorry for Hussein and called him in now and again to share our soup of an evening.

That's how I found out he worked close to our president, Gramman, General Avo Gramman. I happened to find out that Hussein worked in the administrative building next to the Palace. Hussein would not tell you what he did. He was ashamed or cautious or both.

One evening, he was in with us and the radio was going. The announcer said that by General Gramman's orders five thousand extra troops were to be sent to fight in the war against Skochne, on the borders of our country. I didn't care for that news, not one bit. Nor did Pazin. Pazin said the boys were being sacrificed.

"We have to protect ourselves," said Hussein.

"Protect rubbish! Skochnens never attacked us," said Pazin.

Hussein went off in a bit of a sulk to get a drink down the street. Not like him.

237

And it was not like him to leave his brief case on the floor, leaning against the table leg.

Pazin and I had a look in it. All sorts of documents and timetables and memos. Symptoms of a miserable life, said Pazin. Pazin works outside, on the city's gas pipes.

And there was a little sort of diary, with telephone numbers printed in it.

At the bottom of the list was another number, pencilled in.

"That one probably gets you straight through to Gramman," said Pazin, with a laugh. "Knowing what a little sneak Hussein is."

"We could soon find out," said I. Fool that I was.

So that was how it all started.

I rang that number. A lacky answered.

"Put me through to Gramman," I said.

It must have been a secret number. Otherwise, the lacky would never have done it.

Next moment, I was talking to the president himself.

Of course I was taken aback — well, terrified. I had no idea. But I let him have it.

"Look here, mate," I said to him, "my nephew is one of these poor lads you are sending to Skochne to get killed. You're mad. Leave the bloody Skochnens alone. Let them and us live our own lives in peace and quiet."

In a sinister voice he asks, "Who is this talking?"

"Never you mind who it is. It's the voice of the people speaking to you in your rotten ear." By this time, I knew I had done for myself. I was already as good as dead.

"Where are you speaking from?" Dreadful voice.

"I'm in Building Sixteen." That's what I said, and I put the phone down.

I sat there trembling. I felt sick. I clutched my head. I had to get myself a glass of vodka. I had spoken to the... no, it was too terrible!

At least I had had the sense not to tell him I was in Building Twelve. These massive great building blocks of apartments are called New Cowgrange. Numbered from One to Eighteen. You might think they would be numbered from One at one end, Two,

Building Sixteen

Three, along to Eighteen, in numerical order. That would make sense.

Not here. The buildings are numbered in the order they were built. Since they were built more than ten years ago – and now already delapidated – why should anyone care about what order they were built in?

I had an awful night. Could not sleep. Could not believe what I had done. That's what years of oppression do to you.

I was ragged in the morning. Still there was bread to be earned. I had to go and work at the creche up-town. Do a bit of cleaning. Out I went, well wrapped up. This was February. Half-expecting to be shot on the street.

Got on the bus. Crowded as usual. Folk saying nowt.

Looked out at the dreary prospect we were passing. Building Six. Then Building Eleven. Building Two. All much alike, dreary to behold. Next, Building Sixteen.

Building Sixteen was not there.

Just a big flat square of rubble where the building had been.

Other bus passengers saw it had gone. None of them dared say anything. Would not catch your eye.

But it had gone, the entire building. Levelled overnight.

Gramman didn't hang about, did he?

It was so awful, I shat myself. Just a bit.

Maybe everyone on the bus did the same. Out of fear.

The whole building and its inhabitants gone.

Pazin walked to work on his own flat feet. Saving bus fare. The Gas Pipes Protection Company Office was a mile away through town. But nearby was a Protection Cabin standing on the other side of the road to where Building Sixteen used to be… Pazin called in to say Hello to Andy March. March was about to go off duty, and having a mug of tea before he went.

"What happened to Building Sixteen, for Chrissake?" Pazin asked.

"Do you want a mug of tea? Kettle's just boiled."

"Wouldn't say no."

The men were talking quietly. They illegally let out part of the floor to an old woman who was sleeping there now, on a bit of rug. The cabin stood on a stretch of waste ground. The gas men had fenced off a bit of the land and kept chickens there. They got the odd egg now and again.

March said, lowering his voice still further, "I saw them doing it. Watched them. They put dynamite in the basement and dynamite at the four corners. All done fast. Then off she went! Building quivered like jelly, fell down flat on itself. I didn't half feel queer, I can tell you."

He poured lukewarm water over the used teabag and handed the mug to his friend.

Pazin took a sip of the tea. "Any survivors?"

"None. Our old mate Abu Kaine lived there, poor bugger."

Abu Kaine had led the big gas strike for better pay at the beginning of the year.

"Poor bugger," Pazin echoed. "Look, why don't we have a whip round among the blokes, give Abu a good funeral?"

"You need a corpse for a funeral."

"Well then, give him a good send-off. We ought to, oughtn't we?"

"Good idea, mate. I'll chip in five dachts for a start."

They stood there thinking their thoughts, drinking their tea, while the old lady slept on.

"Better get back to the missus then," said March, setting down his empty mug.

"How is Sluski?"

"Lively as ever," March replied, in a neutral tone.

Gaspod Hussein worked in the big glass-fronted administration building next to the Palace. His desk was one among many rows of desks. Men and some women sat at every desk, silent, studying their screens.

Hussein stifled a yawn. Already the secret police were on to the Case of the Traitor's Trail, which had led to the demolition of Building Sixteen. His screen said, "A secret coven in the building was planning an attack on our beloved President. It was therefore considered best to destroy the building before the coven struck."

Afterwards came the instruction to name everyone you knew, however remotely, who lived in Building Sixteen.

A supervisor patrolled between the rows of desks. Hussein thought it advisable to make up several names of people. It might have looked suspicious if he simply typed in None.

To the rear of the huge room stood the Interrogation Office. People left their desks and went in turn into the Interrogation Office. By three in the afternoon, it was Hussein's turn.

He entered and found himself facing a big man of dark complexion with a large beard and moustache. His eyes bulged with high blood pressure.

"I think I should inform you first of all that I am," said Hussein, "a Statepeeper Second Class. I operate secretly and there are matters I cannot divulge."

For answer, the big man slid a sheet of paper across the metal top of his desk.

"Read this," he ordered.

At the top of the page ran a familiar legend: Are you a Muslim (state which group), Christian, Jew, Buddhist, Irish, Black British, Black American, White English, Kurd, Asian, Inuit? Tick appropriate box.

Below ran a series of statements with which the examinee had to agree or disagree.

All Skotchnes deserve to be beheaded.
All Christians should be shot.
All mosques should be burnt down.
All women should bear children before their nineteenth birthday.
Sharia Law should supercede all other laws.

And so on, to the bottom of the page. Hussein agreed with every statement, for safety.

I came home late. I had managed to buy a section of goat's neck and a parsnip and was pleased with myself. In the foyer I saw Pazin's handwritten notice advertising our landing for rent 'to suitable client'.

Pazin was home. He had taken his boots off and was resting his stockinged feet on the edge of the table. He was reading the 'Daily Sun'.

"They've printed a list of the latest conscripts to the army."

"Anyone we know?"

"Yes, as it happens. Gaspod Hussein himself! Due to be sent up north any day! Because it says here that the Skochnes carried out another daring raid and destroyed the town of Berwick."

"Probably lies." I removed my head scarf and sat down on the edge of the bed. I told him what I had managed to buy in the market. "I'll start cooking in a minute when I get my breath back."

"We'll celebrate. Andy March and I have collected thirty-two dachts for a send-off for Abu Kaine."

"Pretty good...Fancy old Gaspod..." I stuffed the goat neck in my pot and threw in salt and chillis and sliced parsnip on top of it. "Good feed tonight, Paz!"

"A bloke's coming up any minute to look at the landing. Don't let him see what you're cooking or he'll want some of it."

"He's not going to get it."

I could hear the screaming starting in the apartment next door. I put the gas on to drown the noise a bit.

"Anything new on the Sixteenth Building business?"

He laughed. "They aren't after you yet, you cheeky thing!"

A shout came from the stairway. The lift had been out of action all month.

A tall man with a handsome dark countenance entered.

"I may need to rent your landing for a short while," he said, addressing Pazin.

Pazin jumped up.

"By god, it's Abu Kaine!"

"Allah alive, it's old Pazin!"

The two men embraced.

"Abu, I thought you were bloody well dead."

"I'm the luckiest guy," he said. "I wasn't in the Sixteenth last night."

"Where were you then?"

He lowered his voice. "Andy March was away on night duty. So I was in there, shagging his wife."

"Good for you." Pazin paused. "I've collected thirty-two dachts for your funeral. Now what do we do?"

Abu Kaine started laughing. "We share it between us. Have a real spree."

So that was what they did. Of course this was long ago, back in Twenty-First Century England.

Dust
Richard Christian Matheson

Son of the legendary Richard – *Shrinking Man, I Am Legend* – Matheson, Richard Christian Matheson has carved out an extraordinary writing career of his own. Based in Malibu, Richard has written and produced hundreds of TV episodes and is a major Hollywood screenwriter. His short stories have appeared in the likes of *Penthouse*, *Omni*, and *Twilight Zone*. His collections include *Mediums Rare*, *Scars*, *Dystopia* and *Pride* (with Richard Matheson). Richard is also an accomplished novelist - his first novel was the superb *Created By* - and has a particular interest in the music scene due to being a drummer for an alternative rock band. Just recently he adapted his father's short story 'Dance of the Dead' for the US TV series *Masters of Horror*; the episode featured *Nightmare on Elm Street* star Robert Englund.

"Though sci-fi in approach," Richard observes, "'Dust' is a fear metaphor. It details what cannot be easily detected nor predicted and microscopes how obsession escorts paralysis. Is the main character really where the story finds him? Or strapped to a bed, mind in black somersault?"

Dust

Two minutes since he'd blinked.

He clutched his coffee frozenly. Sweat trickled. His eyes followed as the dust drifted onto the booth table, warm and slow. He grabbed a menu and propped it against the window, blocking the klieg of sun. Quickly scanned the coffee shop for angry eyes. Eyes that didn't understand. Stupid eyes shifting in blank, doomed faces.

He lifted the bleached mug, sipped coffee and suddenly tasted a crawling tickle on his tongue.

It was in there.

He spit the black liquid onto the table top and watched the dust floating. Swimming.

Multiplying.

There was no way to stop it. He'd tried; every day he'd tried. Even harder at night. Trying desperately to sleep when the sun had gone down and the dust hid in darkness.

He would lock his apartment tight, doors and windows sealed, and go to work to capture the marauding downpour. Standing in a corner of the room, not moving, flashlight gripped. He would listen and wait for minutes. Once for hours; not wanting the dust to sense his presence.

When he finally heard it in front of him, its horrid tinkle like far away sleighbells, he would shock the dust by thumbing on the flashlight and blinding it. Then, he would start the vacuum cleaner, and stare in hunter's fixation as the dust screamed, sucked into a long nozzle he held in his hand.

Smiling at the agonized shrieks, he would move slowly through the apartment, passing the nozzle back and forth, its fat throat swallowing the helpless dust until the slaughter was total; the room safe for sleep.

But he didn't sleep well. He knew the dust would be back by morning, sneaking in through cracks and vents as he twisted with nightmares.

It couldn't be stopped. It was falling everywhere, twenty-four hours a day; an endless supply of smothering, swirling horror. No matter where he went to escape it, to fool it and hide, it would always be there, drifting to the ground like invading parachutists; fearless, secret.

He watched the sunbeam that had moved to the side of the menu. Its yellow straightness was a perfect landing strip for the dust which floated closer to the ground, making noises he'd come to hate. The amusement of the dust; laughing, ridiculing. The arrogant sounds it made as it fell closer, ready to land, ready to join the billions of others. The plans it had; he heard those, too. He'd heard them from the start, when there had been only advance parties descending from the sky. Nobody else seemed to question it. But he'd always known more would come and that time only made it worse, offering the perfect means to chart the inevitable suffocation.

He left the table, positioned goggles, placed a handkerchief over his mouth and walked out onto the city street past a store window. He glanced up. Dust coated the window and its weightless eyes watched him. He hurried on and approached a pedestrian crossing where he waited. He looked down to see dust on the tips of his shoes and bent quickly to wipe it off with the handkerchief, feeling the dust's sticky voltage on the cotton. He threw the white square onto the sidewalk, then lit it on fire with matches from his pocket. As flames rose, he moved closer to hear the dust burning to death.

That night, he decided to fight the dust using different methods, knowing it must be deceived so it couldn't predict his strategy; his advantage. At just past eleven, he rose in darkness. He had been waiting, feigning sleep, listening since sundown to the dust's hidden murmurings. It was secreted in the weave of the curtain fabric, and he heard it scheming, watching for his unguarded sleep. He moved in silence to the tattered curtains, a thick board raised over his shoulder. The sound of the board striking the drab material over and over was mixed with the panicked screams of the dust as it grabbed at one another, forming stunned clumps which clouded helplessly.

When he'd forced it all out, he grabbed his vacuum and started it, holding the nozzle in sweaty hands, sweeping it through the air. The sounds of tiny death filled the apartment, screaming and crying until nothing could be heard. He figured several hundred thousand had died. Finally, he slept, relaxed snores drawing him through what little night remained.

Dust

By morning, the city stared at a murky sun which had turned almost brown and he rose to fight the dust. He pulled open his curtains and drained white at what he saw. Moving in, from the west, was a mile-wide wall of dust, a bronze wave that curled closer. He dressed in silence, knowing what he must do. The air-tight jumpsuit was zipped, heavy boots pulled on. The portable battery-pack vacuum was harnessed to his back. Goggles positioned. He pulled on gloves, clutched the vacuum nozzle, went downstairs and kicked open the front door.

As he walked through the silent city which had been dead for half a century, his mind flooded with images of his children and wife. Friends, and parents. Dogs. Christmas. Laughter. The viral clouds which swept the Mars settlement had destroyed them; taken everything. Fighting the dust was the only thing that kept him sane.

He turned on his portable vacuum and walked slowly toward the brown storm, which howled closer, killing everything it touched.

He had survived. He would survive.

He would win.

SUNDANCE
Robert Silverberg

Born in Brooklyn, New York, in 1935, Robert Silverberg is the prolific and applauded author of many SF novels and stories, with multiple Nebula and Hugo awards to his credit. A voracious reader since childhood, began submitting stories to science fiction magazines in his early teenage years. He attended Columbia University, receiving an A.B. in English Literature in 1956, but he kept writing science fiction. His first published novel, a children's book called *Revolt on Alpha C* appeared in 1955, and in the following year he won his first Hugo, as 'Best New Writer.' For the next four years, by his own count, he wrote a million words a year, for magazines and Ace Doubles. Further novels included *Invaders from Earth*, *Lost Race of Mars*, *Regan's Planet*, *Conquerors from the Darkness*, *The Gate of Worlds*, *Nightwings*, *The World Inside*, *Son of Man*, *The Desert of Stolen Dreams*, *Valentine Pontifex*, *Star of the Gypsies*, *Project Pendulum*, *At Winter's End*, *Nightfall*, *Child of Time*, *Kingdoms of the Wall*, *The Positronic Man* and *Hot Sky at Midnight* to name but a few. He has published more than twenty collections of short stories, including *Next Stop the Stars*, *To Worlds Beyond* and *The Shores of Tomorrow*. Silverberg married Karen Haber in 1987, his second wife – also a science fiction author. The couple reside in Montclair, a small, wealthy enclave in the middle of Oakland, California.

Sundance

Today you liquidated about 50,000 Eaters in Sector A, and now you are spending an uneasy night. You and Herndon flew east at dawn, with the greengold sunrise at your backs, and sprayed the neural pellets over a thousand hectares along the Forked River. You flew on into the prairie beyond the river, where the Eaters have already been wiped out, and had lunch sprawled on that thick, soft carpet of grass where the first settlement is expected to rise. Herndon picked some juiceflowers, and you enjoyed half an hour of mild hallucinations. Then, as you headed toward the copter to begin an afternoon of further pellet spraying, he said suddenly, "Tom, how would you feel about this if it turned out that the Eaters weren't just animal pests? That they were *people,* say, with a language and rites and a history and all?"

You thought of how it had been for your own people.

"They aren't," you said.

"Suppose they were. Suppose the Eaters – "

"They aren't. Drop it."

Herndon has this streak of cruelty in him that leads him to ask such questions. He goes for the vulnerabilities; it amuses him. All night now his casual remark has echoed in your mind. Suppose the Eaters ... supposed the Eaters ... suppose ... suppose ...

You sleep for a while. and dream, and in your dreams you swim through rivers of blood.

Foolishness. A feverish fantasy. You know how important it is to exterminate the Eaters fast, before the settlers get here. They're just animals, and not even harmless animals at that; ecology-wreckers is what they are, devourers of oxygen-liberating plants, and they have to go. A few have been saved for zoological study. The rest must be destroyed. Ritual extirpation of undesirable beings, the old old story. But let's not complicate our job with moral qualms, you tell yourself. Let's not dream of rivers of blood.

The Eaters don't even *have* blood, none that could flow in rivers, anyway. What they have is, well, a kind of lymph that permeates every tissue and transmits nourishment along the interfaces. Waste products go out the same way, osmotically. In terms of process, it's structurally analogous to your own kind of circulatory system, except there's no network of blood vessels hooked to a master pump. The

249

life-stuff just oozes through their bodies as though they were amoebas or sponges or some other low-phylum form. Yet they're definitely high-phylum in nervous system, digestive setup, limb-and-organ template, etc. Odd, you think. The thing about aliens is that they're alien, you tell yourself, not for the first time.

The beauty of their biology for you and your companions is that it lets you exterminate them so neatly.

You fly over the grazing grounds and drop the neural pellets. The Eaters find and ingest them. Within an hour the poison has reached all sectors of the body. Life ceases; a rapid breakdown of cellular matter follows, the Eater literally falling apart molecule by molecule the instant that nutrition is cut off; the lymph-like stuff works like acid; a universal lysis occurs; flesh and even the bones, which are cartilaginous, dissolve. In two hours, a puddle on the ground. In four, nothing at all left. Considering how many millions of Eaters you've scheduled for extermination here, it's sweet of the bodies to be self-disposing. Otherwise what a charnel house this world would become!

Suppose the Eaters ..

Damn Herndon. You almost feel like getting a memory-editing in the morning. Scrape his stupid speculations out of your head. If you dared. If you dared.

In the morning he does not dare. Memory-editing frightens him; he will try to shake free of his newfound guilt without it. The Eaters, he explains to himself, are mindless herbivores, the unfortunate victims of human expansionism, but not really deserving of passionate defense. Their extermination is not tragic; it's just too bad. If Earthmen are to have this world, the Eaters must relinquish it. There's a difference, he tells himself, between the elimination of the Plains Indians from the American prairie in the nineteenth century and the destruction of the bison on that same prairie. One feels a little wistful about the slaughter of the thundering herds; one regrets the butchering of millions of the noble brown woolly beasts, yes. But one feels outrage, not mere wistful regret, at what

Sundance

was done to the Sioux. There's a difference. Reserve your passions for the proper cause.

He walks from his bubble at the edge of the camp toward the center of things. The flagstone path is moist and glistening. The morning fog has not yet lifted, and every tree is bowed, the long, notched leaves heavy with droplets of water. He pauses, crouching, to observe a spider-analog spinning its asymmetrical web. As he watches, a small amphibian, delicately shaded turquoise, glides as inconspicuously as possible over the mossy ground. Not inconspicuously enough; he gently lifts the little creature and puts it on the back of his hand. The gills flutter in anguish, and the amphibian's sides quiver. Slowly, cunningly, its color changes until it matches the coppery tone of the hand. The camouflage is excellent. He lowers his hand and the amphibian scurries into a puddle. He walks on.

He is forty years old, shorter than most of the other members of the expedition, with wide shoulders, a heavy chest, dark glossy hair, a blunt, spreading nose. He is a biologist. This is his third career, for he has failed as an anthropologist and as a developer of real estate. His name is Tom Two Ribbons. He has been married twice but has had no children. His great-grandfather died of alcoholism; his grandfather was addicted to hallucinogens; his father had compulsively visited cheap memory-editing parlors. Tom Two Ribbons is conscious that he is failing a family tradition, but he has not yet found his own mode of self-destruction.

In the main building he discovers Herndon, Julia, Ellen, Schwartz, Chang, Michaelson, and Nichols. They are eating breakfast; the others are already at work. Ellen rises and comes to him and kisses him. Her short soft yellow hair tickles his cheeks. "I love you," she whispers. She has spent the night in Michaelson's bubble. "I love you," he tells her, and draws a quick vertical line of affection between her small pale breasts. He winks at Michaelson, who nods, touches the tops of two fingers to his lips, and blows them a kiss. We are all good friends here, Tom Two Ribbons thinks.

"Who drops pellets today?" he asks.

"Mike and Chang," says Julia. "Sector C."

Schwartz says, "Eleven more days and we ought to have the whole peninsula clear. Then we can move inland."

"If our pellet supply holds up," Chang points out.

Herndon says, "Did you sleep well, Tom?"

"No," says Tom. He sits down and taps out his breakfast requisition. In the west, the fog is beginning to burn off the mountains. Something throbs in the back of his neck. He has been on this world nine weeks now, and in that time it has undergone its only change of season, shading from dry weather to foggy. The mists will remain for many months. Before the plains parch again, the Eaters will be gone and the settlers will begin to arrive. His food slides down the chute and he seizes it. Ellen sits beside him. She is a little more than half his age; this is her first voyage; she is their keeper of records, but she is also skilled at editing. "You look troubled," Ellen tells him. "Can I help you?"

"No. Thank you."

"I hate it when you get gloomy."

"It's a racial trait," says Tom Two Ribbons.

"I doubt that very much."

"The truth is that maybe my personality reconstruct is wearing thin. The trauma level was so close to the surface. I'm just a walking veneer, you know."

Ellen laughs prettily. She wears only a sprayon half-wrap. Her skin looks damp; she and Michaelson have had a swim at dawn. Tom Two Ribbons is thinking of asking her to marry him, when this job is over. He has not been married since the collapse of the real estate business. The therapist suggested divorce as part of the reconstruct. He sometimes wonders where Terry has gone and whom she lives with now. Ellen says, "You seem pretty stable to me, Tom."

"Thank you," he says. She is young. She does not know.

"If it's just a passing gloom I can edit it out in one quick snip."

"Thank you," he says. "No."

"I forgot. You don't like editing."

"My father – "

"Yes'"

"In fifty years he pared himself down to a thread," Tom Two Ribbons says. "He had his ancestors edited away, his whole heritage,

Sundance

his religion, his wife, his sons, finally his name. Then he sat and smiled all day. Thank you, no editing."

"Where are you working today?" Ellen asks.

"In the compound, running tests."

"Want company? I'm off all morning."

"Thank you, no," he says, too quickly. She looks hurt. He tries to remedy his unintended cruelty by touching her arm lightly and saying, "Maybe this afternoon, all right? I need to commune a while. Yes?"

"Yes," she says, and smiles, and shapes a kiss with her lips.

After breakfast he goes to the compound. It covers a thousand hectares east of the base; they have bordered it with neutral-field projectors at intervals of eighty meters, and this is a sufficient fence to keep the captive population of two hundred Eaters from straying. When all the others have been exterminated, this study group will remain. At the southwest corner of the compound stands a lab bubble from which the experiments are run: metabolic, psychological, physiological, ecological. A stream crosses the compound diagonally. There is a low ridge of grassy hills at its eastern edge. Five distinct copses of tightly clustered knifeblade trees are separated by patches of dense savanna. Sheltered beneath the grass are the oxygen-plants, almost completely hidden except for the photosynthetic spikes that jut to heights of three or four meters at regular intervals, and for the lemon-colored respiratory bodies, chest high, that make the grassland sweet and dizzying with exhaled gases. Through the fields move the Eaters in a straggling herd, nibbling delicately at the respiratory bodies.

Tom Two Ribbons spies the herd beside the stream and goes toward it. He stumbles over an oxygen-plant hidden in the grass but deftly recovers his balance and, seizing the puckered orifice of the respiratory body, inhales deeply. His despair lifts. He approaches the Eaters. They are spherical, bulky, slow-moving creatures, covered by masses of coarse orange fur. Saucer-like eyes protrude above narrow rubbery lips. Their legs are thin and scaly, like a chicken's, and their arms are short and held close to their bodies. They regard him with bland lack of curiosity. "Good morning, brothers!" is the way he greets them this time, and he wonders why.

I noticed something strange today. Perhaps I simply sniffed too much oxygen in the fields; maybe I was succumbing to a suggestion Herndon planted; or possibly it's the family masochism cropping out. But while I was observing the Eaters in the compound, it seemed to me, for the first time, that they were behaving intelligently, that they were functioning in a ritualized way.

I followed them around for three hours. During that time they uncovered half a dozen outcroppings of oxygen-plants. In each case they went through a stylized pattern of action before starting to munch. They:

Formed a straggly circle around the plants.
Looked toward the sun.
Looked toward their neighbors on left and right around the circle.
Made fuzzy neighing sounds *only* after having done the foregoing.
Looked toward the sun again.
Moved in and ate.

If this wasn't a prayer of thanksgiving, a saying of grace, then what was it? And if they're advanced enough spiritually to say grace, are we not therefore committing genocide here? Do chimpanzees say grace? Christ, we wouldn't even wipe out chimps the way we're cleaning out the Eaters! Of course, chimps don't interfere with human crops, and some kind of coexistence would be possible, whereas Eaters and human agriculturalists simply can't function on the same planet. Nevertheless, there's a moral issue here. The liquidation effort is predicated on the assumption that the intelligence level of the Eaters is about on par with that of oysters, or, at best, sheep. Our consciences stay clear because our poison is quick and painless and because the Eaters thoughtfully dissolve upon dying, sparing us the mess of incinerating millions of corpses. But if they pray –

Sundance

I won't say anything to the others just yet. I want more evidence – hard, objective. Films, tapes, record cubes. Then we'll see. What if I can show that we're exterminating intelligent beings? My family knows a little about genocide, after all, having been on the receiving end just a few centuries back. I doubt that I could halt what's going on here. But at the very least I could withdraw from the operation. Head back to Earth and stir up public outcries.

I hope I'm imagining this.

I'm not imagining a thing. They gather in circles; they look to the sun; they neigh and pray. They're only balls of jelly on chicken-legs, but they give thanks for their food. Those big round eyes now seem to stare accusingly at me. Our tame herd here knows what's going on: that we have descended from the stars to eradicate their kind, and that they alone will be spared. They have no way of fighting back or even of communicating their displeasure, but they *know*. And hate us. Jesus, we have killed two million of them since we got here, and in a metaphorical sense I'm stained with blood, and what will I do, what can I do?

I must move very carefully, or I'll end up drugged and edited.

I can't let myself seem like a crank, a quack, an agitator. I can't stand up and *denounce!* I have to find allies. Herndon, first. He surely is onto the truth; he's the one who nudged me to it, that day we dropped pellets. And I thought he was merely being vicious in his usual way!

I'll talk to him tonight.

He says, "I've been thinking about that suggestion you made. About the Eaters. Perhaps we haven't made sufficiently close psychological studies. I mean, if they really *are* intelligent – "

Herndon blinks. He is a tall man with glossy dark hair, a heavy beard, sharp cheekbones. "Who says they are, Tom?"

255

"You did. On the far side of the Forked River, you said – "
"It was just a speculative hypothesis. To make conversation."
"No, I think it was more than that. You really believed it."
Herndon looks troubled. "Tom, I don't know what you're trying to start, but don't start it. If I for a moment believed we were killing intelligent creatures, I'd run for an editor so fast I'd start an implosion wave."
"Why did you ask me that thing, then?" Tom Two Ribbons says.
"Idle chatter."
"Amusing yourself by kindling guilts in somebody else? You're a bastard, Herndon. I mean it."
"Well, look, Tom, if I had any idea that you'd get so worked up about a hypothetical suggestion-" Herndon shakes his head. "The Eaters aren't intelligent beings. Obviously. Otherwise we wouldn't be under orders to liquidate them. "Obviously," says Tom Two Ribbons.

Ellen said, "No, I don't know what Tom's up to. But I'm pretty sure he needs a rest. It's only a year and a half since his personality reconstruct, and he had a pretty bad breakdown back then."
Michaelson consulted a chart. "He's refused three times in a row to make his pellet-dropping run. Claiming he can't take time away from his research. Hell, we can fill in for him, but it's the idea that he's ducking chores that bothers me."
"What kind of research is he doing?" Nichols wanted to know.
"Not biological," said Julia. "He's with the Eaters in the compound all the time, but I don't see him making any tests on them. He just watches them."
"And talks to them," Chang observed.
"And talks, yes," Julia said.
"About what?" Nichols asked.
"Who knows?"
Everyone looked at Ellen. "You're closest to him," Michaelson said. "Can't you bring him out of it?"

Sundance

"I've got to know what he's in, first," Ellen said. "He isn't saying a thing."

You know that you must be *very* careful, for they outnumber you, and their concern for your welfare can be deadly. Already they realize you are disturbed, and Ellen has begun to probe for the source of the disturbance. Last night you lay in her arms and she questioned you, obliquely, skillfully, and you knew what she is trying to find out. When the moons appeared she suggested that you and she stroll in the compound, among the sleeping Eaters. You declined, but she sees that you have become involved with the creatures.

You have done probing of your own – subtly, you hope. And you are aware that you can do nothing to save the Eaters. An irrevocable commitment has been made. It is 1876 all over again; these are the bison, these are the Sioux, and they must be destroyed, for the railroad is on its way. If you speak out here, your friends will calm you and pacify you and edit you, for they do not see what you see. If you return to Earth to agitate, you will be mocked and recommended for another reconstruct. You can do nothing. You can do nothing.

You cannot save, but perhaps you can record.

Go out into the prairie. Live with the Eaters; make yourself their friend; learn their ways. Set it down, a full account of their culture, so that at least that much will not be lost. You know the techniques of field anthropology. As was done for your people in the old days, do now for the Eaters.

He finds Michaelson. "Can you spare me for a few weeks?" he asks.

"Spare you, Tom? What do you mean?"

"I've got some field studies to do. I'd like to leave the base and work with Eaters in the wild."

"What's wrong with the ones in the compound?"

257

"It's the last chance with wild ones, Mike. I've got to go."
"Alone, or with Ellen?"
"Alone."
Michaelson nods slowly. "All right, Tom. Whatever you want. Go. I won't hold you here."

I dance in the prairie under the green-gold sun. About me the Eaters gather. I am stripped; sweat makes my skin glisten; my heart pounds. I talk to them with my feet, and they understand.
They understand.
They have a language of soft sounds. They have a god. They know love and awe and rapture. They have rites. They have names. They have a history. Of all this I am convinced.
I dance on thick grass.
How can I reach them? With my feet, with my hands, with my grunts, with my sweat. They gather by the hundreds, by the thousands, and I dance. I must not stop. They cluster about me and make their sounds. I am a conduit for strange forces. My great-grandfather should see me now! Sitting on his porch in Wyoming, the firewater in his hand, his brain rotting – see me now, old one! See the dance of Tom Two Ribbons! I talk to these strange ones with my feet under a sun that is the wrong color. I dance. I dance.
"Listen to me," I say. "I am your friend, I alone, the only one you can trust. Trust me, talk to me, teach me. Let me preserve your ways, for soon the destruction will come."
I dance, and the sun climbs, and the Eaters murmur.
There is the chief. I dance toward him, back, toward, I bow, I point to the sun, I imagine the being that lives in that ball of flame, I imitate the sounds of these people, I kneel, I rise, I dance. Tom Two Ribbons dances for you.
I summon skills my ancestors forgot. I feel the power flowing in me. As they danced in the days of the bison, I dance now, beyond the Forked River.
I dance, and now the Eaters dance too. Slowly, uncertainly, they

move toward me, they shift their weight, lift leg and leg, sway about. "Yes, like that!" I cry. "Dance!"

We dance together as the sun reaches noon height.

Now their eyes are no longer accusing. I see warmth and kinship. I am their brother, their redskinned tribesman, he who dances with them. No longer do they seem clumsy to me. There is a strange ponderous grace in their movements. They dance. They dance. They caper about me. Closer, closer, closer!

We move in holy frenzy.

They sing, now, a blurred hymn of joy. They throw forth their arms, unclench their little claws. In unison they shift weight, left foot forward, right, left, right. Dance, brothers, dance, dance, dance! They press against me. Their flesh quivers; their smell is a sweet one. They gently thrust me across the field, to a part of the meadow where the grass is deep and untrampled. Still dancing, we seek the oxygen-plants, and find clumps of them beneath the grass, and they make their prayer and seize them with their awkward arms, separating the respiratory bodies from the photosynthetic spikes. The plants, in anguish, release floods of oxygen. My mind reels. I laugh and sing. The Eaters are nibbling the lemon-colored perforated globes, nibbling the stalks as well. They thrust their plants at me. It is a religious ceremony, I see. Take from us, eat with us, join with us, this is the body, this is the blood, take, eat, join. I bend forward and put a lemon-colored globe to my lips. I do not bite; I nibble, as they do, my teeth slicing away the skin of the globe. Juice spurts into my mouth while oxygen drenches my nostrils. The Eaters sing hosannas. I should be in full paint for this, paint of my forefathers, feathers too, meeting their religion in the regalia of what should have been mine. Take, eat, join. The juice of the oxygen-plant flows in my veins. I embrace my brothers. I sing, and as my voice leaves my lips it becomes an arch that glistens like new steel, and I pitch my song lower, and the arch turns to tarnished silver. The Eaters crowd close. The scent of their bodies is fiery red to me. Their soft cries are puffs of steam. The sun is very warm; its rays are tiny jagged pings of puckered sound, close to the top of my range of hearing, plink! plink! plink! The thick grass hums to me, deep and rich, and the wind hurls points of flame along the prairie. I devour another oxygen-plant, and then a third. My brothers laugh and shout. They tell me of their gods, the god of warmth, the god of food, the god of pleasure, the god of death, the god of holiness, the god of wrongness, and the others. They recite for me the names of their kings, and I hear their voices as splashes of green mold on the clean sheet of the sky. They instruct me in their holy rites. I must remember this, I tell myself, for when it is gone it will never come again. I continue to dance. They continue to dance. The color of the hills becomes rough and coarse, like abrasive gas. Take, eat, join. Dance. They are so gentle!

I hear the drone of the copter, suddenly.

It hovers far overhead. I am unable to see who flies in it. "No!" I scream. "Not here! Not these people! Listen to me! This is Tom Two Ribbons! Can't you hear me? I'm doing a field study here! You have no right-!"

My voice makes spirals of blue moss edged with red sparks. They drift upward and are scattered by the breeze.

I yell, I shout, I bellow. I dance and shake my fists. From the wings of the copter the jointed arms of the pellet-distributors unfold. The gleaming spigots extend and whirl. The neural pellets rain down into the meadow, each tracing a blazing track that lingers in the sky. The sound of the copter becomes a furry carpet stretching to the horizon, and my shrill voice is lost in it.

The Eaters drift away from me, seeking the pellets, scratching at the roots of the grass to find them. Still dancing, I leap into their midst, striking the pellets from their hands, hurling them into the stream, crushing them to powder. The Eaters growl black needles at me. They turn away and search for more pellets. The copter turns and flies off, leaving a trail of dense oily sound. My brothers are gobbling the pellets eagerly.

There is no way to prevent it.

Joy consumes them and they topple and lie still. Occasionally a limb twitches; then even this stops. They begin to dissolve. Thousands of them melt on the prairie, sinking into shapelessness, losing spherical forms, flattening ebbing into the ground. The bonds of the molecules will no longer hold. It is the twilight of protoplasm. They perish. They vanish. For hours I walk the prairie. Now I inhale oxygen; now I eat a lemon-colored globe. Sunset begins with the ringing of leaden chimes. Black clouds make brazen trumpet calls in the east and the deepening wind is a swirl of coaly bristles. Silence comes. Night falls. I dance. I am alone.

The copter comes again, and they find you, and you do not resist as they gather you in. You are beyond bitterness. Quietly you explain what you have done and what you have learned and why it is wrong to exterminate these people. You describe the plant you have eaten and the way it affects your senses, and as you talk of the blessed synesthesia, the texture of the wind and the sound of the clouds and the timbre of the sunlight, they nod and smile and tell you not to worry, that everything will be all right soon, and they touch something cold to your forearm, so cold that it is a whir and a buzz and the deintoxicant sinks into your vein and soon the ecstasy drains away, leaving only the exhaustion and the grief.

He says, "We never learn a thing, do we? We export all our horrors to the stars. Wipe out the Armenians, wipe out the Jews, wipe out the Tasmanians, wipe out the Indians, wipe out everyone who's in the way, and then come here and do the same damned murderous thing. You weren't with me out there. You didn't dance with them. You didn't see what a rich, complex culture the Eaters have. Let me tell you about their tribal structure. It's dense: seven levels of matrimonial relationships, to begin with, and an exogamy factor that requires – "

Softly Ellen says, "Tom, darling, nobody's going to harm the Eaters."

"And the religion," he goes on. "Nine gods, each one an aspect of *the* god. Holiness and wrongness both worshiped. They have hymns, prayers, a theology. And we, the emissaries of the god of wrongness – "

"We're not exterminating them," Michaelson says. "Won't you understand that, Tom? This is all a fantasy of yours. You've been under the influence of drugs, but now we're clearing you out. You'll be clean in a little while. You'll have perspective again."

"A fantasy?" he says bitterly. "A drug dream? I stood out in the prairie and saw you drop pellets. And I watched them die and melt away. I didn't dream that."

"How can we convince you?" Chang asks earnestly. "What will make you believe? Shall we fly over the Eater country with you and show you how many millions there are?"

"But how many millions have been destroyed?" he demands.

They insist that he is wrong. Ellen tells him again that no one has ever desired to harm the Eaters. "This is a scientific expedition, Tom. We're here to *study* them. It's a violation of all we stand for to injure intelligent lifeforms."

"You admit that they're intelligent?"

"Of course. That's never been in doubt."

"Then why drop the pellets?" he asks. "Why slaughter them?"

"None of that has happened, Tom," Ellen says. She takes his hand between her cool palms. "Believe us. Believe us."

He says bitterly, "If you want me to believe you, why don't you do the job properly? Get out the editing machine and go to work on me. You can't simply *talk* me into rejecting the evidence of my own eyes."

"You were under drugs all the time," Michaelson says.

"I've never taken drugs! Except for what I ate in the meadow, when I danced – and that came after I had watched the massacre going on for weeks and weeks. Are you saying that it's a retroactive delusion?"

"No, Tom," Schwartz says. "You've had this delusion all along. It's part of your therapy, your reconstruct. You came here programmed with it."

"Impossible," he says.

Ellen kisses his fevered forehead. "It was done to reconcile you to mankind, you see. You had this terrible resentment of the displacement of your people in the nineteenth century. You were unable to forgive the industrial society for scattering the Sioux, and you were terribly full of hate. Your therapist thought that if you could be made to participate in an imaginary modern extermination, if you could come to see it as a necessary operation, you'd be purged of your resentment and able to take your place in society as – "

He thrusts her away. "Don't talk idiocy! If you knew the first thing about reconstruct therapy, you'd realize that no reputable therapist could be so shallow. There are no one-to-one correlations in reconstructs. No, don't touch me. Keep away. Keep away."

He will not let them persuade him that this is merely a drug-born dream. It is no fantasy, he tells himself, and it is no therapy. He rises. He goes out. They do not follow him. He takes a copter and seeks his brothers.

Again I dance. The sun is much hotter today. The Eaters are more numerous. Today I wear paint, today I wear feathers. My body shines with my sweat. They dance with me, and they have a frenzy in them that I have never seen before. We pound the trampled meadow with our feet. We clutch for the sun with our hands. We sing, we shout, we cry. We will dance until we fall.

This is no fantasy. These people are real, and they are intelligent, and they are doomed. This I know.

We dance. Despite the doom, we dance.

My great-grandfather comes and dances with us. He too is real. His nose is like a hawk's, not blunt like mine, and he wears the big headdress, and his muscles are like cords under his brown skin. He sings, he shouts, he cries.

Others of my family join us.

We eat the oxygen-plants together. We embrace the Eaters. We know, all of us, what it is to be hunted.

The clouds make music and the wind takes on texture and the sun's warmth has color.

We dance. We dance. Our limbs know no weariness.

The sun grows and fills the whole sky, and I see no Eater now, only my own people, my father's fathers across the centuries, thousands of gleaming skins, thousands of hawk's noses, and we eat the plants, and we find sharp sticks and thrust them into our flesh, and the sweet blood flows and dries in the blaze of the sun, and we dance, and we dance, and some of us fall from weariness, and we dance, and the prairie is a sea of bobbing headdresses, an ocean of feathers, and we dance, and my heart makes thunder, and my knees become water, and the sun's fire engulfs me, and I dance, and I fall, and I dance, and I fall, and I fall, and I fall.

Again they find you and bring you back. They give you the cool snout on your arm to take the oxygen-plant drug from your veins, and then they give you something else so you will rest. You rest and you are very calm. Ellen kisses you and you stroke her soft skin, and then the others come in and they talk to you, saying soothing things, but you do not listen, for you are searching for realities. It is not an easy search. It is like falling through many trapdoors, looking for the one room whose floor is not hinged. Everything that has happened on this planet is your therapy, you tell yourself, designed to reconcile an embittered aborigine to the white man's conquest; nothing is really being exterminated here. You reject that and fall through and realize that this must be the therapy of your friends; they carry the weight of accumulated centuries of guilts and have come here to shed that load, and you are here to ease them of their burden, to draw their sins into yourself and give them forgiveness. Again you fall through, and see that the Eaters are mere animals who threaten the ecology and must be removed; the culture you imagined for them is your hallucination, kindled out of old churnings. You try to withdraw your objections to this necessary extermination, but you fall through again and discover that there is no extermination except in your mind, which is troubled and disordered by your obsession with the crime against your ancestors, and you sit up, for you wish to apologize to these friends of yours, these innocent scientists whom you have called murderers. And you fall through.

My Repeater
Stephen Gallagher

Stephen Gallagher studied Drama and English at Hull in the 1970s before making a couple of student films. He then worked briefly as a documentaries researcher for YTV, then in Granada TV's presentation department with the aim of becoming a drama director. While he was there he made amateur 16mm movies and sold radio plays to ILR for bargain-basement production. He sold a spinoff novelisation of one of the radio serials, then wrote *Chimera*, his first novel (which would later be turned into a mini-series for TV). In that same period Stephen wrote a string of 90-minute Saturday Night Theatres for Radio 4 and four-part stories for two consecutive TV seasons of *Doctor Who*. Upon leaving Granada he went freelance in 1980, then worked flat-out for the next few years, mostly making sales to radio and to American fiction magazines, before starting to turn out a novel a year from the mid-80s onwards.

Bestselling titles such as *The Valley of Lights*, *Oktober* (which was also turned into a successful TV mini-series starring Stephen Tomkinson), *Down River*, *Rain*, *The Boat House*, *Nightmare, With Angel* and *Red, Red Robin* followed, and Stephen also did more TV work for series such as *Murder Rooms* and *Bugs*, as well as creating the ITV show *Eleventh Hour* which starred Patrick Stewart. His most recent fiction titles are *White Bizango*,

British Fantasy Society: A Celebration

Out of His Mind – a collection of short stories for which he won the British Fantasy Award in 2005 – and *The Spirit Box*. His website is www.stephengallagher.com

Stephen says: "For some years before I joined the BFS I was a member of the BSFA, and I've a lot to thank both organisations for. For me they've been like access nodes to a global subculture of the like-minded and similarly-warped. And I mean that in a good way. It's quite a feeling to know that you can be alone in some distant part of the world and have a good chance of hooking up with a bunch of local people with whom you're very likely to have at least some friends in common. They may think you're some kind of a stalker when you get in touch, but that's all down to how you present yourself.

"Of course there's no organisation without organisers, and I've never really been one of those, so I feel a debt to those visionaries who started reaching out and making connections in the first place and to those competent, unselfish people who've ensured that the whole thing's been kept going. It's through fandom that I've made some of my best, my closest and my most long-lasting friendships. Without the BFS I'd just be a nutter in an attic, typing. With the BFS I'm still a nutter in an attic, but I'm typing with that warm sense of validation you have when you know there may be no-one else in the room, but you're never entirely alone."

What can I say? It was a job, and I was glad to get it. The money wasn't great, but I had no skills and nothing to offer beyond a vague feeling that I was meant for something better. My mother knew someone who knew the owner, and I got a message to go along and show myself. I started two days later. Training was minimal. Customers were few in number.

I'd been there six weeks when I saw my first returnee.

My Repeater

He must have got off the bus at the far end of town, and it had started to rain on him as he'd been walking through the centre. I saw him coming up the road. The road was called Technology Drive, and it had been built to run north out of town and into the hills. Ours was the only building on it. You walked about two hundred yards to get to us, with open scrub on either side. If you wanted to follow the road further you could, but there was nothing much to look at unless you wanted to see how the weeds had broken up the concrete.

He walked with his head down, and with his hands in the pockets of his brown overcoat. The rain was light but he walked as if he was taking a beating.

He looked vaguely familiar. But at that point I hadn't considered the possibility that any of the people I'd been dealing with might ever come back.

He came in and went straight to the ledge under the window where we kept the boxes of forms. He didn't have to ask for any help. When he brought the paperwork over to the counter, the boxes had been filled in and the waivers were all in order and I'd little more to do than run through the questionnaire and then take it all through to my boss for his approval.

Morley was in his little back office, where he spent most of the days reading old magazines. He had a desk, a chair, and an anglepoise lamp that couldn't hold a pose without slowly collapsing. I think he had a framed picture on the wall but I can't for the life of me remember what it was of.

"Customer, boss," I told him, and showed him the papers.

He looked them over, and then tilted his chair back a couple of extra degrees so that he could see through the doorway to the main part of the shop. He stared at the waiting man for a moment, then gave me a nod and returned his attention to his reading. Most of his magazines were old technical publications, filled with page after page of fine print. They carried long lists of obsolete gear and they looked about as much fun as telephone directories.

I went back to the counter, and worked out the charges on the spreadsheet. The further back in time you wanted to go, the more it cost. Then there were other complicating factors, like bodyweight and geography.

When we'd sorted out the payment, I gave him a keycard to put in the machine.

"Booth five," I told him.

He went inside and closed the door. I made all the settings and locked off the switches, and then there was nothing else to do but press the big red button.

"Are you ready, sir?" I called out to him.

"Get on with it," I heard him say.

So I got on with it. It was no thrill, just a routine – any buzz had gone out of it very quickly. But something jolted me in that moment as I realised why he'd seemed just a little bit familiar. It was the target settings that I recognised. I'd set them before. He'd been in about twelve days previously and he'd specified exactly the same destination.

But he'd been at least ten years older then.

It was a nothing job in a run-down travel bureau in a town in the middle of nowhere. I could have been stacking shelves in a supermarket or earning merit stars in a fast-food franchise, but instead I was sending a small group of losers back in time to relive their mistakes. I know that's what they did, because the same bunch of people brought us so much in the way of repeat business.

There must have been hundreds of bureaux like ours, small-town operations all scraping by as the last of their investors' capital dwindled. They'd been set up as a franchise network when the technology had first become available. They were like those long-distance phone places where you buy time at a counter and they assign you a booth while they set up the call; only here, you paid your money to be sent back to a date and a place of your choice.

Anyone could walk in and do it.

But only a strange few ever did.

My Repeater

The predicted boom had been a bust. I suppose it was like space travel. Full of romance and possibilities until it became achievable, and a matter of doubtful value ever after.

Here's what I learned when I talked it over with Morley:

He laid his magazine face-down on the desk and said, "I bet there's something in your life that you'd change, if you could."

"That's got to be true of everybody," I said. "Hasn't it?"

"So why don't you consider going back?"

I suppose the correct answer was that it would be a huge and scary one-way trip, and to make it would involve abandoning the life I now had. And for what? No certain outcome.

But what I said was, "You don't pay me enough."

"I'm not talking about the cost of it," Morley said. "Say I offered you a free one. Would you consider it then?"

"That would depend if you were serious."

"I'm serious. You're hesitating. Why?"

"I haven't thought about it that much."

"Think about it now. It sounds like a great idea. But why doesn't it *feel* like a great idea?"

"I don't know," I said. "It just doesn't."

But the more I thought about it, the more I thought I understood. It was obvious that I would never successfully go back and fix everything with Caroline Pocock, the proof being that she despised me so thoroughly in the here and now. Whatever I might try to amend, that was the known outcome.

I said, "Does that explain why the only people I see coming through that door seem to be life's born losers?"

"That's exactly what they are," Morley said. "They're the ones who can't accept what became common knowledge after the first few years. Which is that you gamble everything, and nothing changes. Nothing significant, anyway. The status quo is like one big self-regulating ecology. All that happens is that the balance shifts and whatever you do to try to upset it, it just sets itself right."

"How does that work?"

"Nobody knows. The rules are beyond grasping. If you go back to meet yourself, you won't be there. The past that you return to may not even be the past you left behind. Whatever you try to alter, somehow it all still comes out the same. Or else it's different in a way that suits you no better. There's a whole new branch of fractal mathematics that tries to explain it and what it all comes down to is, there's an infinite number of ways for something to go wrong and only one way for it to go right."

I said, "So the overall effect is like, when you pee in the swimming pool and nobody notices."

Clearly this was an analogy that had never occurred to him, because he stopped and gave me a very strange look before carrying on. He wasn't a healthy-looking man. He had pale eyes and grey-looking skin. His hair had lost most of its colour, as well. He dressed as if he didn't care about his appearance, in clothes that most people would have bagged up and sent to a charity shop.

He said, "The people who set these places up thought they'd make a fortune. Most of them went bust within ten years. The rest of us squeeze a living from the same bunch of hopeless romantics who think they're the ones who'll beat the system." He gestured toward the public area beyond his office door. "You've seen enough of them by now," he said. "They keep coming back. They're older, they're younger, they're just in a loop thinking, *I almost did it then, I'll do it for sure next time.* Next time, next time. They scrape up the money and they come limping back. They can't even see how they've thrown away the lives that they set out to fix."

That first returnee of mine was back within the week.

This time, he was much older. I mean, seriously. He was recognisable but he looked as if he'd spent the last couple of decades scavenging for his life in a war zone. Maybe I exaggerate. But not by much. He didn't seem to have washed or shaved in ages. I could smell him from across the room. He just stood there holding onto the wall by the door, as if that last long walk up the road had taken everything out of him.

I said, "Hi."

He fixed on me. I wondered if he was drunk, but when he spoke I was fairly sure that he wasn't. The messages were just taking their time to get through.

He said, "I'm sorry. I've come a long way."

"Can I get you anything?"

He shook his head, and then moved over to where the forms were and pulled out a chair. I made a mental note to tell Morley that the whole area would need a scrub-down with disinfectant and then I realised, with gloom, that the job would fall to me.

I watched the man. The one I now thought of as My Repeater. I'd seen other returnees by now, but he'd been my first. It wasn't so much that he was now old, more that he'd become old before his time. He looked as if he'd been sleeping rough, and I wondered how he'd managed to get his latest stake together. By years of begging and spending nothing, by the look of him.

He brought the paperwork over. I held my breath.

"Just a few last details to get," I said.

"I know," he said.

I went through the usual questionnaire as quickly as I could and when he emptied the money from his pockets onto the counter, I had to force myself to pick it up. The grubby notes were in bundles, and there was a lot of small change. I felt as if I wanted to scrub the coins before touching them.

It always had to be cash. Travellers weren't creditworthy. They walked away from their futures when the Big Red Button was pressed, leaving no one to pay off the debts.

I said, "Do you want to take a seat while I count this?"

"I'll just wait here," he said.

And he did, too. He leaned on the counter and watched, with me breathing as shallowly as I could and trying not to rush it so much that I'd make a mistake and have to do it again.

Only days before, I'd seen him in good health. Now he was a shocking wreck. I couldn't imagine what he'd been through and I didn't want to ask. The part that I couldn't get my head around was that although the change seemed like a magical stroke that had happened in a matter of days, it wasn't. While his younger self had been standing before me, this older version had been somewhere out there, probably heading my way. They were *all* out there, at more or less the same time – every one of his repeated selves, going over and over the same piece of ground. Never meeting, never overlapping, co-existing in some elaborate choreography managed by forces unknown. Causing no ripples, accomplishing nothing, scraping up their cash and heading right back here. The person he was, and all of the people he would ever be. Fixed. Determined. Tripping over the same moment, again and again and again.

I felt a sudden and unaccountable sympathy. It bordered on tenderness, and it was an awkward and unfamiliar feeling; doubly hard to deal with, considering the scent and the state of him.

Lowering my voice so that Morley wouldn't overhear, I said, "Second chances don't come cheap, do they?"

"You give it whatever it takes," he said.

He looked so bleak and downcast that it made me sorry I'd spoken at all.

I had an idea, and I pitched it to Morley.

I said, "If we kept one file on each repeater, it would save us having to cover the same ground every time."

"You lazy little bugger," he said.

"I'm not being lazy," I protested. "I thought I was being efficient."

"So somebody comes in here and we face him with a file that shows half a dozen returns that he doesn't even know he's going to make yet. What's that going to do to him?"

"Stop him from wasting his life?"

Morley said, "Watch my lips. It's already happened. Nothing's going to change it. All you can do is add to his misery."

And that was the last of my employee suggestions.

I got an hour for lunch, and some days my old school friend Dominic would turn up and we'd walk out along Technology Drive until we reached its lonely end way up in the hills. There we'd sit on a rock and throw stones at bottles until it was time for me to go back.

I must have seemed down that day, because Dominic said, "What's the matter with you?"

"Morley," I said.

"What about him?"

"He's depressing me."

Dominic knew Morley. Partly because it was a small town and everybody knew everybody, if only indirectly, but also because in my first week Morley had made one of his few front-of-house appearances to tell Dominic to stop hanging around the shop and making conversation with me.

He said, "Morley depresses everybody. Even his daughter took her own life rather than listen to his conversation."

This was a surprise. "Seriously?" I said.

"Far as I know."

"When?"

"Years back. When Dinosaurs Ruled the Earth."

I didn't know what to say to this, so I pitched a few more stones at the bottle we'd set up. One of them caught it a glancing blow, and knocked it over. It didn't break, but it fell amongst the remains of countless others that had.

"Who says so?" I wondered aloud as I went over to set it up again.

"My mum," Dominic said. "She used to know him, in the days when he was a human being."

On the walk down, he told me what he knew of the story, which was very little... just that Morley's daughter had written a note and then opened her wrists while stretched out fully-clothed in the bath. She'd cut them lengthways rather than across which, according to Dominic, was proof that she'd meant it. She'd been nineteen. No-one knew for certain what her reasons were. Morley had burned the note.

Technology Drive was like an abandoned airstrip. Just being there made you feel guilty and excited with the thrill of trespass, and for no reason at all. It was as wrecked and overgrown as any

273

Inca road, and in its time had served far less purpose. We picked our way down it, stepping from one tilted block to another. The drains had fallen in and all of the roadside wiring had been dug up and stolen. There was also about seven miles of buried fibreoptic cable that no thief had yet been able to think of a use for.

They talked of it as the Boulevard of failed business plans. The cargo-cultists' landing strip for a prosperous future that never came. Crap like that.

Nineteen years old.

I wondered what she'd looked like.

The afternoon was uneventful. That evening, I borrowed the car and went out with Dominic. We spent most of it in the Net cafe attached to the local Indian restaurant, and then after I'd dropped him off at home I contrived to drive past Caroline Pocock's house a few times, which is no mean trick for a place down a cul-de-sac. Then I parked and watched for a while. I didn't know which window was hers, but long ago I'd picked one at random and by now I'd convinced myself that it was her bedroom. I stayed there until her father came out in his pyjamas and stared at the car and then I took off.

It was after one in the morning when I passed the end of Technology Drive and saw lights in the Bureau's windows. I stopped the car and walked back to the junction. Someone was moving around inside.

Burglars? Looking for what? There was nothing in the place worth stealing. I didn't get too close because I didn't want to be seen. I stayed back in the darkness and waited for another movement. After about a minute, I saw who was in there. It was Morley. He wasn't doing anything much. He was just mooching around.

I saw him polish the glass panel in one of the booth doors with his sleeve, I saw him straighten one of the disclaimer signs on the wall. He mostly looked as if he couldn't quite bring himself to go home.

I couldn't imagine why. He lived on his own. There'd be no one waiting there that he might want to avoid.

My Repeater

I didn't get to bed until after two o'clock. I had a restless night. My thinking kept going around in the same circles. If life is lousy and you go back to change it, all that happens is that you fulfil the pattern that delivered your lousy life. Your choices are no choices at all. It seemed all wrong but think about it long enough, and you'd be scared even to breathe.

After all of that, I overslept and had to scramble.

I was late getting in. Morley was there already. I don't *think* he'd been there all night. He muttered something sarcastic and went off into the back office. The fact of it was that he could have run the place single-handed and saved himself the cost of my miserable wages, if he'd chosen to. What he had me doing was mostly dogsbody work. When I wasn't behind the counter I pushed a mop or answered the phone. The technology, though it was getting pretty old, was maintenance-free and the operation of it was idiot-proof.

I think it was just that he didn't like to go out there and face the clientele any more.

Around ten-thirty that morning, a taxi drew up outside and this young male of around my own age got out. He was well-dressed and had a sharp-looking haircut. You could tell just by looking at him that here was someone from a good family with money, and that he'd been favoured by the education system. Almost everyone from my school slouched, and their mouths hung open in repose. He stood looking the building over as the taxi pulled away, and then he came inside.

He spent twenty minutes or more reading through the forms before he brought them over to the counter.

He said, apologetically, "You'll have to help me with these. I can't work out what I'm supposed to do."

"Sure," I said, and I started to go through everything with him. He'd filled in some of the stuff, and he'd left blank the parts he wasn't clear about.

This time, I knew it way before I saw the name.

"You've never done this before?" I said.

"Nope," he said. I tried not to stare at him. Here, in the midst of his pattern of recycling visits, was the visit that began it all. He was bright, springy, full of confidence. The only giveaway was a

275

dangerous-looking light in his eyes, but it was like the nerve of a bungee-jumper getting ready to go. In his own mind he knew exactly what had to be done, and he was about to step out and do it.

I went to get Morley's approval on the paperwork. My thoughts were racing.

Back at the counter, the young man was waiting. He was tapping out a drumbeat on the counter's edge with the fingernails of both hands.

"Everything all right?" he said.

"Everything's fine," I said with forced brightness.

"When do I go? Do I go right now?"

I lowered my voice and said, "Can I say something to you first?"

My repeater stopped his nervous drumming and looked at me; polite, puzzled, curious.

I said, "Walk away from this. Get on with your life. Whatever you think you're going to change, I can tell you for certain it won't work."

"Thanks for the advice," he said. "But I know exactly what I've got to do."

So then I did what I'd been warned against. "Just one moment," I said.

Then I went and got the records of his last few visits. The ones that I'd witnessed, but that he'd yet to live through.

I laid them on the counter for him to see.

He looked at them. Then he looked at me. The light in his eyes was still there, but it had changed. He wasn't so certain any more, and I could see that he was scared.

"What's all this?" he said.

"That's you," I said. "That's your entire life if you don't walk away."

He stared down at the papers again. They all carried his signature.

I've got him, I was thinking. *It was a risk, but it's working.*

"Fuck you," he said. "Do what I've paid for, or get me your supervisor."

But Morley was already coming out of the back office. "All right," I started to say, "forget I even spoke." I could hear the desperation in my voice as I started to backtrack, but it was too late.

Morley said, "What's the problem?"

"I thought you people gave a service," my repeater said, and he pointed toward me. "Since when was it his job to interfere in my private business?"

Morley looked down, and saw the files on the counter.

"There's been a misunderstanding, sir," he said then, raking them toward him and dropping them under the counter without giving them a second glance. Then he looked at me and said, with a considerable chill factor, "Go and wait in my office."

I went into the back, but I could still hear them talking.

"*Booth four, sir,*" I heard Morley say. "*I hope it works out for you.*"

"*I reckon it will,*" I heard the young man say.

A couple of minutes later, the young man was on his journey and I was on the carpet.

"What do you think you're playing at?" Morley said.

"I was just trying to save him a load of grief."

"He's *got* a load of grief. Sometimes it's just a person's lot to live it out."

"You didn't see his face when he looked at his file."

"I told you, *no* files. Didn't you hear me?" He rammed the point home with his forefinger in my chest, stabbing me with every word. "You don't... show... the clients... their... fucking... files."

"If you'd only stayed out of it," I pressed on, "I'll bet you anything I could have convinced him. I was almost there. I could have rescued a wasted life."

"You know nothing," Morley said, but I was warming to my theme now; now that there was no chance of being proved wrong, I was starting to believe that I'd had control of the situation prior to Morley's interference.

"I bet he was just about to turn," I said, "and then you had to come wading in."

"He's on rails," Morley said dismissively. "We're all on rails. Knowing it won't make any difference."

"But what if things *do* change?" I argued, and suddenly the doubts that I'd been unable to articulate all fell into place like jointed plates.

"What are you talking about?"

I said, "Maybe things change all the time and we just don't know it. Maybe your daughter wouldn't be dead now if you weren't too pigheaded to go back and fix what went wrong."

Bad move.

I knew then that I'd gone too far. I also knew that it was too late to take it back.

Morley just stood there and closed his eyes. I could see the whites flickering where the lids didn't quite meet. He took a shuddering breath and swayed a little. I thought for a moment that he was starting a fit, but it was just that I'd never seen anyone in the grip of such bone-shaking, overwhelming anger before.

He said, "Get out of my place."

He was barely audible. My hands were shaking as I gathered my stuff together and as I was going out of the door that he held open for me, I couldn't bring myself to look back at him.

I heard him say, "I've forgiven you an awful lot since you came to work here. I can see now I let you get away with too much."

"Sorry," I said.

"Not sorry enough," were his last words to me.

I couldn't eat that night, and I felt so sick about it all that I couldn't tell anyone why. It wasn't just that I'd never been fired from a job before. And it wasn't because I'd failed with my repeater, because I'd been onto a loser there from the beginning – the very evidence that I'd tried to show him had been proof in my hands that he'd continue. I just wished I could have taken back what I'd said to Morley about his daughter.

But there it was. You can't change what's passed.

Unless.

Unless I was right. For some odd reason I kept thinking about the spreadsheet we used to work out the charges. When you changed one little thing deep down, everything shifted around as a result. It made a whole new picture.

Maybe we're just talking about the spreadsheet of everything.

My Repeater

There's no past as such, there's just the big '*is*'. No final, bottom line, just an endless middle. Updating all the time, undergoing constant changes in the always-has-been. Our certainties rewriting themselves from one instant to the next. For every miserable repeater, maybe there are a thousand happy and successful travellers whose journey simply vanished from the record once their misery was removed and the journey became unnecessary.

Not a bad leap. For someone so young, naïve and stupid.

I know that there are brain-damaged people who live entirely in the moment, whose memories fade in the instant they're formed. They need a notebook so they can keep checking on who they are, where they live and where they're from, who all these strangers around them might be.

Maybe this whole time thing's just a magic notebook.

And we're just the readers who believe all we see.

The next morning, I confessed to my mother about losing the job. It was that, or go through the pretence of getting dressed and going out early with no reason. She wasn't as surprised as I thought she'd be, but she asked about my unpaid wages. I hadn't even thought about them, and I really didn't feel like facing Morley again. But then when she started to talk about going with me to make sure that I got what I was due, I made hasty arrangements to go back alone.

The building on Technology Drive was all closed up. I looked in through all the windows but nobody was there.

So I went away, and returned late in the afternoon. By then someone had called the police out. Two uniformed officers had turned up in a van, along with a man that I recognised as the owner of a big womenswear shop in the middle of town. I mean it was a big shop, not that it sold stuff to big women. It was called "Enrico et Nora" and he was Enrico. I didn't know it at the time but he was Morley's sleeping partner in the business. The policemen were getting ready to break the door in.

I said, "Can I ask what's going on?"

279

"It's bolted on the inside," Enrico said. "Who are you?" The police wanted to know who I was as well, so I told them.

Then they brought this heavy thing on handles out of the van, and used it to batter the door in.

Nobody said I couldn't follow them inside, so I did.

I'd walked through the same door every working day for the past couple of months, but now it didn't feel right. All the lights were on, even though it was daytime. I was tensed for something awful. I know it may sound melodramatic, but it felt like the kind of scenario that precedes the discovery of a lonely death.

One of the officers had his head inside one of the booths. He pulled it out and said, "How do those things work?"

"It takes two people," I explained. "One to travel and one to operate from the outside. There's a system so one person can't do both."

They started looking in each of the booths, I'd guess in case Morley was lying in one of them.

But I was looking over at the counter.

The anglepoise lamp from Morley's office was standing on it. When I glanced over into booth five, I could see that there was one of our keycards in the activating slot. Back on the counter, the lamp was positioned in such a way that the edge of its metal shade rested squarely on the Big Red Button.

He'd have had maybe a minute to get himself into the booth as the lamp slowly descended.

The settings on the machine meant nothing to me, but I could imagine where they'd led. I don't know if he'd aimed to get there hours before, to prevent the child from killing herself, or months before, to divert her from wanting to.

I told them all about it.

And even as I was telling them, I looked out through the window.

I knew that he couldn't have succeeded, of course. I knew it because I lived in a world where Morley's daughter lay long-dead in her grave and I'd seen the damaged plaything that loss had made of her father. If he'd gone back and saved her, then none of that could ever have happened. But it had.

I could see a figure heading up Technology Drive, walking from where the bus had dropped him off. I couldn't see his features yet, but I could read the determination in his stride.

Next time, his attitude seemed to say. *I almost did it then, I'll do it for sure next time.*

The police went into the back to look through the papers in Morley's desk. Enrico went looking for a phone to call his lawyer. I moved around to my usual place behind the counter.

And there I waited, to see which of my repeaters it would be.

Partial Eclipse
Graham Joyce

Graham Joyce has won the British Fantasy Award for no less than four of his novels. He grew up in the mining village of Keresley, near Coventry, and attended comprehensive school in Bedworth, Warwickshire, before going to college in Derby where he gained a degree in Education and a teaching certificate. During this time he was writing and kept diaries. Later he gained a Masters Degree in modern English and American literature from Leicester University, where he also met his wife Suzanne, a law student. After marrying, the couple went to live on the Greek island of Lesbos, and then Crete, where Graham focussed on his fiction writing. It was in Greece that he wrote his first novel, *Dreamside*, which was published shortly afterwards. A string of highly respected books followed like *Dark Sister*, *House of Lost Dreams*, *Requiem*, *The Tooth Fairy*, *The Storm Watcher*, *Indigo*, *Smoking Poppy*, the World Fantasy Award-winning *The Facts of Life,* and *The Limits of Enchantment.* He is also the author of the novella *Leningrad Nights*, the children's book *Spiderbite* and the young adult novel *TWOC*. He now resides in Leicester with his family, though he teaches writing at Nottingham Trent University. You can visit his website at www.grahamjoyce.net.

"I have many FantasyCon memories," says Graham, "from arriving at my first almost fifteen years ago to form firm alliterative friendships with a number of lovely writers, editors, artists, small-press publishers and the rest. Somehow the society was supposed to be a professional organisation of like-minded genre enthusiasts but it's always seemed to me more like a group of great pals, presided over by elder-statesmen like Ramsey Campbell, Pete Crowther and Peter Coleborn and cemented by dozens of sprightly young things like myself.

"I've learned most of what I know about publishing at the bar and the curry house, and I find out more every year by coming back. Together we've moaned about the hotel beer and drunk too much of it because the company was brilliant; bitched about advances in a world we can't tear ourselves away from because that's the way it is; stuffed ourselves with bad *biriyanis* and *chicken kormas* and made deals we wouldn't have while sober; laughed like stoned coots at some publishing fuckup or other; watched each other's careers follow curly trajectories worthy of early British space-rocket tests; sat in bars and advised, praised, warned, predicted, disputed, winced, snarfed, snarled and howled but never been bored. (Oh except for that bloody awful old-age-pensioners' raffle thing. If we could get rid of that we could talk more brilliant trash at FantasyCon.)"

I know that Myra goes to bed every night and whispers, "Dear God please let the aliens come back."

It's morning, and a diffuse winter sunlight bleeds through the curtains. I roll over in bed and stroke the warm, tanned swelling of Myra's belly, feeling the quickening under the calloused pads of my fingers. It's just a tiny vibration, not unlike the attack note on the E-string. Myra opens her eyes sleepily and smiles at me. It's all beautiful. I want it to be beautiful. But now every expectant mother and father wants their infant to be born with an alien inside them.

"Anything?" I say.

She gives a tiny shake of her head, *no*. Just as she has done for nearly seven years now. Just as I do when she asks me.

"You?"

But she doesn't really have to ask. She knows that if the answer was yes then I would have woken her to tell her. Instead, so we don't have to think about it, I stroke her belly, because I know that by running the heel of my hand along the rim of her thrilling pink pot I can make the baby kick. And it does. *She* does.

"I saw her foot!" I shout. I can still see it. Or maybe it's an elbow, but anyway it tracks along the curve of Myra's belly, rippling flesh as it goes, and then withdraws.

"You're convinced it's a girl," she says. "You're wrong."

Myra's awake now. She'll have to get out of bed. She's about a week away from her time, and I know the baby is pressing on her bladder. But as she swings her legs out of bed she pauses, strokes her huge stomach, and says, "There was a moment. In the middle of the night ..."

"Yes?" I hardly dare breathe.

"No, it wasn't anything really. It was just ..."

"Tell me."

"I can't say for sure. I had to go to the bathroom, and it was in that moment when I was waking up, half-asleep, I thought I heard my baby calling to me. Would that count?"

I lie back, thinking, *Would that count?* Would it count? I don't know.

"I mean," says Myra, "I know he *can't* call to me, so it might have been a dream. Or I might have simply imagined it because I so badly wanted to dream?"

I nod, but it sounds to me like no, it doesn't count. You see, there have been these rumors about pregnant women dreaming. "New wives' tales," you might call them. We've been yearning for it to happen since Myra's pregnancy was first confirmed.

Nothing.

I get up and ready myself for work. I can hear our daughter Mandy stirring in her room. Myra sees me select the Blucher. I love the unusual workmanship. The belly is spruce and the back,

Partial Eclipse

waist, and neck are polished maple. The hole is slightly elliptical, shaping a delicious ooze and throb in the resonance.

She raises her eyebrows as I lay the guitar in my battered carrying case and gently lock the clasps. "We're re-recording Teppi's early piece." God, it's hard to sound enthusiastic.

"Not that old thing! Didn't you do that a couple of years ago?"

"Six years ago," I point out. "And we're doing this much slower. Slow. Very slow."

"Surely there's more you could do than that!" And she looks at me, because she knows it makes me sad. She kisses me, and off I go to work.

* * *

Floyd picks me up. He has his cello in the boot, so I lay the Blucher gently in the backseat. "I've got one for you," he says brightly.

My heart sinks, and I stare at the stalled traffic ahead. "Go on."

"He's six years old. Last week he drew hundreds of people in Manchester. Hundreds. The week before that, Leeds, and you couldn't get a seat."

I've heard all this routine before. "What does he play?"

"That's it. He's not a musician. He's a storyteller."

"Give us a break, Floyd! Six years old?"

"He's in town tomorrow night. You and Myra, me and Zelda."

Like I say, I've been down this road before with Floyd. Mostly with kiddie musos, admittedly, but with the occasional storyteller too. It is a road of stony disappointment every time, but Floyd is a sucker. He wants to believe. He needs to. Maybe I'm mean, but you wouldn't get me to part with the price of the tickets any more, and Floyd knows that. There are too many spivs fleecing decent, hopeful people like Floyd and Zelda.

Floyd reads my thoughts. "My treat," he says. "Now then, do you know what we're doing today?"

"Sure." It's getting even harder to sound bright. "Early Teppi."

285

"Aw, fuck!" says Floyd. "Not Teppi again. That really has spoiled my day." And he leans hard on his horn just to prove it, scaring a hapless cyclist.

And even though I try hard to fake it, I have to admit that down in the recording studio it's a fucking bore, all day long. It's not Teppi's fault. Teppi is wonderful, complex and varied. But it's not enough. Even if I had never heard Teppi before, even if I hadn't recorded him faster, slower, *con brio,* who cares, we just can't make ourselves bleed for him. He, like all the others, takes the awful blame for not being *new.*

Floyd tries. We all try. Mid-morning I see Floyd's shiny black skin, like an aubergine, perspiring from the point on his receding hairline as he works his cello for the complicated fifth. A crackling voice from the control box cuts in and we're told to take a break. Moments later I walk into the washroom and I hear Floyd weeping. He's bent over a basin so he doesn't know I'm there. I leave before he sees me.

While waiting for Floyd to emerge from the washroom I talk with Vanessa. Always bright, always jolly, Vanessa is a brick. Superb pianist. Before the aliens left, Vanessa had a dazzling career ahead of her, with three recordings of her own steely jazz-rock compositions under her belt. Of course, that was nearly seven years ago, but she doesn't seem to let it get her down.

Floyd swings out of the bathroom, chipper, all smiles now that he sees Vanessa, so he pours himself a cup of Darjeeling and treats us to one of his jokes. Old jokes, of course. He knows Vanessa will laugh. He knows I will, too. Gosh, it's a very old one. So old I see the punch line labouring up the hill like a cart horse ready for the knackers, and unfortunately I laugh a moment too soon.

The following evening we put on best bib and tucker and turn up at the De Montfort Hall, where this six-year-old is expected to perform. Myra is somewhat uncomfortable, being so big, but she doesn't want to disappoint Floyd and Zelda. Anyway, she knows we won't get out so much after the baby arrives.

"Oh, let me!" Zelda admires Myra's bump, placing the flat of her palm on the underbelly. Zelda has beautiful long manicured fingers. She and Floyd have kids of their own, but they're almost

Partial Eclipse

grown-up. "It's a boy," she says. "You're carrying at the front." That's what they said about Mandy. Nobody really knows. Then Zelda stoops and puts her cheek against Myra's bump, as if she's trying to listen through the distended skin and into the womb. "Oh please let him dream!" she says softly.

We're caught. Trapped. Left dangling by Zelda's overt remark, and we all look away. A disembodied voice on the PA tells us that the performance will commence in three minutes.

"Come on," Floyd says.

I think he looks slightly angry.

We take our seats, and I'm amazed that the hall is full to capacity. I mean, we've all been hoaxed and duped and gypped and bilked so many times over the last few years you'd think it impossible to fill a hall this size ever again. But no. As I swing round checking for faces I might recognize, I see there's not a single vacant seat. The house lights go down, there's some nervous coughing, the curtains open.

First a warm-up act, a seven-piece jazz ensemble. Floyd looks at me as if to say, not bad but not good either, though we're both pretty stern critics. I recognize the opening piece but I can't put a name to it: Floyd will know. The fact is my mind is on the kid, and I don't like it.

I don't like the idea of this six-year-old having to carry the weight of expectation – and the inevitable disappointment – of the 1500 people in the audience. I think of my own six-year-old Mandy, at home with her babysitter, and how I would never allow her to be put through this.

But there's big money in it, and even when it goes wrong the promoters and, presumably, the kid's parents get to pocket the admissions charges. Because nothing can ever be proved conclusively, can it?

Polite applause dispatches the ensemble and the stage is rearranged for the kid. Big chair in the middle, overhead microphone, one chair either side for what I see in the program are the kid's "guardians" rather than his parents. I point this out to Myra.

"Cynical," she says. I think she means the manipulation of the

287

kid but she adds, "You're so cynical." She strokes her bulge. I know the chair isn't comfortable for her.

The kid comes on and he's a funny-looking thing. He's wearing a starched collar too big for his neck. He's pale under the limelight, his hair is plastered to his head and his ears stick out like wing nuts. Poor little runt. But he looks precociously unflustered by the size of the audience. His "guardians" take their seats either side of him as the kid is introduced by the emcee. Polite applause dies down and the kid waits, creating a tension in the hall, and I know, I just *know,* he's been coached to do this.

He leans forward slightly and says, "Once upon a time."

And the audience goes wild. Rapturous applause. This is irony, you see. Laid on with a teaspoon. From a six-year-old. It's a little message for critical observers like myself, for the skeptics and the doubters and disbelievers. It's post-post-postmodern. Or something. From a six-year-old sprog. And the audience laps it up.

It takes a while for this little riot to die down before he launches into the story proper. And I have to admit it, he's not bad for a six-year-old. He delivers well, his story is pacy, he's got good kiddie timing, and he speaks clearly. What more could anyone want?

The one thing we all want. The one thing we would willingly sacrifice all the above qualities to have.

I identify the story after just a few minutes. Most people in the audience don't yet, but they will, because the narrative pattern will occur to them. It happens to be an old Romanian folktale, about a bear who walks through an anonymous landscape meeting other animals, challenging all of them to guess what he has under his hat. How do I know it? Because two years ago we re-recorded almost the complete collection of Moldovan's work – faster or slower, I can't recall – and there was a libretto borrowing from the tale. Floyd has clocked it too, because he turns to me with an expression of apology on his face. I smile back thinly.

I mean, what are we supposed to do? Interrupt the proceedings and denounce the six-year-old in front of 1500 people? Jump to my feet and shout, "This isn't original! I spy a Romanian folk tale!"

Nah. In any event, there is already a sense of slumping attention in the audience. Many have worked it out for themselves. The familiar narrative pattern, linked with inauthenticities in the manner the kid has been trained to deliver, will give it away. But an audience in denial is an astonishing thing, and the kid holds it for twelve minutes before ending the tale.

The audience applauds loudly, but – and it's a significant *but* – not so loudly as they greeted his opening line. The emcee proposes a break, and promises us another performance by the ensemble before the prodigy will offer us a second tale.

Not for us. We're out of there, as are a reasonable percentage of the audience judging by the bustling cloakroom activity. "Well," says Zelda, helping Myra on with her coat. "I hadn't heard it before."

"Me neither," says Myra huffily.

Floyd's levitated eyebrows exhort me to say nothing. We adjourn to The Long Memory for a drink before home.

And a drink turns into seven or eight, as it must. There has been a lot more drunkenness these last few years, a lot more alcoholism. Drink and drugs: they give a semblance of dreaming, don't they? Helping us to remember. An approach to dreaming. A dullard's kick against the thick, thick ice.

"A man walks into a bar," says Floyd.

We're trying to invent a joke again. It's a dead loss, because there hasn't been a new joke in almost seven years, but we're pissed as newts in a pickle jar so we try anyway. Floyd says, start with the old structures, it makes things easier.

"A man walks into a bar ..."

"Says, 'ouch!' " Zelda chips in.

"Old. Very, very old," Myra says. She's not drinking because of the baby. Her tolerance for our "hilarious" drunkenness is wearing thin. She's already reached for her coat.

"Really?' Zelda protests. "I thought I'd just made it up. I really did." She's slurring.

"A man bars into a walk." Floyd says.

"Give us a break!" Myra almost screams. "Come on, Jonathan, take me home."

I think it's the interpreting I miss most. Though an interpreted dream is a punctured dream, at least in those days you could be certain of a steady supply, and the fun was in the mystery, the guessing, the deconstructing, the reassembling. We can all out-argue Freud when we own the theater.

We say goodnight to Floyd and Zelda; lush, slobbering kisses all round. They stay for another drink as I shamble out of the swinging doors of The Long Memory, supported by my heavily pregnant wife. I complain bitterly about being made to leave early.

"It was time," Myra says. "You know what will happen after the next drink. Floyd will get weepy. Then Zelda will get weepy because Floyd is weepy. Then we'll all have a stupid argument the subject of which no one will remember. Come on, stand up."

"It's only the booze," I say as we reach the car.

Myra gets into the driver's seat. She can barely fit her bump under the steering wheel. "The thing is," she says, tickling the ignition into life, "in knowing when it's time to go."

Time to go. The aliens presumably knew it was time to go. Everyone can remember the moment when they quit the planet. When they quit *us*. And just as with the Kennedy assassination, everyone knows what they were doing at the time it happened: they were sleeping.

The aliens appeared to everyone in a dream. Not the same dream exactly, but almost. You see, the aliens had to take some form in which to say farewell. For some it was a grandmother, for others a long-lost friend; for others still, a pet dog they'd had as a kid: for me my beloved collie, Nelly, long dead. But the message was the same. *Thank you for hosting us,* they said. *We're very grateful,* they said. *But we've had enough,* they said.

They were apologetic that their stay was so brief. Five hundred thousand years residing inside our heads was, for them, a regrettably short stay. The twinkle of an eye. It was short but interesting, they said. But they dearly hoped that we had enjoyed the fruits of their

presence as much as they had enjoyed an exhilarating ride. Everyone remembers being addressed in the same way, whether by grandmother or dog. Polite, somewhat formal, slightly abashed. Then the dream image had transformed into a cube of black light on a black background, before infolding into complete absence. The world awoke to a stunned comprehension of what had happened.
Since which time no one has dreamed.
Not a flicker. Lacunæ on a global scale. A collective lobotomy.

* * *

Back home, Myra climbs into bed as I gargle with mouthwash and brush my teeth and try to sober up a bit. I know if I flop into bed the world will spin and I'll feel the nausea, so instead I go into my daughter's room and watch her sleeping.

I perch on the edge of Mandy's bed, just watching her. In the moment of observing her sleep her room becomes a peaceful chapel or a quiet temple. Wind chimes tinkle softly at the window open a little to the night air. I sense her sleeping spirit at large, roaming, restless, looking for something, a Neverland, a Narnia. She's flying, but she can't find anywhere to land. I love her so much I could cry. She's six years old, and she has never dreamed.

I have this confession to make: in the dark, at night, while she's sleeping, I whisper things in the delicate conch of my sleeping child's ear. Any things. Remembered fables. Old tales. Strange stories. Religious parables. Fragments. Anything that occurs to me. Heaven knows why, but the other day I heard myself saying *Allah is great, there is no God but Allah and Mohammed is his prophet*. Then I sang her a song in French about dancing on the bridge of Avignon.

Trying to create dreams for her. Trying to pierce the shell, hole the ice.

It took us a while to work out that the aliens hadn't *stolen* our dreams. The aliens *were* the dreams. It was difficult to understand initially, generations of us brought up on notions of aliens as basically humanoid with latex rubber heads, or with eggshell-blue skin, or as disembodied human brains encased in a pink gas.

The aliens residing in the consciousness of humanity for half a million years were a benevolent virus. They needed symbiosis, a host to achieve sentience, and that is what we gave them. What did they give us in return? Stories, music, religion. Tools, scientific ideas. Jokes, connections. The synaptic fire.

After their departure they became known to us as Prometheans. Since then our stories have dried up. Our music has frozen. Our science is arrested. No one has had an original notion in seven years. We are lodged in the mud of time, fossilized. We are consigned to limbo, and the cold wind of uncreation howls in our ears like a demon. Our species, all of humanity, has become the preterite, the passed over. Our psychic teeth, pulled.

And at nights I whisper in my child's tender ear, trying and failing to incubate the glory of dreaming.

* * *

Myra wakes in the morning and, with a struggle, sits up in bed. I blink my eyes open, and she shakes her head, *no*, again. She hauls herself to her feet and walks naked to the bathroom, magnificent and comical, the morning light shining on the stretched skin of her huge pot. She mutters something about swollen feet, and I wonder if our baby is going to arrive on the seventh anniversary of the departure of the aliens.

We are post-dreaming now, of course. Almost a new way of dating human history, ante- and post-dreaming. For academics, at any rate. The huge joke (I use the word loosely) is that in the entire field of intellectual endeavour only certain academics – critical theorists, social commentators, and cultural analysts – proceed as if nothing has happened, busily producing unfathomable papers on post-dreaming society.

Of course, not everyone buys the idea that we've lost it. Creativity, I mean. Originality. Innovation. Breakthrough. Those slavering puppies up at the University, for example, publishing their breathtakingly incomprehensible theses and self-serving tracts. But they're about the only ones. Hence the spectacle of six-year-old prodigies conning huge audiences desperate for the succour of the new.

Myra is thinking about something. She returns from the bathroom stroking her belly, two deep vertical creases between her eyebrows. "Out with it," I say.

She sits on the bed again, but with her back to me. "What if," she begins; "what if there were not innumerable aliens?"

I think I know what's coming. It has occurred to me already.

"I mean," she continues, "it would be odd, wouldn't it, if there were exactly the same number of aliens as there were people, and they just happened to match up, one apiece as it were. Are you with me?"

"Yes. Go on."

"So what if really there was only one alien. Inhabiting all of us. And that single alien decided to leave us. That would make more sense, wouldn't it?"

"It's a thought," I say, trying to sound light.

"Then that single alien who left us. Might that be what we've always called God?"

This is too complicated. I don't want to think about this, so I just kiss Myra and go downstairs to make some coffee.

* * *

Is this the end? Have we arrived at some feeble conclusion to human history, terrible in its banality? Not the nightmare end. Not the four horsemen. Not the holocaust, nor the nuclear winter, nor the global warming, nor the asteroid storm. Just this exhaustion. Just this absence. Like a watch spring run down.

I think this might be worse than the apocalyptic ending. The absence of poetry, of music, of narrative; this muted fanfare; the end of the never-ending movie. Not by fire or ice, but by indifference. An indifference that leaves us at the mercy of eternity.

Mandy is up and awake. Warm spring sunlight streams through the windows. She has the door open and is running for the swing I erected for her under the big old lilac tree. I leave the coffee to bubble and follow her out. The lilac flower is rampant, intoxicating.

Mandy sees me. She giggles. "Push me, Daddy! Come on!"

And I push her back and forth, and she moves from shadow into light with each swing. She wants to go dangerously high. "Faster, Daddy, Faster!"

Then I see the expression change on her face, and I step back to allow the swing to slow. "What is it?"

She spits something into her hand, and it's with relief I see it's only a milk tooth, slightly bloody at the root. It's her last one. She hands me the milk tooth as if she's trusting me with a precious stone or a talisman. I'm not sure what to do with it.

"Push me again! Higher! Higher!"

* * *

First contact was something we speculated about for a hundred years. Of course *they* would be carbon-based, even roughly humanoid; of course *they* would somehow vocalize; of course *they* would occupy the same plane of time and space. Not intersecting like this. Not like a finger of smoke inserted into the brain. How could we have guessed that *first contact* was already made perhaps half a million years ago?

Mandy swings from shadow into the dappled morning sunlight, giggling, calling for me to push her higher and higher, and I clutch Mandy's milk tooth, a droplet of dew in my fist, and I think: *Is it one alien? Or is it one for each of us?* And I wonder what I'm going to tell Mandy come the day she asks me.

Myra comes out to us in her silk kimono, sleepily pushing a stray curl behind her ear. Mandy jumps off the swing to let her mother sit, a sincere gesture but one copied from adults around her these last couple of months. But she wants to push Myra on the swing.

"Gently," Myra says. "Just gently. I don't want to go high."

I go back in and bring out the coffee on a tray. Mandy pushes Myra gently back and forth on the swing, babbling happily, and I notice Myra is frowning. She mouths something at me and points to her ear, indicating I should listen.

"... And she said they were sorry. It was a long time. They wouldn't normally have gone such a long time and they didn't like to leave for longer periods than they had stayed, but they couldn't help it and anyway a long time ago is the same as the near future for them and tomorrow is half the length of only a part of yesterday and – "

I stop Mandy from talking and I stall the swing. "Who? Who said this?"

"Nelly," says Mandy still intent on pushing Myra back and forth; and the overpowering scent of the lilac makes me feel giddy and I say, "Who is Nelly?"

"Don't be silly Daddy, you know Nelly. She's a dog. She was your dog when you were a little boy. Have you still got my tooth?"

"Yes, yes, I've still got it here," and I'm holding this tray of coffee and I don't know what to do with it. "When did Nelly tell you this?"

"In the night while I was asleep, Nelly came and told me she was sorry to be away so long but she was back and all her friends would come back –

"Jonathan!" says Myra, but I'm too interested in what Mandy is saying to look up.

I sweep Mandy up in my arms and hurry back inside, where I switch on the television. Mandy is still speaking. "– And I had a little talk with Selina in Mummy's tummy because I know she's a girl though you don't know and – "

"Jonathan!" Myra calls from the garden, but it's all over the television. Reports flooding in from Auckland and Fiji, from Vladivostok and Brisbane, from Osaka and Jakarta! And from Islamabad and Nairobi, from Israel and Cairo, Eastern Europe,

295

anyplace where people go to sleep and wake up before we do, and nearer to home, too, people waking from dreaming, rushing out into the streets in tears and madness just to try to recount what has happened to them in the night, not everyone, to be sure, but millions, yes, millions of people, maybe half the global population, dreaming dreams, gut-spilling their experiences as the report sweeps across the globe like the shadow of an eclipse, or a tsunami of unparalleled joy, or a single unbearably beautiful musical note resonating around the planet and I don't know if it was all a warning, or a punishment or an aberration but whatever it was we are going to be allowed to dream again, dream and create, and I know that this time we need to be more careful but my heart is bursting as I understand implicitly that we are to be given back our wings.

"*Jonathan!*"

I rush back out into the garden and Myra is gazing at me with a strange expression, half desperation, half appeal, and her kimono has fallen open and the sunlight flares on a mercurial rivulet along her thigh and it has started and I want to put down the coffee and to listen more to Mandy and to watch the sensational news reports on TV and to get my wife to hospital and I want to hand back the tooth and I'm staring, staring at the heraldic trickle, the catch-light of the silver manifesto, unable to do anything, paralyzed by the torrent of words my daughter is speaking while I am drunk on lilac and imminence.

"Jonathan," Myra says firmly, hauling herself out of the swing, "just put the coffee down."

So I put the tray of coffee down on the grass and I go and get the pre-packed bags and when I've got the car ready Myra and Mandy get in.

"Selina will be my sister, won't she?" says Mandy.

"Yes. Fasten your seat belt."

"Selina will have lots of dreams, won't she?"

"Yes," I say, sparking the car into life.

Mandy thinks for a bit. "Is Selina coming now?"

"Yes," Myra says. "You're very sure it's a girl, aren't you?"

"Yes," Mandy replies, "because in the night they told me that another half a million years is starting. Have you still got my tooth?"

I say yes, I still have her tooth. It is still squeezed in my fist like a token of some miraculous covenant as I drive us to the hospital, because the baby is coming.

AFTERWORD
By the Editors

Paul Kane was born in Chesterfield, Derbyshire (UK) in 1973 – the same year *The Exorcist* was wowing audiences at the cinema and Stephen King's *Carrie* was accepted for publication. He began his professional writing career in 1996, providing articles and reviews for news-stand publications, and started producing horror, dark fantasy and science fiction stories in 1998. His work has been widely published in many magazines and anthologies on both sides of the Atlantic, in all kinds of formats. His collections *Alone (In the Dark)*, *Touching the Flame* and *FunnyBones* have been highly praised by writers, critics and trade magazines alike and his latest novella is called *Signs of Life*. In 2005 he featured in the documentary *Assembly of Rogues* alongside Ramsey Campbell, Graham Joyce, Christopher Fowler and Simon Clark, talking about his work.

He has a B.A. and M.A. from Sheffield Hallam University and in the past has also worked as a photographer, an artist, an illustrator/cartoonist and a professional proofreader. He is currently working as a lecturer in Art and Creative Writing at Chesterfield College in the UK and serving as Special Publications Editor for the British Fantasy Society. His latest writing projects include a film script, two graphic novel adaptations of his stories, another novella and his first novel. His *Shadow Writer* site, launched on Hallowe'en 2001, can be found at www.shadow-writer.co.uk

Marie O'Regan is a horror and dark fantasy writer based in the Midlands. She has had stories published widely in such magazines as *Dusk, Dark Angel Rising, Here and Now, Midnight Street,* and in anthologies like *The Alsiso Project, When Darkness Comes* and *Terror Tales,* alongside Peter Straub, Simon Clark and Stephen Laws. Marie is also the Chairperson of the British Fantasy Society and has edited their publications *Dark Horizons* and *Prism* in the past. Her first collection *Mirror Mere* came out in April 2006 to much acclaim, with authors like Muriel Gray and Kelley Armstrong calling it 'satisfyingly nasty' and 'a delicious batch of tightly written, shivers-up-the-spine chillers'. Forthcoming from her are a novella, film scripting work, and a full-length novel. You can visit her website at www.marieoregan.net

---

Though both of us are relative newcomers to the British Fantasy Society, in the last few years it has become a major part of our lives. In fact, we owe the BFS a huge dept for bringing us together as both a writing and editing partnership, and also as a couple. We met for the first time at a FantasyCon in 2003, even though we had been in e-mail contact for a couple of months, and met again at the Christmas Open Night of that same year. Our friendship grew and we continued to see each other at Open Nights and FantasyCons, as we took up the posts of Special Publications Editor and Chair of the BFS. Until, finally, we made our relationship official at – you guessed it – another BFS do in 2005. Now we are getting married and couldn't be happier. All in all it was a bit of a BFS romance.

But also during that time we have got to know most of the people in this book, either in person or by e-mail, and discovered what a lovely bunch of folk are a part of this organisation. Hearing all their anecdotes and reminiscences of years gone by just makes us sorry we weren't around for those times. So we'd like to thank everyone who has written or let us use a story for this very special celebration book, and of course BFS stalwart Stephen Jones for his introduction. We hope you like what we did with it.

And we hope that you, the reader – whether BFS member or not (and if not, why not?) – like what we've done too. After all, you're what makes the BFS the unique body it is. The dedication to promoting the horror, sf and fantasy genres that everyone involved with the BFS has is quite overwhelming, and it certainly spurs us on to do bigger and better things. If we've helped in some small way to spread the word, then it's all been worthwhile.

Finally a quick note about the charity aspect of this anthology. As people who have contributed to it know, all profits from the sale of this paperback will go towards maintaining the BFS and also to one of the charities that FCon is involved with this year. Actually, it was at the same gathering we officially became a couple that Bob Wardzinski, proprietor of Talking Dead books, approached us and asked if the BFS would consider donating to a charity he and a lot of other genre writers (some of them also in this book) support: The 'Black Dust' Nqabakazulu Charity Project, a school in South Africa. So thanks everyone for buying the anthology in the first place (again, if you haven't and have just skipped to the back to read this, then why not?) and for helping both these worthy causes.

See you at the next British Fantasy Society event, we hope…

Paul Kane & Marie O'Regan
Chesterfield
June 2006

Join the British Fantasy Society today!

A bona fide British Institution, the Society exists to promote the genres of fantasy, science fiction and horror. Many well-known authors are counted amongst its members, not least its president, the legendary Ramsey Campbell!

The British Fantasy Society organises regular Open Nights throughout the year, as well as the phenomenal weekend FantasyCon event, where the winners of the British Fantasy Awards are announced.

Members enjoy many benefits, such as a quarterly fiction magazine (*Dark Horizons*), a bi-monthly newsletter (*Prism*), free copies of BFS Publications and discounts for events.

So what are you waiting for? Subscriptions are just £25 (UK), £30 (Europe) and £45 (Rest of the World) per year. Cheques payable to British Fantasy Society, 201 Reddish Road, South Reddish, Stockport. SK5 7HR.

Or join online at the BFS Cyberstore:
http://www.britishfantasysociety.org.uk/shop/info.htm